THE
takedown

THE
takedown

carlie walker

BERKLEY ROMANCE

New York

BERKLEY ROMANCE
Published by Berkley
An imprint of Penguin Random House LLC
penguinrandomhouse.com

Copyright © 2023 by Carlie Walker
Excerpt © 2023 by Carlie Walker
Penguin Random House supports copyright. Copyright fuels creativity, encourages diverse
voices, promotes free speech, and creates a vibrant culture. Thank you for buying an authorized
edition of this book and for complying with copyright laws by not reproducing, scanning, or
distributing any part of it in any form without permission. You are supporting writers and
allowing Penguin Random House to continue to publish books for every reader.

BERKLEY and the BERKLEY and B colophon are registered trademarks of
Penguin Random House LLC.

Library of Congress Cataloging-in-Publication Data

Names: Walker, Carlie, author.
Title: The takedown / Carlie Walker.
Description: First edition. | New York: Berkley Romance, 2023.
Identifiers: LCCN 2023013975 (print) | LCCN 2023013976 (ebook) |
ISBN 9780593640395 (trade paperback) | ISBN 9780593640401 (ebook)
Subjects: LCGFT: Romance fiction. | Novels.
Classification: LCC PS3623.A35884 T35 2023 (print) |
LCC PS3623.A35884 (ebook) | DDC 813/.6—dc23/eng/20230503
LC record available at https://lccn.loc.gov/2023013975
LC ebook record available at https://lccn.loc.gov/2023013976

First Edition: October 2023

Printed in the United States of America
1st Printing

Book design by George Towne

For Claire and Pete—this book wouldn't exist without you

prologue

CHRISTMAS EVE

You can tell a lot about a family by the outfits they wear on Christmas Eve. When I was growing up, we were sweatpants people. Casual people. I'd dress in gray cotton from head to toe, and my sister would sidle up next to me on the couch, eating goat cheese with a spoon. There was no big sit-down dinner, no fancy candles. We'd turn on the TV and gorge ourselves on finger food.

This year is different.

It's different in so many ways, I'm not even sure where to begin.

Let's start with dinner. All around the table, my sister has laid out the best silverware (the gleaming forks and serrated servers) alongside Grandma Ruby's handmade ceramic plates. Soon, they'll be loaded with mashed potatoes and turkey and all the perfect-smelling things.

Still, I have to fight a lurch in my stomach.

We never eat like this, at a long table with fresh pine boughs and vases wrapped in tinsel. We never hear the faint slap of wind outside, punctuating our awkward silences.

The biggest difference, though, is him.

Sipping champagne near the end of the table, my sister's fiancé catches my eye and winks. *Asshole.* I grit my teeth so hard that I can feel my dentist wince, and I take a swig of wine in an exaggerated, breakneck way. My jewelry clinks together. It's Grandma Ruby's. She told me to borrow some bracelets, because this is a special occasion; I'm supposed to look "Christmas nice." We have guests.

Over the turkey, I stare back at Johnny. Hard. I realize that he'd make the best poker player in the world. His face is *exceptional.* Not a single shaved whisker of it betrays anything that happened last night. In his white linen shirt, freshly starched, he looks as saintly as an altar boy. Or one of those fluffy polar bears. Sure, polar bears might seem like they'd drink Coca-Cola and snuggle up with you on chilly nights, but get too close and they'll rip your fucking throat out.

Just eat the food, I tell myself. *Just eat the food and say nothing.*

Normally, I'm good at keeping my mouth shut. Blending into the background—when I need to—is easy for someone like me. But tonight . . . the screws are loosening. After everything that's happened, I can feel myself breaking down.

I push back my chair a little.

"What are you doing?" my sister, Calla, whispers, leaning in to me so no one else can hear. Panic flits across her eyebrows. Yes, her eyebrows. They're as chunky as mine, and they're magnificent. She used to worry they looked like caterpillars. "I said no speeches. And . . . you're sweating. Why are you sweating?"

"I'm not sweating."

"Sydney, it's dripping down your face."

Haphazardly, I dab my forehead with one of the cloth napkins and tug my turtleneck an inch lower. This is the last time I wear reindeer wool! The stuff does not breathe. "I'm just going to say a few words . . ."

"No! No, *please*. You're—"

She reaches for the sleeve of my sweater like we're six years old, trying to yank me back to the seat. But I'm faster—*ha!* Rising unevenly, half dragged down at the elbow, I wobble to a stand and clink my wineglass with a butter knife. It makes a comedically tinny sound, like a fairy coughing.

"I'd like to make a toast," I say. My smile is warm, friendly. My voice is gracious. The carbonation bubbles in my sparkling wine.

A hush falls over the dining room until the only sound is "You're a Mean One, Mr. Grinch" thrumming from the speakers. Seems appropriate. There's a Grinch at this table. But he's not going to change by the end of the movie. His heart will always stay just a *little* too small.

"Johnny," I say to my sister's fiancé, raising my glass in his direction. "I don't need to tell you how lucky you are to be loved by someone like Calla . . . but I'm going to tell you anyway."

Everyone at the table titters.

Even Johnny. Even Calla. Even the other guy at the end of the table, who shall remain nameless right now. I don't want to think about him. I don't want to think about the gentle brush of his lips, or the roughness of his palms, or how he looks in bed, covers hugging the angles of his hips.

Currently, he's sitting back in his chair, hand to his mouth, this apprehensive smile peeking through his fingers. He's hanging on my every word.

I shake my head almost imperceptibly and steamroll on. "Calla might be a big fan of holiday sweaters, with the sparkling thread and the bells, and she might be more than a little afraid of teeny-tiny hamsters—"

"Class pets are *unpredictable*," Calla says, unable to stop herself from grinning, her face half-covered in her hands.

"But don't let that fool you. Genuinely, she is one of the fiercest people I know. And the best. Anyone who's met her will say the same thing."

Calla tilts her head at me in a polite way that says both *I love you* and *Sydney, are you drunk?* And yes, yes, maybe I am a bit, but this is important. I'm not done with the speech. Not yet.

My eyes dig into Johnny.

"When it comes down to it, I would do anything for my sister. Anything. I'm lucky to love her, like you're lucky to love her. So . . . raise your glasses."

Around the table, seven glasses surge into the chandelier light. Everything is sparkly. We look like a Christmas card.

"To Calla and Johnny," I say.

"To Calla and Johnny," everyone echoes, including the man at the end of the table. Nick. (Fine, that's his name. Nick.) Of course, I choose this moment to catch his eye. He gives me this gentle, sincere nod, like *Nice speech, Syd,* and I think about mistletoe and the dimples on his lower back and—oh yes—how I've seduced him for the government.

My throat constricts.

I think I might hate him.

And I have no idea how this is going to end for either of us.

"Be good to each other," I add with a final, choked flourish. "Or else, Johnny, I may just have to break every bone in your body, and all that good stuff. Okay? Who wants turkey?"

1

UPPSALA, SWEDEN
FIVE DAYS EARLIER

I can't just approach him and ask to cut in. That would look sus-picious. Instead, I've placed myself at the edge of the dance floor, and I'm sipping a glass of champagne so slowly that I'm hardly tasting it. What matters is my mouth. He should be looking at my mouth. On my lips is a thick coat of crimson lipstick. The color perfectly matches my dress: a strapless, thigh-slit gown that says, *I am your Christmas present.*

Every once in a while, Alexei spins his partner and cocks his head my way. It's subtle. But I notice things. Noticing things is my job. His gaze tracks from my ankle all the way up the bare skin of my thigh, and finally to my mouth. Automatically, I part my lips; my eyes capture his, sparkling for a calculated two seconds, before dipping shyly down.

I'm not shy.

I'm just smart. And well trained.

Also, itchy. Fingertips gripping the champagne glass, I ignore the prickle that's creeping its way under my wig. Maybe it goes without saying, but I prefer my own hair: a dirty-blond bob that almost dusts my shoulders. Unluckily for me, Alexei "The Bulgarian" Borovkov—my target—has a thing for brunettes. It's in the file. All four of his girlfriends (four *simultaneous* girlfriends) have long, dark waves. So tonight, that's what I have.

I take another ludicrously slow sip of champagne—and wait.

Half of this job is waiting, keeping your cool under pressure.

Swishing the alcohol through my teeth, I survey the ballroom for the sixteenth time. Strings of fairy lights dangle from the ceiling, sprigs of greenery crest the snow-flecked windows, and a massive cut-glass chandelier shouts, *Fancy!* It's the kind of place I couldn't imagine myself in as a kid. Christmas bingo night at the Moose Lodge, maybe; a winter ball with tickets double the price of my first car, never.

There are two clear exit routes. Several bodyguards, milling around, attempting to look inconspicuous. And a man in the corner wearing an earpiece. Not one of our guys. One of Alexei's. At the far end of the room, a string quartet plays "*När det lider mot jul*," a Swedish carol that's heavy on the violin, and my stilettos tap until the end of the song. Everyone applauds the violinist—then it's go time.

I don't even need to steel myself.

It's habit, muscle memory, my mind and body in sync.

Alexei takes another step back from his partner, bows, and shoots a look straight at me. For a second, it's like we're the only two people in the ballroom.

Now, all that's left is to reel Alexei in.

A slow lip bite should do it, like I'm thinking about how he might taste—but I stop mid-bite. I've caught myself. I'm so innocent! Alexei sees this and immediately struts over in his white tie and coattails, exactly like I knew he would.

"You are beautiful," Alexei says. He speaks in heavily accented English and extends his white-gloved hand, confident that I'll take it. My fingers slip gently into his, like I'm this fragile little bird—not, say, a deceptively strong CIA case officer who could incapacitate him swiftly and silently. Beneath the dress, I'm all power and muscular curves. A handler once described me as "more striking than beautiful." Emphasis on the *strike*.

Alexei pulls me to the center of the dance floor as the quartet revs up again. A slower song this time, with more cello.

"You're Bulgarian?" I ask in English, affecting a Swedish accent. The ballroom is in Uppsala, a half-hour train ride from Stockholm, so a Swedish alias makes the most sense.

Alexei grins, drawing my chest to his chest, and I make sure I don't stiffen. Make sure I'm breathing smoothly, normally. His neck smells like blood oranges, with a hint of leather, and his custard-blond hair is slicked behind his ears. In heels, I'm only two inches shorter than him. We match up. "Smart girl," he says after a click of his tongue. "You recognize my accent, then? You speak Bulgarian?"

"I speak six languages," I say honestly. It's the first and only truth I'll tell him all night. "But my Bulgarian isn't so good."

"My Swedish isn't so good." Alexei's lips quirk. "I bet there is a lot we could teach each other . . . ?" He leaves the question open, waiting for my name.

"Annalisa," I lie.

Annalisa Andersson. A socialite from Gothenburg. She's a Virgo. A horseback rider. Likes gin and Dubonnet with a slice of lemon.

It's funny how much you can know about a person who doesn't exist.

And how little you can know about a person who does.

Alexei's fingers intertwine with mine in a way that—years ago—would've sent a chilled spike down my back. "You are here all alone, Annalisa? It is no good to be alone at Christmas."

Alone at Christmas.

In my line of work, people hunt for vulnerabilities. What Alexei doesn't know is, he's tiptoeing uncomfortably close to mine. My family briefly flashes in front of my eyes—Calla, Grandma Ruby, Sweetie Pie, even Dad—before I blink and they're gone. They can't be here right now. Alexei is not what you'd call "a good guy." For the last three months, he's been financing arms deals against NATO allies. Give him anything less than total concentration, and I'll be flying back to the States in a body bag.

Reaching up, I trace the sharp ridge of Alexei's jaw and whisper directly into his ear, "I'm not alone anymore, am I?"

I can feel his heartbeat quicken through his shirt. His throat bobs in a discreet gulp, and I've got him. I know I've got him.

Ninety-five percent of the time, my work for the CIA isn't like this. Usually, I'm given a very specific set of instructions: Recruit foreign spies. That's it. That's what I do. I identify them, study them, and ally them with the US government. I've been posted all over Northern Europe and the former Eastern Bloc. Long, cold months of meeting assets in back rooms and bars—and then, sometimes, assignments come out of nowhere. *Son of a Bulgarian billionaire, touring Europe, attending a charity ball in Uppsala. Someone's persuaded him into handing over his father's money to buy missile components. Audio and satellite surveillance so far unsuccessful. Need to find out who he's meeting later tonight.* Suddenly, I'm trading in my cargo pants for a government-funded gown. I'm dancing, song after song, before slipping my hands under Alexei's suit jacket, tracing the slope of his chest. My fingers are nimble, delicate, skilled.

Alexei is practically purring. "You know," he murmurs, "you look like that American . . ."

I'm careful to avoid any tension in my shoulders.

". . . actress," he finishes, which is very preferable to *American spy.* "What is her name? The one with the face. The round face. Dark eyebrows, hair of blond."

"Round face . . ." I pretend to think, distracting him more, my fingers roaming the sides of his body, and—*there.* I stick the miniature audio recorder into the lining of his jacket.

"Ah!" Alexei says, as if he's been stung by a baby wasp, and my muscles ready themselves to block an attack. Internally, I relax as he bleats out, "Ah, I cannot remember her name. You are such a good dancer, my mind is gone."

With a flick of my eyelashes, I thank him.

We don't get wins like this very often: a mission that goes so freakishly smooth, it's like a training exercise. Alexei might as well have been a Farm instructor acting the part of a billionaire. It irks me: the suspicion that the assignment might've gone a little too well. But I was as diligent as possible—and I'll be just as watchful on the way home. When the tech team finally pings my earpiece to confirm that, yep, they can hear everything through Alexei's bug, I deploy a blunt, evergreen excuse.

Need to pee! Goodbye.

Bypassing the bathroom door, I duck down the opposite hallway and slip into the coatroom unnoticed. Everything's choreographed, methodical. I double-check that I'm alone—then I absolutely blitz through the next part. Wig off. Black parka on. High heels off. Rubber ankle boots on. I yank a well-worn pair of cargo pants over my dress, tucking the silken fabric into my waistline. Twenty seconds, that's all it takes, and I'm street ready. Swiping my rucksack from the corner cupboard, I walk slowly but purposefully out of the coatroom—and into downtown Uppsala.

Cold wind and snowflakes nip past my ears, reminding me of Maine: snowshoeing in December; toes freezing before a campfire; that first lick of winter. I yank up the hood on my parka, obscuring the sharp angle of my hair; if anyone starts to trail me, all they'll see is the shape of a person: sleek, possibly athletic, relatively tall.

Luckily, no one follows me to the train station. No one suspicious boards my carriage. No one looks over my shoulder while I pretend to read *Plaza Kvinna* magazine. In the train bathroom, I puff out a tired breath and run my wrists under the tap, scrubbing, until the makeup disintegrates and the black outline of my crescent-moon tattoo becomes visible again. Sometimes this tiny, tiny tattoo feels like the only true marker of who I was.

Splashing a palmful of warm water onto my face, I gaze into the mirror and drag a paper towel over my sticky red lips. Do I look happy?

Maybe that's the wrong question. This job was never supposed to make me happy.

This job was supposed to make me . . . what? Untouchable?

Back in Stockholm, I stop at the first open convenience store and buy a loaf of Swedish cinnamon bread, devouring a third of it on my walk home. Not *home*, exactly. The Stockholm Riverside Hotel has just been someplace to crash for the last two days. It's fine. Way better than the station house in Macedonia, or that hostel in the Balkans. The vending machine makes a decent espresso (if you only care about the caffeine level; *so-caffeinated-that-I-can-predict-the-future* is about the right dosage for me). The hotel carpets are IKEA blue, paintings of extra-furry cows line the halls, and no one really asks any questions besides the occasional "How are you finding your stay?"

Which is good. Obviously.

In the wood-paneled lobby, I shift the grocery bag into the crook of my arm, press the elevator button to 3, and step in at the *ping*. My ankle boots stomp down the hallway, leaving a trail of snowy powder, and when I reach my room (306, by the caffeine delivery machine), I wrench off a mitten, searching deep in my parka for the key.

What's my family doing right now, six days before Christmas, at home in Maine? I can't help thinking about them.

Also . . . I hear something. *Someone.* Right now, in my hotel room.

The noise hits me like a dart to the neck. There has *never* been anyone in my hotel room before. Never, never. Definitely not after a mission.

I knew the assignment went too smoothly! Did someone see me plant audio surveillance equipment on Alexei? Have I been compromised? *Who the hell is in my room?* Bracing myself, I set down the bread, unshoulder my backpack, and reach for my gun. On the other side of the door is a female-sounding voice—and the blare of the television. The intruder is watching something. A game show, maybe? Can that be right? Every few seconds, a bell goes off, like *Ding, ding, ding, you've won a prize!* And the person inside my room lets out a loud, raucous laugh, like Miss Piggy in the Muppets.

This has every hallmark of a trap. And not even a particularly good trap. Shouldn't she, at the very least, be hiding in a closet, ready to spring out and knife me?

Even so, I can't stand out here forever. There's two months' worth of intel in that room, and it's not like I can abandon it. My handler would kill me. If the person in my room doesn't try to kill me first . . .

Suddenly, the television stops.

Then the voice calls out, "That you, Sydney? In here, please."

Her accent is American. Midwestern, by the sound of it. Another trick? My training kicks in like a reflex. Two deep breaths. Compartmentalizing any fear. Grabbing the pistol in my waistband, I sidestep the cinnamon bread and beep the door unlocked. I crack it open, peek inside. Blue carpets, blue walls. A pair of well-worn running shoes, placed by the door, exactly where I left them. Immediately, though, I'm met with the unmistakable scent of meatballs. In a . . . nutmeg-y cream sauce? Which is something that I did not order and have never brought into this room. I round the corner, past the entryway, into—

"Oh, good. You're here."

The woman in my room barely looks at me. She turns her head vaguely in my direction, just enough for me to see the harsh line of her profile. Short, chestnut-colored hair falls around her face. Everything about her says *windswept*, even though she's comfortably seated at the dining table by the TV. She must be about forty years old. Forty-two? Forty-three?

More importantly, I have no idea who the heck she is.

Or why she's ordered so many meatballs. The table's crowded with a platter of smoked salmon, a bowl of spaghetti, and what appears to be venison. Or reindeer?

"I was a bit hungry, so I just ordered everything." The woman shrugs, snapping a room service menu shut and fully looking at me now. Her eyes are hawkish, bright, and might scare the average person. "You eat meat, yes? Should've ordered double, but I didn't know when to expect you back, exactly. Orange juice? There's more food coming. Keep your ears pricked for a knock at the door . . . Aren't you going to sit?"

She gestures at the other dining chair.

"I'm sorry," I say, not sorry at all. Sarcasm bleeds through my voice. "Who are you, exactly?"

"You're not going to shoot me, are you?"

My gun stays in position, pointed at her head, but the slight fear-taste dissipates from my mouth. "Not unless you try to shoot me first."

"Good," she says with a wave of her hand. "That would be very messy. Too much paperwork, and it would probably make the news if you couldn't find somewhere to stash my body quick enough. Not many dumpsters in this city. You'd have to drop me in the river. But then, of course, the river is frozen, so you'd have to drill a hole. Quite time consuming." Grabbing the remote, she changes the channel, watches for roughly twelve seconds, then flicks a finger toward the TV. "What do you think is going on here?"

Nothing as weird as what's happening in here, I think. On-screen, a domestic scene unfolds. It's some sort of Swedish soap opera. Never taking my eyes off the woman with the meatballs, I listen for a short while, as Helga—I think her name's Helga—learns that her lifelong love, Sven, has cheated on her. On their wedding day. With her sister.

"Family drama," I say evenly. A muscle in my jaw feathers. Every few seconds, my eyes flick toward the closet, waiting for an assailant (Alexei? Alexei's contact?) to burst from my winter gear.

"Ah." The woman sniffs and rubs her nose. "I know all about family dramas. I'm supposed to be in Finland right now." She tilts her head toward the neighboring room, as if Finland were just next door. "Skiing holiday. I hate skiing. Too much snow. My son sprained both his wrists on the first day. Would you believe that? *Both* wrists."

"That's . . . awful," I say with just enough empathy, moderating my words. *If you even have a son.* Is she lying to me? Her body language is casual, unassuming; she seems truthful, but those things can be faked. Learned. My mind turns over her vowels, wondering if I can pick any holes in her American accent. Maybe she's putting it on. Is she FSB? Covert ops? At the same time, I wonder if my laptop is still locked in the dresser drawer.

"Yeah, well, it'll give him something to complain about. My

son does love to complain . . . Seriously, though, drop the gun. I'm unarmed, see?" She pats down her woolen sweater, which looks so Finnish, it's like a gift shop souvenir. There are lingonberries on it. "Nothing under the table, either, see? Check the closet if you want. Check under the bed. There's no one here. Just you and me and some meatballs, hmm? We're on the same side."

I huff, a wedge of blond hair falling over my eye. "I'm not just going to trust that you're—"

"Sydney Swift," she says, leaning back in her chair. Her hands fold neatly in her lap, like a school librarian. "Twenty-six years old. Case officer for the CIA. Excellent with languages. Currently turning a defected Albanian criminologist into a workable asset— and just getting back from a Christmas party. Billionaire's son, I believe? Something about missiles? You attended high school in Cape Hathaway, Maine, where you . . . let me see if I remember this right . . . played the flute in the marching band and won the All-State Debate Championship two years in a row. May I show you a picture?"

My mouth dries. *How . . . How in the . . . ?*

Slowly, from underneath the meatball dish, she produces a photograph, sliding it with two fingers across the table. The image shows a sixteen-year-old girl with sun-kissed hair, strong eyebrows, and a mouth full of braces. Her intelligent eyes flick, cat-like, toward the camera.

She's clutching a debate trophy.

She's *me*.

"Studied international relations at Bowdoin," the woman plows on, "then Georgetown. Graduated with honors. Your mother passed away when your little sister was a baby—car crash, very sudden—so you were raised by a grandmother and a single father. At The Farm, you scored the third highest in your class in asset recruitment and the second highest in defensive driving. On your personal phone, you have more pictures of a dog named 'Sweetie Pie' than you do of human beings. No current romantic relationship. In fact, very single. How am I doing so far?"

She's nailed everything. Absolutely everything. My last boyfriend and I broke up at 2 a.m. in the Langley parking lot, after he told me it was too difficult dating a spy. And he *was* a spy.

I grind my teeth.

"Fairly well?" the woman says. "I know. Time to sit down."

Her name is Gail Jarvis. Supposedly. Supposedly she is *the* Gail Jarvis, an associate deputy director at the FBI. From her pocket, she slowly produces her badge along with a prerecorded video message from my handler, who doesn't *look* like he's under any duress. (Although admittedly, it's hard to tell; Sandeep is a notoriously upbeat person.) Five minutes into our talk, I return my gun to my waistband, moderately confident that Gail isn't about to strangle me with chicken wire. At least, not imminently. Outside the room, partygoers stamp by, yelling in Swedish about office party drinks, and room service knocks on the door, delivering two bowls of yellow pea soup. Gail tips the server and, without making any sudden moves, totters back to the table.

"Oh yes," she says, taking a few sips with a spoon. "That really is good. Rich. The Swedes do know how to make a nice soup, I'll give them that." Then she gets back to business. "So I've laid out the beginning of it. Essentially, I need you to come work for me."

"Temporarily," I recap, hand under my chin. My fingers drum against my cheekbone. We're in a chess match, Gail and I. Her move.

"Temporarily," she says.

"As a sort of interagency transfer?"

"Correct."

I give her a look like *Gail, you know that none of this makes sense*. It involves one squinted eye and a slight mouth tilt. When she doesn't seem to read the expression, I come out and say it, blunt as always. "This doesn't make sense."

Gail stabs a meatball with her fork. "Which parts specifically?"

Should I let her keep the fork? It doesn't pose much of a threat, although theoretically I could take down someone with less. "Let's say you are who you say you are," I begin, threading my hands together and resting them on the table. I've never been in this exact position before, so I'm leaning on my confidence. "Say you really did just happen to be in Finland 'on vacation.'" I use air quotes here. "Which is one heck of a coincidence . . . Why break into my hotel room? Why me? You haven't even told me what the assignment is. Why not select one of your own agents?"

"Can't." She twirls the meatball in cream sauce, making me hungry again. "Things are coming into the FBI and they're not *staying* in. Even the smallest detail of this case is too important to leak. I have suspicions about people in my department."

A too-long pause follows. The FBI doesn't half beat around the bush. "And?" I press. I like to get to the point. "Why do you need me?"

Gail bites through a meatball and swallows thoughtfully. "Well, first of all, you're a woman. I trust women. Not all women, of course, but whenever I'm voting, I vote women, straight down the ballot." She makes a sharp hand motion, like she's slicing through butter.

"That's not an effective way to vote." Even so, one corner of my mouth curves into a reluctant smile. There are so few women in upper-level intelligence roles, they might as well have their own secret handshake.

Gail shrugs. "Works for me. And I did not, as you claim, 'break' into your hotel room. No damage. Just a stolen key from that mess of a lobby. Now, I would say I want you for the job because you're the best. But that would start our relationship on a lie. You know that the CIA and the FBI fight like parakeets, so you aren't my first choice. I have no idea if you're the best. Your file says you're competent in the field, but really, I need you because you're the only one who can reasonably do the job."

In my stomach, mild dread mixes with curiosity, forming a sort of frothy cocktail. This always happens right before my handler doles out an assignment. It's like standing at the open edge of an aircraft, parachute strapped to your back. The ground ripples in a patchwork beneath you, and your breath catches in your throat. "The job is . . . ?"

"See these bags?" Gail responds by way of answer. One of her fingers tugs on the skin below her eyes. It's bluish and papery. "All this case. This *one* case. It feels like I've been following this family for half of my career. First the grandfather, then the father, and now the son. Johnny. Johnny Jones. Ring any bells?"

It does. Organized crime. A family out of Boston. "Should it?"

Gail sucks her teeth. "Oh boy."

"Oh boy, what?"

"I was hoping you knew."

"Knew what?" I ask, irritated.

"You should probably take a deep breath."

"I am breathing."

"Yes, but you aren't breathing *deeply*."

Okay, my patience has expired. I'm blunt again. "Just say it."

To her credit, Gail does begin to spit it out. "The Jones family is harder to crack than the Italian Mafia. They used to be real broad-spectrum criminals. Gambling, auto theft, racketeering, corruption of public officials, you name it. Started by running everything through a chain of coffeehouses. The grandfather? They called him the Coffee King." She pauses for what seems like dramatic effect. "The last year and a half, though—silence. Everyone thought they'd gone completely underground. Until I started putting the pieces together. Connecting crimes throughout the country, across the Eastern and Western Seaboards and parts of Canada. *Heists.* The family is running heists now."

"Jewelry stores?" I ask, all business, pushing her along.

"Jewelry stores, museums, banks, private residences—millions and millions of dollars. You remember the art museum robbery in St. Louis three months ago? The one where two civilians were shot? *That's* them. I've spent nearly eight years trying to infiltrate their network. I was beginning to think that it couldn't be done, at least not in my lifetime. And then, last week, Johnny Jones—the son—announced he was engaged."

A trickle of panic slopes down my back. "Okay . . ."

"To your sister."

What she's said doesn't make sense at first. Her words don't sound like *words.* I think the television has short-circuited, but nope, it's just my vision. There's a definite blurriness at the edges. "No," I say automatically.

Gail lifts her eyebrows like, *Well, it's true.*

The tips of my fingers go numb, and memories bubble up like acid: Calla and me in elementary school, with our matching lobster-shaped lunch boxes. Calla sticks the tip of her tongue out at me, then says, "Race you to the swings!" Little sister. Best sister.

"That's . . . that's impossible," I tell Gail, unable to keep the tremor from my voice. Which is something that never happens to me. "You're joking."

"Do I look like the type of person who'd pull a rubber chicken from my pocket?"

"No," I repeat, less to her and more to myself. I see Calla and me, on vacation with Grandma Ruby in Acadia National Park. Calla and me, collecting dust bunnies from the attic and calling them pets. The two of us, curled under a quilt after Dad left, me whispering that I'd never let anything bad happen to her ever again. A wave of nausea crashes against my ribs. "No, Calla would *never*—"

"Calla *has*," Gail interrupts. "I'm sorry she didn't tell you. But the fact remains, your sister is set to marry into one of the most evasive crime families that America has ever produced. And you're going to gather intel on them."

My chin dips, leveling Gail with a stare. "Are you asking me to spy on my sister?"

"See, there we go. Just as your file says. You *are* smart."

Her condescension is like a push into the ice-cold river, and this . . . all of this . . . it's pulling me under. "No. No, I'm not going to do that. You can't ask me to do that."

Gail frowns in a deep line. "Of course I can. I just did."

"She's my *sister*—"

"Who's marrying a suspected felon," Gail supplies. "Yes, I'm well aware. And you may believe that Calla's innocent, completely ignorant of the circumstances—and that's fine. Let yourself believe that. But here are the facts, Sydney. The last heist the Joneses pulled off, a man in his eighties was shoved so hard to the ground, he cracked his skull in three places. He's been in a medically induced coma for over a month, might never wake up, and his dog misses him. Should I show you a picture of his dog?"

My stomach gutters. I know what she's doing. "Stop."

Gail doesn't stop. "His name is Puffin. He's a chocolate Lab, very sad eyes. And another woman in her thirties, she was hit with a stray bullet. Still in the hospital. *Could* survive it, but there's a chance her two kids are going to wake up on Christmas morning without a mother."

A searing ache crawls into my throat. "Gail."

"There's a pattern," Gail plows on. "Every heist is bigger, more dangerous. Each time, casualties increase. Now, we've heard two pieces of chatter in the last forty-eight hours. First, that the Joneses' next heist is on New Year's Eve. And second, it seems that someone in their organization has purchased fifty pounds of C4 on the black market."

Fifty *pounds*? That's . . . enough to blow up a whole series of banks. A whole street. And on New Year's Eve, with the crowds? "Jesus," I whisper.

"This is much bigger than your family," Gail underlines. "With that much C4, *thousands* of people could get hurt. What's the target? What are the Joneses' plans? How can we stop them before they pull off their worst attack yet? Calla's bringing Johnny home to meet your grandmother for the holidays, so you'll have an opportunity to find out. Goody, goody, family time! Pack your bags for Maine."

2

What does one buy a crime lord for Christmas?

Nose scrunching, I lift the cotton tea cozy and examine it. Tiny reindeer waltz across the fabric in a pattern. This is a no. My basket is already filled with way too much Toblerone, and I've snatched up two knitted sweaters, a tin of Holiday Spiced Black Tea, and a T-shirt emblazoned with the Swedish royal family. I was planning on drop-shipping something from Amazon, but since I'm actually going *home* for Christmas, I should arrive with presents in hand. Really thoughtful presents, like . . .

My vision catches on the LOVE FROM STOCKHOLM ARLANDA AIRPORT mug. There's a Viking on it, belching a greeting.

Again, not quite what I'm looking for.

All around me, airport patrons peruse the gift shop, so light and carefree and—by the looks of it—well rested. I didn't sleep a wink last night. Around 3:30 a.m., my handler confirmed that my mission with Alexei was a success—and that Gail was telling the truth. She really does work for the FBI. Calla really is marrying Johnny Jones.

How the hell did this even *happen*? How'd they meet? How long have they been dating? When's the wedding? Does Calla know her fiancé is wanted for alleged criminal activity?

She can't.

I rub my eyelids, telling myself *no way*. Calla is a habitual rule follower. She's the type of person who actually reads the terms and conditions before a software update. Once, in the fifth grade, we were hand-delivering Christmas cards to our neighbors; she refused to open their mailboxes because of mail fraud. What if we accidentally tampered with their junk flyers? And she's kind. I once saw her cross an eight-lane highway, on foot, to save a turtle. She swerves for pigeons. She recycles with the type of fervor usually reserved for Olympic sports.

I know my sister.

I know her.

But that little voice staggers around inside my head, the one that always comes out when I'm tense, when I'm questioning someone's motives: *Do you, Sydney? Do you really?* Anyone is capable of anything, aren't they?

Can I trust my judgment when it comes to the people I love most?

"Just these," I say, dumping my basket by the register. How was Calla acting when we last met? Normal, right? Herself? It was four months ago, on a quick trip back to the Northeast. I was meeting a contact near the Boston Public Library, so I stopped by Calla's apartment that Saturday morning—brought bagels, coffee, peace offerings. *I'm sorry I've been so busy. I suck.* She gasped when she saw me, pulling me into a tight hug, and we talked on her couch for two hours. About her job at the local elementary school. About her students and their tiny vegetable garden and how she was thinking about adopting a cat.

Hardly anything about me.

I've gotten good at dodging those kinds of questions.

On many levels, my sister and I are the same. Organized, meticulous, driven. Honey-brown eyes and thick lashes from Dad's side of the family, sharp cheekbones and a wide smile from Mom's. But Calla's much more trusting than I am. More open. She leads with her heart, while these days I'm more like that aloof cat she wanted to spring from the shelter: warm sometimes but also wary. When you let your emotions get the best of you, when you let people in too deeply, that's when shit hits the fan.

"Lot of Toblerone," the cashier observes.

"Big holiday," I deadpan, unwrapping one and taking a bite.

Halfway to my gate at the airport, I remember something with a jolt—riffling through my backpack and fishing out my non-burner phone. Calla's last voice mail is dated almost a week ago. Her voice chirps through the speaker.

Hey, Syd. It's me. Remember me? Your sister? Around your height, brown hair, a scar on my knee from when we both jumped off the swings? Okay, now that you have the right mental picture . . . you've been particularly absent lately. Call me, please? I have some . . . I have some news. No one's died or anything. It's not bad at all, but just . . . call me back, Okay? Okay, love you, bye.

You didn't even call her back, I think, a lump threatening to rise in my throat. There was the Oslo trip, then Stockholm, and my alias changed twice—but *shit*, that's no excuse. Three years in the CIA, and I thought I'd be better at this by now. Balancing this job and my family. Keeping in touch with Calla, with Grandma Ruby. When I disappeared into my work, I never meant to slip away from *them*.

The corners of my eyes sting before I blink away the pain. It's the middle of the night in Boston, where Calla lives, so I dash off a text (**Sorry I missed your call, promise I'll talk to you when you're awake**), thrust the phone into my suitcase, and take out two pieces of lingonberry gum, chewing them with more than a touch of violence. I should probably try harder to mold myself into the picture of holiday cheer, but every time I think: *Rudolph! Snowflakes! Hot cider in a manger!* I also think: *Your little sister is marrying a crime lord, and you were too busy to answer the goddamn phone.*

The first year after I joined the CIA, I was still taking care of Calla. Not in big ways. Just little things: chipping in for classroom supplies, reminding her to put extra air in her tires before a cold snap hit. For all her organization skills, Calla sometimes forgets about *herself*—and I'd help her remember. I'd ship her vitamin C tablets and a bottle of zinc during flu season. I'd have bags of rock salt delivered to her condo in Boston, because one year she didn't order them, slipped on the sidewalk ice, and broke her tailbone.

When did I stop watching out for her in all the ways that mattered?

Why'd I let that happen?

Calla and I grew up in Cape Hathaway, Maine, which is exactly as picturesque as it sounds. We rode to elementary school on our bicycles, picked wild blueberries like kids in an L.L. Bean catalog, and trick-or-treated under the northern lights. Every year in Cape Hathaway, the weather changes aggressively after Halloween, heralding the end of late tourist season and the official beginning of winter. I know that some Mainers like to complain about snow (it's too cold, too wet), but I can't get enough of the stuff. Calla did this to me. For the first snowfall, she'd always wake me up in the dead of night, dragging me to the driveway and ordering me to hold out my hands: "You have to eat the first snow-flake you catch. It's lucky."

"You made that up," I'd say.

"Maybe." She'd shrug. "Maybe not."

And we'd stand there, boot to boot on the concrete, not know-ing that years later—when Calla was fourteen, when I was sixteen—we'd watch Dad leave. We'd watch his pickup truck plow lines in the snowy driveway, and we'd wave, mittens in the air. He was just going on a camping trip, wasn't he? He was just leaving us for a little while . . .

My breath hitches as the plane lands and I see all the snow out the window. A four-foot-high blanket coats Portland. It's 4:36 p.m. and already past sunset, but with the city lights, I can still glimpse tendrils of steam rising from the buildings. A gentle mist rains down on the city. The late-afternoon air is thick and freezing. Good thing I packed my thermal gloves.

And my Taser.

At the airport's rental car center, I select a car that says, *I am not a threat to you, Johnny Jones, and I am definitely not a spy*, and then proceed to counter-steer as the Prius ice-skids toward my home-town. Unfortunately, right now, I couldn't look more like a CIA case officer if I'd written SECRET SPY on my forehead. In Maine, my wardrobe was all gold hoops and colorful, paint-speckled sweatshirts; this morning, I'm wearing a black turtleneck, black snow boots, and black jeans that hug the curves of my muscles. I've also had two triple espressos to stay sharp. Caffeine is running through my veins like miniature greyhounds, and every time I blink, I see Johnny's face. Last night, Gail sent me headshots, along with two gigabytes of files to peruse, and yes—I could sort of understand why Calla fell for him. Physically, that is. Soft curls, surfer-blond hair. Shoulders like a linebacker. His eyes are piercing.

Because he would literally stab you, Sydney, I think, gripping the steering wheel. Hidden in those two gigabytes was Gail's personal research, plus all available surveillance images of the past three heists. Black-masked men wielding pistols, taking potshots at civilians before slinking away with millions.

Johnny's men. Johnny's guns.

Gail believes so, anyway. She's tracked networks of his associates across the country, tying them back to within a mile of each heist. Johnny's never physically there at the scene (his alibis are locked down tight; he gets other people to do his dirty work), but his metaphorical fingerprints are all over the plans. What's missing is ironclad evidence to link him to the crimes—and to stop the worst attack yet.

I take a sharp, confident breath, knowing I'll fix everything before New Year's Eve, and jack up the temperature on the heated seats. Outside, it's negative seventeen degrees. At least I'm not freezing in my wool socks and Swedish-bought parka. I even find that I'm humming along to carols on the radio, pressing my foot a little harder on the gas pedal; I'm okay. I can handle this, like I always handle my cases. Nothing has to change.

Houses whip by. Multicolored twinkle lights glint under the frosty sky. The farther I travel away from Portland, the more elaborate the displays. Someone's handcrafted sleigh, complete with twelve blowup reindeer. In another yard, a menorah grows so tall, it tangles with the tree limbs. When I hit Cape Hathaway, the holiday cheer explodes.

My hometown takes the festive season seriously. Arguably too seriously. We are in an unofficial competition with the lobster-fishing town next door, and every year must conspire to outdo them in the Joyfulness Department. The stakes are life or death ... at least, they are if you ask my Grandma Ruby. She's in charge of half the window displays on Main Street, and it is glitter city down here. Glitter and tinsel and sparkly wreaths. Hip-height light-up candy canes line the sidewalks. And every house is dressed to the nines, with candles in the windows and ribbons on the doors. Giant animatronic Santas wave at you with snow-swept beards.

Swerving a left down Cook Lane, I drum my fingers against the wheel and recap the plan. It reads precisely: *Swipe Johnny's phone and implant a tracking virus that Gail provided, trail him, determine his New Year's target, and thwart the heist. Merry, merry Christmas, yay. Stop the bastard from marrying my sister by any means necessary.* Calla will marry a crime lord over my dead body.

Hopefully not literally.

I mean, that would *really* be un-jolly.

Just as I'm pulling into my old neighborhood, my burner phone rings. "Hello?" I answer.

It's Gail. "Good, you've arrived. Calla and Johnny's flight has been delayed. In around forty-five minutes, they'll pull up to the house with Marco, one of Johnny's bodyguards. Sixteen minutes ago, your grandmother Ruth—"

"Ruby," I correct her. "Grandma Ruby."

"Ruth, Ruby. Potayto, potahto. Anyway, she left for the local supermarket, so I just wanted to let you know that the seeds have been planted. A technician was in and out earlier. No need to plant anything yourself."

"Wait . . ." I shake my head. The FBI bugged my house? I shouldn't be surprised, and yet—the presumptiveness is a slap in the face. "That wasn't part of the plan. You never discussed that with me."

"Oh." Gail pauses. "I thought that was assumed."

My grip tightens on the phone, and my bluntness takes over.

"They're private citizens, Gail. My family. We don't have any warrants. Why would I assume we'd place my *Grandma Ruby* under audio surveillance?"

"So I see we're not talking in code anymore."

I run my tongue along my teeth. "You called it 'planting the seeds.' Who's going to think we're talking about gardening?"

"We are talking about gardening. I grow tomatoes in the summer. Very relaxing hobby." Gail clears her throat. "I know it might be tempting, but please remember what we discussed. You cannot, under *any* circumstances, tell your sister about this mission."

"We didn't actually discuss that, either."

"It was implied."

And she's right, it was. Doesn't mean I haven't been wrestling with the choice. In fact, that's why I was bleary-eyed the whole night. Could I let Calla in on the details of the assignment? Could I tell her about Johnny? The sun was rising over the Stockholm rooftops when reality bulldozed me: *No, Sydney, you can't.* I'm absolutely sure that Calla isn't a part of Johnny's organization, but . . . fifty pounds of explosives, on New Year's Eve? I couldn't risk that kind of threat to human life.

"We need enough evidence to take down Johnny before you blow your cover," Gail continues, "and I have zero confidence that Calla will keep up the façade if she's read into the situation."

There's that, too. Loading so much sensitive information on Calla, in a rushed and high-pressure way, would only place her in a more compromising position. "Well," I hedge, still debating myself, "she might play along if—"

"Sydney? *No.* Now, just make the fiancé trust you, understand? Good luck." Then she hangs up.

I stare at the phone, understanding why—as Gail claims—the CIA and FBI fight like parakeets. Also, if they've planted bugs, it means that the FBI is watching me, too. They don't entirely trust me. Why would they? My sister is set to marry into the Jones family. Which means *I* could be a part of that family . . .

The Prius jolts as I curve into the driveway, snow sifting under my tires. My grandma's house—*my* house—looks exactly the same: It's nearly a hundred years old, all big, bold windows and yellow-chipped wood, so it stands out like a ray of summer sunshine in the dark, wintry setting. Icicle lights dangle from the downstairs porch, and fir garlands wind their way around the columns. There's my old bedroom, by the juniper tree, still studded with Dad's old bird boxes. Calla and I spent so many hours in that tree, peering out with binoculars to keep an eye on the neighbors' cats. What were they called again?

Milton and Cat Benetar, I remember, still on edge from the phone call. On edge from being home, too—all the memories clawing their way back. You can see my pulse thumping in my neck. I've just checked in the rearview mirror.

I take a breath, hold it, release it.

Okay.

Parking, I yank my suitcase from the trunk and fish out my spare house key, hoping my grandma hasn't changed the locks. Sure, I could wait for her in the driveway. I know my Grandma Ruby. She doesn't peruse the aisles; she decisively selects. Groceries will be chucked into the cart with fruit-smashing speed. She'll be back in fifteen. But the driveway is my least favorite part of this whole house—I can almost see Dad's truck tire tracks—and it's freezing out here, snow beginning to fall in chunks . . .

Luckily, the key fits. The lock turns.

And the love of my life is waiting for me, just behind the door.

Her name is Sweetie Pie. Her fur's dappled black and white, like an Appaloosa horse, and her eyes are that warm, milk-chocolate brown that makes you go weak at the knees. There's a saying about soul mates. Everyone gets one in their life—and chances are, it'll be a dog. Looking at this good girl, jowls pink and blubbery, her tail wagging at the mere, unexpected sight of me, I think: *True. Oh god, it's so true.*

She rushes at my ankles.

It's like the slow-motion reunion at the end of a movie, like we should be in a field instead of a foyer. Dropping to my knees, I give her the most sugary-sweet voice that I reserve only for dogs. "Sweetie Pie! Who is my *sweetest* Sweetie Pie? It's you!"

Hindquarters wiggling, she gives me two long kisses, dog slobber coating my face in a thick sheen. Her tiny whimpers beg the question: *Where have you been?*

Guilt drop-kicks me. My stomach pangs. "Good question," I whisper back.

If one of my colleagues ever asked why I'd joined the CIA, I'd give them a perfunctory answer: the challenge, a sense of duty. That's not true.

The truth is, my CIA cover has its benefits. No one can hurt you if they barely know who you are.

Now, dogs? Dogs are different. I can be my whole, complete self with them, no hiding. Dogs will never trick you; they'll never be anything but honest.

"I would lay down my life for you," I tell Sweetie Pie, cupping the sides of her face.

That's nice, her eyes say. She gives a satisfactory snort, panting out laughter.

When we were in middle school, Calla and I weren't allowed to have a dog. Dogs made too many muddy footprints. Dogs coated couches with layers of ruffled hair. That, in turn, found its way into your kitchen, and suddenly, you were eating dog fur with your eggs. All of this, of course, was explained by our Grandma Ruby. Who ended up being Sweetie Pie's number one fan. The woman has imprinted this home with Sweetie Pie's likeness.

There are Sweetie Pie oven mitts. Sweetie Pie coasters. A Sweetie-Pie-shaped mailbox that's still the talk of the neighborhood. There's a new oil painting of her over the living room mantel, surrounded by tinsel. She is, of course, both blissfully unaware of her ascension to sainthood and completely accepting of the attention.

"You want a cookie?" I ask her, opening the treat container by the stairs. "You want it?"

Yes! Yes! She does! Her paws happy-stomp the hardwood. Such a familiar sound. The house smell is familiar, too: ground-up clove and fresh ginger, with a hint of pine. Since college, I've set foot in the foyer on only a few occasions, and every time, it's a barrage of conflicting emotions. Happiness for the memories, anger that things can never go back to the way they were. Nostalgia. Feeling like a stranger here and feeling like I never left. I decided to join the CIA right after graduate school, in a moment like this: I came home for one week in the summer, slept on the same bedsheets, ate the same cookies. Immersing myself back into family life was . . . too much. A part of me wanted to feel like my family memories, the bad ones, belonged to someone else entirely.

Now, the rickety banister is wrapped in ribbon, imitating a long, tubular present, and when I touch it, my fingers come away glittery. Another memory. Christmas morning. Green plaid pajamas. Me and Calla, hands aglitter, and—

Someone was just in here. In this house. Planting bugs to spy *on my family*. Not just on Johnny. On Grandma Ruby and Calla, too. The oddness of this hits me in an even bigger way. A stomach-acid-churning way. Calla's innocent. She's not involved in hostage-shooting heists or *any* crime. Ninety-nine percent of me believes that. But isn't there the teeniest, tiniest chance that Calla knows the real Johnny? She sees the good in people, the potential in people, and she might've gotten wrapped up in something that . . .

just spun out of control. What if the bugs capture something that implicates *her*?

That little warning bell clangs between my ears again. What if, after three years of my hardly seeing Calla, some part of her character has changed—and I've missed it?

I'm the officer on this case.

What if I *personally* send my little sister to federal prison?

In my mind, seven-year-old Calla sticks her tongue out at me once more—and the foyer spins. I feel sick. By my feet, Sweetie Pie cocks her head, ears aloft.

"You should be judging me right now," I tell her.

Her head cocks even farther.

"I know, you would never."

And then, decisively, I'm stalking up the stairs. Most bugs are virtually unfindable if you don't know what you're looking for. But I do. I can check on a few spots, see where the microphones *might* be hidden. That way, when I talk to Calla—really, really talk to her—we won't be recorded. If I find any, I might even . . . rearrange some of the bugs. Move them to different areas of the house. Places where *Johnny* might be, but Calla won't.

That makes no sense. I realize that as I prowl into the guest room, mastiff-terrier mix at my heels. Sweetie Pie thinks this is a game. The most fun game! *I* zip around like a bouncy ball, and *she* follows me with her gaze, tail zipping as fast as a bumblebee.

Where would the technician hide the bugs? Where would I hide them if it were me?

My gaze scours the shelves. Like the rest of the house, the guest room is decorated for a cozy Christmas. A garland of paper snowflakes hangs across a row of picture frames. An Elf on the Shelf stares back at me from between two hardback books. He looks judgmental.

"I know, I know," I mumble at him, pulse ticking up despite myself. What would Grandma Ruby say if she knew that I was spying on her? Yanking books from her shelves, sneaking around her home? *She'll never find out*, I think, but the idea has slipped under my skin. It settles there. Makes me itchy.

I'm never like this on missions. I'm impenetrable. I check my emotions at the door. Then again, Sweetie Pie is never *behind* any of those doors, and here, I'm not undercover. I'm the seven-year-old girl who skinned her chin tripping on this rug; I'm the twelve-year-old kid who made forts with fresh-washed sheets pulled from *this* linen closet. I open the door quickly before thinking, *No, no—the shower.* They've probably bugged the shower.

Something I never understand in movies: Criminals always whisper their biggest secrets in the shower. They turn on the water so "no one can hear." *Bullshit.* You think the CIA doesn't have waterproof technology? You think the technical team can't filter out the sound of a little water? There's got to be a microphone somewhere in the bathroom.

At this point, Sweetie Pie decides to reinvestigate the biscuit tin downstairs, perhaps to see if she's left any crumbs behind. Good. It's stupid, but I don't want Sweetie Pie to see me like this, double-checking the bottom of the toothbrush holder, riffling through the medicine cabinet, and finally, climbing past the shower curtain to search above the tub.

I remember taking baths in here as a kid. I remember this shower curtain. My grandma's been buying the same one since 1997. It has ducks on it. There's nice-smelling soap in here, too. Very woodsy cabin meets the seashore. The corners of my eyes squint, and I look carefully for a small black dot. My hands rove the tiled ridge above the shower. *No, no . . . Not feeling anything . . . No.* But I do notice something else.

Something way, way worse.

The sound of footsteps. Footsteps headed toward the guest bathroom.

A pang settles in my stomach as I realize it's too late. Too late to climb out the bathroom window. Too late to leap from the tub. The door flies all the way open, the guest robe fluttering on the hanger, and I see the blurry outline of a man through the ducks. He totters across the bath mat and removes a pair of headphones from his ears, setting them carefully on the sink.

Well, fantastic.

Who the hell is *he*?

He's definitely not a burglar. It's obvious by the casual way he's entered the bathroom. This man is a guest in my grandma's home. A guest who has no idea that a CIA-briefly-turned-FBI officer is hiding in the shower. Is he part of the Jones family? What's the danger level here?

I calm myself by taking silent, steady breaths—and hoping that all he's planning to do is brush his teeth. Maybe he won't even turn around. Or maybe he'll see my outline and think, *What a strange shower curtain. It looks like ducks and a twenty-six-year-old woman, hunching with a razor in her hands.* (Just in case, I've reached over and grabbed the razor by the soap. *His* soap, I'm guessing? His razor?)

Quick. A cover story. I prepare a cover story, why I could possibly be waiting fully clothed in the bathtub, as his hand reaches out, around the curtain—and turns on the water.

I do not shriek. I am a statue. An increasingly wet statue. Cold water plummets from the showerhead, drenching my turtleneck, and I think, *This is about to happen. All my training, and I've really screwed up this badly. He is really taking off his clothes, and I'm in the bathtub, waiting for—*

"I'm not looking!" I shout as the curtain swishes open. Which is obviously a lie. My eyes are comically wide. Simultaneously, the man shrieks, "Jesus Christ!" Like the Son of God is hiding in his bathtub.

"Not looking!" I repeat as I wince at him through my fingers, trying to work out which file I know him from.

He's . . . tall. Very toned.

Unfortunately, he is also very naked.

3

There's a long, thin scar on his abdomen and a series of freckles by his left hip. He has a lean but sturdy body, like he'd be very skilled at lugging suitcases. Or perhaps bags of stolen goods, pinched in a heist. His hair's short, wavy, so dark it's bordering on black—and no, I definitely do not look down. That's an invasion of privacy. Also, unhelpful to me. The FBI doesn't have his . . . you know, his . . . *lower region* on file. What finally clicks everything into place is his posture. I recognize the way he's positioned: at an angle, one shoulder slightly in front of the other, like he's about to block a punch.

Nick! Nicholas Fraser.

That's his name.

Everything in his file comes zipping back. Nick Fraser, twenty-eight years old, born in Ottawa to Canadian American parents. Dual citizen. Former bodyguard to Johnny "the Coffee Prince" Jones, now his head of security. No recorded criminal history, but a close friend of the Jones family. Recreational rower. Attended

Northeastern for undergrad, where he met Johnny, his freshman roommate.

He also matches the partial description of a suspect in the Buffalo, New York, heist.

Good. I know how to play this now. I know the key actors and where I stand. Even if where I'm standing is in a puddle of water, thin beads of it slowly dripping down my face.

In a flash (literally, I guess), Nick grabs the fuzzy blue bath towel off the rack, wrapping it around his waist. It has happy little clouds on it. Like with the duck shower curtain, we've had the same towels since I was twelve.

"What . . . ?" Nick asks me, searching for the words. Because what *do* you say to a stranger who's just Jack-in-the-Box-ed you in the shower? At least I didn't pop out and yell *boo*, but this is still egregious. Now that I've identified him, the horror of what I've just done is pinpricking my spine. Mistakes on the job aren't a habit for me. Far from it.

I can navigate this, though. Dodge and swerve suspicion.

Deep breath, and—

"I am *so* sorry." Covertly, I drop his razor by the soap dish. Probably won't be needing that if he didn't attack me straightaway. "I didn't know that anyone was going to be . . ."

Nick raises a chunky eyebrow at me and asks in a slightly hoarse voice, "You didn't know that anyone was going to be showering . . . in the shower?" There's a hint of amusement in the corner of his mouth, and it *almost* sounds like he's about to laugh. But his body language is ultra-tense. As it should be. If someone were hiding in *my* shower, I would probably punch them in the throat on instinct.

"Right," I say, wiping wet hair from my face. I must look like a recently bathed dog, fur slicked down. In fact, that's probably why

Sweetie Pie went back downstairs. Nothing good happens in the bathtub. "I'm guessing you're staying here? Let me just . . ." With as much grace as possible, I step out of the tub, my shoes squishing on the mat. My sweater is dripping. My black jeans are completely soaked. Time to play innocent. "I'm Sydney, by the way."

Nick huffs out a solitary laugh. It's warm, nonthreatening, and the smallest fragment of a smile breaks through. He has the kind of instantly likable face that might disarm other people. I don't buy a single ounce of that charm.

"Yeah, I know who you are," Nick says. The faintest trace of a Canadian accent breaks through his vowels. "What I don't know is why you were waiting behind the shower curtain."

My face gives away none of the truth. Instead, I press my lips together and wring out the ends of my hair into the tub. Water makes a *plink, plink* noise as it hits the drain. "This is super embarrassing, but I heard footsteps and there was no car in the driveway. I thought someone might've broken into the house, so I hid. When you came in, I realized you were actually *taking* a shower, and most burglars don't pause to remove all their clothes . . ."

At this, Nick half cringes. Deep grooves form in the corners of his eyes. There's something very approachable about them, something that tries to draw you in, which—*Nope. No way in hell.* I've seen his type before: those obnoxiously attractive men who think their good looks will give them a pass. "I'm Nick," he says, not extending a hand. Because his right hand is firmly holding up his towel. "Johnny's friend? I'm staying here for the holidays. Last-minute thing."

"Not a burglar, then?" I ask, doubling down on the innocent persona. In my mind, though, I'm sending thought daggers at Gail. *Gail! He's staying here for Christmas? You didn't brief me properly.*

"God, no," Nick says, head rearing back. I notice the thin, faded scar on the cleft of his chin—and that he must be a full six inches taller than me. Without a doubt, the Joneses brought him in as "the muscle." Light glistens over the panes of his abdomen, which is—frankly—obscene.

He's still talking, his voice bouncy. "Your grandma asked me to get a turkey pan from the attic while she was at the super-market. Very nice person, by the way. Really sharp, too. But I'm sure you know that. Why am I telling you that? Anyway, I had my earbuds in. Got a little too into my audiobook. And then I'm in here, pulling open the curtain . . ."

"Ah."

"Yeah." Nick scratches his temple. "All right, so . . ."

"So I'll leave!" I clap my hands once. It's calculated. I need to look like I really am mortified, not just determined to get away from him. "Sorry! I'm terrible."

Swinging open the bathroom door, I find Sweetie Pie on the other side, gazing at me knowingly. *Never go in the tub*, her eyes say to me. *That is the first rule of tub life.*

Now you tell me, I want to mouth back, grabbing my suitcase from beside the bed.

"Hey, Sydney?" comes Nick's voice from the bathroom.

Jesus Christ, *what?* I swivel around, still soaking. My wet foot-prints imprint the carpet. Back to innocent. "Yeah?"

"It was . . . uh . . . interesting to meet you."

"Oh," I say, knowing all of this will be caught on film. I assume there's video surveillance alongside the audio. Someone's prob-ably critiquing my performance. Better make it good. I smile. "You, too."

Then, with a shake of his head, Nick closes the door.

Alone in my room, except for Sweetie Pie, I pitch my suitcase onto the desk and wipe a hand slowly down my face. That could've gone worse. I salvaged it. Didn't locate any of the bugs, though. There's probably one in here, hidden in my debate trophies. On my childhood dresser, they sit gleaming in a neat little row, next to a collection of porcelain dog figurines. Different sizes, different breeds. One of them has a chipped tail that's been reglued half a dozen times. I have joint custody of the Doberman with Calla.

"This is going to be brutal, isn't it?" I ask Sweetie Pie.

And she looks at me like, *Yes, yes, whatever you say.*

It should tell you something that my biggest confidant is a highly flatulent dog. She's farting now. Probably from the cookie. I lovingly plug my nose and zip open my suitcase with one hand. No time to dry my hair, but at least I can change out of these wet clothes—and recalibrate my plans for the week. Now Nick's here. Nick I'm-so-charming Fraser. Head of security. In my grandmother's guest room.

My nose pinches at the thought of him.

I'd prepared for just a bodyguard. Marco, a thirty-six-year-old ex–Navy SEAL with a head tattoo. *That* was the file I'd memorized last night. Where is he? Is he still coming, too? More people in the house mean more uncertainty, more gazes to dodge when I'm trying to snag Johnny's phone or sneak a peek in his suitcase. But I can easily adapt.

One slight fumble with Nick is fine.

It won't happen again.

If anything, I can use him for information. Draw him closer like he was trying to draw me.

Slipping out of my sweater, I riffle through my old dresser drawer, pulling out something that's fully approachable: a light blue sweatshirt with a frayed but presentable neckline. Bright yellow paint flecks the sleeves. My grandma owned a house-painting company for decades, and in my sophomore summer, the two of us recolored half the colonials on Perkins Cove. I yank on the sweatshirt. See! That's cheery. Gives the illusion of vulnerability.

"Kitchen, Sweetie Pie?"

She tippity-taps, and I follow her downstairs, waiting for the back door to burst open. Waiting for Grandma Ruby. It's going to be so strange seeing her in person again. I haven't had much time to call her lately, and when she's holding the iPhone for FaceTime, I get to see only the bottom third of her face. It's more like Chin-Time. Last month, I spent the entire ten-minute conversation speaking to a Sweetie-Pie-shaped couch cushion and couldn't find it in my heart to tell her.

Clock ticking, I grab a gingerbread tree from the Tupperware box by the fridge and bite off the stump, chewing. Grandma Ruby definitely made these. She always puts extra ginger in the mix. I could eat about a hundred. In fact, I eat two in quick succession, wondering what's taking her so long at the supermarket. Eventually, Nick makes his way down the stairs (I pick up on the tread of footsteps this time) and joins me in the kitchen.

We hold eye contact for a moment before he looks away sheepishly, and—*Oh, screw you, Nicholas. I'm not falling for that.* Based on my experience, *sheepish* and *besties with a crime lord* aren't compatible descriptors. "I really am sorry," I tell him, taking another bite of gingerbread and speaking through the corner of my mouth. "That will *never* happen again."

Nick laughs through a wince. "Jesus, I hope not." His Canadian accent slips out; that might be the only endearing thing about him. "I'd like to live past twenty-eight."

"Scare you that badly, huh?"

"I like to think I'm a brave guy, but I might've seen my life pass before my eyes."

"Do you . . . want a cookie?" I ask, knowing I've just said the same words to Sweetie Pie.

"Sure, thanks." He takes one, turns the gingerbread tree over, and examines the icing, like he's confused by the frosting pattern.

It has white sprinkles and zigzags. "You know, I'm not great with silence. Whoever said there's such a thing as comfortable silence is . . . well, they've never met me. So I was thinking, should we just start over and never mention what happened upstairs for the rest of our lives?"

Not great with silence? If he was a bodyguard, half of that job was spent in abject speechlessness. So either he was unsuited to his job, or he's a flat-out liar. My money's on liar. "Could we?" I ask, making sure it doesn't sound like *I hope you choke on your Christmas cookie.*

Nick smiles in a way that tries to put me at ease. I don't let it. "Nick," he says, extending a hand. He has rough palms, like the coarse side of a sponge.

"Sydney," I say, then add seriously, "I really didn't see anything. You know. Back there."

Nick runs a hand over his freshly shaved jaw, stopping by the freckle right above the corner of his pretty mouth. "I thought we *just* agreed not to mention it," he teases.

I mime zipping my lips. "It's done."

"Good. Now, Calla said you weren't coming home for the holidays." Eyes full of energy, Nick pulls out a stool from under the countertop and sits, one hand under his chin. His just-about-black hair is damp from the shower, and he's wearing a hunter-green sweatshirt that says CHRISTMAS SWEATER in bold, white print. The sleeves are pushed up his forearms, which are a mix of muscular and lanky, and tanned like the rest of him. It all feels so disgustingly choreographed, like he's used to playing the nice guy. *Had a lot of practice there, Nicholas?*

"This a big surprise, then?" he asks.

"*Huge* surprise," I say, snapping a limb off the gingerbread tree. "This Christmas is full of them."

And . . . I despise this. Literally could not hate it more. Sitting here with him, in my grandmother's kitchen, those family vacation magnets staring back at me from the fridge; they're trying to lull me into a false sense of security. How can anything bad happen here? How *did* anything bad ever happen here? My middle school artwork is framed on the walls.

"For me, too," Nick says, rapping his knuckles lightly on the countertop. When's the last time he punched someone with those? "The surprises, I mean. I wasn't planning on spending Christmas here. I thought I'd just take the week off, hunker down in my apartment, and tackle some books I've been meaning to read. Although *thank you*," he jumps in to add. "Your Grandma Ruby's great. I just met her, and five minutes later, she's already inviting me to next Christmas."

Keep my grandma's name out of your mouth, I think. Still, I force out a smile. "Yeah, that sounds like her."

Nick leans in conspiratorially. His dark brown eyes fade into gold around the edges. "I feel like I can say this to you, now that your grandma's not here, but I'm not really a big Christmas person."

Another lie. With one eyebrow raised, I point to his CHRISTMAS SWEATER sweatshirt.

"This?" Nick thumbs the cotton. "Airport purchase. Thought I'd try to blend in. Is it working?"

I nod, reluctantly playing along. "I *think* so. You have very good airport purchase control. I just bought a year's worth of Toblerone."

"Oh, you can never have enough Toblerone," Nick says without missing a beat.

"Thank you."

"Or those U-shaped neck pillows. Actually . . . I take that back. You can definitely have too many neck pillows."

"Eight?" I ask, keeping my annoyance in check. "Twelve?"

"Six," he says, "arbitrarily."

I sniff out a laugh and urge myself to keep going. Maybe if I lay enough groundwork, I can gather some early intel before Johnny arrives. "You're right about Grandma Ruby, by the way. She goes big for all the holidays. Fourth of July, Arbor Day. We have one of those giant animatronic Easter Bunnies for the front yard."

Nick faux shudders.

Did he seriously just do that? What kind of game is he playing? "I'm sorry, did you shudder?"

"The Easter Bunny," he says. "You said *animatronic*, but you also could've said *demonic*, and I would've heard it the same way." He gestures to his muscular thighs, and I wish I could bleach them from my vision. "It has long legs! It's pink!"

"So we're not a Christmas fan, not an Easter fan. How are we feeling about Groundhog Day?"

"Love it," Nick jokes annoyingly. "Punxsutawney Phil is a national treasure."

"Arbor Day?"

"I'm Canadian. Can't get enough of it. Let's plant those trees."

"To be fair," I say, enduring the bit, "that bunny decoration does scare the shit out of the neighborhood kids. They egged our house three years in a row."

Nick raises one of his thick, dark eyebrows. "Is that an Easter metaphor? Easter eggs?"

"I don't think they're that perceptive," I admit. "Last year, for Halloween, Grandma Ruby said that one of them dressed as a loaf of bread with zero trace of humor. He was just really, really serious bread."

"Mmm," Nick says, pressing his lips together. "Sourdough, probably."

It's such a dad joke, and he looks almost embarrassed for making it. It pisses me off *to my core* that for a split second, I give a real chuckle. I want to slap myself. I quickly rein it in as Nick grins fully at me, like he's surprised with this conversation. Who knew that shower girl could initiate such good bread banter? He goes on, rubbing a hand over the back of his neck. "Hey, I just wanted to say up front, sorry if I'm cramping your style here. I'm sure spending the holidays with some random guy isn't what you expected." He's looking sheepish again, full lips half twisted to the side, and *Oh, come on. Stop pretending like you're not on the naughty list.* I've seen the surveillance footage; that suspect from the New York heist looks a hell of a lot like Nick, from the side.

"Nah," I say, appeasing him. "It's good that you're here. More people for our holiday week games competition. How are you at Pictionary?"

"As a matter of fact," Nick says, taking an extra-dramatic pause, "I am . . . terrible."

"Charades?"

"Couldn't be worse."

"Perfect," I say brightly, nudging his hand. The hand nudge is premeditated. Even though, as with the Grinch, I wouldn't want to touch him with a thirty-nine-and-a-half-foot pole. "You can be on Calla's team."

At this, he chuckles and finally snaps off a piece of his cookie. By her dog bowls, Sweetie Pie pauses for a second before taking a drink, loudly sloshing; Nick offers her a silly "hellooo, hellooo" as I fiddle with the silver ring on my thumb, preparing to steer us in a different direction.

"So," I ask, "what's he like?"

"Who?" Nick asks, chewing his cookie.

"Johnny." His name comes out casual, light. As if I'm talking about laundry. Or the weather. Then I give Nick a calculated bit of honesty. We're taught to do this in the CIA: to open up a little when needed. To give our targets the impression that they know us. It usually doesn't hurt this bad. "I didn't even know he and Calla were together, much less getting married."

Nick half chokes on the gingerbread, coughing up a few crumbs. "What? Really?"

"Really. Just found out."

A long puff of air escapes Nick's lips. He sits back on the stool, hands running up and down his dark jeans, like he's trying to draw attention to his muscles. Gross. "I had no idea. So Calla didn't . . ."

"Nothing," I supply. "Not a word. Though, I'm not the easiest person to get in touch with."

"Right," he says. "You travel a lot, don't you? With the Department of Education?"

"I do," I say, a little surprised—and angry—that he knows this about me. Immediately, I ready myself for the well-rehearsed script. My cover story is that I'm an educational researcher based in Washington, DC. Whenever I have to leave the country to "survey an international school" or "attend a conference," no one questions it. "Traveling's a shit excuse, I know."

Nick considers this with a perplexed look, then settles back into his easygoing confidence. "I could've sworn Calla said . . . Well, anyway, Johnny and I go way back. I don't have any brothers, my family's small, so he's kind of it. We rowed together at Northwestern, did a lot of volunteer work together, too."

This shouldn't set my teeth on edge, but it does. I've seen evidence of this volunteer work—all the charities that the Jones family donates to. There are pictures of Johnny breaking ground at a new children's hospital, of him petting puppies at the pound. If I had to guess, it's part of the reason why Calla was attracted to him in the first place. And it's a façade. The more volunteer work the Joneses do, the stronger their alibis become; the more people in South Boston jump to protect them.

I tilt my head to the side. "Johnny's one of the good ones, huh?"

Nick stares at me oddly for a second, like he's trying to work something out, before nodding earnestly. "Yeah, he is."

Liar, liar, pants on fire. "What's his family like?"

Maybe I've taken a step too far, too fast, because Nick leans even farther back. He is by no means a small man. I'm five foot nine, so he must be pushing six-three. He has a rower's body. My eyes are clocking the strong build of his arms, the sinew and muscle beneath his sweatshirt. The fabric stretches tightly across his chest. And it happens naturally—the calculations. How I'd take him if things went south. Fist to the throat. Hurl him up against the wall. My body pinning his body.

"His family's complicated," Nick finally says, "to be honest."

"Complicated how?" I push, feigning general, sisterly interest. If he didn't call me on the last question, he won't call me on this one.

"In a way that a lot of families are complicated." Nick shrugs those powerful shoulders. "They'd do anything for each other, even if his dad and his grandpa used to butt heads over the family business."

Ah, there it is. I sit back on my stool, mirroring Nick. Sometimes, the best way to interrogate someone is to fill the room with silence. Keep your lips zipped. Wait for the other person to talk. If Nick actually has a problem with silence, then he's an interrogator's dream.

"You've heard of Morning Kick?" he asks.

Who hasn't? Morning Kick is a popular coffee chain in the Northeast, Midwest, and Southern California. They're not quite a Dunkin' Donuts rival, but over the past eight years, they've astronomically increased their market share and their customer base. I've had their espresso a few times—and I read all about them last night. What customers don't know is that the owners of Morning Kick often serve their caffeine with a side of actual violence.

"That's Johnny's family's brand," Nick says, with ironic timing.

Unfortunately, before he can say another word, the garage door opens. I hear the tug-tug-tug of the motorized chain. My grandma is parking her car and is just about to trudge into the laundry room. The back door springs open, bells jingly on the knob, and she arrives in a cloud of fresh linen scent, plastic grocery bags dangling from her hands. It looks like she's bought half the vegetable section; green onions poke out, rubbing against the sleeves of her L.L. Bean coat.

Or is that . . . Dad's old L.L. Bean coat? Did she take it out of storage?

She sets down the bags in the laundry room, begins to step out of her snow boots—and spots me with a gasp. I've stood up from the kitchen stool. I've set down the battered remains of my cookie. And my throat is tickling at the sight of her: my grandma in her snow-dusted beanie and paint-speckled scarf, motionless in the laundry room doorway, a smile breaking over her face like sunlight.

I should've called her more. I should've come home more.

I should've tried harder.

"AHHHHHHHHHHHHHHHHH!" she cries out, breaking through the whispered hush. She's fast: a puff of white hair and a red flash of cashmere. Her boots stamp snow across the tile as she drops the grocery bags and leaps for me, knifeless. I say knifeless because, if I didn't know this woman, I'd think she was sent to assassinate me. She is perhaps a little too vocal for your run-of-the-mill hit person, but she's also a spitfire: eighty-two years old, a former woodworker, and the first person to show me how to throw a punch. "It's a valuable skill," she told me and Calla one winter in our garage. "Take this seriously. Never tuck your thumb under the rest of your fingers, and get your whole body behind it."

Now, I can barely get out a subtle "Surprise!" before her arms are wrapped around me, so tight. Her hair smells of kelp-and-jasmine shampoo, and this, too, tickles a long-buried emotion in my throat.

"Surprise," I say again, and Grandma Ruby rocks me back and forth.

"Oh, Sydney Bean! This *is* a surprise. The most *wonderful*, wonderful surprise. It's a Christmas miracle! I was decorating the top of my dresser just last night, and I found that little moose ornament you made me in elementary school—and I thought, what if Sydney were here? And now you *are* here. Just imagine that."

I am. I'm imagining everything. I'm thinking about how I'd feel if I'd come home for Christmas *on my own*. Not like this. Not on command from some stranger named Gail. Inside my brain, there's a big part of me that's screaming, *Liar! Liar! Sydney, you are a deceitful little liar.*

"You look too thin," Grandma Ruby says, pulling back. Her hands cup my cheeks, her grip surprisingly strong for her age. Throughout my childhood, she was the one to open the pickle jars.

"I've gained, like, fifteen pounds since you last saw me," I reply through my squished face, and in the background, I can see Nick put a few fingers over his mouth to hide his smile. *Ugh.* Looks like he's loving this big, happy family reunion. Or at least he's pretending to. And it irks me, my two worlds clashing: job and family. When you're a spy, you have to open up and share bits of your life strategically; but you are not, under any circumstances, open about *everything*.

For Nick to see me like this? With my grandma? It's exposing. Damaging. My family knows the before Sydney; they've seen the soft underlayer.

Grandma Ruby releases me, grinning. True to her name, she's wearing her signature ruby-colored broach; she never leaves the house without a splash of red—her power color. Like she's dressed for Christmas year-round. "I feel like the luckiest grandmother alive," she says, trademark spark in her eye, just as someone else walks through the door.

No, not just someone. *Him.*

Johnny Jones is traipsing out of the laundry room, a fistful of bright silver CONGRATULATIONS balloons in one fist. Did he buy the balloons himself, *for* himself? In the other hand, he's balancing a store-bought cake with white buttercream frosting; a swirl icing on top decrees TOGETHER FOREVER. It's a really domestic scene, let me tell you. So damn delightful. I don't clench my fists; I'm supposed to be decking the halls, not Calla's fiancé.

Together forever. Like hell they will be.

"Look who I found at the supermarket!" Grandma Ruby says, pointing to Johnny. Johnny, with his smug face and his stupid balloons and his eager, pleasant smile. He's only slightly taller than me, but his frame crowds the doorway. Ice-blue eyes, tamed blond curls, and a white corded sweater, like he's fresh out of a Ralph Lauren catalog. In fact, he could *model* for a Ralph Lauren catalog. All he needs is a yacht. And a polo pony. If you looked up WASP in the dictionary, you'd find his picture: extremely clean cut, with a plush blue scarf under an expensive winter jacket. It's designer. How much did he pay for that? Eight hundred dollars? A thousand?

And where does he keep his cell phone?

I could swipe the phone, upload the tracking virus, and return it in under a minute flat.

"Is that *Sydney*?" he says to me, as if he's greeting a six-year-old. As if he's playing Santa Claus in a Christmas pageant, and I'm the surprise guest that someone's pulled onstage. He doesn't wait for a cue. He simply waltzes over and throws his arms around me in a rather painful way, lifting me clear off the ground. We spin. It cracks my back. I hate him.

"It is so good to *meet* you," he says. Somehow, his Boston accent is a lot thicker in person than it is in his audio files. You could spread it on bagels. In this alternate reality—where I'm not a CIA case officer, just a sister home for Christmas—I also don't know who the hell he is. I play it like that.

"Okay, thank you, that's enough," I say lightly, grabbing on to the countertop.

"Wow," Johnny says again when my boots touch the floor, stepping back to appraise me. His eyes really take their time. He swipes two hands down his clean, clean scarf, returning it to smooth perfection; he has the precise air of a Connecticut frat boy, mixed with a dash of mob. There's a *loudness* about him, from the volume of his voice to the one-two punch of his spiced cologne. "I've heard so much about you!"

Matching his vocal volume, I give the customary reply of "Good things, I hope!" while inside I'm thinking, *Can't say the same about you, bucko.* My brain actually inserts the word *bucko.* I have never used *bucko* in my life.

Why'd Calla have to pick him? What's wrong with—I don't know—your nice, standard veterinarian? Or a midwife. A midwife who reads to the blind.

"'Course, 'course, all good things." Johnny thwacks me on the shoulder, hard, as Sweetie Pie rushes in to greet him with a hearty sniff to his crotch. Her nose really *digs* into the khaki. She's an intelligence operative, too, gathering all the scent information her snout can contain.

Bite, I think. *Bite.*

(She would never.)

"Well, aren't you friendly," Johnny says to Sweetie Pie.

"Oh, you betcha!" Grandma Ruby says, tapping her temple,

right under the burst of white hair. "Smart as a whip, too. She watches *CSI: Miami* with me and always barks right before they discover the evidence. Don't you, good girl?"

Johnny gives the appropriate chuckle at this, then switches his audience to Nick, calling to him from across the kitchen. Loud, loud, loud. "So good to see you, man! You get in early?" Johnny ventures over, dipping and dodging like a football player in practice—as if he's about to tackle Nick instead of embrace him. They do a wide bro hug, throwing their arms out and slapping each other's backs. "Marco's just helping with the bags and then he's off."

Nick frowns into the hug. The expression looks almost unnatural on his face, but just seeing it—I feel like I know him a bit better. The underneath Nick. The angrier, dumb-muscle Nick he's been hiding from me. "He's not staying?"

Johnny shakes his head exaggeratedly. *Every* movement he makes is inflated, larger than life. "Nope, gave him the week off. It's Christmas. You know he's got a kid. Angela? You've met Angela! At church a few Sundays back. She's got braces like Vinny's kid. Vinny says you owe him a round of drinks when you get back to Boston, by the way, and you missed poker last week. Just a message! Don't shoot the messenger. Anyway, we can manage without Marco. Calla's just—"

Here. Calla's here.

I see her and my stomach twists.

My sister is steadying herself, one hand on the washing machine, like I'm the Ghost of Christmas Past and she can't quite believe I'm in the kitchen. She doesn't seem to notice when she drops a bag of oranges, a few tumbling into the cleaning supplies. Her hair's a little shorter than when I saw her last, chestnut brown and falling across her shoulders in carefully constructed curls.

She's wearing a pearly white headband and puffy snowman earrings.

Immediately, I'm sixteen years old again, my sister's head on my shoulder, and we're talking about Dad. *Was he serious? Was he really not coming back?* He'd sold his truck at a roadside car lot, taken all the camping supplies from Grandma Ruby's house, and as far as we knew, he was somewhere on the Appalachian Trail. Just walking. Away from us. Being a dad was too much for him. Two teenage girls were too much for him. But it made me stronger, I think—for Calla. I told her that, with Grandma Ruby's help, I'd watch out for us now. *Don't worry. Let me worry.*

For years, it stayed like that. I barely let anyone else in below the surface, but Calla—my little sister—we joined soccer teams together and went to Bowdoin together and I kept my promise. Then, the CIA. Then, station houses and new aliases and schedules without a moment to catch my breath. And maybe . . . maybe I stopped knowing how to talk about my life with her—what details to bring up, what to keep hidden. Is it possible that, in the last three years, she's learned to keep things from me, too?

"Hi," I say with a shrug, almost like I'm apologizing. *Will you forgive me for not being the sister I could've been?*

"Oh my *god*," Calla says, bursting forward. It's a very hug-centric evening. Except, this time, I go fully in, squeezing her with everything I've got. Her earrings tangle with my hair.

"I've missed you," I say, telling myself not to get choked up.

And she responds in a whisper that makes my blood chill, "I need to talk to you *immediately*."

4

We should go outside. Into the yard. *Way* past the listening devices currently implanted in our house.

Calla does try to drag me by the hand upstairs. (The hand thing is new. She's a kindergarten teacher now. I imagine there's a lot of hand-holding in that profession; at least mine aren't sticky.) But I think quickly, gripping *her* hand instead—and pulling her toward the front door. Won't she drive around our neighborhood with me? I've barely seen the Christmas decorations. "Come on, please?" I beg. "It'll just take a second. I want to know if the Wilsons still have that big inflatable reindeer. What did we name him? Pudding?"

She'll go for this. She'll relent. My other option was to entice her with a frozen yogurt run. Random? Yes. Effective? Totally.

"Okay, fine," Calla says. "Pudding. But we have to be really quick, so—"

The wind eats up the rest of her words, icy air pelting down our throats, but I manage to engineer her into my rental car, practically pushing her into the passenger seat and clicking shut the door. Once I'm in the driver's seat myself, I switch on the engine, blast the heating, and turn to her. "You were saying?"

Her bright red holiday scarf is still wrapped tightly around her neck. She loosens it, reaching out and lifting a piece of my hair. "Why are you so soggy? Syd, it's freezing out here. Your hair's going to turn to icicles."

I brush off her last comment, letting her hand drop as I pull out of the driveway on this Christmas lights charade. "What were you going to say? And are we just ignoring the fact that there are two random men in our kitchen?"

Calla bites her lip, her snowman earrings blowing back with the force of the heater. Our mailbox wreath flashes by the window. "I'll get to them. It's just... Do you have any idea how many times I've tried to reach you in the last month? I know you're bad about answering the phone, and I usually don't blame you—but this time it was really, really important. You know what? I went to your apartment."

This stops me cold, even as I act naturally. "You... went to my apartment."

"Or what I thought was your apartment," Calla says, gaining steam. Little red dots are starting to appear on her neck, just above her scarf. "I booked a ticket from Boston to DC. I brought a bottle of champagne and a big bag of Swedish fish to your building, and your doorman told me I couldn't go up because *you didn't live there.* Where do you live, Sydney? I mailed you a Christmas card. It came back RETURN TO SENDER."

There are so many elements to unpack in her statement. The Swedish fish? That's our thing. It's always been our thing. A callback to when we were little, and we'd spend hours after school watching cartoons and chewing stale candy from Grandma Ruby's kitchen stash. Sometimes Dad would join us, lounging out in his wool socks, laughing at all of our cartoons; sometimes it felt like he was a kid, too. Less like a dad, more like an older brother. I'm not sure he ever knew quite what to do with us, almost on his own, a widower at thirty-eight. The one time he tried to give Calla a ponytail, he used a vacuum cleaner hose: just sucked all her hair into a bundle and tied it with a thin, rubbery band.

He didn't do the discipline or the "fathering." Just the fun. Grandma Ruby was always the gentle disciplinarian, the one we ran to, the one who stayed.

I swallow soundlessly. "I moved a few weeks ago to be closer to work. I didn't—"

"*Please* don't lie to me," Calla interrupts loudly, which is how I know she's serious. Calla almost never raises her voice. She's lit up equally with holiday spirit and fury, icicle lights from the houses flashing behind her. Her eyes look—just slightly—like she wants to break all my Christmas cookies. "I mailed you that card in November."

Of course she mails her Christmas cards in November. She would do that. That is the kind of person Calla is: dependable, thoughtful, the first to wish you a happy holiday. And she's right. I am lying. I moved four months ago into an unlisted apartment near the Lincoln Memorial. No one's been inside it but me. (And an Uber Eats delivery guy, once, when my kitchen sink was overflowing.)

I hate lying to her. I hate lying to anyone.

"I had my mail stopped before then," I hedge, making a turn around the cul-de-sac. Pudding the reindeer is nowhere to be seen. "I'm sorry, I didn't—"

"I'm getting married," Calla says without the slightest hint of a pause, thrusting up a hand. The engagement ring on her finger doesn't just sparkle; it announces itself. It's like one of those flashing beacons they use to advertise a car dealership. My stomach gutters, remembering the jewelry store from the Jones file. Johnny didn't . . . Johnny didn't give her a ring from one of his *heists*, did he? Would he be that stupid? That arrogant?

Is she literally wearing evidence on her finger?

Those diamonds from the Tampa, Florida, heist never showed up on the black market . . .

"You don't look surprised," Calla says, some of the anger fizzling out of her. It's more disappointment now. "Why don't you look surprised?"

Pulling to a halt at the next mailbox, I grab her hand gently, examining the ring in the half-light of the car, physically unable to stop whatever my face is doing. I thought I'd be able to keep up the act, to not break character. To treat this holiday like every other mission of my career. But I'm slowly realizing . . . easier said than done. "Look at the size of that thing. People always say that in movies, and I really *get* it now."

"Sydney!"

"Okay, fine." I drop her hand, flustered—and settle back into my part. "I just met Nick, and we were talking about it downstairs . . . I can't believe my little sister's getting married." It's true. So is the genuine emotion in my voice. I remember when Calla married our G.I. Joes, and her biggest crush was the fox version of Robin Hood. How'd we get here from there?

Calla's brown eyes soften a bit, and her fingers yank at the sleeves of her sweater. The black outline of a crescent moon tattoo, same as mine, peeks out from above the cuff. "This is kind of the point where you congratulate me."

"Congratulations," I say, throwing in as much warmth as I can stomach. I'm happy that she's happy. But I'm not happy that she's happy with *him*.

Snow starts falling on the windshield. Big globs of it *splat, splat, splat*. I stare at the oversize snowflakes, sifting through options of how to play this. I can't just jump in with *Are you* sure *Johnny's the one? Two thousand percent sure?* Before I settle on something, Calla adds, "It probably sucked not to hear it from me, but I really was trying to tell you! I didn't want to do it over a text or in a voice mail. You're my maid of honor, and—"

Damn it if my eyes don't get a little foggy. "I am?"

"Syd. Of course you are. You're my sister, always, forever, to the moon and back, whether or not you answer my calls in a timely manner . . . I *love* you, Jelly Belly."

Jelly Belly. For my childhood love of jelly beans. The nickname hits me in the solar plexus. Calla hasn't called me that in years. Maybe not since . . . not since the last time we saw a Cape Hathaway Huskies baseball game together. Our end-of-summer ritual, never missed, until it was. Calla never really liked baseball, so I thought it would be okay to let that one thing—that hard thing—go.

I inhale and let it all out, ignoring every single one of the Christmas lights. "Love you, too, Calla Lilly."

Calla leans back against the headrest and scrounges up a smile. "Sweetie Pie's going to be the flower girl. We just have to train her not to sniff Johnny's crotch in front of the entire wedding party."

"That would add to the ceremony, honestly," I say before steering us back on track, my pulse picking up again. "When's the wedding?"

"We haven't decided yet," Calla says with another lip bite. "Probably in the spring. Johnny's family has a big house in Boston. We thought we'd have it there. Classy, but simple. Family focused." She pokes me with a finger. "You could've called to say you were coming home."

"Mmm," I say, calculating how the FBI might set up surveillance *inside* the Jones compound. Hopefully we won't need that. Hopefully I can secure enough intel this Christmas, and the wedding will be over before the cake's even ordered. "I wanted it to be a surprise."

"Well, it is. I'm very surprised." Just then, she straightens in the passenger seat. When I look over again, something sparks in her pupils. Pure joy and inspiration. "Sydney, you're *here* for Christmas."

"Yes . . ." I say, unsure where she's going with this.

"You're staying through Christmas Day, right?" The sparks grow, like miniature sticks of dynamite, ready to explode. Shrapnel everywhere. Wear a helmet. "And Nick's here. You two are going to get along so well. He's Johnny's best man. And Johnny's parents just said they're coming for Christmas Eve."

I twirl my finger, asking her to rewind. "Johnny's parents are going to be here, too? In our house?"

But she isn't really hearing me. She's lost in an idea. The red blotches on her neck are growing in the excitement, and I'm getting the very distinct and terrible impression that one of the most significant conversations of my life is about to happen in a Prius. "All the decorations will still be up," Calla says, speaking faster and faster, "and since—sorry—I have no faith that you'll be back in the Northeast anytime soon, even with advance warning, and I *really* want you by my side . . ."

No. No, she isn't.

She isn't going to say it. Calla is too meticulously organized for anything this spontaneous.

"Johnny and I should get married *this* Christmas, don't you think? We could have an impromptu Christmas Day wedding."

She said it. *Shit, shit, shit.* "Nooooo," I breathe, feeling like the car is caving in. This isn't Calla. Who is this impulsive, devil-may-care person? "No, I'll be there. I'll be there *in the spring.* Or the summer! Summer's even better. You said it yourself, it's freezing outside. It's Maine. You don't want a winter wedding."

"I do, actually," Calla says, as if the thought's appealing to her more and more. "You know I love Christmas, and it's easier for you this way. Less work for all the maid of honor things. Plus, I am *never* spontaneous, and it would just be so romantic—"

"Know what's romantic? Advance planning. Vendor spreadsheets." My chest is tight. I know my sister. I know my sister, don't I? "Calla, this isn't . . . this isn't you. Don't you want to schedule it all out?"

"Not this time," she says, adamant. "I've realized over the past year that I hold on to things so tightly, and I'm also so *rigid* in my relationships. I promised myself, with Johnny, that it's going to be different in every way."

Well, that's for damn sure.

Calla reaches out and holds my hand as we stop in front of our house again. "I want this."

"You just thought of this."

"You owe me," she bats back. "I know it's happening fast, but this really is what I want. To get married here, at the house, with my family." She gestures out the window, where our yellow colonial stands in all its Christmassy glory. There's a dancing felt reindeer in one of the windows; it looks like it's doing a drunken, slightly risqué jig. Somewhere inside the kitchen, Grandma Ruby might be pouring herself a glass of chardonnay, getting ready to outdo the reindeer.

"I don't need fancy," Calla says. "I don't need the elaborate table settings or the expensive dress. I have everything I need, right here. Grandma Ruby's a certified justice of the peace! She can marry us."

Like fucking fuck she will.

"What about Johnny?" I'm foraging for an excuse. Any reasonable excuse that I can say out loud. "Maybe he'll think it's too soon? Maybe he wants to get married at his parents' place instead? This is a lot to put on him, Cal, and he might not—"

Calla shakes her head. "I'll have to run it past him first, of course, and we'll have to talk it through, but I think he'll be happy if I'm happy. And he really does try to make me happy." It's like she feels the need to prove this, plowing on. "He's even started learning about art history so we can go to all the museums I like and actually talk in depth about the paintings. I mean, what other guy would do that? Johnny . . . Johnny's stable, and he's really emotionally intelligent, and he loves me. I promise—I *promise* you, Sydney—you'll love him, too."

It's the first promise she's ever made to me that I know she can't keep.

"Come on," Calla says with one last squeeze of her hand. "Let's tell everyone the good news."

When Calla and Johnny unleash the "good news," there's an instant, joyous uproar. Mostly from Johnny himself. He hoots and pumps his fist, twice, like our kitchen is a New Jersey nightclub. Nick pours five glasses of cider from Cape Hathaway Farms, which Grandma Ruby's brought up with a little shimmy from the cellar. Tears stream down her cheeks as she offers Calla her wedding dress (which, as far as we know, has been mildly pillaged by attic raccoons), and Sweetie Pie dances on everyone's feet, thrilled to be a part of whatever the hell is happening. As for me? I watch Johnny swing Calla wildly in his arms, self-congratulatory balloons tangled all around them, and try not to ignore the churn in my stomach.

If I didn't know who he was—who the real Johnny was—I *might* think they were a nice couple. Very much in love. He bops the tip of her nose, all cutesy, with his finger, and there's an easygoing air between them, like they've known each other for much longer than a few measly months. Does he really love her? Probably. It's impossible not to love Calla. But does Calla have any doubts about *him*?

Or his friends? Like Nick?

"God, I love weddings," Nick says, sidling up next to me, running a hand through his hair. He's just popped another cider cork in a vaguely sexual way, and he offers me a tall, thin glass.

My, aren't we polite?

"Thanks." I take the glass, half numb, adding *Nick's cell phone* to the plan. I'll upload the tracking virus to his phone as well. Tonight. After everyone's had a bit too much to drink. Trailing Calla inside, I've already planted a dime-size tracker under the bumper of Johnny's rental car.

That way, anywhere the car goes, I can follow.

"You been to one lately?" Nick asks, taking a sip of his cider. The glug skates down his throat.

"I'm sorry." I shake my head, preoccupied with Calla and Johnny. "One what?"

Another slow sip from Nick, Adam's apple bobbing. "Wedding."

"Ah," I say. "No."

"You're missing out," Nick says, still in joking mode. "Cake, the Chicken Dance, talking to random relatives, what's not to like?"

I'm only half listening to him. I can't take my eyes off my sister. How she's leaning into Johnny, so comfortable.

When I was recruited for the CIA, I knew I'd learn everything there was to know about reading people: their body language, their motives, the things they try to hide. I knew that the CIA would provide a cover that I could slip into. There, I wouldn't have to be the real Sydney, the whole Sydney; no one would get to know me unless I let them. And I didn't have to let them.

Problem is, when you abandon your old life, it's hard to keep an eye on it.

I used to want the distance. Not from Calla. Just from . . . everything else. Now, I'm kicking myself for it.

"Sydney Bean?" Grandma Ruby shuffles over to Nick and me, pointing at the record player in the living room. "Would you mind putting on something festive?"

"Sure." I nod a little too forcefully. "Sure."

Grandma Ruby runs her thumb along the rim of her glass, like she's trying to make it sing. "Something on your mind, pumpkin? You've had that same look since you were a baby and you were trying to figure out how to pet a dog."

This—*this* is why she's so good at blackjack, why no one bets against her at the senior center anymore. She's quietly perceptive. Sharp. She can read people better than most CIA officers in the field.

Outwardly, I cheer up, eyes brightening. I need to be as merry looking as the rest of them. Nick's outdoing me with his stupid CHRISTMAS SWEATER sweatshirt. "Just happy for Calla, that's all." I slip away from Grandma Ruby and Nick as nonchalantly as possible. "I'll pick something good. Go celebrate! Go!"

At my back, Nick gives me a perceptive tilt of his head, wavy black hair shimmering under the kitchen lights. Despite the happiness on his face, his security professional mind might be picking apart my performance. I make a sharp turn into the living room, thinking, *So! This is what an out-of-body experience feels like. My sister in the breakfast nook with a crime lord. Marrying him. This Christmas.* By the stereo, I lean on my tried-and-true techniques for relieving anxiety. Everyone in the CIA has anxiety. We just know how to hide it better, how to harness it, and how to manage it in times of extreme crisis.

Silently, I box-breathe. Four-second inhale, four-second hold, four-second exhale. Repeat, repeat, as my fingers flick through old records, landing on a band called The Squirrel Nut Zippers. My dad . . . my dad used to play their Christmas album every holiday. He'd turn the volume up loud and do the *Pulp Fiction* dance, limp-wristed, just to make us giggle. He could really *do* Christmas, with the reindeer antlers and fake stomps on the roof; he'd actually get up there and trick us. Nearly slipped on the ice one year. Grandma Ruby had to tell us Santa was a bit clumsy.

I almost smile at this, the memory of Calla and me, necks craned up to the stomping sound—but then, ten Christmases later, nothing. Silence. A lot of people joke about just walking off one day, disappearing into the woods, but our dad—well, he put his money where his mouth was. As far as I know, he's still walking.

I run a smooth finger over the record. He liked saying the band's name. Zippers. Zippy. Zip-Zip. Zzzzzz . . .

My phone vibrates in my back pocket.

An encrypted text from Gail: Call me ASAP.

I might hear from my CIA handler once a week. Gail is oddly communicative.

Slapping on the record, I duck out of sight, climbing the creaky wooden stairs all the way up to the attic, not even bothering to flip on the lights. It's private up here—and inside-of-the-fridge freezing. The cold starts numbing my fingertips, my eyelids . . . My eyelids are getting heavier. When was the last time I slept? Thirty hours ago?

Never mind. Doesn't matter. I stand near the boiler for warmth and for a noise barrier.

"Sydney," Gail says when I dial her. Her voice is crisp. "I'm not sure whether I should say congratulations, maid of honor, or offer you a Kleenex. Metaphorically speaking."

I lean back to thwack my head—once, twice—on one of the

attic rafters. You know the Christmas song that goes, *He sees you when you're sleeping, he knows when you're awake?* That's not Santa. That's the FBI. It doesn't surprise me: There are bugs in the kitchen.

Gail goes swiftly on. "Needless to say, the landscape has changed slightly. Especially on your end. I thought we had more time, at least until New Year's Eve, but once they're married, Calla's plausible deniability diminishes significantly. Of course, it's not a wife's responsibility to know everything her husband is up to, but . . ."

"I'm *telling* you," I stress, still managing to whisper. Sound carries in this house, and I don't want Johnny to hear me above the boiler. Or Nick. Or the attic raccoons. "I don't think that Calla knows about the heists. She wasn't hiding anything with her body language." Not that I could see, anyway. *But you don't always see what's right in front of you, do you, Sydney?* "You don't think we should bring her into the fold? Tell her who her fiancé really is and what's about to go down on New Year's Eve?"

"Absolutely not. We've spoken about this. We'd risk compromising the entire investigation. If your sister is innocent, by some miracle, there's no way she could keep up the charade after we tell her. And then what?"

"Maybe we could put a wire on her," I push gently, still wrestling with the choice. The spontaneous wedding—the swift switch in personality—has made me question my gut, but she's . . . she's *Calla.* "Who knows what Johnny might tell her if she prods him a little when they're alone? We could give her a script, work in a specific question about the next heist that feels organic. Maybe tell her to ask him about her engagement ring. Did you see the ring?"

"I've seen the ring."

"Okay, so—"

"So I'll say it again: We *cannot* risk getting found out. We'd need much more information before making that sort of leap."

She's right. She is. Keeping this from Calla is my choice, too. "Then I'll get the information. I'm planting the tracker on Johnny's phone tonight, and I'll keep working on my sister."

It sounds like Gail sucks her teeth. "No."

The flatness of her response throws me. "No?"

"A targeted approach is always better than a scattershot one," Gail says after a moment's pause. "No need to go poking holes in everything willy-nilly. Keep tabs on Johnny. Send me the intel from his phone and a close-up image of the ring, and I'll see if it matches any of our records of stolen items. Keep a line of communication open with Calla, obviously, but it's clear that you two aren't as close as you once were, and my gut is telling me there's a smarter way to go about this."

Her comment slices its way into my stomach. It curdles there. True, Calla and I aren't as close as we were, but hearing it out loud—from someone I met a little over twenty-four hours ago—is particularly brutal. "How's that?"

"Nick," Gail says, in the same way one might say *duh*. "You two clearly have some sort of . . . chemistry."

The comment is a face slap. "With the *Canadian* guy?"

"What's wrong with being Canadian? My grandmother was half Canadian."

I shake my head furiously. "Nothing. That wasn't a comment about his nationality. Just about him."

Gail waits a third of a beat. "Since you haven't jumped in immediately with a rebuttal, I think you agree about the chemistry."

"Actually, I unequivocally disagree."

"Too late," Gail says. "The pause was noted."

My jaw clenches. I see where she's going with this. "So you want me to . . ."

"Make him like you," Gail finishes, providing the answer I've already guessed. "Listen. Nick is closer to Johnny than anyone. Who knows more than the former bodyguard? Add to that, Nick's new role as head of personal security and his friendly history with Johnny. This could be the break for us, Sydney. Nick has dated women in the past, and *you're* a woman . . ."

Seduce him, she means. Seduce Nick Fraser.

I massage my forehead, which is beginning to feel like an ice cube. A throbbing, painful ice cube.

I'm confident about my abilities, but did it really have to be *him*? Besides the fact that I trust the guy about as much as a rabid wolverine, Nick's goal is to protect Johnny and the Jones family at all costs. My goal is to take down Johnny and the Jones family at all costs. Not exactly a match made in heaven. Also, it isn't an even playing field. I'm *me* here. I'm only half undercover in my own house, in my hometown. So many things about me are already out in the open; I can't dole them out strategically.

There's no barrier. No protection.

I need that.

Besides, who knows if Nick will play along? Who knows if he's even attracted to me? What if he finds me as obnoxious as I find him?

Apparently, Gail interprets my silence as insubordination. "Your organization does unseemly, unethical, and grotesque things nearly every day. The CIA makes political prisoners disappear. They facilitate illogical coups on foreign soil. All I'm asking you, Sydney, is to flirt with the man over a chicken."

I frown into my palm and say bluntly, "I legitimately lost you with the chicken."

Some paperwork shuffles in the background, as if Gail is multi-tasking. "Christmas chicken! Or turkey. I mean turkey. Turkey, ham, pimiento loaf, whatever your family serves at holiday dinners. Just be whoever he wants you to be. Get him to open up and trust you. I know he works in the security world, so he might spot warning signs—tread carefully—but he was *already* starting to open up in the kitchen, even after that disastrous shower stunt. I think we have a decent chance."

She isn't wrong. I peek over my shoulder, triple-ensuring that no one's followed me into the attic, then whisper over the sound of the boiler, "What about Johnny's family? If they come in early for the wedding, can you assemble a task force to swoop in and—"

"Yes, yes, it'll be handled. Don't worry. Go back to the kitchen. Your grandmother is about to make some sort of pie with . . . cayenne peppers?"

"Cayenne pecan pie," I say, distracted. "She's obsessed with spice."

"Mmm. Now, Sydney?"

"Yes?"

"Don't fall for the target."

Seriously? Fall for Nick? My brow fully crinkles. I'm used to the distrust. The CIA never fully trusts you—that's what all the polygraph tests are for—but usually I don't get this shit right before a mission. "Zero percent chance of that."

"It's happened before, historically. With other agents. Sometimes the lines get a tad blurry. It's difficult to tell what's real and what's fake."

"Well, I'm not other operatives. If I can recruit foreign spies, I think I can handle some guy in an airport sweatshirt. You're forgetting that I've done this before."

"Not like this. Those were far different circumstances."

"Gail." I harden myself. "Everything will be under control."

5

In a training camp outside Williamsburg, Virginia, I learned how to tail a target from a distance. I learned how to maneuver an ATV in a high-speed chase, how to position your body in a parachute jump—and the steps to take if you're cornered in a hostile crowd with nothing but the clothes on your back. I'm good at recruiting assets. I'm good at navigating maps, back alleyways, and tricky conversations. Theoretically speaking, I should have no problem maintaining a nearly weeklong fake flirtation that culminates in the transfer of vital intelligence.

Even if it's with someone as repulsively criminal as Nick.

But I am worried, just slightly, about doing all of this as *me*. In my hometown, surrounded by my family. Despite what I've told Gail, I'm actually finding it kind of hard to be my previous self and my agent self at once—and it isn't a one-and-done deal, like with Alexei. I can't switch on the sex appeal and bail an hour later, disappearing on a Swedish night train.

The best I could do here is a very slow and slide-y Prius.

"Okay," I tell myself, clapping my hands once in the attic.

"Okay." If seducing sidekick Nick is the best strategy we have, then I'm all in.

Less than an hour later, Johnny, Nick, Calla, and I are going out.

There aren't many bars in town. In winter, the population of Cape Hathaway shrinks to just under seven hundred. The lobster boats pull in for the season, and the mom-and-pop ice cream stands shutter their windows. All that's left is cold wind on the water, slapping the mossy, black rock—and a tiny inn by the sea, with dim lighting and a formidable whiskey list. This time of the year, Hathaway House is strictly for locals; it's for anniversary trips and date nights, for couples snuggled into cozy booths. Oil paintings of ships and stormy seas line the walls, and the ambience is *just* slick enough for my purposes.

Our only other choice was the Moose Lodge.

With the taxidermied raccoons.

So this will really have to do.

"This place get a lot of traffic?" Nick asks, shrugging off his brown Barbour jacket and hanging it on the edge of his chair. His mask is slipping. He isn't as calm or as lighthearted as he was in the kitchen; in fact, he's mildly on edge, his brow knitted in an annoying little furrow. On the drive here, Johnny kept thwacking his shoulder and telling him, "Loosen up, Nicky boy, it's Christmas. Marco's off duty, and so are you." But even now, as we're perched at a rickety high-top near the bar, I can tell that Nick is fighting his protective mentality. His gaze keeps flicking over to Johnny, whose arm is wrapped loosely around Calla. Johnny's laughing like he wants the whole bar to hear him; he's shooting the shit with the bartender and ordering Calla a holiday-themed drink. It is called, dubiously, "Santa's Surprise."

Frankly, I trust that drink even less than I trust Nick. Which is really saying something.

"'Traffic' and 'Cape Hathaway' don't really go hand in hand," I say, eyeing him. "If you asked, 'Does this place get a lot of knitting circles,' then it would be a different story."

Nick massages the ridge between his eyebrows. Not for the first time, my gaze stops on that faded scar on his chin; how'd he get that? A fight? *Bet you did.* "How many people like to knit in a bar?"

"More than you think."

He drags a hand down his face, then shakes his head like a dog. No, not like a dog. I *respect* dogs. "Sorry, I'm sorry. I'm usually a lot more fun than this, I promise. I just get worried about the job. Johnny's just said that he doesn't want a bodyguard at the holidays. Wants it just to be about family. We're in a town that's so small, no one would care about him here. He's probably right, but . . ."

"Oh, he is right. Our closest thing to a celebrity is the guy who keeps freeing all the lobsters at the grocery store."

Nick snorts, cracking a smile. "Even I've heard about him, the legend."

"The man, the myth." Unshouldering my own parka, I smooth out the sweater beneath it. I've picked the trendiest, most approachable turtleneck in my suitcase: a black one, with shiny gold buttons. Some might say I should've gone for a more obviously sexy outfit, but seduction—I think—isn't always about showing the most skin. Sometimes it's about making them wonder what's *underneath* the wool.

Nick's shallow, I bet. He'll take the bait.

"So how do you normally spend the holidays?" I ask, leaning forward over the table and wrapping my hand around a just-ordered glass of whiskey. Its oaky scent floats in the space between us, tickling my nose. Nick's gone for an old-fashioned, and he's swapped his CHRISTMAS SWEATER for an actual sweater: an all-black number that hugs his shoulders in a try-hard way. His wavy dark hair is a touch damp with melting snow, and he smells of that woodsy-meets-sea soap that I should've clocked him with in the shower.

He's put in some effort for tonight. Good.

"Depends," Nick says, after peering over my shoulder to double-check on good-time Johnny, who's indulging in a predrink sambuca shot, knocking it back with an *ahhhhh*. "What year is it?"

I pretend to consider this heavily, tilting my head back and forth. "Nineteen . . . ninety-nine."

"Then I'm falling asleep every night wishing for a tricycle from Santa Claus," Nick deadpans.

"Did he deliver?"

"Still waiting."

"Damn." I click my tongue. "Tough luck."

"What about you?" he shoots back, still leaving his drink untouched. One of his eyebrows crooks in a flirtatious way, and I read the rest of his body language in a covert sweep. Open. Easy. Just what I want for the mission. "In fact, let me ask this: Why have I been instructed to"—he uses air quotes—"'make sure you don't leave the state' this Christmas?"

A flush of heat threatens to rise to my cheeks. I play it off. "Oh yeah? Who told you that?"

"Calla," Nick admits, voice climbing a little as "A Holly Jolly Christmas" bursts into the speakers in the background. "Then your Grandma Ruby. I'm supposed to keep an eye on you. I think they're afraid you're going to disappear before the wedding, pull a Runaway Maid of Honor."

"Great movie," I say, light and airy. The thought of my family agonizing over me sends a fizzled pang into my stomach, but "running away" isn't exactly what I did. I lock those emotions up tight, resting my chin in my palm and drumming my fingers on the side of my cheek. "How are you going to keep an eye on me, then?"

I look up, meeting Nick's gaze with the tiniest hint of mischief. It catches him off guard. I can tell, because Nick *has* tells. I'm learning them rapidly. When he's surprised, one corner of his mouth ticks up. His pupils widen ever so slightly. His head rears almost imperceptibly back.

"Anyone ever tell you that you're kind of intense?" he asks, squinting, after a moment's pause. He's matched my angle, leaning forward. A slow, borderline sexy smile works its way up his lips. *Does that actually work on other girls, Nicholas?*

"I may have been told that," I admit, slowing my voice to a purposeful beat.

Nick's eyes slide to Johnny, then back to me, his foot jiggling under the table. "It's weird, I keep forgetting that I don't already know you. Calla's been telling us Sydney stories for months."

She has? Whiskey swirls in my glass as I sip and swallow. The vintage is so strong, if I cough, fire might spurt out. "Like what?"

"Like the Maine State Debate Championship."

It's so unexpected that I bark out a laugh—and hate myself for it. "No. Oh god."

Nick's brown eyes glimmer. Can't stand the glimmering. "I have *questions*."

"If Calla told you the story," I respond, still hanging on to my smile, "then you know the story. You don't have questions."

"I *do*," he insists. "The more I think about it, the more questions I have. So you get up there, onstage, in front of all those people . . ."

The metaphorical microphone lands in my lap. The case officer part of me wants to shunt it far into the next room. This is the exact opposite of a sexy story. This is not what I'm going for. But Nick is giving me these ridiculous puppy dog eyes, like *Please, Sydney, please tell the story*, and—goddamn it, Nick. Fine! Okay. I should give him what he wants, for the mission.

My nose scrunches. "I get up there, and I'm calm," I say, aiming to fly through this disaster tale and return to business. "I've won the championship three years in a row, and I know everything there is to know about the legalization of internet gambling. That was the topic, by the way. Gambling. My team was assigned pro, and Jimmy 'the Encyclopedia' Buchanan's team was up first. Jimmy struts up there with his side swoop, looks down at his coach, and winks. Then, all of a sudden, the moderator is asking him about the ethics of cloning."

I can tell that Nick is listening intently, fingers pressed to his stupidly full lips. "I love this part."

"The ethics of cloning! Which is something that Jimmy, apparently, knows all about. He's got statistics. He's got anecdotal evidence. He's memorized quotes from obscure philosophers that play right into his point: In the future, clones will be a necessary addition to society. And I'm sitting there, knowing that my team had been sabotaged. Maybe Jimmy's coach paid off the moderator, I don't know, but I'm seventeen years old, I've been reading about *internet gambling* for the last six months, and for what? To stand up at the podium and embarrass myself in front of two hundred people?"

"Hell no!" Nick says, getting into it. His fist pretend-bangs the table, like he might punch an innocent civilian.

Shoulder to shoulder, Calla and Johnny turn to assess us, probably wondering what the commotion is all about, but I keep right on going. "Hell no!" I repeat with equal, calculated gusto. "So when it's my turn, I walk carefully up to that podium and say the first thing that comes to my mind. Which is to tell a story about what would happen if I cloned myself, eighteen thousand times."

"Why eighteen thousand?" Nick seems genuinely curious. He runs a thumb over his faded chin scar as he thinks. "Where did that number come from?"

"Population of Augusta," I explain. "Maine's state capital. That's where the debate was held. I figured it would add weight to my argument. Keep in mind that I was also heavily involved in marching band at the time. There is nothing more dramatic than marching band. So yeah, I did go into excruciating detail about some of the clones' . . . choices."

"Choices," Nick echoes. "Those were some bold choices."

"You have good clones, you have bad clones." I tuck my hair behind my ears. "Would one of those clones have a personal vendetta against Jimmy? *Maybe.*" I decide to offer up another piece of my past. Just a small thing. Something that will make it look like I'm sharing, without giving away much at all. "Funny thing is, we actually dated after that."

"Yeah?" Nick asks, chuckling. It doesn't feel like he's forcing it. *Good.* This is working.

I nod seriously. "Very end of high school. He tapped me on the shoulder when I was out Christmas shopping, told me we should put the 'debate stuff' behind us, then said, 'Do you celebrate Boxing Day? Because you're the whole package.'"

"He did not."

"He did. In fairness, I like a good line."

"Hit me with your best worst one," Nick says, lighthearted.

"You sure?"

"I'm ready."

I take a second to think before dropping my voice to a husk. "If you were a president, you'd be *Babe*-braham Lincoln."

Nick nearly spits out the first sip of his old-fashioned. "See, that one's not bad at all. That would work on me."

"What's yours?"

"The actual worst one?" Nick sets down his glass, twirls it slowly on the table. He clears his throat. "On a scale of one to America, how free are you tonight?"

"Four," I deadpan.

"See, you're not *actually* supposed to give a number."

"Huh," I say, refusing to drop his gaze, just as he's refusing to drop mine. Two can play this game. And I'll play it better. "Maybe that's where I'm going wrong . . . Do you get to use that line a lot? Out in . . . Boston? Is that where you're from?"

"Boston via Ottawa," he confirms. "And never. Besides the fact that it's a terrible line in almost every conceivable way, I barely leave my apartment unless I'm going out with Johnny. Right now, I do my job, I listen to audiobooks, I get a full eight hours of glorious sleep."

"I wouldn't know about that," I say, a little too candid. "I can't even remember the last time I got eight hours of sleep." Before Nick jumps on this, I shift back to: "What's the last good book you listened to? I mean, *really* good book."

He considers this by dragging a thumb over his mouth. "This sounds super pretentious, but probably *The Great Divergence: China, Europe, and the Making of the Modern World Economy*. It made me re-think the speed of economic development in the West."

I do my best not to blink. That . . . contradicts the dumb-muscle image I had of him, throws me off an inch. "So you're a nonfiction person."

"Wouldn't say that. I like a bit of everything." He pauses, clearly enjoying the back-and-forth. I'm glad. One step closer to eating out of the palm of my hand. "What about you? Not neces-sarily books, but . . . what do you like?"

It's such an open-ended question that, for a whole half second, the only thing that pops into my mind is *tacos*. And petting Sweetie Pie. My existence outside of work is extremely limited; I can't even remember the last time I binge-watched any TV.

For the last three years, my life—almost exclusively—has been about protecting people from dangerous men. I look at guys and sometimes all I can think is, *How many ways can you hurt someone?*

How many ways can you hurt someone, Nick?

"Hey-yo!" Johnny shouts, suddenly behind us. He's clutching two glasses of foamy green beer in his hands, his spicy cologne settling over my neck. I avoid tensing my shoulders like a cat that's just been scruffed. "Nick's telling the truth, by the way. Guy's like a priest."

Nope, I think, giving Nick a quick once-over—from his leather boots to his dark, playful eyes.

No, he most definitely is not. Show me a priest who has a jaw like that.

"Cheers!" Calla says, waddling up to the high-top with her own frothy, gingerbread-scented drink. Oh, so the two beers were *both* for Johnny. "Isn't this place amazing? Sydney and I have been coming here since we were kids. Not to the bar, obviously, but there's a restaurant upstairs. They do a really nice Sunday dinner. Turkey, mashed potatoes, the whole works."

"*Love* mashed potatoes," Johnny adds helpfully, taking a messy glug from the first beer. "Dining hall at our old college had the best ones. You could get, like, twelve pounds of mashed potatoes for a meal. I'd roll out of there."

"Sydney ate nothing but cereal for a year," Calla says, bringing me back into the fold.

I'd forgotten I'd told her that. "Freshman year," I add with a nod. "At one point, I think I was about sixty percent Honey Nut Cheerios."

Johnny tips his glass against mine, rims clinking, beer spilling a little. "I was a Froot Loops guy, so I hear you."

Johnny is . . . almost smooth. A bit self-effacing. On the one hand, he makes you seem heard. On the other, he has this ridiculously big energy; he'll expand to fill any room he enters, leaving you little space for air. And it hits me all over again. Right there, as the music changes to "Winter Wonderland." *Marriage*. Calla is going to *marry* this deceptively friendly frat boy look-alike with the clean, expensive shirt. He's going to drag her so far into his world that she'll wake up one morning and think: *How did I get here? And why is there a two-million-dollar pallet of cash in my basement?* I'll keep working on sidekick Nick. But right now . . .

"So," I say, pasting on a smile and casting a line out to Johnny. I imagine one of those overly bright lamps shining into his pupils. "How'd you two meet?"

Calla places a delicate hand over her mouth, answering after she swallows. "Do you want to tell the story?" she asks, turning to Johnny.

"You tell it better," he says in an infuriating *aw shucks* way, nudging her shoulder with his. "I'll fill in if you miss anything. Nick will, too. He's heard it enough times." Reaching over with a quick jerk of his hand, Johnny musses Nick's hair, like an annoying big brother.

"I think all of South Boston's heard it," Nick jokes, batting him away. "*Vinny* was telling it the other day."

"Was he?" Johnny laughs in an explosive way. Mirth never reaches his eyes. "To who?"

"His butcher. We were picking up some meat for sandwiches."

Johnny faux-pushes Nick. "Why is this the first time I'm hearing about these sandwiches? Anyway, Calla. Sorry. The story."

Calla's teardrop earrings swing as she faces me, while I'm still stuck on *butcher*. That spark of light is in her eyes. "Okay, remember how I said I was going to take a pottery class? I was feeling so stressed at work, after flu season and all my kids getting sick—half of the support staff was out, too, and we couldn't get any substitute teachers—and I just needed something to refill the well. Something creative, just for me. There's an art studio around the corner from my apartment, Funky Pete's—"

"Pete's not all that funky," Johnny adds at near-full volume. One of his curls falls over his eyes, like a tiny dashboard angel. "He's eighty-seven. Calls himself Peter. Nice guy, real Protestant."

"Catholic," Nick mumbles.

"Then why doesn't he come to our church, then?" Johnny says, half joking, but his mask is slipping a little, just like Nick's did. There's something a bit rotten underneath the loudness of Johnny's charm. "I tell the guy he can sit in our pew, what does he do? Never shows up."

"So, I go in," Calla continues with the story, "and sign up for a six-week pottery course. First day, guess who's there?" She jerks her thumb at Johnny, who gives her an almost imperceptible dip of his chin. "Honestly, I'm thinking, 'This guy just wants to hit on a bunch of single women,' but then we start throwing pots and he's got such *concentration*—"

"You need to concentrate," Johnny says with his big, white smile, the mask firmly in place again. "Those wheels will rip your thumbs off."

Internally, I wince. There's something stomach-churning about "rip your thumbs off" in a how'd-you-meet story, when one of the people involved may or may not have actually ripped off someone's thumbs. Oddly, out of the corner of my eye, I see Nick cross his arms and tuck his thumbs into his armpits.

"But it was more than that," Calla says, still enthused. "I've never seen a man like him so . . . so . . ." Her hand hooks at her chest, like she's trying to snatch the words from her soul. "So *invested* in making a mug. You know he cried when his pottery broke in the kiln?"

He did what, now? I'm all for men expressing their emotions (really, I am; I think it's a vital part of a well-functioning society), but does this add up with *Johnny*, the thumb ripper?

"No," Johnny says, sitting up a little straighter. His chest puffs almost comedically, buttons straining. "It wasn't like that. I wasn't sobbing or anything. Eyes just got misty, that's all."

As I observe him, it continues to click—why Calla fell for Johnny. He has all the trappings of softness, the outward signs. He's in touch with his emotions. He throws clay when he's not volunteering at soup kitchens, or running his family's coffee empire, which (I've looked it up) focuses on ecologically sustainable practices. If he finds a baby to hold somewhere in the next twenty-four hours, it'll make the perfect picture. He is not—to give a completely off-the-wall, totally random example—the type of guy who'd hire masked thugs to rob an art gallery, shooting an elderly security guard in the foot.

Calla's hand navigates to his shoulder again. "Well, your passion was beautiful. We got margaritas that night after class, at this little hole-in-the-wall Mexican place on the south side, and we talked for hours about his family—"

My spine tingles at *his family*. Keep talking about his family!

"Your nana," Calla continues, "and how she had to be so tough after your Pop-Pop died, and naturally I started talking about Grandma Ruby—"

"'She dances like her feet are on fire,'" Johnny chimes in, waving a hand across the air, like he's tracing his name in lights. "That's what you said to me. I think I fell in love right there."

Calla blushes under the heat of his gaze. "After that, we were pretty much joined at the hip."

Some margaritas and a grandma anecdote. That's all it took?

Must've been some seriously strong tequila.

My sister eyes me expectantly across the table, silently urging me to *say something, Sydney*. I know this is the part where I'm supposed to offer my well-wishes—my confirmation that *Yes, you're so cute together, what a perfect origin story.* But the lie lodges in my throat. It's hard to keep up the act when this isn't acting, when I'm me, when I'm home, when it's *her.*

The silence lasts a beat too long. Nick jumps to the rescue.

"We should do a toast." He lifts up his glass, bicep flexing under the cotton of his sweater, and this is the first and only time I'll be grateful to him. To him, and his irritatingly toned biceps.

"What should we cheers to?" I add, summoning my voice again. It comes out neutral, with an imperceptible undertone of panic.

"Our health," Nick deadpans. "In the hope that those green-colored drinks don't kill anyone."

Johnny laughs (*because ha-ha, murder!*), and I performatively clink his glass, whiskey rippling. "To 'Santa's Surprise.' Here goes—"

"Ahhh," Nick says, running a hand across his chin, "know what? We should do this for real." He clears his throat, like he can't decide whether to be serious or not. He chooses serious, starting out slowly. "Cheers to . . . to having people around for Christmas. Good people. And cheers to you, Sydney, for taking us out to this bar, and making us feel at home."

His words stop me cold.

Or, rather, stop me warm. What the hell was that? It was so achingly sincere that I want to squirm. Nick is glancing at me now, full lips pressed in the middle, looking so *innocent*—like he's never stepped a toe out of line in his life. And I think about it again: How I'd take him down. Precisely. Elbow to the jugular.

I mouth "Thank you" at him, happy that the Nick plan, at least, is working.

Each of us takes a sip of our drinks, and talk naturally transitions to the wedding. I listen closely, noting which members of the

Jones family might attend in addition to Johnny's parents. Cousin
Andre, cousin Thomas, and another relative that I'm familiar
with, named Vinny . . .

Vinny texts at least three times during the conversation, and
so does Andre. I get the sense of them as a unit, unable to function
without one another—and shiver to think what they're all like in
the same room. Hope I'll never have to find out.

Just before 11 p.m., there's an unexpected swell of people: a
gaggle of carolers stamping toward the bar, fresh snowflakes on
their velvet costume capes. When a rowdier group of late-night
drinkers follows them, a muscle feathers in Nick's jaw. He recom-
mends that we might want to take the party elsewhere. Or better
yet, pack up and go home. I'm okay with this. More than okay,
actually. It's now thirty-three hours and counting since I've had a
single wink of shut-eye.

But Crime Lord Johnny doesn't want to go home.

His energy level is too damn high. He's made friends with the
bartender—it seems like he can sweet-talk anyone—and the bartender is dredging up the karaoke machine from the summer
storeroom. To which I say, *Shoot me! Shoot me right in the spleen.* If
anything can make this holiday more uncomfortable, it's Christmas karaoke.

"Babe," Johnny presses Calla, resting his chin dramatically on
her shoulder. "Babe."

Calla shakes her head adamantly, eyes closed. Her brown curls
wriggle and jump. "Nuh-uh. You know I hate karaoke. If you want
a duet so bad, do it with Nick."

"Or Sydney," Nick suggests, tilting his head suggestively
toward me.

"Or *Nick*," I say, flicking my gaze pointedly back at him. An
almost seductive smile plays in the corner of his mouth. In my

mind, I have him pinned against the wall; he tries to flip me, but I press my knee into his thigh, holding him there.

It's a standoff until Johnny taps in Nick—literally tapping him in, fist to his shoulder, like they're swapping in a boxing match. Begrudgingly, I'm amused when the two of them take "the stage," which is—essentially—a bare patch of carpet near the end of the bar, where servers wheel out the lobster roll station in summer. Leaning back in my chair, legs crossed, I watch Johnny swipe through song choices (so many classics, like "Santa Baby" and "I Want a Hippopotamus for Christmas"), and I swear, if he's up there singing the hippo one, *that's* how I'll know this is truly an out-of-body experience. I'm dreaming. None of this is real.

For his part, Nick decides to go with the flow. He shimmies his shoulders, like he's warming up for a road race. To make Johnny laugh, Nick even stretches his hamstrings, hooking his ankles to his butt. *Ugh. How is he so flexible in such tight jeans?*

They're really doing this. Microphones are in hand. The song is almost selected. And Johnny's left his coat, draped over the high-top chairs alongside Nick's, the slight bulge of two cell phones in their pockets. It'll be difficult tapping the phones in front of them, but they look distracted enough—and as long as *I* look distracted enough, too, they won't suspect a thing.

"What do you want to do for your bachelorette party?" I hard-whisper over the table to Calla, slipping my hand into Nick's coat first. Hidden in my palm is a USB plug-in, no bigger than my thumbnail; click it into place, and it'll upload an untraceable virus onto any phone—encrypted or not. From there, Gail can monitor all incoming and outgoing calls, track any searches, dig into calendars . . .

Calla dismisses the bachelorette party with a polite wave of her engagement-ringed hand. "Oh, you don't have to throw me one."

"'Course I do." Inside the Barbour jacket, which smells oppressively of Nick's cologne, I feel out the edges of his phone. Click in the USB. Wait. "Maids of honor throw the bachelorette party. That's how it works."

"Yeah ..." Calla hedges, tugging at her sweater sleeves. "But it's really last minute, and I don't know who can come other than Grandma Ruby, so it'll just be—"

"Family," I finish matter-of-factly. "Family works."

She hesitates, her lips twisting to the side, then says in a clear-cut voice: "In that case, no penises. No penis balloons. No penis pasta. No glow-in-the-dark penis necklaces."

I cringe, covering for my hands, which are extracting the USB—and sneaking into Johnny's coat now. "What about me says I'd willingly purchase penis pasta?"

"Honestly, nothing. I just know that's what people do."

"What people?"

"You know, people! The *people*—out there." She gestures in front of her, ironically toward Johnny, who doesn't seem like the penis pasta type, either. "Sorry, I just thought I'd have more time to think about all of this, but I'm getting used to the spontaneous thing. Especially when I *genuinely* believed I'd marry—"

"Robin Hood," I supply.

Calla cracks up. "Is this where we start finishing each other's—?"

"Burritos," I say, finding my rhythm with her again. She's smiling. I'm smiling. And it kills me a little: that while all this is going on, I'm phishing for intel. A few more seconds and the virus will be fully uploaded, but inside I'm thinking, *Liar. Liar. Sydney, you're a dirty little liar.*

Honestly? The longer I'm in the CIA, the more convinced I am that my job isn't the best way to do good in the world. How can you do "good" when you're actively doing *bad*? I know it's not that simple, but there isn't a day that goes by when I don't think about quitting. No one quits, though. That's the impression they give us. You die before you leave the CIA.

"I promise," I tell her, "I'll think of something good."

"Text Nick if you need help coming up with ideas," Calla says, crossing her legs, hands on her knees. "He doesn't know Cape Hathaway at all, but he really wants to pitch in. Best-man-type stuff. I gave him your number. Hope that's okay?"

"Yeah," I say, unplugging the USB, thankful for her in more ways than one. She's just made my job a little easier. While also, you know, giving me an outrageously difficult job in the first place. "Yeah, that's—"

At that second, one of the microphones squeals, and everyone in the bar (around twenty people, by this point) groans and snaps to cover their ears.

"Attention!" Johnny taps the microphone once, twice, sound pounding like a heartbeat. Then he erupts with the gusto of a TV evangelist, pointing at Calla from across the room. "You see that BEAUTIFUL WOMAN over there? Well, I am out of my mind happy to say we're having a CHRISTMAS WEDDING! She's going to be my WIFE!"

Big claps of joy explode throughout the room, and Calla looks so blissfully joyous that I almost wish I had a tranquilizer dart. Right now, I could headbutt through a concrete wall.

"This song," Johnny says in a mock low voice, like an Elvis impersonator, "is dedicated to her."

When Mariah Carey's "All I Want for Christmas Is You" bursts from the speakers, a croaking, borderline hysterical laugh builds in my throat. Zero percent of this image jibes. One of the most dangerous men in America is clutching the microphone with both hands, pouring his vocal soul into a diva's Christmas anthem, as his former bodyguard harmonizes in the background. There are

actual *mmmmm*s of harmonization. Unfortunately, Johnny's singing ability best resembles one of those shrieking YouTube goats;
the word *tune* does not seem to be part of his vocabulary. But
Nick . . .

Dammit if Nick doesn't sing like an angel.

Over Johnny's goat screams, his voice charges into the room.
Pure baritone and straight from the solar plexus, the kind of talent
you might pause by a church door for, just to hear it a little longer.
Jesus. How does Nick sound *this* good?

All around the bar, people are joining in the song. This might
be a caroler's dream come true. The highlight of the season. A
well-dressed man and his tall, muscled friend are providing quite
the show, and everyone is eating it up.

"Do you like Johnny?" Calla leans over and asks me, as the
song winds to a close with an emphatic *and YOU, and YOU.* "He's
just so *fun*, and you know I didn't have this huge social life before.
He's really brought me in, introduced me to all these new people,
and—please tell me you like him."

"He's . . ." The word drags up my throat. "Great! He's great."

6

How's your sleep? CIA psychologists always ask you that. *Are you restless? Yes? No?*

Same thing on the polygraph tests. It flickers with a quick *tick, tick, tick,* swishing in thin, black lines across the screen, and sometimes I say *yes.* It depends. It was worse when I was younger. Ever since I joined the CIA, learned tools that helped me cope—or, at least, helped me bury myself in work—I sleep better. At the station house, some nights, I'm out with the light switch. Other times, though, I'm awake at three thirty in the morning, flicking through cable channels, wondering if my melatonin gummies will ever kick in. They're bears. Tiny, sleepy gummy bears. I've taken two just now. Calla, Johnny, Nick, and I got home from the bar twenty minutes ago, after a car ride filled with stories about Calla and Johnny's first dates (a riverboat cruise, dinner at the Ritz in New York), and I'm trying—unsuccessfully—to wind myself down. Every time I even think about closing my eyes, there's Nick's voice.

Singing Mariah Carey.

Obnoxiously well.

Where'd he learn to sing like that? Objectively, he's a good singer; just as objectively, he's attractive. Doesn't make me impressed. If anything, I trust him even less now. I don't like people who surprise me. Shaking my head—shaking Nick *out* of my head—I swipe off my mascara with a wet cloth, then scrub my cheeks until they're rosy and red like Santa's. In the car, I finagled a close-up picture of Calla's ring and sent it to Gail, along with a coded note about the virus uploads. Now, all I can do for the rest of the night is wait, see what the trackers unearth, and scrub.

I only pause when a *knock-knock* rattles the door. I'm in the bathroom at the end of the hall, where—when I was twelve years old—Calla cut my bangs with a pair of construction paper scissors. I asked her to do it. Our mom had bangs in one of her old photos with Dad, which we found wedged in the downstairs bookshelf. I told Calla to *keep going, keep going,* until all that was left was a frayed edge of hair, sticking straight up like a peacock's crest. Maybe it's because I'm exhausted, but for some reason, I jam my toothbrush in my mouth and open the door, expecting Calla to be on the other side.

She isn't. Nick is.

Sidekick Nick, in a worn gray T-shirt and black sweatpants, a plastic toiletry bag clutched under his arm.

"Hi," he says, back to sheepish, and *ugh, you again?* I thought he was asleep. Shouldn't he be in the guest room? In *his* bathroom, with the duck curtains and the razor? Doing, like, push-ups or something? Instead, he's staring at me in my mismatched pajamas (plaid pants and a way-too-big T-shirt from the Library of Congress that reads, A BOOK LOVER NEVER GOES TO BED ALONE).

"Hey there," I say. Let me tell you, it is impossible to sound seductive with a toothbrush rammed in your mouth. I'll settle for unassuming.

"I just gave Calla and Johnny the guest room," Nick quickly explains, looming tall in the doorway; the small bathroom night-light does its best but barely highlights the length of his silhouette. He runs a slow hand through his dark hair. "Calla's old room has a much smaller bed, so I'm in there, and I was going to use the downstairs bathroom, but your grandma's sleeping on the couch—"

Ah, right. Says it's better for her back, like sleeping on a hard plank outdoors. Plus, she enjoys dozing off to the merry-merry cheer of the Christmas tree, lights flashing her into a sleep stupor. So that means . . . Nick is right next door to me now. We share a wall. *Perhaps like he will with Johnny in prison!* my inner voice adds.

"I didn't want to wake her," Nick finishes in a polite whisper, like he deeply cares about my grandmother's well-being. *Yeah, right.* He bites the pillow of his bottom lip. "I saw your light on. Do you mind if I use your bathroom when you're done?"

I shift from one foot to the other, telling myself not to look a gift horse in the mouth. Or a gift Nick, I guess. The more I mull over his case files, the more questions I have. Was he a part of all the heists? Just the one? Based on what the FBI has gathered, each heist has at least five men on the ground. Does the group change every time? Where are the Joneses selling their stolen goods?

And—most importantly—where are they hitting next with fifty pounds of C4?

Removing my toothbrush, I push the minty paste into one of my cheeks and talk as normally as I can. "Suuure. Need to brush your teeth? Just come on in now."

When Nick tilts his head, I realize—annoyingly—that I've already memorized him. I'd have no problem describing every angle of his face to an FBI sketch artist. The freckle above his lip and the scar on his chin. The precise thickness of his eyebrows.

Why does that bother me so much?

"You sure?" Nick asks.

"Yeah." Steeling myself, I step aside, giving him space to walk by. A smoky pine scent crashes over me as he brushes past my shoulder. That soap of his again. It irritates my nose. In the almost dark, I offer him the toothpaste tube, even though he probably has his own.

"Thanks, but I—" He gestures into his toiletry bag, fishing out his toothbrush and a tube of Crest. Sensitive brand. Gentle whitening. The same as mine. "Well, hey, look at that."

"If you pull out the same floss as me, I think that makes us friends."

Nick laughs. "Never heard that rule before, but I believe you." His fingers reach into his bag, obscuring the floss. "Are you ready for it?" he asks, like he's about to perform a magic trick.

He whips out Wegmans own-brand floss with a theatrical flourish.

"That is so *niche*," I argue, hamming it up.

"Wegmans brand? With the glide-and-slide? Are you kidding me? It is the *only* acceptable kind."

"Agree to disagree."

We brush in abject silence for the next sixteen seconds, but then, true to his earlier statement, Nick can't stand the quiet. He speaks around his toothbrush. "Hey, were you all right earlier? In the kitchen, when Calla told us about the wedding. And then at the bar when they were talking about how they met. You looked kind of . . . sick."

"Did I?" I say, noncommittal, treading carefully. Inside, I'm cursing him. Grandma Ruby almost interpreted the look on my face, but she's known me my entire life. How did *this* guy? The paranoid part of my brain wonders: *Does Nick have a file on me, too?* As Johnny's head of security, he might. What would it say? My online life is a fabrication. My job at the Department of Education is a fairy tale.

"Must've been a surprise," Nick says, brushing, before passing me an irritatingly sympathetic glance in the mirror. "I don't blame you. This is turning into one hell of a holiday."

I spit daintily into the sink and fix him with a look, deciding to spin this into a joke. "What if I told you that I looked sick because I'd . . . eaten some bad shrimp on the plane?"

"Bad shrimp," Nick repeats around the toothbrush, dubious.

"Yes."

He's blunt now. "Then I'd have to question what kind of person would trust plane shrimp."

"Yeah, that's fair."

"Did you know that raw shrimp can contain over seventy different types of bacteria?"

"I . . . did not." Pause. "Nick, are you a germaphobe?"

"You mean, am I a completely reasonable person who acknowledges the existence of germs that are everywhere, then yes."

"How the heck were you a bodyguard, then?" I ask, half happy that I've diverted the conversation. "You have to touch everything."

"My secret weapon," he says, deadly serious, "was hand sanitizer."

"I respect that," I say, "even though I'm an eat-off-the-floor person. Three-second rule."

Nick looks aghast. "Please say you're joking."

"I'm joking," I say, not joking, and wipe my mouth with the washcloth, hopping onto the countertop by the seashell nightlight. Time to kick the flirtation up at least ten notches above floor shrimp. "So," I say tentatively, "tell me about yourself, random man in my bathroom."

Giving one of his slow smiles, Nick appraises me, packing up his toothbrush and rinsing out the sink. "What do you want to know?"

I shrug, the T-shirt slipping purposefully down my shoulder. Cool air tickles my skin, and I see him scan the bareness for just a second. "Anything." I raise a coy eyebrow. "Secrets, preferably."

Nick runs a hand over his mouth, a laugh in his throat. "Secrets, huh? Don't have many of those."

Liar, I think. "Liar," I tease, crossing my ankles.

He shifts over a few inches, so we're face-to-face, and presses his lips together in a sigh. "I might have one or two," he says, deliberating. One of his hands works its way down the side of his neck, and the bottom of his shirt lifts up half an inch, exposing a tan slice of stomach. "Last year, I got pulled over on Route 1 for speeding."

He's led with an actual crime? *Idiot*. I sit up straighter and ask the natural follow-up. "How fast were you going?"

"Seventy-seven in a seventy-five. Massachusetts police will get you for anything. But that's not the secret. It's more the *reason* I was speeding. I wasn't paying attention, because . . ."

"Because . . . ?"

Nick leans back, arms crossed, like the secret is about to bowl him over. "I was too busy blasting Taylor Swift."

Can't help it. I snort with a burst of unexpected glee. Is that the truth? Or a calculated attempt at vulnerability? To make him seem more approachable, warmer, less threatening. Won't work on me. "Wouldn't have pegged you for a Swiftie."

"I'm much more a George Strait, Leonard Cohen, Bob Dylan type of guy, but every once in a while, the mood strikes."

"Is that how you're such a good singer? Cruising down Route 1, belting out 'Bad Blood'?"

He waves this off, modest. Modesty might come across as sincere to anyone else, but I'm suspicious, picking it apart. The corner of his mouth is turning up again, and *god, just stop it with the mouth.* "I'm not that good," he says.

"Nick, come on." My forehead scrunches. "Michael Bublé wants his voice back."

Nick drags his teeth over his bottom lip, as if he's reluctant to admit something. "Church choir," he finally says. "Eight years."

Guy's like a priest, Johnny had said. Maybe this fits in one exceptionally small way. I cock my head at Nick, remembering those photos in his file—him and Johnny's men, crowded into the same pew at church. Fucking hypocrites. "Eight years. Wow. That's a long time."

"It is," he says, nodding, dark hair illuminated in the half-light. "It was never for me, though. It was always for my grandmother. I wanted to play the acoustic guitar instead, or maybe, like, the ukulele. Don't laugh! You can't tell me that 'Somewhere over the Rainbow' doesn't give you a lump in your throat. But singing made my grandma happy, so . . . do I get a secret now?"

My mind highlights the grandmother thing. Puts a pin in it for later. "From me?" I lightly kick the cabinets with my heels. "Thought you knew all the stories."

"Still have questions," Nick says, tapping his own wrist on the spot where the crescent moon outline is on mine. "What's your tattoo mean?"

Why'd he go straight for that? My thumb rubs at the shape as I forbid any irritation from seeping across my face. Nick picks up on my moment's pause, waving off the question with a soft hand. "Know what? Don't answer that. You don't have to answer that."

Then why'd you ask it? Shaking my head, I recover easily, tucking two chunks of blond hair behind my ears. If there's one thing

I'm good at, it's skirting around personal questions. "No, it's fine. Calla and I just went hiking a lot when we were little. Camping under the moon and all that. It reminds me of being a kid."

Half-truth, half-lie.

I almost follow it up with, *Do* you *have any tattoos?* Even though I know he doesn't. And *he* knows that I've seen the length of his naked body, half wrapped in a towel: the tan slope of his waist, the way the cloth hugged his hips, freckles, a dark trail of hair.

Instead, I look up at him through my eyelashes. "You get another question. Hit me with it."

Nick doesn't waste any time. It's like he already had the question prepared. His lips part. "Why didn't you tell anyone you were coming home for Christmas?"

The words seep in, twisting and stabbing a little. How did he know exactly where to hit me?

My shoulders scrunch as we stare at each other: me still on the countertop, him right in front of me, the air heavy between us. This bathroom is minuscule. Starting to feel like purgatory. One big step forward in the dim light and we'd be chest to chest. The closeness amplifies the question, makes it pinprick my skin.

My face is neutral. Voice is neutral. "Like I said, I wanted it to be a surprise."

"Yeah, but that's the thing." Nick appraises me with his dark eyes, inching forward. *Stalking* forward. Invading my space like a challenge. Maybe he's smarter than I've given him credit for, this guy. His eyebrows cinch in the middle, as if he's confused. "It seemed more like a surprise to *you*."

We're so close, I can feel the heat pulsing off his skin. And I have those thoughts again: the what-ifs. What if he attacked me from the front? What if I slammed him into that towel rack? So I'm back to the half-truths. That's what I'm trained to do when I'm in a tight spot. Give an inch but leave the mile.

Even the half-truth, though . . . it's more personal than it usually is. It hurts. "Maybe it occurred to me that spending Christmas alone was a shitty idea, and I just wanted to see how everyone was doing. Sweetie Pie, Grandma Ruby . . . Calla. I haven't been the most present sister lately."

The night-light throws a yellow glaze over Nick's hard jaw. "Don't be so tough on yourself," he says, tapping my knee with the back of his hand. My knee that could *easily* slam into his groin. "No one talks about their sibling like Calla talks about you. You must've done something right."

I nod, tamping down my annoyance again. What the hell does Nick know? "Thank you."

"Don't mention it." He's still holding my gaze, refusing to drop it like I did to him at the bar. He shifts infinitesimally forward, and—suddenly, this feels easy, too. Suspiciously easy. The sudden heat that's building between us. The way he's studying me. Yes, Sweetie Pie is farting audibly downstairs, and yes, we're bathed in the glow of a cheesy seashell night-light—but the heat is *there.* It's there in the gentle sweep of his eyes, which look like they're categorizing the curves of my mouth.

"Sydney, do you think I could take you out to dinner?" Nick asks, just as sudden, in a quiet, sensual way that makes me wonder who's seducing whom. Darkness curls around him. "I don't want to get in the way of your family time, though. So whenever works for you, if you're interested."

"Yeah," I say, matching his intensity. Yanking the reins back with full force. "I might be interested."

Nick smirks in a way that probably works on other women. "Maybe tomorrow? Should we say tomorrow and see how it goes?"

"Tomorrow," I agree, glad that everything's going according to plan, and before I lose any momentum, I take a calculated risk: pushing myself off the countertop and closing the space between us. My fingertips find his arm. Rising up on my tallest tiptoes, I kiss him softly on the cheek, lips caressing the slight stubble of his skin. I've surprised him. His body goes rigid for a second, taut muscles tensing further, before he relaxes into it.

I leave with a bounce in my step. "Night, Nick."

He stares after me, chest slowly rising and falling. "Night, Sydney."

B ack in my twin-size bed, I crash almost immediately, sliding into that empty void where my melatonin gummies kick in, where I usually have strange, incoherent dreams.

This one's different.

The bathroom is billowing with steam, and someone's behind the curtain, whistling. My subconscious realizes: *That is Taylor Swift.*

I mean, it's not Taylor Swift *behind* the curtain. It's Nick. He's bopping along to the tune, his tall frame jamming behind the ducks.

"Come in," he says, lighthearted, as if I've knocked on the door instead. Annoyed, I reach for the curtain, sliding it back inch by inch to reveal Nick, fully clothed, standing under the rushing water. In dreamland, this is nothing out of the ordinary. It is absolutely not weird that he's wearing the CHRISTMAS SWEATER sweatshirt, lathering the sleeves with a bar of pine-scented soap. Bubbles pop and spread against the fabric.

What the hell am I even doing here?

It feels like I should be . . . moving. Leaving. Scuttling away from him.

Just then, Nick slaps his head theatrically with his palm. *Duh!* He should be showering *without* his clothes! Idiot. I know this. He knows this. A moment of urgency passes between us before—

slowly, holding eye contact with me the whole way—he peels off the sweatshirt, leaving only the wet plane of his glistening chest. My breath catches painfully in my throat, and that pisses me right off. He is all slopes and angles, trim and tight. When I was awake, I did notice the long scar on his abdomen, the exact placement of the freckles on his hip, but it was clinical. I was trying to place him in a tall stack of files.

Dream Sydney isn't clinical. She notices the trail of hair, leading down below his waistline, and the sculpted way his muscles flex. He has two perfect dimples on his lower back. "You joining me?" Nick asks, voice husky now, unbuttoning his pants where the dark hair dips, and I—

—wake up like a bomb's exploded, shooting up in bed, sheets tangled against my legs. My heart's pounding like a marching band drum, and I am *boiling*. Way, way too hot for winter in Maine. A thin sheen of sweat covers my body, pajama shirt sticking to my skin, and I peel it off in one swoop, chest heaving in the thin morning light.

Fuck.

7

The dream does not put me in a good mood. I'm going to chalk it up to the melatonin gummies. Nick's attractive, factually speaking, but he isn't attractive to *me*. I promised Gail professionalism, promised myself that I wouldn't get caught up in his charm—and I'm still immune to it.

In fact, the thought of him—real-life Nick—makes my skin itch.

I shower, washing away any trace of the dream, and slip into another pair of dark jeans. Rough-toweling my hair, I pace my room, flipping through every piece of Nick intel that I can absorb. Nothing's come in from the virus implant yet—Nick and Johnny went straight to sleep last night and have barely picked up their phones since—but at five twenty-two this morning, Gail confirmed that Calla's engagement ring wasn't a match on any of the FBI's stolen goods databases.

I'm just as frustrated as I am relieved; that would've been an easy win. Johnny might be too loud, too in-your-face, but he isn't stupid.

Neither is Nick. I'm learning that. One of his files explains that he was salutatorian of his high school. Scored in the 97th percentile on the math section of his SATs.

Still stalking back and forth, phone in hand, I click on another Nick folder. It shows he pays his taxes on time. He has zero parking tickets. He's never been married. His grandparents are deceased, and his parents are divorced. Not much info on his American mother, even less on his Canadian father. Nick has an undergraduate degree in economics that he—for some reason—chucked aside to be Johnny Jones's bodyguard. He jogs on weekend mornings. He rows on the Charles River at least fifteen times a month, in sunshine and in snow. There's a photo of Nick in his boat, backward baseball cap smashing down his hair, beads of sweat dripping down his neck.

Gross, no.

I scroll right past that—and venture outside the contents of his folder. Social media isn't my go-to place for reconnaissance (the foreign assets I recruit hardly ever have internet profiles), but in rare cases, it's good for establishing a baseline. It tells you how to approach a target based on how the target views themselves.

Nick views himself as . . . hungry.

His profile features a whole lot of ice cream photos. Cones and sundaes and triple scoops. In Boston, he lives across the street from a shop called Lick of Luck, run by a couple of Irish octogenarians who whip up their own specialty flavors. Nick's tried them all. Here's a picture of him with Owen and Catriona (the owners), arms wrapped around them, in front of a poster for a brand-new flavor: "Nick of Luck." It has pistachios in it.

That is, unfortunately, my favorite kind of ice cream.

The picture with Owen and Catriona sharply contrasts with the next images, where the real Nick explodes off the screen. Raucous photos of Nick, Johnny, and some of the boys: I recognize

Andre, Conrad, Marco, Sal. Most of them are untagged. Drinking in pubs and bars in Boston, looking like a bunch of assholes with their beers and we-get-away-with-everything grins. Is that Vinny? That's Vinny, throwing his arm around Nick. He's got a tight buzz cut and a face that looks like he'd bite you and enjoy it.

You're going down, too, I think, still flicking. Much farther down in Nick's profile are a few nicely cropped dinner photos with people who aren't octogenarian ice cream moguls or garden-variety thugs. In one, Nick's kissing the cheek of a twenty-something woman with close-cropped curls. *Run, girl. Run.* In another, he's sharing a vegan hot dog with a tennis pro named Bobbie. Only one other person appears regularly on his profile. Nick's grandmother. His "Nan," as he calls her. Here they are at a Red Sox baseball game, a bucket of popcorn between them, and—no. *No.* The picture triggers something, my own memories of baseball games with Calla and Dad, my own family tradition, which I shove back down. Focus on Nick's nan instead. She's short, adorable—and my guess? Didn't know that her grandson protects a criminal.

Speak of the devil . . .

The *chop* of metal sounds outside my window, and I curl my fingers around the blinds, peeking through. Nick's in the back-yard, splitting wood for the fireplace; he's wielding the axe with expert care, his neck glistening with sweat, like in the rowing photo. If he sees me, he doesn't let on—just pauses to unzip his winter parka, revealing nothing but a plain white tee. He lifts the edge of it, wind against his muscled stomach, and wipes the beads of sweat off his forehead.

Oh, come on.

This is just ridiculous. He's going to get frostbite.

Scowling, I flip the blinds closed and listen to see if anyone else is awake. Downstairs is the scent of Grandma Ruby's famous peppermint candy cane scones (buttery, sweet, like Christmas in gluten form), alongside the sounds of voices: Johnny gently teasing Calla about her fifth-grade yearbook pictures. I'm alone up here.

Good.

Within fifteen seconds, I've dug out a pair of latex gloves from my backpack. I know this house. The creak and squeal of each floorboard is locked in my memory, so I step lightly in all the right places, slipping out of my room, easing open the guest room door and popping inside. The Elf on the Shelf is, once again, giving me the judgmental eye from the bookshelf. Tiny recording devices are still possibly hidden in this room.

No time for a bug sweep . . .

My gaze whips back and forth. Despite her newfound impulsivity—which I'm convinced isn't really her—Calla is still meticulously tidy. Her suitcase is neatly tucked in the corner, clothes probably pressed and hung in the closet; her Christmas gifts are already wrapped and arranged on the desk. Johnny, on the other hand, is more scattered. Two designer suitcases lie open on the floor, eight-hundred-dollar sweaters sticking out like tongues. Had a housekeeper when he was growing up, I'm sure. Probably never had to clean up after himself in his life.

I nudge one of the sweaters to the side with my foot. Hopefully, all of Johnny's stuff will end up bagged and tagged in an evidence locker.

That's what I want for Christmas.

Silently snapping on the gloves, I dip inside the first suitcase. Cashmere sweaters. A *Men's Health* magazine from the airport. A baggage tag from Boston Logan international. Aftershave, dirty boxers, a packet of tissues (maybe for when he breaks another mug in the kiln and has to fake-cry about it)—and *ah, what's this?*

Unzipping one of the hidden suitcase pockets, I yank out a black switchblade, flicking it open. Its metallic swish sounds so cold in the warmth of the bedroom. I'm going to go out on a limb here and say this is *not* for carving the turkey.

The knife isn't what I'm looking for—I'm searching for a laptop or a tablet, any larger communicational device that I can mine for intel about the next heist—but it's a literally sharp reminder of just how dangerous this man can be. The FBI crime scene photos from his last heist ping in my brain. A pool of blood drying on an art gallery floor.

Take the weapon, a voice in me says. *Throw it out the goddamn window.*

But then, footsteps.

Shit. Someone's headed toward the stairs.

I've left myself enough leeway to cover my tracks this time. No one will find me huddled in the shower or (worse) stuffed into this oversize suitcase. It looks tight in there. And I'm not that flexible. Rushing the switchblade back into the suitcase, I snap off the latex, wedge the gloves in my pocket, and stride calmly out the door. The handle clicks shut as Johnny crests the bottom staircase step.

I give him a believably innocent wave and stare down from the landing, wondering if I need an eye test. Is it just me, or is he . . . wearing my *bathrobe*? From high school. That is my fleece bathrobe from high school, the one with blue and white polka dots.

Johnny motions to the fleece, then pets it, like he's taming a tiger. "Sorry, this okay? Calla said it would be okay. Forgot my robe."

"Yeah, totally fine," I manage, even though I really want to say: *You couldn't have worn one of your fucking sweaters? Or the specifically designated guest robe?*

Spiritedly, Johnny rushes up the stairs, taking the steps two at a time. He looks like he's eaten a carton of eggs before dawn. Just so *chipper.* "I was actually coming up to talk. Would you mind if I borrowed you for a second?" Up close, his breath smells of candy canes. His curls are visibly hardened with gel, so his face looks tougher than last night, when he was belting out Mariah Carey karaoke. "I want to run something past you."

Another believable smile from me. "Yeah, go for it."

Opening the door I just shut and striding through, Johnny pats the mattress, gesturing for me to take a seat at the end of the guest bed. Uncomfortably, I do. Even more uncomfortably, he perches right by my side. We're shoulder to shoulder, his aftershave hitting my nostrils with daggered spikes.

"I want to get Calla a wedding present." Johnny's hands cup the air, as if to demonstrate the largeness of the gift. He's a big hand talker; based on my observations, he's never met a gesture he didn't like. "Something substantial that I can give to her at the altar. Diamond tennis bracelet, plane tickets to Aruba, a horse . . ."

He wants to give her a horse at the altar. Like, physically? In our living room?

"Now that the timeline's pushed up," he says, narrowing his blue eyes, "I need something fast, and all my options are starting to sound generic. I do have one thing that's getting shipped in, but I was thinking we could put our heads together this week. Figure out a second option. Go shopping."

Christmas Shopping with a Crime Lord sounds like a Hallmark movie that I'd skip. "What're you having shipped in?" I pry, cell phone buzzing in my back pocket.

"Oh, that's a surprise," he says, winking at me in a completely unironic way. Besides the bathrobe, he looks like he could be on a political campaign flyer, and—*goody.* Another surprise. Just what this holiday needs. "I'm sure she'll like it, though. Don't mean to toot my own horn, but I have good taste. Picked it out myself."

"Like the ring," I add, trying to butter him up. "It's beautiful."

He enjoys the compliment. "Thank you." He slides a bit closer to me, our shoulders touching with a static spark. "Not jealous that your little sister's getting married before you, huh?"

And there—*that*. That first trace of nastiness, like he couldn't help himself. The way he's said it, it's like a joke. He's just teasing me. But it's meant as a subtle dig. Men like him see competition in everything.

I'm honest. "You know, the older I get and the more I see, the more I'm completely turned off by the idea of marriage."

Johnny frowns. "And why's that?"

"Well," I say lightly as my cell phone buzzes again, "can you ever really know who you're marrying?" I give a tiny shrug, like this is a joke, too. We're both so funny. "But yeah, we can go shopping . . . Looks like I have a wedding gift to get."

"Because I'm getting *married*," Johnny says with a sly grin, smacking me on the back. My god, would he stop doing that? *You don't just get to touch everyone.* "Hey, I just want you to know, your sister is . . . well, she really is the most special girl I've ever met. I never believed in that whole 'love at first sight' thing, but she had me with that nose scrunch she does." He scratches the tip of his own nose, huffing out a laugh. "She's . . . she's made me a better person. And smarter. I didn't think I'd like a girl who's as smart as Calla, but turns out, it gives you more to talk about."

I nod, tight-lipped, reading him. He isn't lying. Don't need a polygraph test to figure that out. But the question isn't *Does he genuinely love my sister?* It's *Does he love my sister enough to keep her out of trouble?* Is a part of him using Calla's goodness, her light, as a cover? Some men, they think they can love a woman and control her at the same time.

"All right," Johnny says, slapping his thighs, "we better get down there. Breakfast calls." When he stands up from the bed, fluffy blue bathrobe opening a little too widely across his chest, he looks back at me. "Aren't you going to check who's texted you?"

"Oh, it's my landlord," I tell him automatically, pulling the lie from the air. "She keeps wanting to know if I'll sublet my apartment."

Johnny shakes his head, exaggerated as always. "Don't recommend that. I've heard horror stories." He waits until I've followed him into the hallway, shutting the door with a loud *click*. "Wouldn't want a stranger in your house, would you?"

At breakfast, I go easy on the caffeine. Grandma Ruby's hazelnut coffee is pretty strong, so three cups will do. I'm sipping, upright by the coffee station, reading Gail's messages like I'm reading the news. Apparently, right before he came upstairs, Johnny puttered out to the driveway and made several calls to a Mid-Coast Maine area code. Mid-Coast Maine? Who does he know in Mid-Coast Maine?

No mention so far of New Year's Eve in any text messages, just a lot of Christmas chatter. Gail sends me screenshots of a few from Johnny to his cousin Andre, asking if he's bringing Christmas presents to the wedding. Is that code for something? Or am I reading too much into it?

"Sydney, off your phone," Grandma Ruby says, urging me to *sit, sit* next to the mountain of candy cane scones. There's also maple French toast, scrambled eggs, crunchy strips of turkey bacon, and no less than seven bottles of hot sauce, including Grandma Ruby's "home brew" recipe, which makes pepper spray look like a soothing mist. She applies it liberally to her eggs and asks if I want some.

I laugh. I could not love her more. "I'm going to have to give that one a miss."

She waves a hand in my direction, like *Oh, Sydney!* "You girls never did get that 'spicy' gene. Well, more for me!"

Nick—who's arrived back inside from his wood-chopping adventure—slides into the seat beside me. He's oppressively close. His hair's messy and he smells heavily of cedar, like an old man's closet.

"Morning," he says, pouring himself a cup of coffee. Hope he burns his tongue. He takes it black, with a side of charming my grandmother. Over the meal, he asks her about her house-painting business, about growing up in Maine, and Grandma Ruby supplies that at her own wedding, one of the groomsmen was kicked by a horse.

"Just, wham!" she says, slapping her hands together. "Right in the behind."

I throw a meaningful look at Johnny. *See? No horses at close-quarter weddings.*

Johnny doesn't interpret the look correctly. "Here you go!" He thrusts the butter in my direction. I accept it like butter is just what I wanted. "Speaking of injuries," he adds, sucking a tiny blob of jam off his thumb. "Has Calla told you about Darlene?"

Tell me Darlene isn't another crime lord.

"She has not," I say.

"Darlene is a hamster," Calla explains, pouring maple syrup on her toast. It pools in glistening globs. "I think being a class pet may not be all it's cracked up to be? She Houdini-ed herself out of her cage right before pickup for winter break, and got stuck inside one of the Lego houses, and by the time I found her, she was *annoyed*." Over the French toast, she extends a hand, showing off two tiny bite marks, imprinted into her knuckle. "Darlene is spending her Christmas holidays with our PE teacher, and then she's being re-assigned to third grade. No Lego houses there. The problem is that I now have a fear of hamsters. The *other* problem is that we don't have a class pet now, and we need to adopt one before there is a full-out mutiny in the New Year."

"Lizard?" Nick suggests, forking his toast.

"Raccoon?" I suggest, raising an eyebrow.

Calla huffs, then nods seriously. "Good thinking. Kindergarten isn't chaotic enough without adding rabies to the mix."

"Don't I know *that* from experience," Grandma Ruby says incomprehensibly, and Calla and I look at each other like *what?* For a second, things feel a smidge normal. Like it's just me and Calla and Grandma Ruby again, eating French toast and joking about our lives. Like Dad might be sitting right at the other edge of the table.

I slap myself out of it.

Then come the wedding plans, storming in. Grandma Ruby agrees with a whoop (and an extended sob) to serve as the justice of the peace. She even has the shoes: black patent leather brogues with gold buckles, like an antique pilgrim. "I'll have to dust them off," she sniffs, beaming, "but they're my good luck shoes! I've married people in them before. I've married *lots* of people since you girls have been out of the house. Lobstermen, tourists, even a former member of the Hells Angels, with the tattoos and the— oh!" She smacks her head dramatically, white hair puffing, before rushing upstairs with extra pep in her step. Quick as lightning, she fishes out her wedding dress from the attic; to Calla's luck (or perhaps misfortune), the fabric has remained untouched by tiny raccoon paws, and the sleeves are just as poofy as they were in 1962.

"It's still got some oomph in it, I think!" Grandma Ruby says, draping it over the couch. "The thought of you wearing it, having a long happy marriage like I had . . . Well, that brings me a lot of joy." She starts suggesting design alterations for the gown, pulling

out her bulky sewing machine. Calla kisses her on the forehead—
right before asking if *I* have a dress to wear for the wedding.

I mumble something about a fancy pantsuit in my closet,
knowing that no such pantsuit exists. We won't get to the point
where I need an outfit. Everything will be sorted by the day of the
wedding.

Satisfied, Calla then asks Nick if he wouldn't mind gathering
wedding accoutrement in town (additional lights for the altar,
handmade white stationery for the name cards, et cetera). Fifteen
minutes later, my phone buzzes with a text. Did you know that your
town has a shop that is both a lobster pound AND a nail salon? Then,
This is Nick, by the way.

My nose wrinkles. But good. He's reached out first.

After breakfast, I tried to scuttle back upstairs to research any
link Johnny might have to Mid-Coast Maine, but Grandma Ruby
caught me by the elbow. She's roped me into phoning distant relatives, spreading the jolly news. I text Nick in between calls. Do
they not have those in Boston?

I'm confused, Sidekick Nick responds right away. Can the lobsters request manicures if they want them? He also texts back a
picture of a poster in the shop window. The poster boasts a drawing of a man with a trout poking out of his pants. Explain?

If only I could.

No, Nick replies, you really do have to explain this.

With nine more relatives on the to-call list, I type as fast as I
can. That's an old poster from the summer. About a hundred years
ago, people in Cape Hathaway wanted to honor the summer fishing
industry, so they started Fisherman's Picnic, which is like a food fes-
tival with games. The main game is the trout toss, where grown adult
humans cut two holes at the bottom of a trash bag, step into said
trash bag like underwear, and hold out the sides, trying to catch a

fish in the pocket. The one who catches the trout from the farthest distance away wins. And the truth is they don't actually win anything but the fish they caught in their pants.

Tell me they don't eat that fish, Nick says.

Gamely, I respond with a fish emoji, a trousers emoji, and a dinner plate emoji. Nick types a germ emoji followed by a shrimp emoji, and that'll do. Enough of him for now. I return to calls.

"Hi, Aunt Meryl. *Hi*, Aunt Meryl. It's Sydney. *Syd-ney*... Your grand-niece? I know, it's been a while. Yep, Calla's getting married... Who'd you hear it from? Oh, okay... No, I don't know if Calla has any mixing bowls. I don't think Johnny has any mixing bowls, either... I'm not sure what their wedding colors are. Green and red, I guess? No, the dress isn't red. It's white? Off-white? They're just getting married at Christmas... I know it's short notice. Mm-hm, *this* Christmas."

Uncle Wilfred promises to send a check, then asks how he's related to us. The Bartlett side of the family is vacationing in Mexico for the holidays and doesn't pick up the phone. All in all, I call seventeen people, inviting them to the wedding at Grandma Ruby's behest; a few of them say they'll look into last-minute flights, which is nice of them.

But I'm praying that no one spends money on a wedding that—surely—is about to be canceled.

I even try to persuade a few of them, in not so many words, to skip it.

Hardly anything I can do about the bachelorette party, though. That's full steam ahead. It's going to be on a boat. A few of Calla's friends are driving up from Boston on the twenty-first, and Johnny will be there with his bachelor crew, too. A joint party isn't what Calla had in mind, but when Johnny hears about the winter cruises around Oak-Bar Harbor, he's sold. There's a cancellation. Space available. I explain to Calla, in a roundabout way, that *maybe* it's not the best idea to gather a bunch of drunk (and lest we forget, criminal) men on a boat together in a small, icy harbor, where a body can easily be dumped overboard and the Coast Guard will take weeks to find it, but Johnny's already made a reservation over the phone.

Grandma Ruby says she won't attend, just in case, as the maid of honor, I want to comfortably invite a male stripper. "I'd check the Yellow Pages," she says, still wonderfully in 1992.

By noon, Johnny and Nick have barely picked up their phones for more than a quick Wordle (Nick) and a Google search for hair gel (Johnny). Not exactly actionable intel. I hate waiting. I could sneak up to my room and research possible heist targets, but right now it's like throwing a dart, blindfolded, at a moving target. I'll go for a run instead, to keep myself centered while intel trickles in.

When I rush downstairs in my jogging clothes—extra-thermal black leggings and a polar jacket that moves well when my elbows swing—there's Nick, back from his errands, lacing up his sneakers on the floor. Half of me is irritated to see him, blocking my way, but also . . .

I can work with this.

"You going running?" he asks hopefully, glancing up at the final bunny loop.

I crouch down on the hardwood next to him. "I was thinking about it," I say slyly, yanking on my own sneakers and tying them tight.

Nick unfolds to a stand. "Can I join you? I haven't been on a run in ages and I'm starting to get kind of antsy." He's wearing a pair of sleek sweatpants and a black hoodie, a winter beanie tugged down over his ears. When I gaze up at him, I see the dream version of him peeling off his sweater in the shower and think that there is no one in the world I'd rather run with less. For the mission, though . . .

"Absolutely." I hop up, grabbing a pair of earmuffs from a bowl by the front door, and slap his stomach with the back of my hand. His abs are not unlike a block of wood. I deeply wish I didn't know that. "As long as you can keep up."

8

I never run with anyone else. Not anymore. Running is a solo endeavor. I don't want to chat and jog. What do people even talk about when they're running? Don't they care that it slows them down?

The only person I ever ran with was my dad—around the cul-de-sac, down toward the beach. He'd push me because he knew I was fast, had a lot of drive in me, even at the end of a couple miles. *Kiddo*, he'd urge me on. *Pick up the pace.* He was a good dad when he wanted to be: kind of chaotic, messy haired, never managing to hold down seasonal work; but I still picture him running backward, belly-laughing on the beach, calling me *kiddo, kiddo, kiddo.* Sometimes, when I'm sprinting at 5 a.m. by the river in DC, I can almost hear his footfall, catch a glimpse of his bearded face.

Calla didn't run with us. In fact, I don't think I've ever seen Calla run, unless it was in a mandatory gym session or after a frozen yogurt truck. She is more of a Pilates, cross-stitching type of person. But when Nick opens the door, Johnny isn't far behind,

saying that *he'd* like a run—and that *Calla, babe, you should tag along.*
He doesn't ask; he insists. There's the faintest hint of a wince from
Calla, who'd just put on her fluffy lounge socks, but she quickly
spins it into an eager, conciliatory smile.

We depart as an awkward foursome, Johnny and Calla in the
rear, Nick and I up ahead.

Nick's a little chatterbox, isn't he? I expect him to fill the silence, ruin the solitude. But his breath just streams out in a long
puff of air. He keeps pace with me as we wind along the snow-
plowed path, past the long-drained swimming pool and the gazebo.
Our sneakers grind against the rock salt, our faces dig into the
cold wind, and I wonder if someone like him sees my neighborhood the way that I do. The way that I am, right now. In the snow,
near the holidays, you can't beat it. This subdivision is seaside
Maine meets a Netflix Christmas movie. Carrot-nosed snowmen
wave at you from lawns. Wreaths wrap around picket fences, half
held up by drifts of snow. There's a manger scene by the frozen
tennis courts, complete with plastic donkeys bending down to lick
the face of Baby Jesus.

"So where is Nick taking you tonight?" Calla chirps behind us,
breaking my no-talking-while-running rule as we curve onto the
main road, toward the beach.

"Sorry, I told her about dinner." Nick shrugs, back to sheepish,
his feet pounding the pavement. When our shoulders jostle together, I remember those images from the Buffalo heist—
bloodstains on the bank floor—and I want to hip-check Nick right
off the sidewalk. "I thought she could give me some recommenda-
tions."

"And?" I say, thinking that in a city like Stockholm, I'd know
exactly where to suggest. Nick and I would sit in a corner booth
at a just-dark-enough bar, with smooth leather seats and crystal

glasses that clinked with our *cheers*. Everything would be precise, sharp, sexy. In Cape Hathaway, Maine, Nick could ... bring me to Al's Off-Season Lobster Shack. Or the grocery store.

"You know your Italian restaurant has a C-minus health rating?" Nick asks.

"Dishies!" Calla and I yell at the same time before I look back at her and whisper "Jinx."

"That was it," Nick says, laughing, like he has the right to insult a town relic. "Dishies. Where they serve no deep-dish pizza. Or pizza of any kind."

"No pizza at an Italian restaurant?" Johnny asks, horrified. He has a borderline psychopathic running style; he barely swings his arms, stiff as the firewood Nick was chopping this morning. Nick, on the other hand, has good form. Hate to admit that. He keeps his face slack and his arms loosely crooked at his side.

Great style for sprinting away from a crime scene.

"Just surprise me," I say, picking up the pace when we hit the near-beach motels. Pastel-colored buildings with long summer balconies whip past us. "As long as you don't take me to the Moose Lodge."

Nick barks out another laugh. "What is a Moose Lodge?"

"An institution!" Calla says, keeping up. It's Johnny who's slowing down.

A gust of wind cuts under my earmuffs. "A hundred bottles of hard whiskey," I detail. "Moose Lodge bingo. Lots of taxidermy."

"As fun as that sounds, I think we'll give it a miss." Nick tugs down his beanie again without breaking his stride, then throws me a look that I catch out of the corner of my eye. "I'm trying to impress you."

Glad he is. Also wish he wouldn't.

"Did I tell you that I had a visitor last night?" Nick asks. "Sweetie Pie is a bed hog."

"What?" I ask, squinting.

"She actually crawled up into bed with you?" Calla asks, beaming.

I'm confused. Usually I trust Sweetie Pie's judgment. "She never does that with strangers."

"She hasn't done that with me," Johnny mumbles, like a sulky little boy pouting in the back of his mother's minivan because we've forgotten his presence.

"I feel honored, then." A warm smile spreads across Nick's face, giving him those deep eye grooves again, and man, I'm getting tired of the nice guy shit. "I grew up with German shepherds. Lots of people were scared of them, but they were just big mushes . . . You know Sweetie Pie wags her tail in her sleep?"

"*Yes*," I say, leading us closer to the beach, scanning for black ice on the pavement. Nick has found one of my only weaknesses, so I let myself be a tiny bit vulnerable. Calculatedly. "It kills me."

"When I woke up," he says, "all four of her paws were stamped into my back, and I was . . ." Still running, he scrunches his arms to his chest, demonstrating his predicament. Maybe she was trying to push him off. I revise my earlier statement about Sweetie Pie's judgment. "Hanging on to the edge of the bed."

"As long as Sweetie Pie was comfortable," Calla says with a nod.

Nick chuckles. The first hint of a five o'clock shadow is starting to appear on his jawline. "Yeah, I didn't move a muscle for about fifteen minutes, because she was still wagging her tail and I didn't want to wake her up. Then I got a cramp. Had to wiggle a little. How long have you had her?"

"Since she was a puppy," I say, then reluctantly offer the whole story as we run. Sweetie Pie was all roly-poly belly and fresh spots. Calla and I'd picked her out at the local shelter; she'd dug her snout through a bundle of shredded newspaper and had come up with little pieces sticking out between her ears. It was love at first bark. "We did one of those doggy DNA tests on her," I finish, "just for fun. She's a mastiff-terrier mix. Six percent German short-haired pointer. Two percent *Chihuahua*." I end with the shock factor.

To his minor credit, Nick obliges me with the appropriate disbelief. "*No.*"

Johnny doesn't give two shits about Sweetie Pie's DNA apparently. He's preoccupied with trying to pass me on the sidewalk. Enough of me leading! *He* wants to be out ahead.

I cut him off at every damn turn and feel the silent rivalry welling up between us.

"I tried to run with her once," I add, aggressively (but innocently!) blocking Johnny and pointing to the pavement, as if Sweetie Pie were loping alongside us. "I know pointers are huge runners. Sweetie Pie made it to the tennis courts, which is like a quarter of a mile, and then refused to move. The neighbors thought she was dead. She stiffened her legs in the air and everything. It was very convincing."

Nick gives this a full grin, like he's pulled off a particularly difficult heist, leaving no fingerprints, and once again, I'm confident that I've got him. Time to slip in a few questions about New Year's Eve.

Increasing the pace even more, we hightail it down to the water, a mix of sand and dark pebbles beneath our feet. Long Sands Beach isn't just deserted in the winter—it's like the set from a postapocalyptic movie where nature has taken over and no more people remain. There's something so violently beautiful about the surf crashing against the rocks. The sky is slate gray with approaching snow. Little puffs of white are already descending from the clouds, but the real storm has yet to come.

"Race you?" I ask Nick, already accelerating, because I think he'll like this, the playful competition. And I need to get slightly ahead of Johnny, so that I can ask Nick a few questions in private.

Nick is less ferociously competitive than Johnny, but he's down for the challenge. "If I can keep up," he teases, throwing my words back at me. The length of his strides increases. Sweat beads on my chest, underneath the polar vortex of clothes, and we're neck and neck until the first bathhouse, where Nick pulls ahead, stopping short by the edge of the water. His hands go to his knees, and he breathes heavily through his mouth. "Damn, Sydney. You're fast."

"You're faster," I say, just as breathless, palms on my hips. I walk it out. Walk it toward him. We've sprinted about a quarter of a mile, and Calla and Johnny are . . . Actually, I can't even see them anymore with the fog.

"How often do you run?" I ask Nick.

"Just on the weekends. I'm more of a rower." He pauses, massaging the pads of his hands, where the calluses have built up. "I try to wake up early and get out on the river before anyone's up. Sounds stupid, but everything else just . . . floats away. It's the closest thing I know to peace." He clears his throat. "Anyway, I used to mountain bike, too. Way back when."

My mind lingers on the *peace* comment, but I push the conversation along. "Did you have a crash or something?"

Nick examines me with a squinted gaze, still bent over from the run. There's something *so* satisfying about recovering before him, about him wheezing long after I've stood up straight. "Yeah, how'd you know?"

I tap my chin. "Your scar here."

"Ah. Yeah. Went straight over the handlebars." He jerks his head toward the water, cold waves crashing. "That's when I took up swimming. The water kind of healed me, and—well, swimming led to rowing."

My brain sparks with a connection. I know how I can get him to talk about New Year's Eve. "You couldn't get me out of the water when I was a kid. Calla, either. But everyone's a big swimmer around here. We even have one of those polar plunges for the New Year."

Nick stands up straight, too, only half recovered from the sprint. "You ever done it?"

"Actually, no. Do *you* want to? Thinking about sticking around for New Year's?"

Nick laughs. "If anything could entice me, Sydney, it would not be the opportunity to freeze my ass off."

"Oh, come on. You're Canadian. Canadians are immune to hypothermia."

"That's scientifically proven?"

I nod, checking for Johnny and Calla. They're still behind the curtain of fog. "Can't argue with science." My feet shift in the sand toward Sidekick Nick. I need a better nickname for him. Something that fully captures his slipperiness. Tricky Nicky? "Really, though. Got any plans for New Year's?"

Nick eyes me flirtatiously, the tip of his tongue in the corner of his mouth. "Are you asking me out?"

"Maybe," I say, nudging him. My skin rebels at the contact, but I'm getting tunnel vision, eyes set on the prize. Any bit of intel he wants to let slip. "Are you working then?"

"Always am," he says, peering out at the water. "I've never done a polar plunge, either."

My gaze travels alongside his, over the icy waves, and the pieces slot together. How I can further this relationship *fast*. Yes, it means momentarily abandoning the New Year's chat, but on the whole, it'll be worth it.

I said I was all in for the mission. This is what all in looks like.

Gathering my resolve, I inhale and face Nick completely. "Here's an idea . . ."

"Uh-oh," he jokes.

Then, without any further hesitation, I unzip my jacket, shrugging it off onto the hard-packed sand. A question rises in Nick's eyes, but I'm far from done. Crisscrossing my arms, I peel off my fleece hoodie, then my tank top, revealing the naked plane of my stomach and a thin cotton sports bra that hardly covers anything in the cold.

Seduction isn't always about showing the most skin.

Sometimes it is.

Nick sweeps a tasteful gaze down my body, quickly, before returning to my eyes. "What are you . . . ?" he says, leaving the question hanging in the frigid air. His Adam's apple bobs. The way he's looking at me has changed. This has just gone from a friendly, competitive run to something else entirely. I haven't miscalculated; he likes the intense parts of me. Shouldn't I play that up more? Be spontaneous. Surprise him.

And pray that we don't get hypothermia.

Or, at least, pray that *I* don't get hypothermia.

"Well?" I raise an eyebrow, thinking, *Come on, take the bait.*

Nick puffs out his lips but meets the challenge, pausing to peel off his own clothes. He does it carefully, slowly. "Guess it's nothing you haven't seen before," he says. The naked parts of him hit the bare winter sun, goose bumps popping on his forearms. Our teeth barely chatter as we strip off our pants together, until we're standing in our underwear on the deserted beach.

He's a briefs guy. Calvin Klein. Black cotton.

Figures. It's basic.

"On the count of three?" he asks, wind whipping against his skin. He has winter freckles. They pop in the sun. That slice of a scar on his stomach glistens, too, and I wonder who was on the other end of that scar. Who Nick might've hurt in return.

"We run in up to our shoulders, we run out," I say over the sound of the surf. "One, two . . ."

"Three!"

Nick doesn't waver. Neither do I. We dash into the surf, ice water splashing against our ankles—and yep, that is absolutely freezing. A prickling sensation consumes my calves, my thighs, waves crashing against my stomach, my shoulders, and Nick is two feet away, muttering something under his breath that sounds suspiciously like a prayer.

"Oh, I hate this," he chokes out with a laugh.

"This may be the worst thing I've ever done!" I shout, mimicking him on purpose. Rigid waves crash against my neck, and we get the hell out of there, arriving like jellyfish onto the shore: wobbly, knees knocking together, breathless. I pretend that the extreme cold has knocked me sideways. "Who . . . whose idea was that again? Yours?"

"I think . . . yours." Nick is taking deep, intentional breaths through a lazy grin. His lips are mildly chapped from the cold. "Here . . . there's . . ." he chatters, leaning down to scoop up my clothes, and I take them with an equally shaky "thank you," waiting for him to grab his own before leading him to the bathhouse. The building is shuttered in the winter, but there's still an alcove by the shower station. A good windbreak.

Calla and Johnny are nowhere to be seen.

"You . . . okay . . . ?" Nick asks, tugging on his pants in the alcove, and honestly, it's hard to get words out when your lips are almost completely numb. I mutter something incoherent, struggling to slip my damp socks back on, and despite myself, let go of a full-body shudder. I've been in colder situations—on assignment, in Romania, last year—but obviously, Nick doesn't know about Romania. Silly little lines of concern run across his forehead.

"Hey," he says, shuffling toward me and rubbing his hands up and down my arms. What's that supposed to do? I'm half naked here. Friction, his skin on my skin, isn't enough. Those rough rower's palms scrape down my arms.

"Let's get your jacket on," he says, gaze raking my face.

And there. *There it is.* The tiniest sliver of an opening.

I feel the relative warmth radiating off him.

And the trust. And the want.

Everything I don't feel. Everything he should.

With slow, deliberate movement, my toes rise, and my lips press against his in a crash of ice and pretend lust. Is he surprised about the kiss? *Good.* Let me keep him on his toes. The timing is slightly off for a natural progression of this "relationship"—it doesn't feel completely right—but this job is all about probability. Weighing up outcomes. We have days, not weeks, not months.

I'm taking the early chance.

Fisting the front of his fleece coat, I drag Nick even closer to me.

A breath shudders through him—*excellent sign*—and his fingertips reach up to trace my jawline. It's a gentle touch, powdered sugar light. The kiss starts out gentle, too. A slow sweep of my mouth against his, capturing the fullness of his lips—and yes, I will concede that he is an objectively decent kisser. The energy between us shifts. This is no longer an innocent, mistletoe kiss. We aren't at a Christmas party, surrounded by friends and family; no one could look at us right now and go *awwwww*. When Nick bites my bottom lip, it's sensual and sharp. Almost like we're fighting.

I want to bite him harder. So very, very hard.

But I'm thinking about what *this* version of Sydney would want. She might have the sudden urge to draw his hips flush against hers; it's like Nick can read that Sydney's mind. His fingers sink into my lower back, pulling me against him, and his tongue slips into my mouth. He tastes of candy cane scones and seawater.

"Sydney . . ." Nick rasps, straight into my mouth, and I answer with an unintelligible sound, wrapping one leg around his body as he presses my back against the cold concrete wall. I'm thinking clinically, methodically, even though his tongue is trying to make me forget this is a mission. Forget I'm doing this for a reason other than I desperately want to. His hips roll forward, and I match the movement, breathless, the heat in my belly traveling lower, lower . . .

Okay, that's enough acting.

I drop my leg, unclasp my hands from behind his neck, and to Nick's credit, he stops immediately. He listens to the movement of my body, taking a full step back.

A surprise to me. Didn't think that any part of him was a gentleman.

"Sorry," I say, clearing my throat.

"No, don't apologize," Nick says, a touch hoarse. He runs a hand over the back of his hair, which my fingers have just mussed through.

"That was—"

"Unexpected," he volleys back. "And nice." His throat bobs again. "You know, I really would take you out for New Year's, if you wanted. Are you sticking around, or . . . ?"

Now we're getting somewhere. "I thought you had plans," I say, coy, sidestepping his question to keep us on track.

Nick huffs out a sigh. "I do. Well, sort of. Vinny, you know,

Johnny's cousin? He was going to throw this big New Year's Eve get-together, but things seem a bit up in the air now. With the surprise wedding. Everyone's thinking about . . . moving things around."

He's said it oddly. Slowly. Like he's contemplating a bigger event than the wedding.

Chills break out along the base of my neck, nothing to do with the polar plunge. Something's occurred to me. A wedding would make a perfect alibi for a heist.

The Christmas presents. Johnny's texts to Andre. Maybe that *was* code.

"Where *is* Johnny?" Nick says suddenly, uneasy, peeking his head out of the bathhouse, and I yank my jacket on. Say we should call them. Go look for them.

But all along, I'm wondering how far I can push Nick on the walk home.

Three minutes later, I have him pinned to the ground.

"Ugghhh," Nick groans.

Palms to his jacket, I still his shoulders with the force of a combat medic. "Seriously, you need to stop moving."

Nick grunts out an expletive, lying face-up on the frozen side-walk. Turns out that he is a black ice detector. He's just detected it with his feet. And his back. And his butt. Turns out, Johnny got a massive cramp near the boardwalk and made Calla turn for home; Nick and I were following their trail. We'd barely gotten past the beach motels before the ice sent Nick flying. "Man," he says. "*Man*, my ass hurts."

Judging by his full-body wince, the pain is at least a six out of ten. I jump farther into triage mode, unpinning him for a hot

second, pulling out my personal cell phone, and dialing Grandma
Ruby. "I'll have someone bring the car and we'll get you back to
the house, all right? Or to the hospital?"

"No, no hospitals." His head tilts back and forth on the
sidewalk.

"*Stop* moving." Can't he follow simple directions? I extend a
finger in front of his face as the phone rings. "Trace the path with
your eyes. Good. That's it . . . I'm not sure if you have a concussion, your pupils are responding, but we'll still see if you need a
doctor. I promise we will fix your ass."

Nick chuckles dryly. "Don't make me laugh, Syd."

Syd? Since when am I "Syd"? That's probably a good thing. A
sign that he trusts me. Or that he does have a concussion and has
forgotten my whole name. Either way, the nickname scrapes an
angry path down my insides; this guy doesn't *get* to know me. "On
the bright side," I try, "everyone loves a good holiday injury story."

Nick winces, crow's feet popping around his rich brown eyes.
"Do they?"

"No. That's really dark. Sorry."

"If I have to sit on one of those tailbone donuts," Nick says, "I
think Christmas might become my least favorite holiday . . ."

Christmas. Holiday. It's the perfect time for a heist, isn't it?
Even better than New Year's. Much lower law enforcement
staffing . . .

Has Johnny really moved the heist up to use his *own wedding* as
an alibi?

The bastard.

On the second try, Grandma Ruby picks up the phone. She
speeds through the streets in her Oldsmobile, helps me load a very
stiff Nick into the back seat, and soon he's stretched out on the
living room couch, light from the Christmas tree dancing over his
face.

"Really, it's okay," Nick says at everyone's concerned looks, even though he is two shades paler than this morning. "I'm fine."

"Well, you don't *look* fine," says Grandma Ruby, and I think I might get my bluntness from her. She's Betty White sweet, but no one at the town council has ever accused her of holding her peace. "You've lost a bit of your razzle-dazzle."

For Nick, it's bad enough that he's bruised (my guess is a rapidly purpling chain from his tailbone up his spine). What's worse is we're all crowded around him like he's a dying man in a nineteenth-century painting. Sweetie Pie tip-taps over and licks one of Nick's nostrils, which I can only assume is dog for *Feel better soon. Or, You have something in your nostril.*

"Are you sure we can't drive you to urgent care?" I ask, gazing down at him, thinking, *Welp, Nicholas, this might be karma for everything that you've done.* There's also, annoyingly, a flash of a moment where I remember the press of his lips on mine. The thought of his teeth scraping against me, of me scraping right back.

"Or the hospital?" Calla asks, biting her thumbnail next to Johnny. She's still in her running gear. "You might've broken something."

"Or have a concussion," Johnny adds, tapping his own temple. Presumably he knows a lot about concussions. Having given them to other people.

A muscle in my neck twitches discreetly.

Nick shakes his head, black hair outlined against a reindeer cushion. There's a bag of miniature frozen corn under his tailbone, carrots and peas supporting his spine. We will not be eating those later. "It's really not that bad. I thought it was, but I already feel better. Don't worry about me."

On what seems like instinct, Grandma Ruby presses the back of her hand to Nick's forehead, like she's checking for a fever.

"I texted everybody," Johnny says, pulling out his cell phone as evidence. "My messages are blowing up. Vinny wants to know if he should come over."

"No," Nick says firmly. "No, he doesn't have to do that."

"He doesn't *have* to do anything." Johnny tuts, dragging the attention to himself. "But we worry about you. You know we worry. Sal's asked the same thing."

"Well, the more, the merrier," Grandma Ruby offers, removing her hand and gently patting Nick's shoulder. "You're a brave boy. Now, let's give the guy some space."

I do not give the guy some space.

When everyone else disperses into the rest of the house, I plunge down onto a footrest by the Christmas tree, wondering if my icy route on the walk home has briefly dented this mission along with Nick's tailbone. Also, I'm not *that* cold; I don't want to see anyone hurt, even if it's someone thoroughly reproachable. "I owe you an apology."

"Oh, for trying to kill me?" Nick bats back, equal amounts of strain and humor in his voice.

A laugh cracks out of me, unbidden. "How was I trying to kill you?"

Nick shifts the bag of butt corn and counts on his fingers. "Shower scare attempt, ice water plunge, ice road walk—"

"When you say it that way . . ." I did select a different route home to extend the journey. A windier path should've equaled more time for Nick to open up. I knew it was shadier, tree-lined; black ice was always a possibility. "I feel like I should point out, though, that if I am trying to kill you, I'm terrible at it."

Nick huffs out a laugh before his face softens even more. "You know I'm just messing with you, right? No way is any of this your fault. But if you feel like making it up to me . . ."

Back to flirtatious, are we? That's a partial relief. "Name your price."

He points to the TV remote with noticeably stiff effort, but his eyes are jollier than his body suggests. "Watch something with me. Whatever you want."

"Yeah?" I grab the remote. "I'm pretty sure that Grandma Ruby still has cable, so our options are probably going to be limited to the news and Hallmark Christmas movies."

"Never seen one," he says.

I blink at him, resettling uncomfortably into my role. "Nick, *no.*"

"That good? What am I missing?"

"You know, it's all like: A twenty-eight-year-old widow who's a well-known children's author buys a dilapidated ski lodge in rural Vermont just before the holidays, but the lodge *used* to belong to the grumpiest grandson of some guy in town, and the grandson is bitter about the loss of his ancestral property, but at his core, all he wants is *love.* He and the author are thrust together by fate, building construction, and Christmas spirit."

"Which movie are you describing?" Calla says, suddenly popping her head into the living room.

"Fake film," I reply.

"*Darn,*" she says, leaving again.

I switch on the TV, start scrolling. "What's your favorite movie?" I ask Nick.

He smirks. "This is where you judge me, right?"

"No judgment. Unless you say something like . . . I don't know . . . *Grease 2.*"

"See, I was going to go with *Good Will Hunting,* but thank you for reminding me that *Grease 2* is, in fact, my favorite movie." Nick points at the framed photo on the coffee table between us. "This is great, by the way."

My stomach pinches, looking at our Christmas card photo from twelve years ago. Grandma Ruby does not have an eye for photography. Give her a choice of three excellent photos and one stinker, and she will—without fail—pick the one where Calla is sneezing, my eyes are closed, and Dad looks newly emerged from endoscopic surgery . . .

Dad. I skate right past his face. Past his salt-and-pepper hair and graying beard. Refuse to focus on any of it. He was wearing that shirt—that red flannel shirt—the day he got in his truck.

"Isn't it?" I say, like the reminder hasn't affected me at all. "We're a photogenic bunch."

"It's nice," Nick says.

"That's your concussion speaking."

"Don't have a concussion. And honestly, even if I did, hospitals really aren't my thing."

I frown. "Germs?"

"Germs," he concurs. "I've also spent way too much time in them. Anyway, the photo's got character. That your dad?"

Goddamn it, Nick. Let it be. I flick through the channels, grinding out, "Yep."

There's just enough bite in my voice that I think he'll shy away from the subject, but he just keeps pushing. "I always wanted a big family."

A big family? I wouldn't describe mine as particularly large, especially with Dad gone, but maybe it is, for Nick. Something in my chest pinpricks. What I say next is half strategy, half . . . just plain human. "I'm sorry about your grandma."

A line forms across Nick's forehead, and it's abundantly clear what he's thinking: *Did I tell you that my grandma died?*

"You just sounded like you were close, and you're not with her at Christmas, and the hospital thing. Should I not have brought it up?"

"No, no, you're good." Nick clears his throat. "Thank you."

I nod. "You're welcome."

Together, we flick through the channels, settling on a movie about a woman from California who inherits a Canadian cabin from her great-great-uncle, only to fall in love with the youngish cranky groundskeeper who (plot twist!) is all sunshine at heart. Also, there are bears. They attack midway through the film, and for a second, I think the story is about to go in a *completely* different direction.

Nick doesn't notice. His eyes are closed. His breath has slowed. I leave him as he drifts peacefully to sleep.

9

An hour and a half later, in the kitchen, there's a tall, tattooed man eating our cereal. On his left hand is an ink-red skull; on his right, the Powerpuff Girls. All across his arms and his throat, the motif alternates: death insignia, cartoons, death insignia, cartoons. "Hey," he says to me, perfectly casual, barely breaking his trance. He's picking the tiny marshmallows meticulously out of his Lucky Charms—with his fingers. There's a miniature pile by the bowl.

"Were you going to eat this?" he asks, finally looking up, grabbing the cereal box, shaking it.

"Oh, no, all yours." I stare at him over the kitchen table. "I'm sorry, you are?"

I know who he is. He's Sal, one of Johnny's men. Sal, come to check in on Nick. He arrived almost soundlessly through our garage and is occupying himself while Nick naps. On his wrist, Bugs Bunny is hanging out with a grenade.

"Sal," he says. One word only.

"Cool," I say, zipping up my parka—and trailing outside. Gail has just sent me an encrypted text. It just says, Call me.

Alone in the Prius, I massage the space between my eyes with my thumb. "Sal's in my kitchen," I say when Gail picks up.

Her voice cracks over the line. "I see that . . . Well, I'll get straight to the point. I've located the owner of the Mid-Coast Maine phone number. His name's Boyd Winters."

"Okay, who's that?"

"No idea."

"What do you mean, no idea?"

Gail tuts. "Just what I said, Sydney. The guy is nobody. Runs a small gift shop that sells candles and bric-a-brac. Lobster magnets, things of that nature. No FBI profile whatsoever. Law-abiding citizen. Unless Johnny's planning on robbing his collection of dried starfish, I'm not sure how he fits into any of this. I was hoping he was a distant cousin of yours, someone Johnny's inviting to the wedding."

I check out the Prius's window. From this angle, I can see the back of Sal's head in my kitchen. "Not the case."

"Well, drat." Gail pauses. "Just keep listening for the name. I'll send one of my trusted associates up to scope out the place, see if our friend Boyd is hiding anything. I got your text about your Christmas Day theory as well. Pushes our timeline up a bit."

My tongue runs over my teeth. "I'm thinking we should feel out the Calla angle a little more. If the timeline's changed, this could help speed things—"

"Sydney." Gail is clipped. "How many times do I have to say it? This investigation is too important to compromise in any way."

"Yeah, I know that," I say, just as clipped. I haven't forgotten about the fifty pounds of C4, waiting in the wings. "But if she is innocent, shouldn't we try to find that out, too? Wouldn't it give us a fuller picture? I'm not saying that we have to tell her. I just think—"

"You're not thinking. Focus on Nick. You're making progress with Nick. Bring him to the pageant tonight."

In all the chaos, I'd forgotten about the Cape Hathaway Christmas Pageant. It's a costume party meets theatrical play put on by the local elementary school. I'm not sure there's been a single year in Grandma Ruby's whole life that she's missed the fun. She plays the piano for the kids and gets *very* into it, sometimes kicking back the piano bench and dancing by the keys.

"Isn't that one of your family traditions?" Gail asks, filling in the blanks. "I've done my research. Plus, I heard your grandmother boasting to Calla that she got you both great seats this year."

"Wait." I frown. "I thought the pageant wasn't until Christmas Eve. It's always on Christmas Eve."

"Things change," Gail retorts in the understatement of the season.

"Even so, I'm not sure Nick's going to be able to leave the couch for a while. He's down for the count."

"Give him some Advil," Gail says. "He'll recover."

"He actually fell down pretty hard—" I start to argue, but the line has already disconnected.

Back in the house, Sal has migrated to the couch and is watching a Hallmark movie with Nick; they're like two peas in a pod. Around the same height, around the same build. Maybe Sal fits the profile for the New York heist even better than Nick? Either way, I slap down a bottle of industrial-strength Advil on the coffee table, then join my sister at the kitchen sink, where she's washing dishes.

I can't *tell* Calla about Johnny, but I can at least *talk* with her.

I offer to dry the cookie sheets.

"That would be great, thanks," she says with a big smile. Her sweater has polka dots on it, just like my high school robe, and I vow to stop her if she starts to say anything even remotely incriminating in this kitchen. I imagine Gail in a windowless van, somewhere outside of town, listening. "Sorry I've been so all over the place," Calla says. "I feel like the wedding has kind of eaten my brain."

"Ah, no worries," I say, grabbing a clean dishcloth. "Hey, I've been meaning to ask you, is the rehearsal dinner the first time you're meeting Johnny's family, or . . . ?"

Calla picks at a piece of burnt sugar with her thumbnail. "No, I've met them. They're nice. Mom's a little strict. Nick calls her 'the Eagle.'"

"The Eagle. Why the Eagle?"

"Mmm . . ." Calla stops picking, considering this. "She just looks like an eagle. Maybe it's the eyes. Picture Meryl Streep in *The Devil Wears Prada*."

"What about his dad?" I ask. A text notification dings in my back pocket. Probably from Gail, telling me to back off.

Calla wavers, head tilting back and forth. "His dad is . . . like Johnny, I guess. He can come off a bit harsh sometimes, but underneath it, he's a real softie."

Oh, is he? To put this in perspective, besides "the Coffee King," his dad's nickname is "Bootsie." He likes to break people's ribs with his boots. "How many times have you met them?"

"Not too many," Calla says, shrugging, "but don't worry. They're really going to bring me into the family."

My stomach sours like custard in the heat. That response, it doesn't even *sound* like Calla. It's like she's parroting words straight from Johnny's mouth.

Another text chimes furiously in my pocket.

"And you want that," I say to Calla, hoping she'll read between the lines. "The whole 'you take this man and his family' thing."

"Of course I do."

My phone starts angrily screaming with a call. I silence it. "Because you really are taking him. You're taking him everywhere. He's attached to you."

Calla frowns. "Thank you for explaining the concept of marriage to me, Sydney."

"He's just . . . not who I pictured you with."

"I know," Calla says firmly, "that's why he's a good match. He's not like anyone I've ever dated. I did that on purpose. You know that saying that the definition of insanity is trying the same thing over and over again and expecting different results? I was tired of expecting different results, so I tried a different type of person . . . Johnny isn't the quiet, sit-at-home kind of guy. We go out, and we have fun, and he's really the life of the party—and that feels nice to be around, you know? He pushes me, too. Which, I'll admit, sometimes I don't like, but overall I think it's good for me. I went *jogging* this morning."

She says the last part in a whisper, like it's a secret.

"I know," I say. "I know you did."

"And he's dependable. He always shows up when he says he's going to, and no matter what he does or doesn't do, I get this feeling like . . . like he's not going to leave me, okay?" Before I have time to process that, she hits me with: "He wants to get to know you, too. Johnny *likes* you, so please . . . try a little harder."

She has no idea how hard I'm trying. "I just think—"

Now the *landline* begins to ring. I didn't even know we had a landline anymore. What year is it? Nineteen eighty-two? Swiveling around, I reach next to the fridge, pick up the receiver, and clack it down again.

Calla throws me a judgmental look. "Did you just hang up on that person?"

"They called earlier," I say. "Telemarketer. Wanted to sell us roofing supplies."

"Oh, you should actually call them back," Calla says, pointing at the phone. "Grandma Ruby needs new gutters." Her back is still rigid from our previous strain of conversation. "Anyway, I know what I'm doing, okay? It wasn't an accident that I was in that pottery class. I was really *trying* to do something different. It was between that, a cooking seminar, and a self-defense workshop, but the other classes were all booked up by the time I got around to it. So, fate."

Plunking down the final pan on the counter, I turn to Calla. "I could teach you."

She eyes me suspiciously. "You want to teach me how to cook? Sydney, you can't even make eggs."

"No, self-defense. I took a class last year—" *Half-truth.* Momentum surges through me. "Here, stand by the table. I'm going to pretend to choke you."

"Oh my god, Sydney."

Maybe I've come out of the gates a little too strong. "It'll be worth it, I promise. Please?"

Eyes hard, Calla drops her sponge, shuffling over to the empty space by the table. "This is not what normal families do. I'm just telling you that right now."

Not a normal family, I think. *Not anymore.* My fingers slip gently around her neck. "Okay, so, grab my hands and try to pry me off of you. If that doesn't work, try to push me."

Calla does, her fingers at my fingers, her palms thrusting against me.

"Harder," I say, and she tries again, feet slipping and sliding, teeth gritted this time. I barely budge. "See? That's what most people do, and neither of those work. You have to raise both of

your arms all the way above your head—good, that's it. Twist to
the side and chop my arms with your elbows. Nice! Okay." Standing in front of her, I clap my hands, my feet positioned shoulder-
width apart. "Now try to punch me as hard as you can in the throat."

Calla scoffs, almost laughing. "I'm not going to punch you in
the throat! It's *Christmas*." She pinches her eyebrows together.
"Also, I would *never* punch you in the throat? Even if it wasn't a
holiday? Jeez, what's gotten into you?"

I squirm. "I'm just trying to make sure you're . . . safe."

"Well, I can take care of myself. I've been doing it for years."
The way she bites off the last few words, I can tell that something
else is coming. Something I might not want to hear. She faces me,
shoulders back, and actually does punch me in the throat. Just,
you know, emotionally. "I think I might ask Dad to come to the
wedding."

I blink at her, not processing, an image of Dad erupting: him,
Saturday morning donut run at the gas station, snow; he points
into the case and asks which one I want. Eating together on the
frozen picnic tables at the edge of our neighborhood. And later, in
summer, at the Cape Hathaway Huskies game, his face beaming
in the stands. "I'm sorry, what?"

Calla pushes out a rush of words. "I hired a private investigator
to find him, and they did. He's at a long-term campground now,
just outside of Burlington, Vermont, and it's . . . it's tradition. Dads
walk their daughters down the aisle, and he—"

My head's fuzzing. "Wait, slow down. You actually talked
to him?"

"No," she says quietly. "No, not yet. I just *found* him. So he's
there. And Burlington's not that far away. I know it's a really long
shot, but maybe if I just let him know that I'm getting married,
he'd want to come."

What Calla's just said . . . I'm not sure I can handle on top of everything else. It's un-handleable. And it's a bad, bad idea. Calling our father? Our father, who hasn't called *us* in a decade? What makes her think he'd even answer the phone, much less walk her down the aisle? He'd only disappoint her, hurt her, hurt her *more*. There's a burst of pain in my chest, and I poke at it, scratch at it, tell her, "You can't just . . . fucking . . . drive out of someone's life, not say a single word to them, leave them, and . . . No. No." Our father is just another person who will fail to live up to Calla's optimism. I'm shaking my head, pulse in my throat, trying to keep my voice from carrying to the living room. "It's not worth it, Calla. Don't put yourself through that."

Calla chews her bottom lip. "I know you've always hated him since—"

"I haven't *hated* him," I argue.

"Hated him, resented him, I don't really know. But it's been a long time, and it was terrible what he did, but I've been thinking about it a lot and maybe we shouldn't have assumed the worst about him. Maybe it's time to start letting go of what happened, Syd. Both of us. It seems like you still have trouble trusting people . . ."

"Well, maybe you should trust people a little less!" I burst out as the landline rings off the hook for a final time. I pick it up and tell Gail, "We don't want what you're selling!"

"Oh," says a man on the other line. "Oh, I'm sorry."

I cringe. "No, wait—I thought . . ."

But he's already disconnected.

Calla hangs up the dishtowels in a neat little line before retreating upstairs. "I won't call him, okay? If it's going to make you that stressed. Case closed."

"Wait, Calla . . ."

She holds up a hand. "It's fine. Don't worry about it. I'll just . . . see you at the pageant tonight."

A couple hours later, it's still eating away at me. The possibility of Dad waltzing into our house again, a decade of dirt on his shoes, to walk my little sister down the aisle. At her wedding. To a crime lord.

Won't happen.

"You look deep in thought," Nick says, nudging my shoulder with his.

"Are you sure you shouldn't be lying down?" I volley back. He shouldn't even be off the couch. He shouldn't be willing to sit through this long, long pageant in a stiff auditorium seat—but *Nick* was the one who insisted he should come.

His jaw clamps and unclamps, probably gritting down the pain. "And miss the Cape Hathaway Christmas Pageant? Never."

Together with Calla, Grandma Ruby, Johnny, and Powerpuff-Girls-tattoo Sal, we're waiting outside the elementary school auditorium as people file into the entryway. Johnny's acting jittery. Pre-wedding stress? Or pre-heist stress? Behind me, his teeth grind, and he's firing off texts that I know Gail is monitoring. I'm watching him in the corner of my vision as, inside, we duck under construction paper Christmas trees and strings of popcorn hanging from the ceiling. Somewhere down that hallway—that one, right there—are my third-grade handprints. I still have a ribbon in the trophy cabinet by the principal's office: FIRST PLACE, DISTRICT SPELLING BEE. Dad won the same thing, when he was a kid in this town, and I—

Shut it down, Sydney. I'm not thinking about him. It's over.

"Were we supposed to dress up?" Nick asks, even though he's dressed just fine. Black blazer. Festive tie that Grandma Ruby found in the depths of her closet, insisting Nick should take the "Christmas pineapple" tie for a spin. I seriously hate to say it, but if Nick can pull off that pattern, he can pull off anything.

"Don't worry," I reassure him, playing my role again. A few elementary-age kids rush past. "If you ever make it back to Cape Hathaway, you can be a . . . green bean casserole or something." The best thing about this pageant is that every kid—whether they're in the play or not—is encouraged to dress up. Kudos go to the kid who's decorated himself as a Christmas ham, complete with circular pineapple halo. (Have I missed the memo about Christmas pineapples?) A girl in a goose costume flaps and honks past me, hot on the heels of a Rudolph. His nose twinkles under the hallway lights.

"With the crunchy onions?" Nick asks, catching my eye.

There's too much warmth in his glance. Good for the assignment, but . . . I don't like it. "Whatever you want." I slap the tickets in my palm. "Should we find our seats?"

What I'll never tell Nick is that I have a long history with this play. Seven years in a row, I was the donkey. Or rather, Donkey. I only added the "the" for gravitas and emphasis. Donkey has no lines, traditionally speaking, just some carefully timed *eeee-aaww*s at theatrically appropriate moments.

Off to my left, a buzz sounds in Johnny's pocket, and he curses under his breath. "I'm sorry," he says, shaking his head and unsheathing the phone from his jacket. "I have to take this. What time does it start?"

"Eleven minutes," says Grandma Ruby, wiggling her fingers. "Time to warm up the old piano hands!"

"Break a leg, Grandma," I tell her absentmindedly, eyes trailing Johnny down the hallway; Sal shadows him like a ghost—and I already know I'm going to follow them both.

Grandma Ruby throws me a pointed look. "Never say that to

a person over eighty, dear." Then she saunters off with all the youthfulness of a spring dove, her red velvet skirt rippling behind her.

The auditorium is packed. Kids, parents, and the other 79 percent of Cape Hathaway's population are settling into their seats. "Should we?" asks Nick, gesturing for Calla and me to go down Aisle 11B first. Scattered caramel corn is already littering the floor; the pageant is serving snacks this year. And eggnog. Spiked eggnog, I think, for the adults. Smells like it. Every once in a while, I catch a faint whiff of booze.

"You know what?" I say, conscious that I'm losing precious time. "I'm just going to pop to the bathroom before the play starts. Don't want to miss a minute of the action."

"Hurry back," Calla says, a little muted after our squabble in the kitchen. "The beginning's the best part."

I nod, feeling Nick's eyes on my face, then weave through the crowd in the opposite direction, ears trained for Johnny's voice. He isn't in the main hallway. I duck into a few classrooms on the east side of the building. Not there, either. Finally, through one of the circular hallway windows—painted into the shape of a sun— I spot Johnny in the parking lot, pacing like a bobcat, cell phone glued to his ear. Chunky snowflakes whip sideways, biting his face. What kind of phone call is so secret that you have to take it outside in a soon-to-be snowstorm?

I know exactly what type of phone call. That was a rhetorical question.

Every ten seconds or so, one of Johnny's hands chops through the air. Sal's standing with his arms crossed, shoulders puffed, keeping watch.

If I can sneak by the flagpole, into that sea of minivans, I should be able to inch up to them . . . Hear what's Johnny's saying. The virus will pick up on who he's calling, but not what's being said.

Parka hood up, obscuring my blond shock of hair, I slink out the lobby doors, footsteps hushed in the snow. Except for Johnny's voice, it's deadly quiet. But I can match the silence. The trick is to maintain a fair amount of distance, just close enough to pick up the words, and—ideally—match your footsteps with the target's. I step directly in Johnny's tracks; his boots are at least three sizes bigger than mine.

"I thought you said it was . . ." he says, obviously struggling to keep his voice down. The wind kicks up, swallowing the rest of the sentence. I use the sudden noise barrier to pick up my pace, staying ducked. When I'm less than thirty feet away, back against a tinted minivan window, I listen over the vehicle, neck craned, pulse rising in my wrists.

Johnny's biting out words. "The van . . . Yeah, the van . . ." A few rattled phrases follow. "Make sure everything's ready . . . . Well, time's fucking running out, isn't it? Just get it *done* . . . Couple of days . . ." Then he abruptly stops.

I hear Sal shuffling forward, maybe placing a hand on Johnny's shoulder. "Boss," he says. "Did you hear that?"

My blood runs cold. Slowly, soundlessly, I curl a mittened hand over my mouth. Stop any of my breath from fogging in the air.

"Hear what?" Johnny says, annoyed, clearly done with his call.

As noiselessly as possible, I lower to my knees, prepared to roll under the minivan if needed. Adrenaline pumps so hard through my veins, my right temple is throbbing.

Sal pauses, shuffles. "Maybe nothing. Maybe . . ."

Johnny's dismissive. "Let's just get back inside. Calla will kill me if I miss this thing. Can't stand to see that girl upset."

Mitten still shrouding my mouth, I remain crouched, watching their feet under the minivans as they trail back inside. Faster than Santa's sleigh, I whip out my own phone and speed a text in Gail's direction: **Johnny phone call 7:06 pm, who was it to? Mention of a van. Next heist . . . highway robbery? Any bank planning a large monetary transport on Christmas Day?** With any luck, Gail will look into it immediately.

I'm feeling lucky. Lucky that Sal didn't pursue his instincts. Lucky that I've snagged an actionable bit of intel. This mission is heading in the right direction, even with Nick.

I can't follow them into the lobby—too suspicious—so I slink around the back of the elementary school, pry open a classroom window with my house key, and climb in that way. Undetected. Ripping off my mittens and my coat. Until I *do* reach the lobby, where—

"Oh, thank heavens!" Grandma Ruby says, rushing up to me. She really is fast for eighty-two. Her face is flushed pink. "Sydney, there you are. We have an emergency!"

A lump surges into my throat, thinking of Calla. "What kind of emergency? Is anyone hurt?"

"No, no, don't be silly. No one's hurt." Grandma Ruby pauses in front of me and clasps my hands in hers, tucking them to her chest. "Donkey is missing."

My eyes squint. "Like, the costume?"

"No, the person. The child."

"There's a missing child?" *Shit*, this is an actual emergency. "When was the last time anyone saw them? Has anyone contacted the police?"

Grandma Ruby presses her lips together. "Maybe I'm not explaining this right. Delilah Hannigan went on vacation to Calgary with her parents and everyone forgot to contact us. She's been coming to rehearsals, so no one knew! No one thought twice!" Grandma Ruby levels me with a glance, squeezing both of my hands in unison. "The play needs you, Sydney."

The pieces fall together in a horrible clash. "Oh, Grandma, no . . ."

"There aren't any lines, pumpkin! You know that! And the costume has always been roomy. Just two and a half hours of your time. That's all we're talking. You were so *good* at it."

"But—"

"Sydney, you were born to play this part. I knew that from the first moment you stepped foot onstage, when you were eleven years old, just as I knew you had my whole heart the moment you were born. At Cape Hathaway General Hospital. You were seven pounds exactly, with a thick head of hair. The nurse passed you to me, my first grandchild, and I looked into your eyes, and I said, 'Hello there, little bean.' It was like you stared right back into my soul."

Love with a side of not-so-subtle manipulation. Grandma Ruby is laying it on thick. She squeezes my hands again, and it's such a familiar movement—the hands I remember, the familial warmth I remember. This is the person who read me adventure novels when I couldn't sleep, who stepped up and raised me and Calla when there was *no one*, and—

I let out a sigh through my nose. "Where's the costume?"

I'd forgotten. I'd blocked it out. This costume is so atrocious, a picture of me inside it might effectively serve as blackmail. Backstage, in front of the floor-length mirror, I stick out one of the donkey legs to the side and drag a hand (or rather, a front hoof) up the fabric. *Yep. This'll do it.* One look at me and Sidekick Nick will tell me any secret he has. Who could resist a woman in a tattered gray onesie with floppy ears and a felt tail? The costume fits, but barely. Ironically, it is fairly tight in the ass region. All I have to do is stand stick straight for every one of my scenes, and the fabric won't rip.

"Places!" the director shouts behind the scenes. "Everyone, places!"

Lips vibrating with a sigh, I tell myself it's just a short period of time—then it's back to business. *Who did Johnny call? What van is he referencing? One he's rented, or one he's attacking?* My mind ticks over his conversation as I line up next to a blond-headed boy approximately half my height. The kid is staring at me with a mixture of awe and bewilderment, like I might actually be a donkey.

"You're a grown-up." He has a voice that's surprisingly assured—and bitter—for his age. His tiny foot stamps. He's dressed as a crab. "This play is for kids!"

I lean over, hands on Donkey's knees. "Do you have a grandma?"

"Yeah?"

"*That's* why I'm here."

He looks puzzled by this turn of events (what's his grandma got to do with it?), but the music has already started with a peppy rush. On the other side of the velvet curtains, Grandma Ruby is pounding the baby grand piano keys. Her Christmas tune is more rock concert than elementary school hymn. It's the type of song that makes you want to rip your wig off.

Well, here we go.

When the curtain rises, everything is black, but soon the auditorium explodes into Technicolor. You'd think we were performing that play about a dreamcoat. Under the haze of flashing, multicolored lights, I zigzag my way around the giant cardboard boxes—wrapped like presents in silver paper—and file behind my friend the crab. This play truly makes no sense. As a kid, I rolled with the various inconsistencies and the comingling of disparate species. As an adult, I question its plot. Or its lack of plot. The play is—roughly—about a lamb who is traveling across a magical land around Christmastime; she meets a variety of animals who teach her about holiday joy. I don't know who wrote it. Someone high. There is no true middle and no true end. But there are snow machines. To the audience's delight, they burst now, spraying us with lumpy, white dust. I spit out a tiny chunk when some lands in my mouth.

Has Calla noticed me onstage yet? Has Nick? Are Sal and Johnny back in their seats? The lights have blacked out the audience. I can't see a thing, and— *Oh, sweet Jesus*, we're dancing. Since when is there a choreographed dance? Grandma!

As far as I can tell, it is a simple one-two step, so I follow crab boy's foot pattern, squinting into the auditorium. There's movement in the middle row. Someone's switching seats. Or getting up from their seat? When the golden lights flash over the audience, I see him more clearly: a middle-aged man in a Santa hat, swaying into the aisle. *One of the kids' parents*, I think. But he's acting kind of . . . strange.

As a CIA officer, I'm trained for the unexpected. Yet, when Santa man starts stomping toward the stage, an openly determined gaze in his holly jolly eyes, a little voice inside me still says: *What the fuck?* He looks smug, too absolutely sure he's about to get away with whatever is about to happen. He's already passing Grandma Ruby at the piano.

A sick feeling starts in my belly, climbs its way up my throat. Is this man an actual threat? Or is he just reliving the glory days of elementary school, hopped up on way too much eggnog? I'm not sure, I'm just not. Murmurs erupt from a few people in the audience, spiking above the piano song. Is this part of the act? Is Santa supposed to rush the stage?

And the kids . . . *God, the kids.* All twenty of them are so merry, so dedicated to their roles, they haven't even clocked the intruder. They're like I was. Innocent. Unaware that anything could go wrong in the world.

"Let me up!" the man yells, throwing one leg over the stage, attempting to lift himself onto the platform. He has the grace of, well, a forty-year-old drunk guy in half a Santa costume—but that doesn't make him any less dangerous. Any less unhinged. Is he armed?

"Hey!" I shout back at him, advancing past the cardboard Christmas tree. My boots thwack against the wooden floor, fear bubbling under my skin. "Get down!"

If he can get off the stage, slip back into the audience, maybe this'll all be fine. Maybe I won't have to do anything drastic . . .

But he's standing up now, wobbling at the edge of the platform. He mumbles something that sounds like "potatoes," followed by a much louder, "YOU CAN'T STOP ME, DONKEY!"

And there's a second when I think to myself, *No. No, this cannot be fucking happening.* Gail and I have a new lead on the case; things are progressing with Nick; there've been a few hiccups, yes, but nothing major. Nothing that would put me or the case in serious jeopardy. And now . . .

I'm five feet away from the man, the stench of alcohol wafting from his breath—and he charges. He's charging. Charging at me? Charging at the kids? *The kids.*

My throat hitches, because I want to cry, and scream, and I— *Cannot* break my cover this way.

I also have no choice.

Blood rushes to my face, protective mode takes over, and I lurch forward, headbutting the man straight in the nose. Gasps from the audience and shrieks from the kids follow a not-so-gentle crunch.

"Son of a—" the guy says, stumbling back, pure shock crossing his face. Shock turns to anger turns to "*bitch*." His right arm shoots out, aiming to grip me around the throat, but he is way too slow for my reflexes. I dodge him, grabbing his arm midair, and in one smooth motion, flip him directly over my shoulder. He lands with a tremendous thud on the stage, groaning about a bill from his chiropractor, and—

The song's over. Everyone's on their feet, staring, gaping.

I have never felt so exposed in my life.

10

So just explain everything from the beginning," the police officer says, handing me an ice pack. I take it obligingly, pressing the coolness to my forehead; it stings. I'm sitting low on a beanbag in one of the third-grade classrooms, my knees almost to my chin. "No need to go fast. At your own pace."

I nod, playing the part: confused, rattled. I *am* rattled. Santa was given a lift to jail for the evening. Turns out, he's crab boy's father; he's going through a custody battle and wanted to take his son home for Christmas. That kills me for crab boy—but what's really churning my stomach, what's making me sweat in this donkey suit, is the memory of Nick's face.

When the lights flickered on in the auditorium, Nick was staring at me. He'd hobbled to the stage, determined to thwart my attacker, but . . . it didn't go down that way. Confusion flitted across Nick's eyes, a muscle straining in his cheek, and he was giving me this *look*, like he'd read me all wrong—and I was a different person entirely.

A bead of sweat trickles down my cheek. I wipe it away with a donkey hoof, laying out the details of the event—not like a CIA officer would. Like a civilian would, with scattered pauses, talking mostly to my knees. If this officer asks any probing questions about my mixed martial arts background, I could be here all night, and I need to get back to my family.

Back to Nick. Explain a few things. Explain them away.

I can still fix this, I think, knot hard in my throat.

"We're all good here," the officer finally says. She's my age, roughly my build. "You really did a brave thing tonight. I don't think this would've ended too badly, but you never know. You protected those kids. Did what you had to do."

"Thank you," I say quickly, rising from the beanbag, glad that the interview, at least, is over.

Outside the classroom, there's no one. Everyone's been forced into the lobby, I think. Or the parking lot? The armpits of the donkey costume are starting to chafe, and all I want to do is unzip, grab my parka from backstage, and start damage control. Methodically. Engage the protocol for a potentially blown cover—because Johnny and Sal must be suspicious. Nick must be suspicious. If I get Calla to vouch for me, to tell them about our self-defense session in the kitchen . . .

But I can't do that.

I can't do that because Nick has—somehow—managed to send Johnny, Sal, and my family home. When I round the corner, it's just Nick in the lobby, hanging out by a trio of glittering Christmas trees. Blue light pulses over the shadow of his face. My stomach gutters. He's standing at an odd angle, favoring his right leg, Johnny's car keys clutched in his hand. "Are you all right?" he asks, voice raw and scratchy. "You're not hurt at all, are you?"

He's saying the right things, but elements of his demeanor feel *off.* His jaw is too tight. His eyes are too hard. There's a stiffness in his body unrelated to his injury.

"I'm fine," I say warily, shuffling up to him, and it *is* possible that the stiffness is from worry. Maybe he was scared for me; maybe he's kicking himself for not getting to the stage first.

That is not it, Sydney, a voice inside me says. Instinct pinpricks my arms.

"No bruises," I add with a slow swallow, pointing to the un-blemished skin of my forehead. A sticky coolness lingers from the ice pack. "See? They cleared me to go home, but . . ." I shift from foot to foot. "You didn't have to wait for me."

"'Course I did," Nick rasps, hobbling to close the gap between us. His fingertips reach out and dust my forehead, sending a sharp shiver down my spine, and for three seconds I barely breathe. Was that a tender movement? A threatening movement? Distinctly hard to tell. His touch doesn't match the look on his face, which is . . . *What? What's he thinking exactly?*

How bad is this about to be?

I test the waters further, offering a light brush of *his* shoulder—and a pun. "Sorry if I made an ass of myself."

Nick shakes his head, irises darkening, his pupils like tiny lumps of coal. He skips right over the joke. No goofball energy here. No slow, ridiculous Nick grin. "You didn't," he says, his full lips pinching together. "We should go."

Not *we should get you home.* Just *we should go.*

The ice in his voice, the hardness . . .

It shouldn't shake me. But I've never come this close before. Never tiptoed toward a blown cover, much less barreled right through it. I inhale, my ears starting to feel like miniature bon-fires. It's a roll of the dice. I could assume my cover is toast, refuse to go with him—or I can play this out until the end. Keep up with the mission until I'm absolutely sure it's gone south.

"You coming?" Nick asks, wrenching open the door to the parking lot.

"Yeah." I nod, bracing myself. Acid roils in my stomach. "Yeah."

Nick hasn't explained why my family left before us. He hasn't explained why he's barely looking at me, why there is such a sudden and impenetrable shift between us. Covertly, with nimble fingers, I switch on the recording function of my cell phone, vowing that—if I have to go down—I'll go down with intel.

I owe the mission that much.

Back in the Escalade, Nick's at the wheel, and I'm box-breathing silently in the passenger seat. Praying. I never pray. The heaters have just roared to life. Hot air puffs against my face as snowflakes *splat* the windshield in vicious chunks.

There's an exercise on The Farm that really dug underneath my skin.

You're alone in a junky sedan. You're sitting there, nice and still. And all of a sudden—five, six minutes later—people swarm you. People in black masks with baseball bats. Your windows are rolled up, and you have to stay there, motionless, breathing, as they bash the glass. As spiderweb cracks form on the windshield, and they're yelling, shouting so loud, and you're wondering how long until everything caves in. Until you're covered in glass and scratches and—

It took all my emotional reserves, even though there was no real danger. No one *really* wanted to hurt me. It was all pretend.

This isn't.

This is when I should've called an Uber.

"Maybe I should've called an Uber," I actually say, pointedly underlining Nick's silence. My voice is unfaltering even as my rib cage hollows out. "Much chattier drivers."

I'm switching strategies on the fly.

My plan now? Agitate him. Annoy the crap out of him like he's been annoying me. Get him to talk however I can. If Nick's planning on confronting me, then it needs to happen *soon*. Before he has the opportunity to strategize with Johnny. Before he has the chance to take me somewhere way off the grid or—God forbid—back to my house, where Calla and Grandma Ruby would be in jeopardy.

"An Uber?" Nick rubs a hand down his face, almost laughing. He throws the car into reverse, backing out of our parking lot space and lurching toward the road. My gut lurches with it. "Honestly? I'd be scared for the Uber driver. Make sure he has good life insurance."

Playing innocent, trying to unsettle him further, I drop my mouth open. "Well, that's unfair."

Nick's voice is full of awe and confusion. "Sydney, you *headbutted* a guy."

"Who rushed at some kids!"

"I know! I know. I'm not talking about *why* you did it," Nick says, changing gears. "I'm talking about how." We speed out of the near-empty lot, the hush of snow beneath the tires. Dark woods flit by—plenty of hidden places to stop and force me out of the vehicle, onto my knees. Every flick of Nick's eyes toward the passenger seat feels like a preemptive strike, digging little holes in me. "I don't mean to profile you, but most people's go-to move isn't the headbutt. You aren't an English footballer in a pub. Did you ever even play soccer?"

Good. Don't have to lie. "I did."

"Really?"

"Really." Blood pulsates in my neck, the space in the car's cabin feeling smaller and smaller. "Shouldn't I be driving? Aren't you hurt?"

At the first stoplight, Nick turns and gazes at me fully, head cocked, as if I were a jigsaw puzzle that someone's assembled a little bit off. Pieces askew. It chills me to my toes. When he speaks again, his throat is hoarse, and his fingers are gripped tightly against the wheel. "Something you want to tell me here, Sydney?"

The metallic taste of fear creeps onto my tongue. I speak through it, swallow, fight to keep my pulse down. "Like what?"

Nick's voice has dipped dangerously low. *Here* is the man that people are afraid of. Always knew he was lurking beneath the surface. "Like why one second you were a donkey, and the next you were James fucking Bond."

The word *catastrophic* comes to mind, but I hold on. Grip with everything I have. "I never thought I'd *use* that stuff," I say quickly. "Didn't you hear me in the kitchen with Calla? I took a workshop—"

"Where you learned an expert level of mixed martial arts in an afternoon?" Nick cuts me off, scowling. "Come on, Sydney. Someone charges you in a setting like that, and you blink. You didn't even blink. It was like you just became this completely different person. That move you did after the headbutt? Your technique? Textbook military. And you weren't in the military . . ." He says the last part almost to himself, musingly, and that's when I really know. I know with a sharp spike inside my lungs: Nick Fraser has looked me up. Much more than a casual Google. "I knew something was up with you, but I *never*—"

"Nick," I rasp, repositioning my cell phone in my pocket, angling the microphone toward the air.

He comes out with it, wiping a hand once more down his face. "Who are you?"

My throat burns. My skin can't seem to decide if it's freezing or boiling, the hot puffs of air drying out my eyes. The curve of Nick's bicep tenses as he turns the steering wheel, and—

This is still fixable.

What evidence does he have, really?

"I think you've got the wrong idea," I say, shaking my head. I've borrowed Calla's earrings. They swing as I *deny, deny, deny.* "I'm not—"

"Can't be the CIA," Nick muses again. His voice has taken on a gravelly quality, like he isn't just surprised but also somehow sad, and . . . he's said it. He's actually said it. *CIA.* "They don't work domestically. Not police, either. The Joneses have the police in their pockets. So that leaves . . . Interpol? The FBI?" Nick pauses with a chest hitch, the car windows foggy and closing in on me. His breath grows heavy and thick. "That's it, isn't it? You're with the FBI."

He could've slugged me straight in the nose, and it would've been less of a blow. Every part of me tenses, my hands gripping my thighs, and I want to *scream.* I've never failed before. Never failed at my job. Not in Sweden, not in Lithuania, and now, in my hometown, on the most important mission of my life, fucking *this?* This happens?

"I'm not sure how you're coming up with these ideas," I say quickly, hanging on. "But I promise you, I'm not even *close* to being—"

"*Please* don't bullshit me, Sydney," Nick says, exasperated, tired. "I know, okay? I know. You left to tail Johnny when he made a phone call at the pageant. This afternoon? When I fell on the ice? You have a *lot* more medical training than you were letting on. You also put a tracker on this vehicle, which I took off, by the way. You're subtle, and you're clearly good at your job—but I know what to look for." Nick huffs as I silently unclick my seat belt, petrified. "And the suitcase. You rooted through his suitcase."

That's it.

That's what gets me. How the *hell* does he know that?

It strips me back, strips me bare. Terrifies me. *Nick knows.* He actually knows. My core starts shaking, adrenaline pumping, and this . . . Gail can *never* find out about this. She'll pull me off the case. No question. And if I'm off the case, then the Joneses might actually go through with their worst attack yet, and—

Fuck.

Never mind working undercover again. Will I even make it back to my house?

"How much *do* you know about me, Sydney?" Nick pushes as that vein in my forehead starts throbbing. "Name of my first dog? Password for my computer? What's my blood type? *Sydney.*"

"Fine!" I burst out, formulating a second new plan. A much wobblier plan. "It's A positive, okay?"

Nick stares openly at me, jaw slack.

But I don't stop. I'm not sure what other choice I have. "My handler knows exactly where I am." *Lie.* "If you try anything, you'll be swarmed in three minutes or less." *Lie.* "If you're willing to negotiate, though, I think we can talk. This is what I do. I give people exactly what they want in exchange for information. So all you have to do is tell me what you want." Then, with one swift jab, I punch open the glove compartment. It's empty.

"What did you expect to find in there?" Nick mutters, sounding incredibly deflated.

I'm honest, my stomach still guttering. "Pepper spray, at least."

"You were going to *pepper spray* me?" Nick squawks.

"I was actually going to keep you from pepper spraying *me.*"

"You really think I'd hurt you?" Nick asks, deep strain in his voice. Shadows race across the windshield. "You really think that little of me?"

Absolutely. Totally. One hundred percent.

When I glance over again, there's a flash of pain in his eyes.

"No," I lie, keeping my voice small. Box-breathing again. "No, I don't think you're going to hurt me."

"Good," he deadpans, clearing his throat. "Because I think it might be the opposite. At this point, I'm just a boy, driving adjacent to a girl, asking her to not break his nose."

I laugh dryly. "Says the guy who breaks noses for a living."

"Again, is *that* what you think of me?"

You and *Johnny*. Johnny, one phone call away. One text. One *Sydney is not who she says.* "Let's not pretend that you're completely innocent," I say, deliberately unsettling again. The last thing I should let Nick think is *I'm in control here.* "I may know things about you, but you've done your homework, too."

Nick snorts, picking up speed. The snowy road curves in front of us. "Looking you up on Instagram is hardly the same thing. I know you like possums. I don't know your social security number."

"It's not like I *memorized* yours," I mutter under my breath, loud enough for him to hear it. The undercurrent of fear is still there, pulsing. "It's just available if I need it."

"And what's up with your Instagram, anyway? Any of that really you?"

"What do you think?"

"I think you follow six accounts and one of them is a mayonnaise company."

Once again, no chuckle or boyish Nick smile. In the space of an hour, all that's disappeared. Now, we burst out of the woods and onto Main Street, which is flooded with Christmas lights and those giant candy canes that Grandma Ruby lined up along the curb. Golden wreaths wrap around the lampposts. Everything is so disgustingly cheery compared to what's happening in here. "When're you going to tell Johnny?" I ask, throat tight.

Nick doesn't waste a second of breath. "What makes you think I'm going to tell Johnny?"

We don't go back to the house. Nick makes a hard left after the Long Sands convenience store, headed in the opposite direction of Cook Lane. My tone is steady as dark water flits past the window. The rough sound of the sea. "Where are you taking us?"

At the next stop sign, Nick whips out his phone, checking for a message or a missed call. Apparently, he's waiting for someone to contact him. *Johnny.* Must be Johnny. "We're going on a date, remember?"

"Oh, right," I say, a laugh burbling from a painful place in my chest. "Cool. Of course we are. Does this date involve duct-taping me to a chair?"

"Only if you want it to," Nick deadpans, pulling into a snow-plowed lot on the other edge of town. "Truth is, I'm waiting for confirmation of something."

"Mysterious," I mumble.

"Mysterious is more your forte, isn't it?" He catches my eye and mimics me, batting his long dark lashes. "*Will you tell me a secret?*"

My face burns, emotion crashing over me like waves. Horror, anger. So Nick knows I was trying to seduce him—and he's throwing it back in my face. Understandable. If I were in his position, I'd do the same thing. But the frostiness still wriggles its way under my skin. Right now, he's in the position of power. I angle myself toward him in the cabin, prepared to fight fire with fire—or rather, frost with frost. "Are you critiquing my seduction methods?" I ask, taunting him a little. "Was there a better way I could've gone about it? Does something really niche turn you on?"

Nick grunts. "Don't even go there."

"Because if I should've dressed up in a penguin costume or something, please tell me now."

His lips crack into the barest grin before he obviously remembers: Smiling around Sydney is a *no* from now on. He puts the vehicle in park, killing the engine. And I look up. A neon orange sign flashes MOOSE LODGE in retro lettering. I smirk. *Oh, boy's got jokes.* Or boy is planning on disposing of me at the Moose Lodge.

Nick gives me a tight-lipped smile. "Shall we?"

Ice ricochets off the car door as I slam it closed.

Nine minutes later, we have our drinks. I triple-check the exits, then bite the maraschino cherry off its stem, chewing aggressively. "So how's your ass?"

Nick glares at me across the table. "Still bruised. Thank you so much for asking." Taking a sip of his bottled beer, he taps his phone. No messages. "Now that I think about it, maybe you *were* trying to kill me."

I scoff, leaning back in my chair, arms crossed. "If I was trying to kill you, you'd be dead."

Luckily, and also unluckily, no one is overhearing this conversation because no one is in this bar. The Moose Lodge is only busy on bingo nights. Busy with humans, anyway. With taxidermy? Always a party. All around the wood-paneled bar, taxidermied animals stare down at us. A moose with a pipe winks from above the jukebox. Two raccoons advertise the menu. A miniature herd of deer look like they've having a conversation, open-mouthed; someone's strung silver tinsel between their antlers.

"What are you waiting for?" I ask Nick, gesturing to his phone. "Run Rudolph Run" blasts in the background. That is legitimately what they're playing. God, I hope they don't catch him.

Nick doesn't answer me.

Grumpily, I slip out of my parka, a rush of warm air greeting my back. Adrenaline is still racing through every vein in my body, but I'm hoping that my loose cannon demeanor will keep Nick on his toes. Level the playing field somehow. I tell him genuinely what's on my mind, alongside *Don't you dare try to kill me.* "You ever wonder what would happen if all the taxidermy in the world suddenly sprang back to life?"

He doesn't even look up from his phone. "No."

"Me neither," I say, sucking on my teeth. I hook my parka onto the stool beside me. "So far, is this the worst date you've ever been on?"

This gets Nick to gaze up. Something flickers across his dark eyes, like he's trying to determine how much to give away. "Surprisingly not."

"Any more information you want to volunteer?"

"Surprisingly not!" he says again, full of sarcasm. "Although I'm not saying this is a good one. At this point, Sydney, you and I probably go together about as well as peanut butter and hepatitis."

I spurt out a bitter laugh. "Am I the peanut butter or the hepatitis in this situation?"

"Neither," Nick says.

Finally, his phone dings. He yanks it off the table and holds it away from my gaze, reading through what seems to be quite a long and detailed message. If Johnny is telling Nick how to dispatch me, he is very thorough. Many bullet points. (Pun.)

Nick's eyebrows bunch together. His lips move ever so slightly as he reads.

"What is it?" I pry.

He says nothing. He's obviously thinking. A muscle in his jaw feathers.

"You know that guy who couldn't stand silence?" I pry further, stomach starting to churn again. "Can I have that guy back, please?"

Nick snags my eyes, thwacking down his phone. "There's no visible record of you working for the FBI. No fieldwork. No desk work. Nothing."

A beat follows as my mind wraps around those sentences. This mission is off the books, and I'm not really an FBI officer. That's why. *But also* . . . "How do you know that information?"

Nick stares at me for a good, long moment before he flips everything—this whole holiday—on its head. "I work for the government, too."

11

It's happening again, the room-fuzzing feeling, like when Gail delivered the news in Stockholm. The tips of my fingers tingle, and there's a sudden rush of blood to my head. The raccoons and the moose and the deer are closing in around me. *What* did Nick just say?

He's peering at me like you might look at a bear in the woods, watching its reaction, determining whether or not it's about to charge. A dimple pops in his cheek. If what he's saying is true, then this man . . . this man has played me. He's played me even better than I was trying to play him. *I work for the government, too.*

The words shoot into me like a bullet in slow motion.

"Sydney?" Nick presses, his tone steady, but I already know him better than that. His tells jump out at me like dots on a map. *Nothing* about him is steady. He licks the seam of his lips because his mouth is drying out. He taps his thumb on the table because he can't stand sitting still. "I think it would be really good if you said something now."

I inhale strongly through my nostrils. *Oh, I am going to say* a lot.

And the first thing is, "Are you *joking*?" I understand now why Nick's dragged me to this terrible bar. No witnesses. An open dialogue. Nothing leading back to Johnny or my family. "I swear to god, if you ask me, 'Do I look like the type of person who'd pull a rubber chicken from my pocket—'"

Nick squints, thick eyebrows quirked together. "A rubber chicken? Why on *earth* would I say that?"

"Believe me." I lift my drink and take an enormous sip, gathering the ice in my mouth and crunching. "I've been down this road before. Not this *exact* road, but the odds of *both* of us working for the government are—"

"Infinitesimal," Nick supplies.

"Exactly." I chew harder, speaking with my mouth half-full. "Run Rudolph Run" switches to "Chestnuts Roasting on an Open Fire," and my goodness, that does not fit the vibe of this conversation. "How do I know you're telling me the truth? Actually, scratch that. More specific question first. Who do you work for? Which agency?"

"CSIS," Nick says, no hesitation, but the lump in his throat bobs up and down.

The Canadian Security Intelligence Service. The Canadian version of the FBI. So he's on the other side of the border. Supposedly. "What's your badge number?"

Nick leans farther across the table, heat pulsing between us. "What is *your* badge number, Sydney?" When I don't budge, Nick takes a swig of his own drink. Beer sloshes inside the bottleneck. "Come on, you can't be annoyed. I'm the one who should be annoyed here. You jump in on *my* investigation, making me lose valuable time following a possibility that—" He gestures in my direction. "Won't give me any leads."

That's when it clicks. It really, really clicks.

My jaw drops a full inch. "You were trying to seduce me, too."

It's not a question. Nick gives me an answer anyway, dark eyes flickering. "I wouldn't really put it like that . . ."

"Oh my god."

"Sydney—"

"Just give me a minute to process that, okay? I'm recovering. I thought there was at least a fifteen percent chance that you were going to try and murder me." I swallow the last bit of ice. It plunks down cold in the pit of my stomach as I rethink every minor interaction with Nick. That night when we were brushing our teeth, *he* knocked on the door. *He* was waiting at the foot of the stairs right before I went running. *He* asked about the polar plunge, slipping the idea directly into my mind. The *back* injury! Is he even bruised? Or was that just a ruse for sympathy?

Jesus Christ. Nick isn't just an exceptional agent; he might be even better than me.

And I'm . . . starting to look at him a bit differently. This stranger, sitting across the table. When I first saw him, shower water pouring on my head, I assumed he was just dumb muscle. Someone I could easily maneuver into the palm of my hand. The muscle part, that's still right. But this new image of him straight-up headbutts me like I headbutted Santa.

If Nick really is in CSIS, if I was being calculatedly seduced, too, then he was never a mark. He was always untrustworthy—just in a completely different way than I'd imagined.

You never really know what's going on in someone else's head, do you?

"Which parts are the lie, then?" I ask, sorting through all that in my brain. Trying to drop it somewhere that feels safe and manageable. My palms are starting to sweat. "Is Nick your real name?"

He scowls through his natural ease. "Of course it is."

"How long have you been undercover?"

"Three years," Nick says. "And I'm sorry if I scared you, but I was trying to feel you out, and this just came out of nowhere. Can you at least tell me who you work for? You realize I just took a big risk blowing my cover on you?"

I do. That doesn't make total sense, either. "Why?"

"Why what?"

"Why'd you do that?" I pin him with my eyes, telling myself not to focus on his jaw. Or the curve of his lips. "I could be anyone."

Nick blows out a frustrated breath. "No, you couldn't be. For one, there's my gut feeling. Two, you're obviously a professional. And three, if you were trying to get information from me, then you must've thought I'd lead you to Johnny. CSIS and the FBI have been investigating the Joneses for years, so it wouldn't surprise me if other organizations were, too. Ergo, someone from the government. Look, I normally don't carry this, but—" He whips out his badge and slides it low across the table. "I have zero reason to fake my involvement with CSIS."

I examine the gold CSIS insignia, some things still refusing to add up—like why he'd risk carrying this badge on an undercover mission, around a bunch of criminals who'd put a gun to his head if they found it. Did he bring the badge tonight for my benefit? Was he planning on blowing his cover?

"How is it possible," I ask, leaning back in my chair, "that we ended up on the same case without knowing about each other? I thought I read about a joint task force. Cross-national interagency collaboration."

Nick nods once. "You probably did. That's still in place, but there've been a ton of leaks out of the FBI. CSIS doesn't trust them with this case anymore. We're keeping things in-house."

I narrow my eyes at him. "But you trust me?"

"Honestly?" he asks, rasping out a laugh. "Not entirely, but I'd *like* to. You're not making it easy right now."

"Well, I've basically just been told that I've lost valuable time barking up the wrong tree, and you have to understand . . ." I cup my drink with both hands. "If you've been working on this for three years, this is a tiny blip for you. This is almost one hundred percent of the mission for me."

"The mission for who?" Nick presses.

What do I have to lose at this point? Almost all of my cards are already on the table. "The FBI," I say. My eyebrows crowd together. "Do you even like Taylor Swift?"

Nick levels me with a gaze. "That is seriously the question you're asking me right now?"

"I'm just trying to figure out how much of you is real." I say this flatly, but it's sincere. What people say and do are separate, a lot of the time, from what they're *thinking*. You can observe someone for years, believe you know them to the core, and they still have this terrible capacity to surprise you.

Just then, the crusty old barkeep toddles over and offers us two drinks on the house. They are frothy, blue, and smell salty like the sea. I trust the taste about as much as I trusted Nick half an hour ago. He must be braver than me, too, because he takes a sip while the barkeep waits.

"It's good," he says, straight-faced, swallowing. "Thank you." When the guy leaves, Nick winces. "He probably thinks this is a date and it isn't going well."

"Well, I think it could be going *better*," I say honestly. "So give me a rundown on the timeline here. If it's been three years, that means you were friends with Johnny first?"

Nick gives a full-body sigh. "That's complicated. Look, I didn't choose Johnny as a roommate in college. It was a random assignment. But yeah, at first, we were close. I wasn't lying to you when I said that. Before I knew the truth, he was a likable guy. Always up to hang out. He introduced me to half my friends on campus, and he also got that I needed to be quiet sometimes. Out on the water, when we were rowing. That sounds like a small thing, but it's not." He palms the line of his jaw, grinding his teeth. "Then again, we never talked about anything big. All we did in college was row, study for finals, go out, and play video games. Unless someone was going to write him up for reckless driving in *Mario Kart*, there wasn't much of a case against him."

"You sure?" I push, matching Nick's expression, eyes narrowed. "You roomed with him for years and you never saw anything suspicious?"

"What, you think I just don't want to throw him under the bus?"

"This wouldn't be a bus. It would be more like a small airplane on the way to federal prison."

Nick guffaws, running a hand through his hair. "You know, you're a smart-ass, but you're funny . . . Okay, the timeline." He sets his hands down on the table, about a foot apart, like he's showing me the beginning and the end. "I graduated college with Johnny. Still didn't know what the Joneses were about. Went back to Canada, took a year, trained for the CSIS in Ottawa. When I turned twenty-four, there was a job opening for a bodyguard."

"For Johnny," I clarify.

"Correct," he says. "My superiors said I should take it. They read me in about the Joneses, who didn't have much of a profile in Canada at that point, but of course, that was before the heists. I was . . ." Nick grits his teeth. "I couldn't believe it. Didn't take it well. It's a hard thing to wrap your head around, that someone isn't who you think they are."

"Yeah, I can relate to that." The rest of it is on the tip of my tongue: the tire tracks in the snow; the last sight of my dad in his flannel shirt; his favorite leather boots, which he left in the living room. Never saw it coming. But I don't know Nick. That's super clear. Even if he understands what it's like to catastrophically misunderstand a person, he doesn't need to hear about any of that.

Another small chunk of ice grinds under my teeth. "So you worked your way up to be his head of security, and the rest is history, but I guess I just don't understand—"

"What's taking so long?" Nick supplies.

"Exactly. And why you'd agree to inform on him if he was such a great friend. You two still seem pretty close."

Nick considers this, running his tongue over his teeth. "Johnny runs two separate operations. There's the legal one and the illegal one. Unfortunately, I landed on the legal side, so it's not as easy as you'd think to gain intel. Plus, Johnny's stupidly, *stupidly* lucky." He pauses, unreadable, taking a final swig of his lager. "Second question, I'm going to pass . . . but I also have something that you should know."

The way he says the last part, I'm absolutely certain I don't want to know.

Certain that whatever factoid he's about to produce is going to knock me sideways again.

I hold my breath. "Okay . . ."

His phone's still on the table; he grabs it, covertly tapping in the password, and scrolls for a second before spinning the screen around. It's a picture. Of Calla. Black-and-white. Surveillance photo. There's a timestamp in the corner.

"What am I looking at here, exactly?" I ask, knowing it's a dumb question; it's also the only thing I can get out of my mouth.

Nick inhales deeply, like this is paining him, too. "Calla, on a gas station's security footage, less than a mile from the scene of the last heist."

You're pacing, Nick texts me around one thirty in the morning. Of course I am. Wouldn't he be, if he were in my situation? Through the wall, I hear his mattress squeak as he rolls over. Or leaves the bed. I'm not sure. He types again before I respond: Are you OK?

I stare at the screen, typing back, Fine.

Obviously, not fine. This is a worst-case-scenario-type situation. That 99 percent certainty of Calla's innocence? The margins are diminishing, and starbursts of pain have started to settle behind my eye sockets. I'm blinking them away. Because still, it . . . can't be. I'd know. I know her better than that. I do, even after years of semi-separation.

Right?

Right. Right.

I know her, I repeat like a mantra, pacing again. *I know her, I know her, I—*

We should finish that conversation, Nick responds.

Immediately after Nick's bombshell, a few people trudged into the Moose Lodge, and it no longer felt like the safest space to share information. Back in the car, I was still processing, scared that any intelligence I provided from my side might further implicate my sister. Calla . . . can't be involved with this. Not willingly. When we were growing up, she told me what she got me for Christmas at least four days before the holiday; she'd burst with the secret. That is not someone who could hide a part in a crime ring. And yet . . . why was she so close to the scene? What was she doing in Buffalo, New York? Even if she is innocent, it doesn't paint a good picture. The legal fees she could rack up, trying to work her way out of this . . .

It makes me nauseated to think about.

That is my *sister.* My sister in that photo.

At home, Nick and I slunk in through the garage, hoping that no one was awake to ask questions, but *I* still have questions. About a million and two of them. Luckily, Sal has found his way to a local inn for the night, so all I have to worry about is Johnny hearing. And Gail, who doesn't know my cover's blown with Nick. Gail, listening through the walls. I yank on my bunny slippers from high school—seduction mode is over—and shuffle silently out of my room, not even knocking before I turn the handle and glide into his.

Nick's stretched out on Calla's old twin bed, his white-socked feet sticking off the end. He's in roughly the same pajamas as he was during our toothpaste talk: black sweatpants, black T-shirt, but I'm noticing him a lot more. The clinginess of the fabric. Ripples down his shirt. He jolts like he was half asleep—or like I've snuck up on him in the shower again.

"Jesus, will you stop doing that?" he asks in a whisper. I barely hear him over the noise. The loud, loud . . . frogs? Rainforest tree frogs. A sound machine blares in the corner, melodious ribbits hopping across the room.

"Sorry," I whisper back. "I didn't want to risk knocking."

He swings his feet off the bed, stands up, and paces closer to me. "Finish the conversation?"

I grab him gently by the elbow, leading him over to the frogs in the corner—and turning up the volume as high as it'll go. Electronic sound barrier. Much more effective than shower water. "Tell me where you think the next heist is. Any leads?"

"Some," Nick says, close to me. So close. I crick my neck up to look at him. "I know *when* it's going to happen. Christmas Day. Vinny canceled the New Year's Eve party; said we didn't need it now that there's a wedding, and that was a big clue. They like to use events as alibis. Charity functions. Book clubs."

I frown. "Who's in a book club?"

"Oh, all of them," Nick says. "Murder mystery."

"You're kidding," I say.

"No, Johnny's full of surprises. Like, he actually loved that pottery course. Even though he was there for an alibi."

I shake my head, voice lowering to a whisper again. "Okay, okay, keep going."

Now it's Nick's turn to frown. "Vinny said something last week. He was drunk, and he was going on and on about explosives. All the things you could and couldn't buy on the black market. And he was talking about how smart Johnny is, and how he has 'big plans' for the end of the year."

Tension settles over the bridge of my nose. "You know they have fifty pounds of C4, right?"

Nick pales. "*And* the grenades?"

"What? What are you talking about?"

"That's what our chatter picked up," Nick says, wiping a hand down his face. "But I guess we missed something. Looks like their next heist is going to blow the rest of them out of the water. I pressed him on it, hard, but by the end of it he was slurring his words and just passed out on the couch."

I swallow, nod. "But Vinny's in the loop?"

"I think he's a third in the loop. Doesn't know everything but knows enough. Haven't gotten the chance to speak with him, because he's been traveling—but I thought we could both press him tomorrow at the bachelor party. Or bachelorette party. Bachelor-meets-bachelorette party." Nick's gaze flicks over my face. "If you want to work together."

I waver, shifting in my bunny slippers. "I'll work with you if you leave Calla out of it. I know what you showed me, but I still don't want to believe that she'd—"

Creak.

The slightest creak. Down the hallway. A door whispering open. Footsteps, a man's tread. It's probably louder than he expects it to be, and I can feel it more than I can hear it: a reverberation over the floorboards. I know this house. And Nick senses it, too—how, in the next three seconds, someone could wrench open the bedroom door, and we'd be here, after my takedown on stage, discussing something. Nick and me, the two of us, alone at almost two in the morning.

Bad optics.

New plan.

It happens in an instant, before we even discuss anything, before we have time to whisper or lock eyes. Nick just knows— exactly what I'm thinking, exactly what we should do. A perfect cover-up requires far fewer clothes. I still don't trust Nick. How could I, after all the deception? But I do trust our mutual idea. Instinctively, I whip off my shirt while Nick peels off his, and then we're clashing. His hands find my hair. My hands find his jaw. The lace of my bra presses against the firmness of his chest, and he pulls me closer, lips claiming mine. When I open my mouth, his tongue sweeps in—so different than at the beach, more feverish, hungrier . . .

And something inside me moans as loud as it rebels. Underneath my confidence, underneath the cover-up, is something feverish that I can't quite control. People might surprise you in bad ways, but on the flip side, I guess there's this: a dangerous flutter in my belly, warmth climbing, and—

Nick is . . . actually kind of hot, isn't he?

The handle clicks open.

Johnny. Here's Johnny.

"Oh, I'm *sorry*," he says, coming up short on the bedroom rug. The sorry doesn't sound genuine, at all, but Nick and I explode apart, caught in the act, embarrassed, mortified. From what Johnny's witnessing, it seems like we are super turned on by the sound of tree frogs. My cheeks are flushed. My chest is spiked with little spots of red. I'm acting, I'm acting, I'm *acting*, remember?

I fish for my shirt on the floor, whipping it up, and covering my chest.

Nick clears his throat, a little overheated himself. "Yeah?"

"Heard you were up," Johnny says. "Just wanted to go over some last-minute plans for the boat party, but I see you're . . . occupied." He gives me a hideous once-over, gaze falling over me like a cold splash of water. "We can talk in the morning, hey, Nicky boy?"

"Night then," Nick says, faux-embarrassed, giving Johnny a short wave.

The door clicks closed again.

And then I'm just standing there, my chest rising and falling, watching *Nick's* chest rising and falling—

"I'll go, too," I say over the rainforest sounds. "See you tomorrow."

The remainder of my questions will have to wait until the next time we're alone. On the drive up to the bachelor-meets-bachelorette party tomorrow? That'll do.

"Yeah," Nick says with a clear of his throat, adjusting the waistband of his sweatpants. "Yeah, tomorrow."

N ick," I say, downstairs the next morning, by the coffeepot.

"Sydney," he responds, matching my let's-not-talk-about-it undertones. Being my agent self and my at-home self is hard enough without . . . this. Whatever this is.

Nick swigs a too-hot sip of his black coffee, filtering it through his teeth. Automatically, I match him, burning the tip of my tongue. An uncomfortable level of tension pulses between us, and I wonder if he's thinking about the press of his lips against my—

"I still can't get over it, Sydney," Calla says. She's sipping her coffee at the breakfast table, shaking her head; she seems to have recovered from our little squabble yesterday, seems to have shoved the dad talk back into a dark drawer, where it belongs. "You took that guy *down*. In a donkey costume." A teaspoon of sugar plunks into her mug. "I bet that's up on YouTube by now."

My nose scrunches. How long before the FBI wipes it from the web?

"Good coffee," Nick says with a lift of his cup, changing the subject.

After breakfast, Grandma Ruby flutters around the kitchen like a moth, spurting out plans. If there's going to be a wedding at the house, we *need* additional fresh Christmas trees. "For the greenery," she says, fishing out a spool of ribbon from one of the cabinets. "Maybe we can place them at the altar? Ooo, wouldn't that be pretty for the pictures?" I gulp another mouthful of coffee before I say something stupid, like, *This wedding is about as good of an idea as filling a bunch of trash bags with gasoline, tossing them in the Prius, and then lighting a match on the way home.*

We take two cars.

I ride with Nick, Johnny, and Calla in the rented Escalade. When I slide into the back seat, memories from last night crash into me—the glove box, empty of weaponry; the line in Nick's forehead as he accused me of the truth; the crush of his lips against mine—and soon we're setting off with a tire screech in the snow. As with everything else, Johnny's competitive behind the wheel— and he's an atrocious driver. Turn signals? What turn signals! Stoplights? Merely a suggestion. Pedestrians? Never heard of them! *Even if you have tinted windows*, I want to say, *people can still see you being an asshole.*

"Hey, learn to drive, will ya?" he shouts . . . at a cyclist. Calla winces. Which is promising. She must notice, at some level, that Johnny isn't the nicest guy?

By the time we arrive at Cape Hathaway Christmas Tree Farm, just over the river on the other side of town, the parking lot is jam packed, and the sky is a cloudless gray. Grandma Ruby took us here the first winter after Dad left. Said we could pick out any tree we wanted. No sadness, no distractions, just acres and acres of Christmas trees. The scent is amazing.

Almost smells like Nick's soap.

Sydney, for fuck's sake. Do not think about Nick's soap.

From a man in a tiny wooden shed, Calla rents a handsaw for the tree takedown, then sidles up by my shoulder. "Remember the last time we came here?" she asks me, glistening metal dangling from her hand. "We picked out that Charlie Brown tree and it didn't have any needles by Christmas."

"Oh, I remember," I say, trying to keep myself in the moment. "Sweetie Pie was terrified of it. And Grandma Ruby chucked it away as soon as all the presents were gone. Poor skeleton tree . . ."

By the farmstand, Nick laughs at something Johnny's just said.

Calla catches me staring. Eyes bright, she nudges me with her shoulder. "How'd the date go?"

She says it in a merry way that lets me know that she absolutely heard about my late-night meeting with Nick. I keep my voice light. "It was good. We got drinks."

"That's really nice to hear. I know you wanted that date even after everything that happened at the pageant, which Grandma Ruby and I thought was . . . a little strange actually, but . . ." Calla frowns. "Are you seeing anyone back in DC?"

"No, why?"

Calla shrugs. "No reason really, it's just . . . Do you realize that I haven't met anyone you've dated since high school? I couldn't even pick your type out of a lineup."

Out of a lineup. Hopefully my type would not be behind bars at a police station. Then again, my usual type isn't that healthy, either: guys who hardly want to know me at all. In college and after, whenever the relationship got too deep, I bailed. It's one thing for a guy to leave you if he doesn't know who you are; you can explain it away to yourself. You can say, *He didn't know what he was missing.* It's another if they understand your quirks, your idiosyncrasies, and leave you anyway.

The safest type of flirtation is a fake one. Maybe that's why I'm . . . minorly drawn to Nick. It's nothing real, never was, never will be.

"No, it's not that," I say.

"Are you on the apps?" Calla asks.

I shake my head. "Nope."

"Can I make you a profile?"

Just then, Johnny's boots crunch in the snow as he approaches us, hand outstretched. "I can take that, babe," he says, prizing the saw from Calla's hand.

Internally, I scowl, thinking of the way his gaze slid over me last night—and how now, he's just so *patronizing.* Calla is a twenty-five-year-old woman. She can handle a saw. She could handle a flamethrower if she wanted.

"Know what?" I mumble. "I'm going to get another saw."

Technically speaking, the rule is one handsaw per family, but I pay the guy twenty bucks and promise to have the second one back in an hour. When I try to pass the saw to Calla, she balks. "Nah, I'm fine. You take it. You're better at this stuff anyway."

"No, you should—"

"It's *fine,*" she says, even though it isn't. "I know what you're thinking, and you shouldn't. I can cut down a tree, and I *like* cutting down my own Christmas tree, but if Johnny wants to do it . . . It's okay. Sometimes you have to sacrifice things in relationships."

"Yeah," I fire back, blunt, "like how many ceramic dogs you have on your mutual dresser. Not things like your ability to express competence."

She pokes her tongue into her cheek. "Just, please?"

"Or how many cats you have," I add, "if your partner is allergic to cats."

"All I'm saying," Calla adds, "is that it's a balancing act."

I suck my teeth. "And what else is he asking you to balance? Next thing you know, he's . . ." *Asking you to lie for him. Steal for him. Commit armed robbery for him.* "Asking you to quit your job."

Calla's eyes widen almost imperceptibly. There's a flicker at the center of her pupils.

"Calla . . ." I say, breathing slowly through my nose. "Did he ask you to quit your job?"

"It's not like it sounds."

"It sounds like he's asked you to quit your job."

"He just knows how much it stresses me out sometimes," Calla protests, voice dropping to a sharp whisper. "And I won't need a salary after we get married, not financially speaking, and . . . maybe I'm not explaining myself well. I'm not sure this is a productive conversation."

"I don't think the problem is *you*, Calla," I say, but she's already stalking off with a quiet "Be nice."

And oh, I will be. I'll be so, so nice.

We find two perfect specimens on the corner of the lot, one next to the other. Grandma Ruby's cornered them like a hawk with prey, shooing away other potential customers. Johnny announces that he's got the Norwegian fir on the left. Saw in hand, he makes the first cut—

And I immediately start on the Christmas tree to the right, slicing into the trunk with a jagged swipe. I arch. I bend. I'm remembering how he tried to knock past me on the run; how he tried to dig under my skin about Calla getting married first. Competitiveness practically oozes from Johnny's pores.

I can't take him down yet. Not fully. But I can knock him down a peg.

Johnny sees me pick up the pace out of the corner of his eye.

I think a part of him knows that it is *on*.

Really cheery music plays in the background; gaggles of kids cavort through rows of pristinely green trees. But make no mistake. This has become a spontaneous battle. My saw slices back and forth, its toothy ridges biting into the base—and Johnny's does the same. Beads of sweat are forming under my black beanie. His curly hair is bouncing in the sunlight.

Back, forth, back, forth, back. It's a symphony of sawing. An orchestra of aggression. I want to make Johnny *wheeze* with effort.

I hear Grandma Ruby say to Nick, "This is much more intense than I'd anticipated. I haven't seen this much tension since bingo at the Moose Lodge."

Johnny steals a glance at me. I see it in my peripheral vision. I'm ahead of him by a good two strokes. *Can't hack it?* a part of me cackles. *That's so sad for you.*

My boots sink farther and farther into the snow. My mittens tighten on the handle.

With a satisfying crack, my tree falls first.

Fresh snowflakes dust our shoulders as we shuffle back indoors, lugging two Christmas trees into the living room. At the sound of the trees thudding by the couch, Sweetie Pie tucks her tail all the way between her legs. Before I can reach over to comfort her, Nick does. His hands travel to her ears, massaging with a "Shhh, it's okay, it's all right," and I concede that—fine, yes—he is good with her.

But I'd like to stop noticing good things about him.

Especially since the boat party's tonight. We have to stay focused and probe Vinny for intel.

In a flash, Calla disappears into the attic and comes down quickly with a box of old ornaments, picking through the plastic and unwrapping a few. "Awwww, Syd, look at this one." She's holding up Sweetie Pie's paw print, from when she was a puppy. Heart legitimately warming, I scooch over to her and take a deeper peek inside the box. There's my sixth-grade woodshop assignment: a tiny Christmas nutcracker with a green feather plume. There's Calla's first-grade reindeer made out of a red lightbulb and cardboard antlers, along with Great-Grandma Pearl's handmade lace snowflakes; the woman went ice fishing until she was ninety-seven years old and lived by herself in a one-room cabin—which she built—like a total bad-ass.

"Noooo," Calla says, pulling out a picture ornament. "Remember when you had a mullet?"

I laugh out loud, examining the miniature framed portrait of young Sydney, who was missing her two front teeth. "The worst thing is, I requested that haircut." From Dad. I remember that part as well. In the backyard, a September day, leaves falling on our shoulders. "I mean, I didn't say 'Give me a mullet,' but I accidentally *described* a mullet."

Calla turns to Nick. "Want to see?"

"He does not," I say.

"He does," Nick says, and then proceeds to smile in a broad, lazy way. "Would it make you feel better if I told you that elementary school Nick wanted to bleach the tips of his hair?"

I pause, eyebrow arching. "Yes."

After the trees are erected in front of the living room window, right where the ceremony will (or will *not*) take place, Grandma Ruby throws a few logs into the fireplace, newspaper sizzling and disappearing beneath the burgeoning flames. Then she suggests, since we're all gathered around anyway, we should do our Christmas games night. Or rather, games midafternoon. The schedule has gone the way of everything else this holiday: It's completely shredded.

Grandma Ruby appoints herself master of ceremonies.

Johnny snags Calla, wrangling her into a gentle—but pointed—headlock.

I'm with Sidekick Nick. Probably should stop calling him that.

"You know, I saw this post about male reindeer," Calla says, legs crossed on the living room carpet. She's wiggled out of the headlock, a little flustered, and has forgone her parka for a thick, puffy sweater and even thicker socks. It reminds me of the old days when we were sweatshirt people at Christmas. When we'd spend whole afternoons lounging on the couch, stringing together popcorn garlands and watching all the *Home Alone* movies. "They don't have any antlers in the winter, whereas the females not only grow antlers, but also keep them year-round. Which means, if all those illustrations are correct, that *women* pull Santa's sleigh."

"Figures," Grandma Ruby muses with a click of her tongue. "Men can't even find pickle jars in the refrigerator. How're they going to find all those houses?" She turns, force-feeding Johnny. "More cookies?"

"Oh, thanks," he says, "but I'm stuffed. I think that four sugar cookies is my limit."

"Nonsense!" I say, loading another one onto his plate—and then onto mine. I take a bite and pray for Scrabble. A nice, calm Scrabble competition in which I E-V-I-S-C-E-R-A-T-E Johnny in a triple-word-score fashion. On top of everything else, he wants Calla to quit her *job*?

Johnny does the honors, riffling around inside a winter hat, stuffed to the brim with board game options. Grandma Ruby's scrawled them all on tiny white slips of paper.

At this point it feels like Russian roulette.

"Let's see . . ." Johnny says, really milking this. With a flourish, he selects a paper from the very bottom. It reads: *Pictionary*.

That's safe. Nothing is safer than Pictionary.

From the garage, Grandma Ruby wheels in a standing board with giant sheets of paper, and Calla grabs a tub full of markers. Nick and I are up first.

When Johnny mouths a taunting "Good luck," I don't let it rile me. I let it fuel me. My team is going to smoke him.

With cupped hands, Grandma Ruby whispers the prompt into my ear. It's easy. It's *SpongeBob*. We can win with that one. Calla starts the clock, Nick leans forward on the couch, and I race to the board, marker squealing as I draw a quick rectangle and fill it with tiny circles, cartoon eyes, bucked teeth, and trousers.

"Cheese," Nick guesses.

Calla side-eyes him. I'm no Michelangelo, but my drawing is *clearly* not cheese. What kind of cheese has square pants? Giving Nick the benefit of the doubt, I add legs, rounded feet, and arrows pointing to the holes in the sponge.

"Twenty seconds," Grandma Ruby says.

"Sandwich," Nick says.

I scribble furiously with my black marker, illustrating Sponge-Bob's environment: a spiky, ovular pineapple; Patrick Star; bubbles in the sea. I even *draw* the sea, a wave over SpongeBob's spongy head. Nick is either guessing wrong to annoy me (why would he do that?), or he lived in complete isolation in the early 2000s. He says, "Ocean." He says, "Starfish." But he does not say fucking *SpongeBob*.

"Five seconds," Grandma Ruby says.

I passive-aggressively recircle the image, over and over again, until it looks like I'm representing a black hole. When the timer goes off with an evil little buzz, I spin around. "*He lives in a pineapple under the sea, Nick!* He lives in a pineapple. Under the sea."

12

—————

W hat was that?" Gail says over the phone, not an hour later. She's stern, like a berating parent. "That was wildly aggressive for a children's game. Not to mention this morning, and last night—dear god, Sydney, last night. That pageant performance."

I drop my voice to a whispering hiss, so no one but Gail can possibly hear—even though I'm waiting, alone, in the Prius. "Do you have eyes on the *Christmas tree farm?*"

"I'm everywhere," Gail says. "I'm like Moses."

The stress of the last few days is catching up to me in a big, big way. "What does that even *mean?*"

"It means that you might try a touch harder to maintain a positive impression on Nick, and to not provide video clips that threaten to go viral on the internet." When I don't immediately offer a counterargument, Gail stills over the phone. I can almost hear her blood stop flowing. "Something's happened, hasn't it? Sydney."

I know what she means. My heart probably should palpitate. I should waver. But it only takes a second to issue Gail a clear, emphatic *no*. (I haven't blown my cover. Not exactly?) A worry is also tickling the back of my mind: If CSIS doesn't trust the FBI, can I trust Gail? Even if *she* doesn't trust the people in her department?

Besides, if I did tell her that Nick knows I'm undercover, I'd be on the next flight to DC. Gail would make sure of it. She'd probably be next to me on the plane herself, loudly chewing some pretzels. I skirt the issue. "I can't talk for long, so . . . I got your text about the bachelorette party tonight."

"Panel under the trunk," Gail says, telling me what I've already checked for: a small black box with a wire. For me. For my dress.

I chew my lip. "Have you picked up any actionable intel from the house?" *Or anything that implicates my sister?* That's the unspoken question. What have the bugs discovered?

Gail sounds nasally, like she has a bad taste in her mouth. "All that I've deduced from the footage is that your . . . your *guest*, the fiancé, enjoys push-ups. Every morning, every day at lunch, and in the evenings. He is also fond of doing them in your robe."

"Oh my god."

"I would bleach that robe, Sydney."

"Two times through the washing machine, at least," I say, wrinkling my nose. "What about the Mid-Coast Maine contact? Gift shop guy, the one Johnny was calling? Did someone check him out?"

"Yes."

"And?"

"And he has twenty different flavors of coastal candles. Flavors, Sydney. That's what he calls them. Like one would choose to eat a candle . . . Otherwise, the business checks out. Maybe Johnny wanted to buy a wedding gift for Calla there, who knows, you two never did go shopping, but . . . my hunch is that something doesn't add up. We have surveillance on them twenty-four seven. There's a live stream. I'll send you a link."

"Gotta go," I tell Gail as Nick traipses out of the house, down the rock-salted front path, recently snow-shoveled. Turns out, Nick shoveled it for my grandma, again—which was a nice gesture, again. I pop open the trunk, and he chucks his luggage inside before lowering himself into the passenger seat with a slow, controlled movement.

Normally, on my solo road trips, I like the spontaneous snacking and the devil-may-care wandering and the feel of the open road. This is different. "I'm listening to that," I mumble minutes later, changing the station back to where I had it.

Nick drops his hand from the radio controls and pokes his tongue into his cheek. He's wrapped his neck in a chunky black scarf, which really underscores his broodier elements. "You realize that this station has just played 'White Christmas' twice in a row."

One hand gripping the wheel, I gesture to the snow falling around us. My windshield wipers *flick, flick, flick*. "They were cementing their point. And it was two different versions of the song. One classic, one country. I'm not sure that counts as a replay."

"That counts," Nick bats back, bordering on flirtatious, his mouth in what I'd call a smirk, and my stomach does a tidy little flip-flop, remembering how his fingertips wove through my hair. At this point, I'm wondering if I should've ridden with Calla after all. A disappointed frown creased her forehead when I said I wanted to take the Prius, instead of all of us traveling together; my excuse had the illusion of practicality. If we hit any trouble with the storm, at least we'd have a backup car. Really, it's so Nick and I can share information in peace.

So *peaceful* in here. Close quarters. No sexual tension at all.

No sleep deprivation, either. Looks like he didn't shave last night. Stubble crests the harsher lines of his face, and I will never admit out loud that this crossed my mind, but Nick might be part of the 0.02 percent of the population who could pull off a mustache. "Everyone knows," Nick says, still with that flirtatious edge, "that the definitive Christmas radio station is the one with Casey Kasem. Holiday top forty."

"Casey Kasem? Isn't he the guy who voiced Shaggy in *Scooby-Doo*?"

"Exactly."

"He's still alive?"

"No. That's why it's the same show every year. It's recorded. Nostalgic." Nick messes with the heating controls, clearing more fog from the windshield. It's 4 p.m. and already dark. Outside, we whip by a farmstand that sells wild blueberries in the summer, and a house with no less than fourteen Christmas gnomes spread out on the lawn, lit up with green and red floodlights.

My hands tighten on the wheel. "Before we get down to business, can I just ask, do you *really* not know who SpongeBob SquarePants is?"

Nick huffs out a laugh. "I'm bad at Pictionary. I told you that."

"No one's that bad at Pictionary," I grumble.

"Your SpongeBob looked like a slice of cheese, okay?" He tilts his skull back against the headrest. "This is a ridiculous conversation. If anyone was listening to us right now, they'd think we were talking in code."

I make a left, sloping down to the highway. Piles of dirty snow edge the entrance ramp. "No one's listening on my end," I say, bypassing his point. "The Prius isn't bugged."

Nick's eyes carve a hole into the side of my face as he picks apart that statement, wincing. "So . . . the house is. Did they make you bug your own house?"

His tone isn't judgmental, just empathetic for me, and somehow that makes it even worse. The fast *whip-whip* of the windshield wipers matches my heartbeat. "I didn't. That was done without my consent. By the time my handler looped me in, it was too late."

"I'm sorry, that must've been tough," Nick says, reaching into the depths of his coat pocket and extracting a small black dot. He plunks the recording device on the dashboard, as if he were setting a whiskey glass onto a bar. "Does explain this, though."

A tiny shock settles in my stomach. "You actually found one? Where was it?"

"Inside one of the elf figurines."

"Which you discovered . . ." I say, once again putting the pieces together, "when *you* were bugging our house." No denial comes from Nick. He just unwraps his scarfs from his neck, as if they're strangling him. "Didn't find any of yours, either."

"Wait a second," Nick says, realization dawning across his face. "Is *that* what you were doing in my shower? Looking for bugs?"

"Afraid so."

"Do you know I peek around the shower curtain now? Every time I get in the tub. I swear. When I go home, I'm ripping out my shower curtain and replacing it with glass."

"I think it's highly doubtful that another person will be hiding in your shower. That seems like a once-in-a-lifetime occurrence." I chew on my lip. "Have your bugs picked up on anything, at least?"

Nick stills in his seat, the corner of his mouth wavering. "Not yet."

"What was that?"

"What was what?" he asks, almost nervous, like a kid who's just been caught opening presents before Christmas.

"*That.*" I motion in his general direction. "You went all stiff, and then you lied to me."

From the corner of my eye, I catch Nick run a thumb along his mouth. "Fine," he says. "If you really want to know—"

"I do."

"You talk in your sleep."

Good thing I'm trained in defensive driving. Sixteen-year-old Sydney would have skidded off the road just now. Merging into traffic, I take the quickest opportunity to throw a disappointed glare at Nick, who jumps in to say, "I didn't know you were coming home! I didn't even know anyone was going to be staying in that room. Then you came into the picture—"

"Literally."

"It's audio," Nick explains hastily. "Not a video. Not that that makes it any better. Look, I'm sorry. I actually am. I'm not even the one who reviews the recordings."

A prickle of hot sweat descends the back of my neck when my dream from two nights ago flashes to mind. Nick, showering in his CHRISTMAS SWEATER, slowly peeling off his clothes . . . "What did I say?"

"In your sleep? I don't know." Nick shrugs unconvincingly. "Nothing important."

"Tell me."

He studies me quietly, all eyebrows and cheekbones. "You said, in a very clear voice, 'That is Taylor Swift.'"

Mmm. Could be better, could be worse. My finger flicks the blinker, and I switch into the fast lane, snow flying under my tires. "Just fill me in on all the high-level information, then. What else do I need to know about the Joneses before we get to the party?"

Nick checks the GPS on his phone, which calculates our arrival at 6:17 p.m. "No way we're getting through even one percent of that in two hours."

"Two hours plus stops. Calla also mentioned something about Christmas shopping by the harbor, so add another . . . hour."

Nick rubs a hand down his face. "Let's start with how we're going to approach tonight." Despite the warning, he turns off the radio completely. "You share your game plan, I'll share mine, and we'll see where we match up."

My game plan. For the party. The party that keeps getting fancier.

I think that Calla wanted a quaint harbor cruise with comfort food hors d'oeuvres—tiny cheese blintzes and macaroni bites—but Johnny has since steamrolled that idea. The party's still on a midsize windjammer boat, rocking turbulently in a pre-storm sea, but I have a feeling that the vibe is now more *Casino Royale* than *Town and Country.* Johnny added a full waitstaff and an ice sculpture. Eavesdropping this morning, I heard the words "champagne tower."

"At least one of us should wear a wire," I say simply. "Wait until everyone from Johnny's side gets drunk. See if they're chatty when pressed, especially Vinny."

"Don't wear a wire," Nick says, almost defensively. I spy the tiniest twitch of his lip, right below his face freckle. "They might check."

"I'm careful."

"It should be me," he says, firmer this time.

I'm just as firm, right back at him. "You don't need to protect me, Nick. I appreciate it, but I really am good at my job. Just . . . go over your impressions about who Johnny's invited. I know everyone's files but extra details help."

Nick looks like he still wants to fight me on the wire issue, but his jaw clamps shut. After a moment, he says, "Marco will be there. Johnny's primary bodyguard. Noticeable guy—head tattoo of a scorpion. A man of very, very few words. Don't expect to get much out of him. He's even less talkative than Sal, who loves his cocktail shrimp. He'll be chewing all night. There's Andre, Johnny's cousin on his mother's side."

"Right. The professional boxer."

"Semiprofessional," Nick corrects me. "He has an anger problem that might be described as 'clinical,' and at some point in the night, he'll try to punch something. Like a wall. Or the champagne tower."

"Sounds like a really fun guy."

"The most fun." Nick lets out a breath, and I think about what he must've gone through, all these years. Undercover life takes a serious toll. What has it cost him? "Last is Vinny."

"Ah, Vinny." Our main target for the evening. "And what do I need to know about Vinny?"

"Vinny will tell you everything you need to know about Vinny, and more. He's a talker. Just focus on him, and he'll be your best bet." Nick readjusts himself in his seat, eyes fully on me. "And Calla's side?"

I'm maybe a little too defensive. "What about them?"

"The dynamics. What're we about to walk into?"

I puff out my lips. "Let's see, Diana is one of Calla's oldest friends. She knits sweaters for teddy bears and sells them on Etsy. Rachel is a youth librarian, and her girlfriend, Kirsten, works at a charity that finds homes for special-needs cats."

Nick is quiet. "Shit."

"Yeah, so the two groups will mesh really well." Deftly, with one hand, I unzip my snack bag of white chocolate caramel corn and move a handful to my mouth, chewing. A few popcorn flecks lodge in the back of my throat, and I *a-hem* to free them, my voice turning husky. "What are you wearing?"

A playful huff comes out of Nick. "You're not trying to seduce me again, are you, Sydney?"

I roll my eyes. "I meant tonight. The dress code keeps changing." We come to a stop on the highway, holiday traffic backing up before a patch of ice. Red taillights flash in front of us. "If we're

going to go there, though, you didn't seem like you'd be that difficult to seduce."

Nick shakes his head, smiling, like I'm being silly. As if everything from his end was just acting. He was seducing me, too,
remember?

A laugh cracks out of my throat. "You're saying that nothing I
did turned you on? You weren't attracted to me at all?"

Again, Nick is maddeningly silent.

At a standstill in the car, I tilt my head at him, teasing. "So if
we were back at the inn that first night, and I pulled you aside and
whispered into your ear, 'Nick, I don't have any panties on, and I
want you between my thighs,' that would've had zero effect?"

Nick presses his lips together, a harsh intake of breath making
his chest rise and fall. "But you didn't say that, did you?"

I'm not even sure what game we're playing here when I add, "I
could've."

"Is that what you like?" Nick asks, eyes mischievous now, holding on to my gaze. "Dirty talk?"

The sudden intensity of what's happening between us is making me sweat. Literally sweat. Moisture is pooling under my parka,
but I refuse to peel back a single layer—emotionally or physically.
I trust him more than when I thought he was a criminal . . . but not
that much. So I backtrack. Sort of. "Most men don't know how to
dirty talk well. It always seems so violent, like—" I put on my
truck stop voice. "'I wanna fuck you so hard your eyeballs fall out.'
No one wants that."

Someone behind us beeps.

Traffic's moving again.

I clear my throat and break his gaze, wondering why the hell I
just said any of that.

One hour in, we make a pit stop off the highway. There are two businesses available. One of them is a gas station. The other is a Morning Kick, their coffee bean logo lit up under the blackened winter sky.

"Absolutely not," I say, making a hard left into the Citgo station. I fill up the Prius and grab a canned cold brew while Nick buys a hot dog with mustard. He does not seem like the type of person who'd be willing to risk his life on a gas station hot dog— especially after the plane shrimp accusation—but it's another reminder that I don't *actually* know him. That people can be unknowable. Maybe his germaphobia is another hoax.

"To answer your question," Nick says between bites, "I'm wearing a tux." He gestures with his free thumb to the trunk. "Packed in my suitcase."

I think about my own outfit—the red dress from the Swedish Christmas ball, crumpled into the secret compartment of my bag. So strange to be wearing it again. Like things have come full circle in the absolute worst way. "Plane shrimp would be safer than that," I say, gesturing to the hot dog.

"It's probably been there for two days," Nick says with another bite. "Two full days of cooking under an ultrahot heater. Nothing could withstand those conditions . . ."

Now that I've said it, though, he looks skeptical.

He doesn't eat another bite, and rolls down the window a crack, wind ruffling his dark hair. "Let me ask you something," he says after a moment. "Do you like your job? This thing we do?"

I shrug, taking a glug of my cold brew. I'm using it to stall a little. No one has ever asked me if I *like* my job—especially not someone in the same profession. It's an unwritten rule. You grit your teeth when things get tough. You endure. "Do you?"

Nick tuts. "Nuh-uh, see, I asked you first."

"I think you wouldn't be asking me if you *did* like your job."

I can feel him studying the side of my face before he sniffs out a laugh. "Touché, Sydney. Touché."

When we arrive at the dock, I'm immediately questioning if I should've put my foot down about the boat. Snow is falling sideways on the cold gray rocks, and the windjammer is making a *thwap-thwap* noise against the shore. It's smaller than the pictures. Older.

Calla gazes up at the boat, suitcase in hand. "It's pretty, isn't it?" She sounds unsurely optimistic.

It is, I think. *Like the* Titanic.

We aren't staying on board overnight, thank goodness—we've all booked rooms at the Ocean Harbor Inn across the road—but a porter comes to help with our suitcases anyway. "Thanks, I've got it," I say, holding my bag tight. Another man arrives at the foot of a long, rickety staircase to greet us formally. He looks nail-bitingly nervous, as if he's been warned what might happen if the evening goes off with a hitch.

Frigid air nibbles at our faces as we climb aboard.

Inside, it is surprisingly swanky. There is, as promised, a tower of champagne glasses, which feels risky on a slow-rocking boat. Art deco chandeliers swing overhead, and plush green carpets race down the halls, back toward a clanking kitchen, where a staff is rigorously preparing canapés. All the glimmer borders on gaudy. It doesn't feel like seacoast Maine. It doesn't feel like Calla.

And she looks . . . expensive.

When the porter gathers her coat, she reveals a gold necklace I don't recognize, and a sweeping green dress with straps criss-crossing at the back. Johnny, for his part, is wearing a smart black tuxedo—and I think I better get changed before the other guests arrive. "Where should I . . . ?" I ask one of the waitstaff vaguely, and she leads me to a small, tidy bathroom with real cloth towels, where I squidge into the red dress, hide the wire underneath my boobs, and double-check my reflection. Smooth hair, minimal cleavage, fabric running over the silk of my curves. Just as long as no recording devices are sticking out, I'm happy. Sort of happy. Good enough.

I charge out of the bathroom door just as Nick exits a galley room, nearly banging straight into me. He's changed as well. An off-white dinner jacket and a starched white shirt mold to the leanness of his body; a black tie pops around his neck. He's as polished as I've ever seen him, including the pictures in his file. My eyes sweep up and down his sleek lines, landing on the expression he's giving me. It's a raw one. I'm not sure he's entirely aware of what his face is doing. It seems reflexive, that heated double-take, the way his gaze skirts over my dress. Over my exposed thigh. Then he catches himself, just as *I* catch myself.

"Nick," I say, as neutrally as possible, hard knot rising in my throat.

"Sydney," he replies.

We part as the guests trickle in one by one.

Diana is doing well. She's still making those teddy bear sweaters. Apparently, she is very big in Japan. And Kirsten arrives early with Rachel, who says that Johnny once sat on the library floor with her kindergarten students, reading them *If You Give a Moose a Muffin*. I want to tell her that he was probably gathering material for his own story, *If You Give a Crime Lord an Alibi* (didn't someone come from the newspaper to take pictures of Johnny's "philanthropy"?), but Nick cuts in and introduces himself, shaking hands.

"You have a very strong grip," says Diana.

"So do you," Nick observes.

"It's the sewing." A little later, Diana makes an offhand

comment about the Johnny-Calla pairing, how odd she finds it—and I'm thinking, *Yes. Yes, Diana.* It's obvious she has a few reservations, too.

We're still waiting on Johnny's gang; I excuse myself, making my way to the nearest server, who's holding out some sort of seafood pastry on a silver tray. The messed-up thing is, I recognize her. I *definitely* recognize her, especially after my second discreet double-take of the night, my eyes tracing the distinctive hawkishness of her face.

"Crab puff?" Gail asks nonchalantly, holding out her tray. She's wearing a tremendously convincing wig that doesn't look *as* convincing on her. It's strawberry blond and permed, à la Julia Roberts in *Pretty Woman.* Nothing about it says "Gail," which I suppose is the point.

"Thank you," I say through gritted teeth, giving her a pretty clear *what the fuck* glance as Johnny mills around in the background. My fingers daintily select the largest puff before I stuff the whole thing in my mouth, chewing hard.

"Napkin?" she asks, once again nonchalant, as if we were perfectly unacquainted, and *Oh, we will be discussing this later.* Don't know how the FBI does things, but in the CIA, it is not standard procedure for the handler to drop by unannounced on covert operations. Unless something major has happened. Or changed. *Has something major changed?*

One of my eyes squints at her.

She gives no indication of a response.

Well, cool. Cool, cool, cool. Maybe, after our conversation this morning, Gail just doesn't trust me. She's dropped by to keep tabs. "Thank you," I say again, snatching a miniature napkin and dabbing without smearing my lipstick. Not that it matters. I could look completely wild tonight and not be the focus of attention. Vinny, Andre, and Marco have strutted aboard, alongside Sal.

Together, they look like a remake of *The Godfather*. Dark suits, serious faces, dubious energy.

Marco can't stop power-posing; every time he stands still, he clasps both hands over his belt buckle and punches his shoulders out. Andre is like one of those kids in a fourth-grade classroom who keeps hopping up from his desk and screaming about sharks. He's everywhere. And Vinny, true to Nick's word, is already chatting away.

"Sydney? Is it Sydney? Come here, Sydney. That's a nice dress you've got there. My ex-wife? You don't know my ex-wife. Her name's Victoria. Unless you *do* know my ex-wife, and in that case, I'm sorry for your trouble. But she had a dress a lot like yours. She moved out to California with the kids, got herself a new guy now, but we're happy we're getting some new members of the family ourselves! Look at you. You and Calla. Johnny boy! How's my favorite cousin?"

Tonight, I'm sticking by Vinny like Gorilla Glue.

When the boat sets off with a jerky pull, Vinny holds my arms for support—and we start talking. *He* starts talking. Vinny, I find out, has two Chihuahuas and a vacation home in Sarasota, Florida. He likes WWE wrestling and pizza on Thursday nights (pineapple, ham, extra cheese). His Mercedes sports car has a six-cylinder engine, which he is inordinately proud of. His legal name is Vinny, not Vincent or Vincenzo, as one might infer. When he sneezes, he does not cover his nose. Champagne flows into him like a reverse fountain. Less than twenty minutes in, Vinny has given me his life story—from his boyhood in South Boston to his all-too-recent divorce—and he is on his fourth or fifth glass of alcohol. So far, though, nothing he's said has raised any major red flags. (About the heists, I mean. Vinny himself is like a walking red banner.)

"So you work with Johnny?" I press, clutching my champagne

glass to my chest. After I mine Vinny for intel, I'll take my drink with me to the bathroom and pour it down the drain, giving the helpful illusion that I'm knocking them back, same as everyone else. "That must be really rewarding, working with family."

Vinny nods appreciatively; he seems grateful for someone to talk to. "You could say that. Although we do get in our little arguments here and there, like all families. But blood is blood, you know? And look at that *face*." He tilts his head toward Johnny, who's lingering scarily close to Gail. His fingers reach out for a second crab puff. "Who could be mad at that face? Johnny's done a lot for this family. Really taken the reins the last few years, now that his grandpa's retired and his old man's winding down. When you're looking at Johnny, you're staring at the future, right in the eyes." Fingers in a peace sign, Vinny fakes a jab at his own eyes, then at mine.

Whoa there, okay.

I take a slow, measured sip, so that the champagne barely coats my tongue—and try to ignore Gail's gaze at my back. It feels like she's critiquing every sentence that comes out of my mouth. "What's Johnny doing that's different?" I ask in a way that connotes low-level curiosity.

"Oh, this and that," Vinny says helpfully, rooting around in his jacket pocket. "Keeps the business running smooth; we used to have all these supply issues until Johnny came around. And there's perks! Spray tan Tuesdays, family trips . . ." With a victorious smile, he plucks an unwrapped maple sugar candy from his coat, pops it in his mouth, and chews. He offers me one. I politely decline. "Suit yourself. As I was saying, Spray tan Tuesdays, and he's really evolving the business, keeping it fresh—"

His gaze snaps toward someone in the distance.

Sal, at the shrimp cocktail table.

"Will you excuse me, angel?" Vinny says.

Angel? *Bleh.*

He totters off after Sal, who's handing him a packet of ciga-rettes. They're about to go onto the deck for a smoke. But I have a hunch that it's more than that, the way they're whispering to each other. Across the room, Nick catches my eye—and I know we're both thinking the same: Trail them. Nick and I, we approach each other, setting down our glasses of champagne on a nearby table, and he asks, loud enough for others to hear, "Want to get some air?"

He's said it in a husky voice, lightly grabbing my wrist, right where my pulse is beating. The look on his face is openly carnal, a dark spark in his eyes—and I get it. We're back to pretending. That's the only way we can convincingly follow. Make it look like we're desperate to be alone.

Quickly, keeping Vinny and Sal in sight, I rise onto my tiptoes and press a kiss right by Nick's ear, letting my lips linger. "Sure," I mouth, in view of everyone, slipping a hand around Nick's lower back, and he does the same with me, leaning closer, wrapping me up in him. I have tunnel vision; I'm in mission mode. But at the same time, the intimacy, the nearness, the way this feels so natural . . .

My heart rate spikes.

We follow at a distance, outside onto the long, narrow deck, where wind whips over the black water—and Nick cradles my shoulders, keeping me warm. If I can dunk myself in the ocean and avoid hypothermia, I sure as hell can stand a little wind, but I like it. I like it too much. I don't want him to stop.

"Around the corner," he whispers into my neck, and there they are, Vinny and Sal, oblivious, on the bow, smoking. Cigarette plumes disappear into the night air.

Their sound carries.

And I hear something distinctly.

I hear Vinny talking about his contact at the FBI.

13

You sure he's clean?" Sal asks, gruff voice in the wind.

Vinny harrumphs. "He's never been wrong before, never led us astray—we pay him enough, that's for sure. I know, I know, it's hard to trust a guy in a suit," he says, wearing a suit himself. "A lot's riding on this. Everything. The whole kit and kaboodle. Damn it, I'm starting to sound like my grandpa. *Kit and kaboodle.* But my FBI guy's running interference. They don't know a thing. It'll work, the same time those wedding bells are ringing. And if it doesn't . . . we're fucked, my man. Absolutely shit out of luck. All those heists? All that money? It's all been for fucking *nothing.*"

Internally, I startle as a door behind me and Nick swings open, a few party guests spilling drunkenly onto the deck, and Vinny and Sal go quiet. Nick tenses his hand around the small of my back, giving me a discreet warning sign: *We should go. Now.* Cold bites at the back of my neck, and my mind spins. Gail was absolutely right—her department is like Swiss cheese. Someone's been feeding the Joneses information, has been helping them maneuver their way around the law.

But it's more than that.

It seems like the Joneses are using the heists to buy something *in particular*. Maybe the previous heists were always to finance something bigger, more dangerous, worse? It's like Nick can read my mind. It's like we're reading each other's. Back inside the party, we share a knowing glance, pupils slightly wider than normal. *How bad is this about to get?*

In the end, no one is thrown overboard. No one seems to suspect that the server with the *Pretty Woman* wig is an undercover federal official. No one even gets seasick, if you don't count Andre, who—instead of *punching* the champagne tower—decided to *drink* half the champagne tower and spent a large portion of the night in the small galley kitchen, pressing the side of his face to the cool tile. Very kindly, Diana smoothed a hand down his back and sung him off-key Christmas carols until we reached shore.

Don't count it as a success, though.

Success is not Vinny's phone number on a cocktail napkin; he handed it to me by the crab puff station. I'm supposed to "look him up" the next time I'm in Boston. Which, at this point, might be to visit Calla in her new multimillion-dollar town house overlooking the Charles River. I'm realizing, as we clamber onto the dock at just after one in the morning, that I'm missing something; it's like the clues are all right there and I can't quite put them together in a way that makes sense.

I inform Gail about Vinny and Sal's conversation as soon as I'm off the boat. I couldn't talk to her in person because I couldn't find her—was she in the kitchen? The bathroom? The text pings back, unsent. No service near the water. It finally sends on the short trudge to the hotel, Nick and I keeping up appearances; he threads his hand through mine, glove to glove.

He squeezes, letting me know we'll work through this.

What are we missing?

"You guys have a good night," Nick tells Calla and Johnny in the lobby of the Ocean Harbor Inn as they disappear upstairs with their suitcases, all happy and giddy and in love. Nick watches them, stress and indignation washing off his tall, dark frame—and my god, I can't stand any of this. All I want is to grab my key, crash into bed, and spend the next six hours working through the possibilities with Gail.

Gail, who isn't responding to my message.

I try again. A second time. A third. No response.

"Reservation for Swift . . . Sydney," I say, first in line before Nick, watching the concierge tap her clackity keys. She's a tall woman in her mid-forties with square red glasses, and when her gaze flicks up at me again, I know that the unthinkable has happened.

"Swift with an S?" she asks. "S-W-I-F-T, like the bird?"

I nod. "Yeah, Swift. Sydney Swift."

"I'm so sorry, Ms. Swift, but we don't have you on file for this evening."

"What's going on?" Nick asks, inserting himself into the conversation. He's hovering at a respectful distance, but I can still feel the heat of him. If I backed up, I'd fit right under his chin.

"Nothing," I say, focusing only on the concierge. "Sorry, could you maybe check again?"

She checks again. Still nothing. "It's *possible* that there's been a glitch in our system. That's happened before, but we had our IT guy come in last week. Normally I'd put you in another room, but this close to Christmas, we're all booked up—and there's a wedding party that's just taken half the rooms . . . You know what? I'm so sorry. Let me get this gentleman behind you checked in, and then we'll figure something out, if you wouldn't mind taking a seat?"

"No, that's . . . that's fine," I mumble, not really caring about the

room, just the assignment. Just what Vinny said. Nick steps forward, trying to catch my eye, and— *Nope.* That is not happening.
I know what those eyes are saying, and it is *not happening.* If the
hotel can't find space for me, I'll stay right here in the lobby with
the hard-looking couches and the free morning mini-muffins.
This isn't going to turn into one of those rom-com bed-sharing
situations.

"Don't be stubborn," Nick says, immediately after he collects
his keycard. "I just talked to her. There's nothing available."

"I'd rather sleep out in the Prius," I say, because we both know
what he's suggesting. Him, me, one room, together. And I . . . don't
think I can do that.

"It's negative twelve degrees outside," Nick grunts, almost
towering over me in his meticulously tailored dinner jacket.
"You'll freeze."

My lips press together. "Then I'll move to the lobby."

"The lobby closes in six minutes. They'll kick you out."

"Then we're back to the Prius," I say.

Nick pinches the bridge of his nose, then lets out a strained,
half-hearted laugh. "Sydney, just get in the goddamn elevator. You
know you can't do *anything* in the lobby, right?" He gives me a
pointed gaze, annoyingly; he understands I'll be up for the rest of
the night, waiting for Gail to respond to my feverish, panicked
messages.

The lights in the lobby flicker off. Wind rattles the revolving
door to the parking lot, snow whipping past.

Begrudgingly, I trail my suitcase behind Nick.

It's a silent ride up to the third floor, completely absent of
Christmas music. Although if I listen *very* carefully, I suspect I
might hear the grind of Nick's teeth. He's anxious. Anxious about
what we just heard? Or about spending the night with me?

I clomp down the hall in my heels, and he fingers the keycard, hovering it over the handle, and a tinny *beep* lets us through the door. Inside, once again, is swanky for Maine. Sparkling white towels and a marbled vanity; a colonial dresser with golden buckles; a writing desk with chunky, handmade stationery. According to the website, every room at the Ocean Harbor Inn is uniquely styled. Ours, fittingly for the tense vibe, is called the War Room. There's a painting of a rather serious horse by the curtain-closed windows and miniature stacks of books about the Revolutionary War on each nightstand.

And a bed.

Obviously, there's a bed. Only one, queen-size, glaring at us from the middle of the room. Tucked at the base is a stiff, striped couch that might accommodate the length of a particularly short six-year-old.

I drop my suitcase on the floor. "It's your room. You get the bed."

"And make you sleep on the couch?" Nick says. "No way. You get the bed."

"Before this turns into a bad script, how about neither of us gets the bed? You squeeze into that weird love seat couch and I'll take the floor."

Nick eyes the carpet dust suspiciously. "You won't be allergic to that?"

I let out a short laugh, half impressed, half losing it after the night we've had. "How do you know I have allergies?"

Nick brushes past me. "Probably the same way you know my blood type."

In the bathroom, he tells me that he's contacted his handler at CSIS as well, informing him about the FBI leak, and that we should sift through our files again tonight—remind ourselves which FBI agents are or were attached to the Jones case. We settle into thoughtful silence, although I know it's going to eat at him.

Nick breaks it almost immediately, as I'm brushing my teeth. He clears his throat. Twice.

"Yes?"

"Nothing."

"Don't do that," I say around my toothbrush, not caring if I dribble a little. This isn't like the first night. I'm not trying to seduce him anymore. We might've kissed twice—no, three times—but we're colleagues. We're here, in this hotel room, because we're stuck together. "Don't clear your throat like you have something to say and then pretend it was nothing. We're past that."

"Fine," Nick says. "You brush too aggressively. You're going to recede your gumline."

I spit. "Is this you bodyguarding me?" I stare at him, agitated. "You look like Santa Claus."

Nick's put half a cup of bright white shaving cream on his face, and he's currently dragging his razor over his jawline. There's something strangely erotic about watching a man shave, but he will never, *ever* know that.

"I'm not going to take that as an insult," he says, maintaining focus.

"Okay," I joke back, "Old Saint Nick."

In the main room, I swing open the minibar fridge to reveal an assemblage of fizzy waters and something orange in a glass bottle; I select the orange one and hold the bottle against the pulse in my neck. *Good. Cool.* It's freezing outside, but stress heat is still flushing up my cheeks. It's one twenty-six in the morning. On the twenty-third of December. That's less than two days to stop the attack.

Clanking the bottle down, I unzip the back of my dress, removing the wires and replaying Vinny's words in my head. Rewinding them like a tape recorder.

I'm missing something, right?

What does this have to do with the Mid-Coast Maine contact? Or the van Johnny hired? Maybe I'm overthinking it. Maybe the van is just their getaway vehicle?

In the bathroom, Nick runs the tap. The whole space is starting to smell like his pine-scented aftershave. The scent should be cloying. There's too much of him here. Changing quickly into my pajamas—a less homely set this time, silk bottoms and a black sweatshirt—I decide to carve out a nook for myself in the corner. Soon, my computer's out and whirring.

In my emails, I click on the encrypted link that Gail sent several hours earlier: live surveillance from outside the gift shop. A virtual stakeout. On-screen, the whitewashed clapboard building creaks in the mild wind; there's a flag on the porch, softly waving. It advertises the candles.

Towel in hand, wiping down the sides of his neck, Nick saunters out of the bathroom as I'm hitting send. Right now, a normal question would be: *Do you snore?* Instead, he says, "You look like you're . . . spiraling."

"A bit." Over my laptop, I can see Nick pause at the foot of the bed, his face scrunched into a concerned look. "Here I am thinking that the heists were to finance their lifestyle, to make the family richer, but it seems like it's all a ploy to *buy* something. Maybe the next attack is going to be their biggest yet because they need the rest of the money fast, but something is just not clicking, like . . . this gift shop. What the hell is up with this gift shop? And this isn't *Love Actually*, okay? This isn't one of those Christmas stories that ends with everyone hugging at the airport. In fact, it might end with Johnny getting arrested in the airport as he's trying to flee the country for Guatemala, or some other country where you can disappear into the rainforest, and my sister would *not* do well in the rainforest. The spiders are enormous—"

"Hey, hey." He crouches down in front of me, eyebrows

crowding in the middle. "I hate this as much as you do. But all we can do is keep going. I'm sure, as we speak, both of our agencies are pulling security footage on Vinny. We haven't been tracking him nearly as much as we've been tracking Johnny. Something will turn up in time. We'll find out who he's been meeting, they'll arrest that guy and get him to talk." Nick puffs out a breath. "What's best for the case is for you to take a break, Sydney. Use this time to rest. You've been running yourself ragged."

"I'm sure I'll survive."

When I keep my eyes glued to the surveillance live stream, Nick stands up, pours himself a glass of tap water from the bathroom sink, and drinks it like he's spent the last twelve weeks wandering the desert. Then he starts talking to me again. "I bet you're tired. You drank three cold brews on the way up here."

My eyes don't leave the live stream. "Honestly? I couldn't fall to sleep right now if I tried. My brain's working at about a million miles a minute, and I've forgotten my gummies."

Nick raises an eyebrow.

"Melatonin gummies," I clarify, hardly looking up. "They help me wind down. Give me really weird dreams, though."

"Ah," Nick says. "*That is Taylor Swift.*" He pauses, running a hand over the back of his neck. The white shirt is clinging to Nick's collarbone. He's taken off his dinner jacket, rolled up his sleeves. "Look, while you're watching whatever you're watching—"

"Gift shop live stream," I supply.

"Gift shop live stream," Nick repeats, a little confused. "Maybe we can use this time to . . . get to know each other better. For the mission. Isn't that what partners do on stakeouts? Things are heating up, and I want us to trust each other. Fully."

Finally, my neck cranes up. The way Nick is gazing at me now, it's like I could say anything to him and he'd listen.

"I can't do that," I say firmly, standing up with my laptop, pacing for a moment before resettling on the bed.

He tries to guess what I'm thinking. "By the time I met Calla," Nick says clearly, slowly, "Johnny had already decided that she was the one. I didn't have time to warn her before she potentially got caught up in all this. I thought if I worked my ass off, I could put him behind bars before he had a chance to entrap her permanently. Then you came into the picture, and I figured, 'Here's another person who's about to get sucked in,' and I felt so fucking *guilty*—"

"But you thought I might know something."

"Yeah, well, you *did* know something, and I—" He cuts himself off, face clouding. "I still don't want this to hurt you," he finishes, eyes boring into mine. "Both of us are trying to take Johnny down, and we're going to need to lean on each other if we're going to do it together."

I shift uncomfortably on the mattress. "Okay, this is going to sound like a line . . . but it's not you. It's—I'm not sure I'm *capable* of trusting you. Or anyone, really . . . anymore."

"Because of your job?"

"Because . . ." My lip twitches. "Because of some pretty complicated family dynamics, and the job on top of that."

Nick nods at this, hands on his hips. "Well, you just trusted me enough to tell me that, Sydney. So that's a start." His eyes survey the room before he seems to decide something, bridging the gap between us and sitting down on the middle of the bed, cross-legged, facing me. "Maybe we should turn this into a game. Getting to know each other."

I slide my gaze to his. "After Pictionary? You're sure that's a good idea?"

He grunt-laughs. "There's no drawing involved, and no

guessing. Definitely no SpongeBob." The clock on the nightstand reads 1:31 a.m. Nick tilts his head toward it. "How about this? Ten minutes. You can keep track. Ten minutes of total honesty. I ask you a question, you ask me a question. You can skip anything you don't want to answer, but if you *do* answer, it can't be a lie."

That . . . terrifies me. My mind tries to poke holes in this with a wisecrack. "Do you have one of those portable lie detector tests in your suitcase?"

"No." He searches my face for a beat too long. "I just know your tells."

Pff. "I don't have any tells."

Nick leans his shoulders over his knees. "You *think* you don't have any tells."

"You met me three days ago," I quip, sliding my laptop to the side. "I think you forget that you don't actually know me."

"Oh really?" he says.

I swallow. "Really."

"You love your family," he says, soft yet matter-of-fact, "but you keep your distance because you're scared of having meaningful relationships with people, because that means you can lose them. They can leave you. You're like Sweetie Pie. You look tough, but on the inside, you're sweet. You like *any* type of bread and hate that cider your grandma bought. You were a nerd in high school—"

Here, I jump in to interject, almost happy that I've discovered something counterfactual. "I wasn't a nerd."

"Debate team, marching band," Nick says, ticking them off on his fingers. "Cute nerd. Accept it. When I asked you if you liked your job? You don't. You probably like the thrill of it sometimes, and the escape of it sometimes, but I think you're just like me. I think you hate the moral compromises you have to make, even though you have to make them all the time. You're afraid of what'll happen if you quit, but you're afraid of what'll happen if you stay. Maybe I'm projecting here, but if that's true, believe me, I get it."

Finished, he throws me a knowing look.

It kills me.

Reaching up to the desk, I take a sip of tap water from the glass; it tastes strongly of minerals. "Know what? Fine. Honesty game."

Nick repositions his legs on the floor, recrossing. "Yeah?"

The two of us have spent so many hours lying to each other, maybe this is a good antidote. And maybe . . . maybe there's a small part of me that wants to know him, that wants to let *him* know the Sydney I was before. "*Only* ten minutes, because I'm still watching the live stream. And I'll probably skip most of the questions."

"Fair enough," Nick says, straightening his back. "We'll start with an easy one. What's . . . the best Christmas gift you've ever received?"

My lips twist to the side. *That isn't so easy.* "Probably this quilt that Calla sewed me one year? It was a project for home economics, and it's like this terrible brown, with all of these strings hanging from it. But she made it for me, so . . ." I shrug, flicking my gaze back and forth to the computer screen. "I love it. You?"

Nick considers this. "There was this one year my grandmother tracked down an unopened box of my favorite cereal from when I was a kid. Cocoa Boulders. Like Cocoa Pebbles, but bigger? And three times the sugar." Nick swigs his water. "I ate the whole box in one sitting and gave myself a kidney stone."

I snort, amused. "How old were you? Fifteen?"

"Twenty-four," he says, then slides right into: "What's your biggest fear?"

Jesus. Can we stick with the cereal talk?

"Is that a skip?" Nick appraises me. "How about your biggest *irrational* fear?"

I run my tongue along my teeth, unwilling to give in this early. I have a bad, bad answer, though. "That a snake will pop out of the toilet right when I'm going to the bathroom."

Nick spits out half a mouthful of water, spraying the bed. He chokes on a laugh. Actually chokes. "That is—*not* what I was expecting you to say. Is that . . . like . . . a thing that happens?"

I'm straight-faced. "Everything has happened to someone, Nick."

Nick shudders. "Okay, you already know my biggest irrational fear. Easter Bunny. It's unnatural. I also really can't stand wet paper. On the side of the road and stuff. Paper shouldn't be wet."

"What about pulp?" I ask, incredulous. "Paper manufacturing? Paper has to be wet to exist."

"That is what makes it *irrational.*"

I smirk, shifting on the bed, mattress squeaking. We are blazing through these questions. I refresh the computer screen, making sure that the live stream is still running. "Your last girlfriend. Was that Bobbie?"

"You're thorough."

"Instagram," I supply. "What happened?"

"Ripped my heart to shreds, to be honest," Nick says, blowing out a breath. It dusts my face on the other side of the bed. He smells clean, minty, with a hint of citrus. "She was, uh, actually engaged to someone else and didn't tell me until we'd been dating for five and a half months."

"Oh, shit."

"Yeah, that was not a fun conversation. I couldn't be a part of something like that." When his eyes flick toward mine, he says, "What about you? Last boyfriend."

His name emerges flatter than I'd intended. "Griffin. We were together for two months."

"And?"

"And there wasn't . . ."

This, my brain inserts. There wasn't this. The back-and-forth. The banter. The intense eye contact over a hotel bed.

"Chemistry," I finish.

"You weren't in love?" Nick asks.

I shake my head. "No."

"Do you believe in love?" He grimaces. "Pretend I didn't ask that in a cheesy way."

The question still hovers between us, heavy. "Yeah," I say finally, vision dipping to the computer for a second, avoiding his eyes, "but I also believe in the inevitable possibility of love being ripped violently away from you if you're not careful enough. Like you said." Nick's lips part to respond to that, and for some reason, I just can't take whatever he's about to add.

"Love," I continue, surprising myself, "is having someone who knows you so well, you can just be with them in silence. When we were younger, Grandma Ruby took Calla and me on this one-night cruise on Prince Edward Island, and we sat next to this German couple at dinner. There were all these courses, and when we got to the cheese course, Calla and I realized that they hadn't spoken to each other since the breadsticks. Just ate their cheese, no talking. And I used to think that was really sad, because they were old, and maybe they didn't have anything to say to each other anymore. Maybe they'd gotten tired of each other. But now I think they could sit and just eat their cheese, and everything was comfortable, and everything was okay, because they knew each other inside and out . . . What is your *actual* biggest fear?"

Nick blinks. "Wow, that was like whiplash."

"Sorry. I figured we only have three minutes left in the game.

Thought I'd get my money's worth." I tip my water glass in his direction. "Biggest fear, you're up."

Deliberation flits across Nick's features. "I feel like my biggest fear changes the older I get. I don't have *one*. I have a constantly evolving series of fears. When I was a kid, it was that my grandmother was going to die. My parents divorced when I was eight years old, and my mom basically jumped ship to another family in Toronto. My dad's a workaholic, so growing up, it was just me and my grandma."

"You loved her a lot," I say, not a question.

"Yeah. She was . . . She was like your Grandma Ruby. Warm. Supportive. Tough. You never dared to argue with her, because she'd fix you with this . . . this *look*." He laughs, but it's sad. "I miss that look. First Christmas I'm not seeing it. When I made that toast at the bar? Thanking you for making me feel at home? I meant it. I was grateful to be there with you. I didn't want to spend the holidays alone."

Something in my belly drops. *Fuck.* We really *are* being honest with each other. "And now? What's your biggest fear now?"

"This," he says, blinking at me.

This? What does he mean *this*?

"Messing up anything about this mission," he clarifies. "I . . . uh . . ." He clears his throat, scratching at the side of his face, uncharacteristically uncomfortable. "I never answered that question you asked me at the Moose Lodge. About why I agreed to inform on Johnny if he was such a great friend. And firstly, you're only friends with someone if you actually know who you're talking to. He hid so many things, by the time I found them out, it was like I'd been catfished. The big switch for me, it was when we were out at this bar, back in Boston, and Johnny got into this disagreement with some kid. He made it out like he wanted to calmly speak to this guy outside. Just talk things over. They were taking forever, so I went to check on them. Stepped into the alleyway just in time to see Johnny punch the kid in the kidneys—and spit on his back. Johnny's hovering over him going, 'Do you know who my family is? Do you know who you've messed with?'" Nick rakes his teeth over his bottom lip. "CSIS contacted me pretty soon after that, told me about Johnny's criminal background. I felt sick to my stomach about everything I heard. If it had just been his family . . . people aren't their families. I would've stuck by him, stuck through it. But it's *Johnny*, too. The amount of lives he's personally fucked up . . ."

I'm motionless on the bed, wouldn't dream of interrupting him. It's obvious: Nick has been waiting a long time to tell someone his story. "I joined CSIS because of a strong sense of moral duty. I wanted to 'make a difference' in the world, and I couldn't see myself working a nine-to-five, and I thought, hey, it'll keep me fit, keep my mind engaged. But honestly? I was also trying to follow in my dad's footsteps. He was CSIS, and we never got along too great, and I thought that maybe I'd—I don't know— understand him better? Feel what he felt when he was on the job? Didn't matter, though. Didn't fix anything. And I keep telling myself that I *am* doing something good, that I'm making people like my grandma safer, but it's like you said—am I? Are we? Is this really the best way to do good in the world?" He looks entirely deflated. "I'm just hoping that I haven't gone through all of this for nothing."

"You haven't," I say automatically.

"You don't know that," he says, voice soft.

It's not my turn anymore, but I can't help but ask. "What's the scar on your stomach from?"

He flinches, his thick eyebrows drawing together. Still wearing his dress shirt, Nick peers down at the foot-long scar beneath the fabric, as if to remind himself that it's there. For a moment, I think he's going to wind down the clock. Tell me *pass*. New question. "It was the first time I truly realized what I'd gotten myself into," he answers, voice gravelly. "I was two months into the job, guarding Johnny. We were meeting one of his 'business associates' at his home in Boston. Needless to say, the deal went south. Guy pulled out his knife. I stepped in front of Johnny, pushed him back—and the knife went clear through. That's why he trusts me so much. Because he thinks I'd die for him." His eyes shift to my wrist. "Your tattoo? What's it mean?"

Now he's giving *me* whiplash. My mouth goes completely dry. He might be the only person in the world who has ever had that effect on me. My fingers trace the half-moon outline. "Why do you want to know about this so bad?"

"That's the first time I found out you existed. I met Calla and she was thinking about getting a new tattoo. She pointed to her wrist and said, *My sister, Sydney, has a matching one.* Then she showed us a picture of you. You were—" Nick chuckles lightly. "You were on this white water raft?"

"Oh god," I say, covering my mouth with my hand. "That was not a good trip."

"Didn't someone get their teeth knocked out?"

I nod humorously. "One of the guys in the back. He didn't hold on to his T-grip, and there was just . . . It was terrible."

"But that's what I noticed about *you*," Nick says. "Obviously the accident hadn't happened yet, but everyone else in the raft looked absolutely petrified. You were going full speed over this rapid, and you had this . . . this . . . war face on. Like you were a Viking shield-maiden or something. While everyone else was leaning back, you were leaning in."

"And you thought," I try, "'That girl is really pretty'?"

"Actually I thought, 'That girl scares the shit out of me.'" He smirks. "But yeah, essentially. Then I asked Calla what the tattoo meant and she just kind of clammed up. Wouldn't really talk about it."

"That's because we *don't* really talk about it. Not anymore." I rub the tattoo. "I think we got it for different reasons, or maybe not, I ..."

Nick sits up straighter. Just like I did for him, he doesn't interject. Doesn't speak. Just listens.

And it's the listening, it's the way his eyes are scanning my face, really *trying* to know me. It's the fact that we have the same job, that he understands what I do, that this room is nearly silent except for the whir of the computer and the merging of our breath, and when I think about somewhere I want to be, it's wrapped under Nick's arm. It's my head in the crook of his neck, and that terrifies me, and—

"I think that tattoo's for my and Calla's dad," I say, not sure where to even begin. Maybe our dad always plunged the tip of his finger into his coffee to make sure it was cool enough to drink. Maybe he used to stick pencils in his mouth, like walrus tusks, to make me laugh. Once, he made a crown for Calla out of a Honey Nut Cheerios box. He was a good father. He was an unprepared father. One of the last words he said to me was my name.

Be good, Sydney bean.

"Our dad decided that he wasn't cut out for solo parenting," I say, something building, scratching, dying to get out. "Or maybe that's not even it. Because he wasn't really a parent. Grandma Ruby filled the caregiver role. Maybe it's more like ... my mom died when I was little, and Dad never really went to therapy or anything, and it might've just ... built up, you know? I've never fully figured it out, but he told us he was going hiking. And he did go hiking. He just never came back. At first we thought he was missing, and Grandma Ruby got really worried, but he was just still out there. I think he did the whole Appalachian Trail in one direction, and then turned around and did it again."

Nick's still silent, still listening.

"And I couldn't contact him," I say, throat burning. "I couldn't really ask him why, and by the time I could, I was so *furious*, so . . . sad that I decided it was easier if we never reconnected. Even though we had a lot of fun together. When I was a kid. He always sort of did his own thing, but he let me tag along. Like camping. I'm not even sure if Calla remembers this, but there was this one night, a few weeks before he left? Calla and I dragged our sleeping bags out by the lake, and we fell asleep under this perfect half-moon. It was the last time I remember feeling truly . . . like everything was okay."

I gulp. My throat has almost dried up completely. And I can't look at Nick, don't want to see myself reflected in his eyes, see him pity me.

"Sydney . . ." Nick says.

"It's fine," I say reflexively, but Nick's reached out, his hand clasping my chin, forcing my gaze up. My eyes to his eyes.

"It's not," he says, one of his thumbs grazing my cheek. "It's *not*."

And maybe that—that, finally, is what does it. Two stupid, simple words that I've needed to hear for half of my life. It's not. It's not okay. It wasn't okay. It's never been okay. And I've just been drifting in this . . . this not-okay-ness, unable to share it with anyone. Afraid to risk someone *seeing* me—because what if they did? And what if they left? And what if it happened all over again?

Nick's hand stays, cupping the side of my face. *Nick* stays.

"What sucks is my dad probably knew me better than anyone," I add, plowing through, and my breath's coming out furiously now. Rugged words. And *relief*. It's like stepping out of a dark shed, fresh rain on my skin. These memories, they've needed air. They've needed someone to hear them; someone who's leaning in instead of away. "And he let me go, and I think ever since I've tried to become this . . . this unknowable person. That's what one of my exes called me. 'Unknowable by definition.' And I've picked this job—this stupid, *stupid* job—where I can know everything about everyone else, read them, study them, pick apart their motives, see the signs, where I'm allowed to be only a fraction of myself, where I'm hiding things because that's the *point*, and I think underneath it all I'm terrified. I'm just terrified that by wanting to be unknowable, I'll actually *become* unknowable, to everyone, and I'll never have that . . . I'll never have that again . . ."

I'm scratching too close, digging too far, into an essential truth about me, and maybe I . . . maybe I shouldn't have . . .

I sniff, looking at the clock. "Time's up."

The only other sounds in the hotel room are the hum of the miniature fridge and the heated *whoosh* of the radiator by the window. Nick breaks the silence, his voice just as ragged as my own. "You want to go for round two?"

14

I blink at him, long and slow. Watch him study me. Watch him part his lips. And I could stop it here. Cut off this conversation. Retreat. But speaking to someone like this, so openly . . .

"Yeah," I manage, straightening the pillows behind my back. "Yeah, okay."

We sit closer to each other this time, computer between us on the bed. And it feels strangely intimate, in the quiet, just the two of us.

Nick tells me that the octogenarian ice cream moguls from his Instagram were his grandmother's best friends; he visits them multiple times a week so they can talk about her. The flavor "Nick of Luck" has pistachios in it; pistachios were Nan's favorite. I fire back with a story about my dad's favorite ice cream shop, by Cape Hathaway Cove, where we used to feed the seagulls. I ask Nick, tangentially, if *he's* ever been in love, and he says yes. With Bobbie, who broke his heart, and a mechanic named Gabrielle, who fixed her own antique cars—and we talk about our first cars, how we learned to drive, who taught us.

The clock ticks. Tells us time's up.

We recheck the live stream—then go again. And again.

"What did your dad say?" I ask Nick, hands under my chin. "When you told him you'd joined CSIS?"

Nick inhales deeply with his chest. "He ... he, uh, didn't really say anything."

"Nothing?"

"Nothing that I was hoping for, at least," Nick says with a sad little smile. "It feels like I've spent most of my life trying to get the guy to notice me. Got good grades, excelled in sports ... I thought if I found just the right thing, he'd say that he was proud of me. Of the man I'd become. Instead, when I told him I was following in his footsteps, he immediately jumped into shoptalk. How hard the road was going to be at CSIS. Maybe that's ... maybe that's why I was friends with Johnny at first. I was kind of desperate for acceptance. When Johnny told me I fit with his crew, I believed him."

"Do you ever see your dad?" I ask, wincing. "Do you ever go home?"

"Not really." Nick swallows. "My dad usually goes to Hawaii for the holidays, this big fishing trip, and I guess I'm technically invited but it never feels like a real offer. My mom sends a Christmas card from her new family every year, and that's just about all the contact I get from her. She came to my grandma's funeral, and there was ... nothing. No affection toward me. And now that my grandma's gone, and her house is sold, there's really no reason for me to go back."

"All the memories are still there," I offer.

"True," Nick agrees. "That can be a good thing, when it doesn't hurt ... What about you? Ever think about telling your family about your career? Must be tough, keeping that secret. You guys are so close."

"We were," I say.

"You *are*," Nick underlines.

"Well, either way, I have thought about it. Extensively. And I kept coming to the conclusion that this was something they couldn't be a part of. I didn't want to drag them into my mess. Because that's what it feels like a lot of the time. Just a big ole mess."

Nick nods empathetically. It's so wonderfully odd—and therapeutic—commiserating with someone who understands the ins and outs of my world. Of *our* world. "What would you do if you weren't doing this?"

"Besides sitting around all day and eating tacos?" I ask.

"No, tacos can be included."

"Well then, I'd probably work at an international relations think tank. Eating tacos. You?"

"I'd be a dog trainer," Nick says without hesitation, and we talk about the tricks that Sweetie Pie could learn, and how our jobs make it difficult to maintain real relationships. Who'd want to get close to someone that you categorically cannot get close to?

The timer buzzes. We go twice more. Again.

And each time, it's like . . . chipping away at something. This profound, bit-by-bit relief. Finding myself, sharing myself, giving as much as I receive. After the first hour, I'm reminded that I used to be a person outside of my job. I used to be a person who baked lemon squares with my Grandma Ruby, who stayed late in elementary school to practice free throws in the gym. I lived for winter. I lived for climbing out of my bedroom window and touching the mountain of newly fallen snow, telling my sister, *Let's build a snowman as tall as the garage.* I lived for this *state*, my neighborhood, my town, the porcupines scuttling through the bushes and the gentle glint of sunlight on Hathaway River. Getting coffee from the same place where we buy our lobster. Quiet grocery store aisles and the sense of self-sufficiency. Thick wool socks and Cape Hathaway Huskies baseball.

I miss wild blueberries in the freezer, left over from summer. And saltwater taffy.

I tell Nick about all of it. And how much I used to love Christmas.

"Didn't you say you weren't a fan of Christmas?" I ask Nick, leaning in. The mattress creaks between us, comforter bunching.

"Yeah, I was trying to make myself believe that." He gives me a tiny wince. "I thought it'd be easier that way. Lower expectations."

"But you're really a fan?"

"Sydney, let me put it this way . . . You know that Claymation Rudolph story about the origin of Christmas? And Rudolph learns how to walk for the first time by putting one foot in front of the other?"

"Yeah?"

"I get an actual lump in my throat."

"*Stop*," I say, batting him with a throw pillow.

"I'm serious! It's emotional!"

My head cocks at him, heart lifting a little higher. "Did you really buy that CHRISTMAS SWEATER sweatshirt at the airport?"

"Ah, now that—that is true."

"I like that sweatshirt," I say, a hint of mischief in my voice.

"Oh yeah?" Nick says, turning mischievous himself. He places a hand on his chin, the pad of his thumb tracing his jawline. "How much?"

"A lot," I admit, wondering, *How is this so easy, when everything else is so hard?* "Possibly too much. It does wonders for your bone structure."

"I'll keep that in mind," he says with a crooked smile, then peers at the clock. It's three forty-seven in the morning. "What are the chances you're going to fall asleep?"

"No chance," I say, swallowing. Honestly, I'm not sure I want our conversation to end, even though my eyes are blurring at the computer screen. "This game has only made me further awake."

Nick seems to consider something. "Would a run help?"

The gym at the Ocean Harbor Inn is surprisingly well stocked. Twin treadmills, a variety of free weights, a thick red mat for sit-ups and Pilates. I packed my running shoes but no exercise clothes, so I'm wearing my pajamas. It's almost four in the morning. Who's going to see besides Nick?

The first minute in, he riffles through the workout equipment, finding a set of stretchy plastic bands and a brand-new pair of boxing gloves. A thick, black weight bag hangs in the corner.

"You kickbox?" he asks me.

"Occasionally," I say, tightening the laces on my sneakers. We've taken a short break from our digital stakeout, leaving the record function on. "I'm more of a mixed martial arts type of person." As I say this, an idea flickers in my belly. My eyes slowly slide toward the mat.

Nick snorts. "Uh, no. Nope. I'm not going to fight you, Sydney."

"It's not fighting. It's *sparring.*"

"Which is a synonym for fighting."

"Do you want a safe word?" I ask, only partly joking, then mimic Johnny's accent: "You afraid, Nicky boy? I'm, like, half your height." Nick has six inches on me and a good number of pounds, but I could use my shorter stature to my advantage, dipping and ducking when I need to . . . "Or is it that you don't want to spar with a woman?"

"You know that's not true," Nick growls.

"Then prove it," I argue, tiptoeing onto the mat.

Nick rolls his eyes and starts unbuttoning his shirt. He's still wearing the same one from the party, with a pair of jet-black sweatpants.

I quirk an eyebrow at him. "What are you doing?"

"Hey, this is a nice shirt," he says, whipping it open. Underneath he's tanned and toned, that scar racing up his abdomen. A quiver goes up my own belly. "I don't want to pop a button. Are you sure you want to do this?"

In response, I hold up my hands, palms flat, ready.

"Are you *absolutely* sure?" he asks.

"Jesus, Nick!"

With a faint sigh, he saunters toward me, onto the mat, and then it's fast—a lightning-quick dip of his shoulder as he tries to plow into me, hoist me onto his back. But I've anticipated this. He thinks he can hook me over his shoulder? Think again. I spin, my back to his back, until we've changed positions. Palms still raised and flat, I inch closer across the mat.

Hand-to-hand fights, my Farm instructor told me, aren't won by circling each other like hawks; they're won with full-body contact, when you have the chance to catch your opponent off balance. Off guard. Be so close that you can smell their skin, so close that you know what kind of soap they wash with, so you can see every tiny freckle on their neck.

Nick has three large freckles running down his throat.

My elbow whips out, and he blocks it carefully—almost gently—feet shuffling to the side. I dip under and, with my shoulder, plow him into the wall; he hits with a fantastic *thud*, rattling a framed picture of the White Mountains. The glass quivers in the frame. "Careful," he heaves, and I am careful. I carefully pin him to the wall. And I remember the first time we ever properly spoke, in the kitchen with those gingerbread cookies, and I thought about how I'd take him down, shoved up against the wall. If I'm honest with myself, even then, something in my belly fluttered.

My eyes dig into his, passing him a message: *If you respect me, you'll fight back.*

Message received.

Powerfully, he twists his arm between us, edging me back, and we start sparring properly. Like real colleagues would in the CIA. He doesn't swing to miss—but he also doesn't swing to harm. We're training right now. Competitively. Block for block. This is an inn chock-full of people, and I'm hoping that all of them will sleep through a *minor* disruption. Our footfall is quick, swift, barely there. Until I catch him unaware, hooking an ankle behind his knees, literally sweeping him off his feet.

I pounce, straddling his hips with my thighs. Our backs flatten the ridges in the mat as we roll, grunting—real guttural stuff, scrounged up from the belly. I realize, belatedly, these are *very* similar to the noises I make when I'm having sex. Nick's cheeks are flushing with the faintest splash of red, and I doubt it's from the workout; we haven't been wrestling that long. Neither of us is truly winded.

My limbs tangle with his limbs; his breath turns hot against my neck. "Sydney," he chokes out, and I'm waiting for him to finish that with something like *Sydney, get off of me, you weirdo,* or *Sydney, this is a little too intense for me,* but what he says is, "Was *any* of it real?"

I pull back, on top of him, face over his face. "What do you mean?"

"You know what I mean," Nick says, voice strained, and I do. That's the thing. I do.

Swallowing hard, I throw it right back at him. "Was any of it real for you?"

"Yes," he says without hesitation or a twitch of his mouth. No lies. His eyes are flaming in the fluorescent light of the gym, and I . . . don't know what's happening right now.

My chest heaves as I take in a few breaths, my hands pinning him harder by the shoulders. For the moment, his fingers are resting on my knees, the heat of him pulsing through the fabric, and I'm stressed out of my mind. Agitated. I shouldn't be feeling . . . this. *This!* Whatever this is!

"That night in the bedroom, when Johnny almost caught us . . ." Nick says, so softly that I almost ask him to repeat it. "And even before then, maybe on the couch watching that terrible holiday movie. Or at the beach. Maybe earlier."

Even earlier?

I inhale slowly. "Sometimes I thought I had you, for the mission, and sometimes I really wasn't sure what you were thinking." My chest goes right on pounding, even though I tell it, *Stop, jeez, enough.* "It was always a risk with you. When we first started, I wasn't even sure if you'd find me attractive."

I'm not fishing, it isn't a line, but Nick scoffs anyway. "Sydney, I'm telling you right now, that is the *last* thing you needed to worry about." He reassesses this, thick eyebrows scrunching. "Maybe not the last thing, considering the situation, but . . ." The rest of his words come out raw. "It's almost unreal how beautiful you are."

Nick's eyes trace the edges of my face. I can feel splotches of red crawling up my neck as he looks at me. I should be able to control it—to tamp down anything that I want hidden—but there it is, the rawness in my expression reflected back in his eyes.

"What was your plan for me?" I ask, breath refusing to come out easy. "Right at the beginning?"

"I just . . . wanted you," he admits, voice gravelly, gaze backing up his words. "I thought I'd do everything I could to make you open up to me, and I was trying to convince myself it was for the assignment. *Only* for the assignment. But it wasn't. It never was. Most of it was just . . . you."

Instantly, the air between us changes. Heats up. I'm in my pajamas, my hair in a half-mangled ponytail, beads of sweat dripping down my unwashed face. Nick doesn't care. There's an undeniable hunger in his gaze that crosses the boundaries of our cat-and-mouse game.

Or maybe we're playing a new game now.

Hesitantly, pulse pounding, I answer him with another move of my own, letting my fingertips crawl up his neck. They draw a line up his throat, to his mouth, and soon I'm dragging a finger across his bottom lip, tugging, before slipping the tip of it into his mouth. The gentle bite of his teeth sends a pulse right down my arm.

No one's sparring now. No one's joking around. Together, we're silent except for the slight hitch of his throat, and the breath that we're sharing. His lips close around the edge of my finger, sucking, and my mouth falls open. That's when I realize: I'm not a little bit turned on. I am *incredibly* turned on.

Through my pajama bottoms, I feel the sudden hardness of him as a growl builds in his throat; this time, it's from a different kind of frustration. Gently, Nick grabs my wrist, bringing my palm to the smooth edge of his face, and he sits up, hitching me onto his hips. I've seen him move. Just now, when we were sparring. I've seen how his body works. All the taut lines, the lean cords of muscle. And I can't help but picture it, how he'd move on top of me.

Nick swallows noticeably, his throat bobbing up and down, and when I lean my head back, his mouth drags a trail across my collarbone. It's hungry. Carnal. This is still a game. Who can make the other groan first. Who can make the other beg.

"Sydney," Nick says. My name is tender in his mouth. "I don't want to fight with you anymore."

A re you sure?" Nick says, back in the hotel room, a muscle feathering in his jaw. I nod as he inches closer, hips hovering above mine, his hands reaching up to cup the sides of my face. Warm fingers. Tender touch. With each little caress, anticipation fizzes in the center of my belly. That parachute feeling. Diving in. If this isn't trust, I'm not sure what is.

With one slow sweep, Nick drags a thumb across my bottom lip, like I did to him in the gym, his eyelashes dark and blinking, and my breath hitches. I'm almost shuddering. I'm realizing with a heart-palpitating, can't-feel-my-face sort of sensation that Nick might know me better than any man has for years. And this is . . . not like before. Not like days earlier, at the beach. There's no hesitation, no questions, no *Is this too early for the mission?* We aren't using a kiss for a calculated cover. When Nick leans forward, I barely think, his breath hot as he parts my lips. The kiss is tender, urgent, like he's taking his time even though he doesn't have nearly enough of it. And that makes me even hungrier. Instinctively, I arch all the way into him, his hands wrapping around the base of my neck, thumbs imprinting into my cheeks—and *god*, he tastes good, like the toothpaste brand we share.

Words skate up my throat. "I had a dream about you. That first night." This elicits the smallest grin, right in the corner of his mouth, and I kiss it, managing, "You were in the shower. You were wearing that Christmas sweatshirt."

He laughs, my palm coasting down his chest, and then it's like he's reading my mind; he grips my hips and hoists me on top of the dresser. "You weren't kidding about that sweatshirt," he whispers, nuzzling into my neck, his lips grazing a pathway up my throat. Goose bumps break out all over my arms. They're the good kind, the best kind, the ones that travel down my stomach, down my thighs.

There's an intensity in Nick's eyes that I've never seen before, his pupils steadily widening. Something in him is ... unraveling. When Nick kisses me again, it's even (how do I describe this?) greedier. The word is *greedier*. He dives in, his tongue sweeping against mine, and this—*this*—is a whole different kind of sparring match. I'm not sure who's winning, but I do know that my muscles are tightening *everywhere*.

Nick kisses even better than he fights.

I lift both arms for him to peel off my shirt. He tugs, but the fabric's tight, too formfitting; it gets stuck just under my armpits, my head like a turtle tucked, and now both of us are laughing. "I wasn't thinking," I say, tugging myself free, which is true in more ways than one. I wasn't thinking that I'd get stuck. Wasn't thinking we'd be doing this. Wasn't thinking, for a moment, about anything but him. In these seconds, Nick Fraser is all-consuming. He is my entire vision: those eyelashes, that scar I'm running my finger across, the look he's giving me now that my shirt's tugged off. Casting a glance down my body, across my stomach, over the lace of my cami.

"Never had a fighting chance, did I?" Nick says, breathing hard, pressure building in both of us, and I'm starting to wonder the same thing about myself. How could I ever think I wouldn't fall for the target when the target was *him*?

Heat spreads in my belly, working its way between my legs, every inch of me begging for him. One strap of my cami slips down, gravity, movement, and Nick lets out a ragged sigh, helping the other strap on its way, until the stiff peaks of my nipples hit the air, and—*fuck*, it's freezing in this room, but Nick's hand is warm as he palms one of my breasts, leaning over to flick his tongue across my nipple.

I liquify. I am snow, melting.

"You like that?" he rasps out, and I whimper, *Yes, extremely, yes.*

"For the record, Sydney," he says, voice dangerously low, "if you'd come up to me that first night and said, quote, 'Nick, I don't have any panties on, and I want you between my thighs,' yes. Yes, that would've had an effect on me. Just the sound of my name in your mouth . . ."

"Good to know," I breathe, pawing at his shirt with almost-shaking hands, and his own fingers carve a line down my back, sending a full-on shiver down my spine. It's frenzied, carnal, before he dips his head and kisses the freckles underneath my breasts, working his way down the middle of my stomach; at the waistline of my pajamas, he hesitates, as if to say, *This all right? May I?* Having this powerful man between my legs, staring up at me, asking for permission . . . it is by far the hottest thing I have ever seen. "We can stop," he breathes out, "anytime you want."

His gaze rakes over my face, possibly searching for those non-existent tells. But I don't want to stop. I want to watch him slowly tug down my pajama bottoms, revealing that while I might be wearing underwear, I also very obviously want him between my thighs. When Nick drops the rest of the way to his knees, slipping the thin lace aside, I'm slick. "So goddamn sexy, Sydney," he rumbles, and I get it now. My name, his mouth—I really, really get it. Then he's kissing me, tongue parting me. His lips hum against my most sensitive spot, making the breath rise quicker and quicker in my chest.

When he slips in a finger, it's heaven. When he slips in another, my hips buck, needing *more.* "Condom?" I manage in an inside voice.

"In my wallet," Nick says with a husky rasp, then seems to catch himself. "It wasn't for you. It wasn't for, I mean, I didn't plan—"

"I know," I gasp as he stands, digging out protection from the depths of his parka, and I undo his pants, plunging my hand into his briefs. Nick closes his eyes when I wrap my fingers around the solid heat of him, pumping slowly.

"If you want that Christmas sweatshirt," he grits out, "it's fucking *yours*."

"Noted," I breathe out, swallowing, my breath tremoring into the crook of his neck, and—*right, the condom.* I snag it from his grip, tearing it open as Nick steps out of his pants, stroking a hand over his significant length. "Do that again," I say, hoarse, a little bit out of my mind, because I want to see how he touches himself when no one's around. With a tighter grip this time, he strokes his cock up and down, a few tendons straining in his neck, and if I don't get this man inside me, I think there's a good chance I might explode. I roll on the condom, our foreheads pressed together. His hands reach to cup my ass, hoisting me up onto the dresser again as my legs wrap around him, pulling him closer. Our noses brush, both of us looking down as he slides into me with a thick, delicious thrust.

"*Sydney*," he says at the same time I cry out, "*Yes*, Nick."

Never. It is *never* like this.

Normally I'm in my head, withdrawing to that place where I'm in the driver's seat. Only me. Only showing what I want to be seen. Or I'm on top, completely in control, with the guy just lying there watching. Nick is in it. He's active. He's so firmly wrapped up in me, and I'm so wrapped up in him, that each thrust of his hips is a revelation. It's a fucking gift.

Everything's going a bit hazy. I don't even know where it's coming from, this new kind of noise I'm making—halfway between a whimper and a groan, like Nick is literally feeding me air; I can't get enough of it, I keep taking. Small gasps. Bigger. My hands tumble through his hair, which is soft, *so* soft, gentle waves springing between my fingers.

"You aren't unknowable," Nick rasps, rolling against me, and I almost miss it. What he's said. The other gift he's given. "You aren't. Unknowable. Sydney."

His lips draw a tender line up my throat.

And I rush over the edge, my fingertips pressed hard into his skin; waves of relief rock my core as Nick groans into my shoulder, following me into the abyss. He trembles, muscles quivering, his breath just as unsteady as my own, and I'm clinging to him, like I'm afraid of what might happen if we fly apart.

I've always hated how my body reacts to an orgasm—that uncomfortable loss of control. The rush of pent-up emotions spilling out. With other guys, I'm able to stem it. Halt it. Go back to that bulletproof Sydney who walked through the bar door. But with Nick? I'm not exaggerating when I say I want to cry.

"I'm okay," I say quickly, shaking my head as he searches my face. "It was good." *More than good.* I'm just about to elaborate, about to open up even more, but humor feels safer. "I meant it about the Christmas sweatshirt."

Nick's laugh is rough and easy. Moving slow, he tucks a stray hair behind my ear and caresses my collarbone, breath floating in waves across my skin. "Take it. It's yours."

My chin crooks over his shoulder, and—"Oh, *shit*."

Nick takes a step back, eyes widening. "What?"

I spin him around by the hips, gaze landing on the purple trail of bruises crowding his spine. "I thought you didn't actually have an injury. I legitimately thought that. I am *so* sorry. You *sparred* with this?"

Shrugging, he tenderly presses around the area with his fingers. "I've had worse."

My heart does a big, uncomfortable leap. "Why didn't you say something?"

"Besides *ow, my ass*?"

"I meant tonight."

He shrugs again. "Didn't want to."

That's when my phone *dings*. Finally. Finally, some communication from Gail. Any news on the FBI mole? Nick and I both jolt, snapping us straight out of the haze, and I lurch for my phone on the nightstand, swiping up the screen to reveal—

That Dishies, the Italian restaurant in Cape Hathaway, is finally going to start serving pizza in the New Year. There's a coupon, inexplicably, with a dancing beaver on it. I'm not even sure how they have my number.

I blow out a breath. "False alarm."

Nick drags a hand across his forehead. "Maybe we . . . maybe we really should try to sleep. We're no good in this state."

"Yeah," I say quickly, "yeah, okay."

I've never required an after-sex debriefing before. Never wanted to stick around and suss out the details because there *were* no details. It was clear what would happen afterward. I'd go home. Back to my apartment or hotel room. Return to work without complications. Mission first. Job first. But now I'm wondering, *What happens?* Where do we go from here?

What *was* this to me? What was this to Nick?

I don't ask. We pass each other one last breathless look before shuffling around the room, gathering our clothes, yanking them on with varying degrees of efficiency; my sweatshirt goes on backward at first. I twist it, jumping into my pajama bottoms at the same time, as Nick reties the waist of his sweatpants. I realize he's as unsteady on his feet as I am, as shaky and wrapped in that post-sex haze. Wordlessly, neither of us takes the floor or the couch. We just slip into the cool hotel sheets, flicking off the lights.

For once, I'm in a hotel room and I don't have to leave the TV on for the voices.

Someone's with me as I fall into an uneasy sleep.

15

In the morning, we rise way too early, restless. We spend an hour flipping through case files, cross-checking Vinny's known associates, before Nick asks if he can buy me a quick breakfast.

I have never, not once in my life, said no to breakfast.

The diner down the road happens to be my favorite type of restaurant: a place where the tables are so sticky with maple syrup, you never risk placing your palms down flat; you may never wrench them up again. Green vinyl booths and a soda-fountain-style counter crowd the space, and there are seven different types of pie listed on the chalkboard—from blueberry to rhubarb. Nick and I order two enormous breakfasts: lobster omelets, hash browns, steaming cups of coffee, and a slice of banana cream pie for the table. It's acceptable to order pie at 6 a.m., if you're anxiously awaiting news. (Or honestly, anytime.)

The food arrives on thick ceramic plates, clunking down on the table.

"Please don't take this the wrong way . . ." Nick says.

"That is my *favorite* opener from a guy," I say, taking a scorching sip of my coffee, prepared to throw my shields up. "Especially after he sleeps with me."

Nick quickly shakes his head, digging into his omelet with a tinny metal fork. "It's not bad. At all. When we were fighting, I was surprised by how strong you were. You are *seriously* strong."

I fork up my own breakfast with a flourish. "I can carry my groceries all in one go."

Nick blinks. "I think that's the most impressive thing you've ever said to me." He checks the soda fountain clock on the wall. "Ten minutes?"

Once we left the hotel, I was afraid that the game might truly be over. *Last night* was the honesty. Nick's body, wrapped around mine. Naked honesty in naked form.

I chew my eggs. "Let's make it fifteen."

We continue to unravel each other, bit by bit, until our omelets are well past cold. The server refreshes our coffees, a buzz working its way into my limbs, and I'm reminding myself what it means to understand a person outside the contents of a file. He knows, now, that I google "world's oldest mastiff" on a frequent basis, my fingers crossed, to see how many years with Sweetie Pie we might have left. I know, now, that he also wants to adopt a dog—an elderly one, with clouded eyes—and give her the last, best years of her life. "I'd want someone to do that for me," he explains, "if I were a dog."

And I like that. *If I were a dog.*

On the car ride home, I actually let him drive. And change the radio station. Twice. He selects a folk Christmas music channel, a Bob Dylan impersonator belting out a gravelly "Feliz Navidad," and I spend the time flicking through recorded gift shop surveillance (there's a dock near the back, and I zoom in on that, with no luck); I jolt when we roll to a stop in the driveway.

"Home," Nick says, cutting the engine, and it strikes me again just how *weird* this is. Three days ago, I was ready to jump-tackle him out of the shower, and now—now what? When I glance side-long from the passenger seat, the frosted window gives him an aura, haloing him with bright, cold light. He looks beautiful. I mean that unsarcastically. As fully as I've ever meant anything.

"I'll get my bag," I say, croaky, checking my phone, clearing the sleepiness from my throat.

There's a saying about spies: that after a long, undercover mission, they "come in from the cold." The field is emotionally snow-swept, treacherous. If you aren't exceedingly careful, it'll give you frostbite. I'm thinking about that now, a thin sheen of cold sweat still clinging to my back, as we follow the snow-blown footprints back into the house, the heater turned up, the Christmas decorations twinkling on the tree.

This is the warmest place imaginable.

I'm still . . . I'm still struggling, aren't I? I'm missing something, aren't I? The van, the gift shop, the C4, the mole in the FBI. Pulling my cell phone from my jacket, I rattle off a text to Sandeep—my CIA handler—and ask if he'll do me a favor. He owes me one. I was the only person who'd play Scrabble with him at the Macedonian station house. Sandeep is a Scrabble fanatic.

In the kitchen, I expect the sharp tap of Sweetie Pie's claws, but there's a pale blue Post-it Note with Grandma Ruby's hand-writing, saying that she's taken Sweetie Pie out for a long beach walk.

"I can . . . make us some coffee," I offer Nick, trying to get my mind right. With the case. With us. To figure out where Nick and I go from here. Because . . . I live in Washington, DC. Nick lives in Boston. He's undercover. I travel all the time. It would never work.

But . . . his words are plowing through me again, looping on an endless cycle: *You aren't. Unknowable. Sydney.*

"Yeah, thanks," says Nick, and it reminds me of the first time we talked in the kitchen, when I offered him that gingerbread cookie, and he wasn't quite sure what to say next. That unsettledness pulses between us. "Why don't I bring our bags upstairs?"

"Okay. Good. Thank you."

Nick lingers by the coffee maker, like he desperately wants to add something else—and I wait for it. Keep waiting for it. But it doesn't come. He simply grabs our luggage with a nod, trailing upstairs, and I'm left in the kitchen, scooping out lumps of fresh-ground espresso.

The landline rings.

I answer it, fully in my head. "Hello?"

"Ruby?" comes a voice at the other end of the line. I recognize it instantly. Every cell in my body recognizes it. He's older, grumblier, but it's him. The sound knocks the breath out of me. My dad. My dad, who was supposed to know me, and can't even identify the sound of my voice.

He thinks I'm my grandmother.

I don't say anything. Can't. Can't summon words. My neck's hot. I'm steadying myself against the countertop with one hand. I'm unprepared for this. After all these years . . .

He doesn't seem to notice that I haven't responded. That Ruby hasn't responded. He just keeps on going. "Look, I'm . . . This is Dean." His tone is ragged, weathered, like he's speaking through twigs; what I remember of my dad is almost larger than life, but this man? This man sounds so small. "I know we haven't . . ." A deep breath from Dad here. "I know we haven't spoken in a while, but uh, Calla called and left a message. Campground director. He gave it to me, and I'm sorry. I'm just so sorry, but I . . ."

I slam the phone down onto the receiver, eyes glazing, pulse hammering, and—

He's not coming to the wedding. Calla called him and he's not coming to the wedding. He's going to disappoint her, and I don't—I don't even—I don't even know what to say to him. What to feel right now. What to feel besides nausea, welling up in my chest.

Dad. I just heard my dad.

And he didn't remember you, Sydney.

A car door slams in the driveway.

In seconds, Calla barrels through the laundry room, boots thundering across the tile. My heartbeat is pounding in my ears, but I still pick up on it through the *thud-thud-thud*: The slight stamp in her gait. She's too stiff. Too uncharacteristically silent. When she sees me, she doles out a tight-lipped smile before whipping open the fridge, pulling out a small jug of apple cider, and taking a drink right from the bottle. And I'll have to tell her. I need to tell her that Dad called.

But how . . . how do I . . . how do I even get the words out? What do I say? How do I tell her that he's going to disappoint her again? Again and again and again, and I take a big, silent sniff of air through my nose and wipe my eyes and—"How was your drive?" That's what training does. I'm almost surprised how good I am. How normal my voice sounds when everything inside me is trembling.

"Traffic," Calla says with a sharp sigh, wiping her mouth with the back of her hand. Her curls are much less springy than usual; the snowmen dangling from her ears almost look like they're melting.

A large lump has formed at the back of my throat, and I can't swallow it down.

Calla shoves the cider back in the fridge. It sloshes as she wedges it tight into the door, between two fancy bottles of wedding wine. Sparkling, white, Californian.

When she turns to look at me, right there in the kitchen, another memory smacks me in the face. I'm living it all over again.

Suddenly, we're kids. Eleven and nine. Dad is out decorating the front lawn. We're playing Sting by the breakfast bar, as loud as the radio will go, whipping our arms out like birds, pretending we're *in a field of gold*. It's Christmastime. I'm limping through the dance because my knees are all bandaged up. (Turns out, it's a risky idea to ride your bike down an icy road when your dad has explicitly told you not to.) Meaty brown scabs goop under the bandages. I want to lift them and peek; I wonder how far I can see inside me, if I can glimpse the whiteness of bone, shining back at me like fish scales. Calla—littler, wiser—slaps my hand away with a gentle swipe. *"Don't."*

"It's not gross!"

"It is!"

"It isn't!"

"You have to *heal*, Sydney." Her face is so tiny and so earnest and—

Pinpricks rise along the back of my neck. Tiny pockets of light are bursting in the corners of my eyes. I'm realizing something. I've been telling myself for years that I'm busy—I'm just so busy with work, with foreign operations and foreign spies—and that's true. I am busy. But I also *made* myself busy. I'm in charge of that. The CIA didn't say, "Join us or else." Every time my sister called, *I* was responsible for not picking up the phone.

The CIA wasn't an escape hatch from my family.

I told myself that, too.

But . . . wasn't it? A little? Didn't it sometimes feel good to protect myself, not just from the world, but from *them*? From all the memories in this house? From the idea that maybe, *maybe*, I couldn't fully trust anyone—even the people I love? And it all just . . . built up. All those years protecting Calla, all those years keeping her close, and I . . . never really dealt with any of my grief.

Just like Dad didn't deal with any of his.

Maybe he was scared to be close to us. Maybe that really was true. Maybe he buried his wife and looked at his girls and said *I'm going to be strong for you* until he couldn't, until he didn't know how. He held it in. I held it in. He fled. I fled.

How could I have hurt Calla like that? How could I have been that kind of sister?

What the fuck have I done?

Johnny stamps through the laundry room next. No bags. No suitcases. They left them in the Escalade. Which means that he parked while Calla rushed out. Did they have a fight? *About what?*

I stand there motionless, like a reindeer in the headlights, thoughts stampeding through my head. *My dad and I, we're the same. We're the same. My god, we're the same.* And I abandoned her again. Calla. Abandoned her by not telling her, not reading her in. Dad should've chosen us. And I sure as hell should've chosen my sister.

"Calla, you can't just walk off like that if—" Johnny notices my presence with an abrupt halt, his nostrils flaring, and I give him a choppy wave. He swallows. "Hi, Sydney."

I can barely speak. Barely breathe. The person who needs the truth the most—who *deserves* the truth the most—doesn't have it. "Hey, Johnny."

"Would you mind giving us some privacy for a second?" he asks me, not particularly rude, just presumptuous to kick me out of the kitchen, my kitchen, that *he's* entered. Both of his hands are perched on his hips, and—

I haven't told Calla about Johnny.

You haven't told your sister, Sydney.

I approached this holiday as a case officer. As a spy. I haven't approached it as a *sister.* Suddenly, I can't feel my face. I start to close the bag of coffee with measured breaths, choking on my words.

Calla doesn't have that issue. Her words are right there. Spewing. "This is *her* kitchen, Johnny. Do you understand that? This is our house. You don't own everything!"

"Baby, you're just stressed," Johnny says, running a hand over his forehead, and *ugh*—the *baby*. The condescension. The *just*. "You need to relax. Why don't you go take a nap or something? You could—you could get your nails done."

This time, I do not rein in my glare. My head fully whips, pupils hard and completely readable.

"Don't look at him that way, Sydney," Calla snaps, reopening the fridge, grabbing the apple cider jug again and clutching it like a newborn. "I'm going upstairs." She delivers the last line with a thinly veiled tremor, flitting away.

Then it's just me and Johnny. I smile at him in a completely straight line.

He pops his tongue into the side of his cheek. "Do you know what that was about?"

"No," I tell him, adding with my eyes, *but I bet* you *do.*

Every year, in the days before Christmas, when the snow has formed an icy crust on the ground, nearly half of our town gathers at the frozen-over lake near Al's Lobster Shack for an afternoon of skating. Hockey practice has just ended, players swapping out their sticks for paper plates at the cookie table, and my throat has never been tighter. We're supposed to meet Grandma Ruby here, but I'm stuck in a thought loop. *You haven't told Calla. You haven't told your sister. You're a bad sister. You're the worst sister. The mission is about your sister, but you've put the mission in front of your sister! You chose the CIA. You chose the FBI. You did not choose her, just as your dad didn't choose her.*

And I'm struggling, grappling with it, can't quite believe that I did that. *I* did that. Me. Following in Dad's footsteps when I was sure—I was *positive*—that I was walking my own path.

After Johnny went to retrieve their suitcases, I took the stairs two at a time and knocked on Calla's door. "Calla Lilly? It's Sydney. Can you open up, please?"

She didn't answer. Another knock, no answer. I tried wiggling the handle. Locked. Was she ignoring me? Or taking a nap with her headphones on? When I texted her, the notification never changed from *Delivered* to *Read*. Okay. That was fine. Totally okay. I should speak to her alone, anyway. Without Johnny skulking nearby. Without Gail listening through the walls. *Gail.* Gail and her wig and her crab puffs. She's going to go ballistic if I tell Calla. *When I tell Calla?*

Now I'm just standing here by the ice. I can't seem to move. Nick gives me a head tilt from one of the benches near the parking lot, where he's sliding on a pair of skates, and my heart clenches. Those moments with him at the Ocean Harbor Inn roll through my mind—the press of his body, the way his fingers interlaced with mine the moment before I fell asleep—and I feel unbalanced. Off-kilter. My trust issues . . . those were always about my dad. They were never about Calla.

She never deserved that from me.

She deserved a better sister.

Can I repair this? Is it too late?

Tying the laces on my old hockey skates, I step onto the ice, gliding over to Calla at the south side of the lake. She's showing off her engagement ring to one of our neighbors with approximately 30 percent less enthusiasm than she showed me. When I catch her eye, I give her a head bob, gesturing toward the middle of the rink. *Skate? Please? Oh god, please?* She gives me a strangely suspicious glance, then shoves on her mitten again, gracefully exiting the conversation and meeting me on the ice, the toes of our skates nearly clashing. There are at least thirty other people skating with us, some slow and stumbling, some whipping by. We slide toward the other side of the lake, away from Johnny. Johnny, at the cookie table. Munching.

"I tried to talk to you earlier," I begin. I can't break the news here, in this public space—but I can lay the foundation. Start to make amends for everything, for the things I can't believe I've done.

For some reason, Calla laughs. It's dry. "That's a first." Her words crackle between us. This is more than a reaction to Johnny, isn't it? More than whatever happened in the car. "Is it something I said, Sydney? Like, I've been racking my brain for three years, trying to figure out why we don't talk like we used to. You text me like you're booking an appointment with your dentist. Like it's just a formality you have to go through every six months, and it might be a little painful."

Air leaves my chest. She could've kicked me in the shin with her ice skate, and it probably would've hurt about the same. "I am genuinely so sorry that I—"

"I already know what you're about to tell me," Calla hedges, stoniness in her voice.

"You do?" Somehow, I doubt that. I really, really need to doubt that. The alternative is that she actually knows who her fiancé is.

"Yes." She halts, spinning to face me, blades clamping against the ice. Her facial muscles tense. "You don't like Johnny."

Well, she did get that right. My neck twinges as I breathe out, cold air snapping at my eyelashes. Honesty. The beginning. Here it goes. "I don't."

Calla rears her head back. "I'm actually kind of shocked that you didn't fight me on that, or try to deny it, or . . . even look *sorry* about it." Hurt barrels its way across her features. "I just don't think it's fair that you can waltz back into my life and judge *my* fiancé, because of what? Because he likes karaoke? Because he wore your bathrobe?"

"You don't think it's *anything* deeper than that?" I push, untangling my wool scarf at my throat, which feels like it's trying to strangle me.

Calla picks up speed, skates slashing the ice. "Here's what I think. I think that, three months ago, I met someone very possibly great—"

Very possibly?

"And he might know me even better than you do. The me *now*, and—hold on, let me finish!"

"I didn't say anything!" I cry, tension rising between us.

"But you were going to!" Calla says, exasperated. We've sped straight to the far side of the lake, lined with ice-crusted trees. When she cuts a stop at the shore, I almost slam into her. "Look. I love you. That's what you don't seem to get. I *love* you. I would do anything for you, and this—this is not an equitable relationship. It isn't. I feel like I keep giving and reaching out, and you're taking the rope and swinging it back into my face."

In my stomach, eels slither. The snow piled on my collar has started to melt in a cold trickle down my back. "I'm sorry that I *ever* made you feel like—"

Calla doesn't seem to want to hear it. "I know that Nick is attractive. I get it. I have eyes. But we've barely spent any time together this Christmas, and I was trying to pretend like it's a mutual thing—like oh, ha-ha, Sydney's just surprised us all but I have my own life, I don't really need her—but I *do* need you, Sydney. I've always needed you. Even if it's just the little things, like reminding me to check my tire pressure. You used to do that stuff, all the sisterly stuff that showed you had my back where I fell short, but you haven't been there for years. Know who has? Johnny."

"Calla," I breathe out, almost no air in my chest. I didn't think . . . I didn't think she really noticed those little things. But of course she did, and I . . . I've broken us. I've broken us in the same way that Dad broke us, haven't I?

"Last night was my bachelorette party," Calla says, voice starting to crack. "You're my maid of honor. You spent half the night talking to Vinny. To *Vinny*!" She's getting a little louder, but we're far out of earshot. Yards and yards away from Johnny. Whenever another skater passes us, it's with a fast, here-then-gone swoosh.

I swallow, steeling myself. "There was a reason for that."

To this, Calla says nothing.

I go on. "There's also a reason that I'm here for Christmas. It's—it's different from what I told you before."

"Well, you haven't really told me anything, so—"

"I was trying to protect you."

"From what?" she scoffs, folding her arms. "You treat me like I'm this precious, breakable thing, but you know what? It's *hard* to be a kindergarten teacher. It's hard to think about what kind of world my kids are going to grow up in, and it's seriously hard to realize that—sometimes—there is nothing I can do to protect them. Every day, I walk into that classroom, and I fight for them. And no one gives me enough credit. I'm not going to shatter, Sydney. If that was going to happen, I would've broken a long time ago. Like, when I saw everyone else with their moms, and we didn't have one. Or when Dad did what he did. I may need you, but I don't need you to *protect* me. See the difference?"

This wallops me. Because suddenly I do. There's ferocity in her eyes, literal blades beneath her feet. Maybe I have . . . not been giving Calla enough credit? In this way, in others.

I straighten, pulse thundering in my ears. "When I say what I'm about to say, you need to not react visibly."

Calla crosses her arms even tighter. "Okay, now you have to just say it. Say it right now."

"You have to promise."

"Sydney!"

"Okay." I let go of a sharp breath and spit it out. "Your fiancé is a crime lord."

It doesn't register. It must not register. She squints one eye at me. "I'm sorry?"

I gather my breath again. "Your fiancé is a crime lord."

"What?"

"Johnny, your fiancé, is a—"

"Stop saying the same thing over and over again!" she bursts out, far too loud. A skater a few yards away slows down to peer at us. "I understand the words that are coming out of your mouth. That's not the problem. I just don't . . . Is this some sort of elaborate wedding prank that I don't understand?"

A sour taste invades the back of my throat. "No. It's the truth. The Jones family owns more than a chain of coffeehouses. They're criminals. They've orchestrated a string of heists all over the country, and in Canada, and they're planning another one, a much bigger one, on Christmas Day, right when you're—"

"No," Calla says, adamantly shaking her head. She doesn't know. *She doesn't know, does she?* Her face is an open book, and for once, I'm fully trusting *myself*. My gut, my instinct about someone I love. I'm embarrassed—horrified—by how much relief fills my chest. "No, this is . . . That's impossible."

"I said the same thing when I found out."

"And how did you 'find out'?" she asks, liberally using air quotes, her mittens hooking in the air.

Another deep breath. Another truth. "I'm in the CIA."

Calla laughs humorously. "No you're not."

"Cal. I am."

"*Syd*," she says. "You're *not*. You're an educational researcher. I've read your papers. I've driven past your office. With the big sign! Off the highway! You're . . ." She examines me, different strains of alarm coasting across her face. "You didn't hit your head or something, did you? When Nick fell on that black ice? I thought you said you were—"

"I didn't hit my head. Calla, think about it." On instinct, my gloved hands wrap around her shoulders, and I look at her straight in the eye. "I'm gone all the time. You know almost nothing about my life for the past three years. I live in Washington, DC. I work for the government. I can take down a two-hundred-and-fifty-pound man without blinking."

"Because you took a self-defense workshop," she deadpans.

"Because *I'm in the CIA*."

A rogue snowflake splats against Calla's cheek. "This feels very much like when Edward Cullen was trying to convince Bella Swan that he's a vampire. I don't like it." She's deflecting. Anyone can tell. Calla's tells have always been obvious. Her face goes practically immobile, expressionless.

I drop my hands, inhaling hard through my nose. "Nothing about Johnny is suspicious? *Nothing*, Calla? There isn't anything you've seen in the past three months that's made you wonder? Even just a little bit? Surveillance caught you near one of the heists, in Buffalo, so if there's *anything* that doesn't seem right to you . . ."

Her pupils flick back and forth across my face. She's so stiff, she's almost vibrating. After a strained thirty seconds, where everything around us almost stands still, she breathes out an "Oh my god."

"Calla."

"Oh my *god*."

"Just . . . please keep your voice down. I know it's hard, but you can't react here."

When she speaks again, her voice is so tense, it's like a squeezed fist. "If this *is* true, which I'm not saying that it is . . . I'm getting married in forty-six hours. I'm supposed to get married in *forty-six hours*, and you had this alleged information, and you didn't tell me? You *kept* it from me?"

Another ice-skate stab, this time to my heart. "Yes."

"Who *are* you, Sydney?"

I'm bleeding. Bleeding out. "You know who I am. At the core. You know me."

"I know who you *were*," she spits. "I know the Sydney who dressed up like a pelican for Halloween when I was nine, and I even know the Sydney who snuck Twizzlers into the movies with me in college, but this Sydney?" She looks me up and down, like she's trying to determine if she'd save me from a fire. Answer pending. "I'm not sure that I do know her."

I gulp down a croak. Because this is not about me. No matter what I'm feeling, it's about Calla. "You will not have to marry this man. We will get you out of this. If you want to get on a flight tonight, I will take you myself. Fly with you. We can place you in a safe house if—"

"Will you *listen* to yourself?" Calla hisses, hardly containing her volume. "I'm not going to a bunker somewhere in Florida. Or Idaho. Or, like, Alaska or something. That is . . . that is not happening. This is not happening. I'm not even sure what you're *saying* anymore."

"Alaska is not as bad as you think," I venture, knowing it sounds pathetic.

"Sydney!"

"Or Idaho."

Calla's hand flies to her temple, massaging it. "I need to leave."

"Good. I'll come with you."

"You're not understanding what I'm saying," Calla says, redness rising to her face. She's already backing away on her skates. "I need some time to . . . Because Johnny isn't . . ."

My panic level rises as I follow her, closer and closer to the crowd. "Calla, whatever you do, you *cannot* ask him about this. Okay? We'll figure this out together, but—"

"Sydney, please just let me be for one goddamn second, okay? I need . . . I need a Christmas cookie or something. My sugar levels are dropping."

I swallow hard. "Yeah, okay."

With those words, she leaves me in the dead center of the ice. Turns out, it's a little longer than a second. After a quick glance over her shoulder, she sprints away from the cookie table, mashing the snow with her skates. I hightail it after her, but when I see her again, it's from a distance; she's alone in the Escalade, peeling out of the parking lot at least sixty-seven miles an hour. Dread gutters in the pit of my stomach.

Good lord, what have I done?

16

What have you done?" is Gail's first question.

I'm speeding back home in the Prius, hoping to find Calla there. The phone's cradled between my shoulder and my ear, and a spike of anxiety has settled somewhere in the region of my entire body. "Wish you'd called me last night. Or this morning. Or any other time, Gail. This isn't really a good time."

"Oh, when would be a better time for you, then, going forward? When should I pencil you in for a nice chitchat?" The other end of the line crackles. It sounds like Gail is in traffic somewhere, the hum rushing by. "Because I think we should probably talk about what just happened at the ice-skating rink. What did you say to Calla?"

I make a tight left onto Main Street, heart palpitating. "Is it customary for the FBI to tail their own agents?"

"I wouldn't call it a tail."

"Do anything interesting lately, then? Go on any boats?"

"You can say what you want about the party, but I was in the area—and our last conversation had left me feeling unsettled."

"You just happened to be in rural, seaside Maine."

"Exactly."

"Just like you happened to be on vacation in Finland," I snort out, carving a right into my neighborhood.

"Well, that was true." She blares her horn at someone, the sound ringing in my ear. "And it's not a crime to worry about the people under my command. You were acting more roguishly than I would've liked, so I came to see how you were getting on, yes. How *are* you getting on, Sydney?"

In response, I skid mildly on a patch of black ice, nearly taking out a mailbox wreath, and then I'm home. Back home. The Escalade isn't parked in the driveway. No tire marks. Only fresh snow. *Where the hell is Calla?* She could've texted Johnny by now. Could've called him. Or potentially, worse, she's leaving him two days before the wedding, when I've yet to gather enough ironclad evidence against him, which means that Johnny can track her uninhibitedly. Outside of prison. Hunt her down. I think I might . . . Yep, a dry heave racks my belly. I retch.

"Did you tell your sister?" Gail asks.

Retch.

"Sydney, did you tell your *sister*?"

Double retch.

"That was not the protocol!" Gail warns on the other end. "That was *expressly* against everything I told you. I have worked too hard and too long for everything to go up in flames like this. If she tips off Johnny, it's all over. *Do you understand me?* Hundreds of thousands of dollars in taxpayer money. You might as well have thrown all that cash in an incinerator. Years and years of work, gone. Not to mention the residual effects, the pain you're inevitably causing to *every further person* who Johnny's thugs hold up at gunpoint. I was calling to tell you that your intel paid off. We rooted out the mole, Vinny's FBI contact, and he's given us everything: They're planning on attacking an armored vehicle carrying over seven million dollars' worth of untraceable bills, much like the Loomis Fargo Heist of 1997."

That comes out of nowhere. "And you . . . believe this guy?" I breathe.

"It all fits," Gail says with a clipped edge. "The gift shop Johnny called, it's within a mile of the armored vehicle's path, and the vehicle will be cruising by at ten a.m. on Christmas Day. We haven't been able to locate the getaway car—the van Johnny spoke about—but clearly that's where they'll load all the cash. We've informed the bank and will stock phony bills in the armored vehicle; the drivers will be federal agents. But . . . Jesus *Christ*, Sydney. If Calla tips them off, then I wouldn't be surprised if the Joneses pull back on the whole endeavor. We'll lose them. We will *lose* them, and—"

"What about the C4?" I interject, shaky. This doesn't . . . this doesn't fully fit. "Where would they use that?"

"Pisgah River Bridge, on the north side of the gift shop. That's what we're thinking. There's a police station right by the bridge, so law enforcement wouldn't be able to access the site of the crime. Not immediately. Harder to give chase."

"But fifty pounds of C4? That could blow up twelve bridges."

There's a quick pause as Gail regroups, and I fish out a napkin from one of the cup holders, wiping the sweat from my forehead. "Sydney, just . . . did Calla give any indication of what she might do next?"

"She said . . ." Close to hyperventilation, I take an unsteady sip from a day-old can of cold brew. "She said she was going to try and prove me wrong."

"Well, that's perfect. That is just perfect. Obviously, she's still going to be loyal to Johnny. You don't get engaged to someone and drop your feelings for them two minutes and a Christmas cookie later. Honestly, Sydney, how did you see that playing out in your mind?"

"Better," I choke out, backing up the Prius again. Where might Calla have gone, if not our house? Where did she use to run off to when we were kids? "Gail, have you tracked the Escalade yet? Flagged any outgoing calls from Calla's cell phone?"

"I will," Gail says, stern, like a tough mother. "But you're off the case, Sydney."

Unsurprising. This is unsurprising. My throat constricts anyway. I still have this horrible, nagging feeling that we're missing something. "Gail, *please*, don't—"

"In a way, this is all my fault. I never should've placed you in a situation where your judgment was going to be tainted. This was almost inevitable. It was too much."

Another dry heave threatens to build as I tear out of my neighborhood again. "I promise, once I find Calla—"

"Once you find her, what? Hmm? What happens then? Turn around, pack up your things, I'll email you a plane ticket back to DC. Domestic flight. Keep up the charade. I know it's two days before Christmas, but I'm sure there's something available in coach if we—"

"You think I'm just going to leave her?" I spit out. "Just shoot that information at her and peace out *two days* before Christmas, right before she gets implicated in the Joneses' worst attack yet?"

Gail seems to consider this heavily. "I think, Sydney, that if you truly cared about your sister as much as you say you do, you would probably have known she was getting married in the first place."

Speechless, I jam on my brakes at the stoplight.

"Plane ticket," Gail repeats. "Promise me you'll get on the flight before you do any more damage."

Head shaking. "No."

"Sydney."

"I'm staying. You can kick me off the mission, but you can't kick me out of my family."

I almost hear Gail purse her lips, deliberating. Wondering if she should argue with that logic. "Well, it's your holiday," she grunts out, making the last word sound like *funeral*.

I call Calla's cell phone. It goes directly to voice mail. Eight times in a row. On the final call, I leave a message, circling around the parking lot of the saltwater taffy store where Calla and I used to buy candy after school; we both had a big sweet tooth. "Cal?" my voice croaks over the line. "It's me. Sydney. Obviously... I know I just dropped a lot on you. The most on you. Ever. But *please* call me back as soon as you can and let me know where you are. I can come get you, and you don't have to speak to me. You don't have to speak to me ever again if you don't want to, even though that would kill me, but I just need to know that you're safe, and you're going to be all right..."

I disconnect the call, shout "*Fuck!*" and slam my hands against the steering wheel. A trio of holiday shoppers, traipsing out of the saltwater taffy store, give me the eye. Deservedly. At this point, I'm twelve taffies short of a box, and I'm running out of places in town to check for Calla's rental car. Could be that she's left Cape Hathaway entirely. When I tried the "Find My Friends" phone option, I discovered that she'd disabled that function. Because of me? Because of Johnny? Did she go back to Boston? Leave the state?

What's going through your mind, Calla?

Besides the one hundred obvious things, like, *My sister Sydney is a traitor. The worst of the worst. Just like Dad.* How could I have been just like Dad?

The Prius accelerates once I hit the road by the beach, waves rising, almost crashing against the sidewalk. All the motel owners have decorated their roofs with strings of lights, half-battered by the storm, still glinting under sliding heaps of snow, and I wonder if Calla's checked herself in somewhere. My neck cranes, glancing into all the driveways, looking for the shadowy vehicle tucked into one of the bays. Nothing. No car at the grocery store, either. No car at the gas station or the lobster pound or the nail salon or the lobster-pound-nail-salon. I haven't even begun to process what this means for my career. My career is insignificant.

By now, my CIA handler will know.

His boss will know.

His boss's boss will know.

And I'm thinking about that Swedish night train, less than a week ago, how I looked at myself in the mirror and wondered if I was happy. Happy people rarely ask themselves if they're happy. If I'm honest—truly, truly honest with *myself*—I think this career is killing me. I think I wanted to hide, wanted to protect myself in all the secrecy, but my god, is *this* how I pictured my life? Speeding down a side road two days before Christmas, searching for my AWOL sister, while I'm personally trying to put her fiancé behind bars?

And before that. Even before that. The all-night sessions poring over the computer, kicking myself, telling myself that if I miss *a single shred of intelligence*, people will die. And it will be my fault. *Your fault, Sydney.* All the meeting assets in shitty bars, coming home alone to an empty apartment, spending weekends in solitude if I get a weekend at all. What would it have been like? To come home this Christmas for *me*. To buy seven different types of goat cheese at the grocery store and watch *Die Hard*—at least twice—with my sister. For the last two years, I've been fantasizing about it. Leaving the CIA. Undoing my choice. Rolling off an assignment and just . . .

Just what?

When I pictured the future before this holiday, it was suspiciously blank. Now little glimpses of it are forming. Tiny fragments. I could adopt a dog. Walk my dog. Call my sister on the phone. Maybe call Nick on the phone. Be available. Visit my family, who I've missed . . . and *shit*, now I'm crying. My throat clogs up, hot tears streaming down the sides of my cheeks as I wrench up the phone again, swerving into a space in the lighthouse parking lot. The South Harbor Light glows in the background, a beacon, a warning, green Christmas garland wrapped all around it.

Dad used to take me here to watch the boats come in, come back home.

I dial Calla's number one last time.

"Hey," I say after her automated voice. My teeth are almost chattering. "Me again. I should have said . . . I should have said a lot of things, and done almost everything differently, but I need you to know that I'm sorry. I am so, *so* sorry, Calla. I thought I wasn't like Dad at all, and I can't believe that I didn't really see that, because it was right in front of me . . . Just like you were right in front of me, and I put my own grief first. You deserved more of me." Here, my voice cracks, a split right down my throat. "From here on out, I promise to be completely honest with you. No secrets. I'll tell you everything. Okay? That's it. I know your voice mail is probably going to fill up, so I won't leave you a million messages, but I just . . . I just need you to know how much I love you, Calla Lilly. That will never, ever—"

Another spike of pain in my throat.

"Change," I finish, dropping the phone.

By the time I return home, it's dark, just after 4 p.m., the sky a purple bruise. No one has plugged in the window reindeer, so there's no slightly risqué jig to greet me. Even the reindeer doesn't feel like dancing. One of the strings of Christmas lights has fallen, dangling off the roof like a villain at the end of the movie. Once again, the Escalade isn't in the driveway. Inside, it's even quieter. No Christmas music. No Squirrel Nut Zippers holiday album blaring from the record player.

Where's Grandma Ruby? Nick?

Johnny answers my unspoken questions. He's perched on the kitchen countertop, by the fridge, his legs swinging down. "They went to pick up some lobster," he says, and I half jump out of my skin. Only the kitchen island lights are on, the rest of the house plunged into darkness. *Has he been waiting for me?* That's my first thought. Johnny has been waiting for me to come home. That's why he's hung back.

In the laundry room, I slowly unzip my parka, clunking the snow off my boots—then tiptoe forward, closer. "And Sweetie Pie?"

"Went along for the ride," Johnny says, his voice totally light. So airy and smooth. "Thought I'd stay here and see if you came back with Calla . . . but it looks like she isn't with you?"

Breathe, Sydney. Breathe normally. "No, she actually said something about going to the spa. Before the wedding. To unwind. Get a massage."

"The spa," Johnny says, unblinking, neutral. *Why is he sitting on the countertop?* He looks like a twelve-year-old boy playing at being a crime lord.

"I was encouraging her," I roll on, hanging my parka over the breakfast table chair. Wetness drips to the tile floor, and I un-puddle it with my sock, a quick swipe of my foot. Casual. "There's a really good one just over the state line. Wentworth by the Sea? Facials, manicures, everything bridal. You said she should get her nails done."

"And you didn't go with her?"

Keep lying. Dig in. "I'm not really a manicure type of person."

Johnny curls his fingertips over the edge of the countertop, gripping. "Any idea when she'll be back? Because I've been calling her. She isn't answering her phone."

"They make you turn your phone off. Phones aren't relaxing." Speaking of not relaxing, the vibe between us has immeasurably soured. Some might call it downright menacing. In fact, if I wasn't a trained CIA officer—just a sister, home for Christmas—I would be heart-poundingly afraid of him. A darkness has cascaded over his face, pupils blacking out his eyes. The smart thing would be to make another excuse and shuffle right out of the house. Wait for my grandma in the driveway. Tell her to *run*. But my wheels are turning. Nick said he's bugged my room. If I can get Johnny to threaten me on tape, if I can get him to admit that he's threatened people, like FBI officers, for his "business" before . . .

Split-second decision.

I take off in the direction of the stairs. A full-out, suspicious sprint.

"What the—?" I hear Johnny mutter as he slides down from the countertop, bootsteps pounding after me. My hand barely trails over the garland-wrapped banister, flecks of blood-red glitter rubbing off on my fingertips, my other arm pumping. "Sydney!"

To my room. My old bedroom. Closed-off space. Let him corner me. Let him think I'm powerless. Whipping inside, nearly slipping on the hallway rug, I jam the door shut, pretending to fiddle with the handle, as if *it won't lock, dammit!* Right on schedule, Johnny's shoulder slams against the door, thrusting it open, and I stagger back. Baiting him. Breathing hard.

"I don't think we were finished with that conversation," Johnny grunts, chest close to heaving. "Do you?" One hand behind him, he clicks the door shut, locks it. *So that's how you lock a door! Takes a man to do it.* "I just think it's really funny how, moments after I see you and Calla having an argument where I'm reading your lips and see the word *Johnny*, she just . . . disappears!" He laughs dryly at this, advancing, his fingers running over the back of one of my ceramic dog figurines; he picks up the Doberman with the broken paw, examining it, as if he's about to smash it against the dresser.

"I told you," I say, backing up even farther, until my spine is flat against the bookshelves. A miniature elf rests somewhere near my ear, one of his eyes replaced with the tiniest recording device, and it doesn't take much acting to sound nervous. I am. Not nervous that he'll hurt me. If he tries anything, I think that'll turn out very badly for him. But I'm trying to lead us down *exactly* the right conversational path. "She's a little stressed about the wedding, and as her maid of honor, I thought—"

Another laugh from Johnny. "You thought it'd be better if she spent some time away from me, is that it? Haven't exactly warmed to me, have you, Sydney?" Harmlessly, he sets the Doberman back on the dresser, other paws intact—but he still takes another few steps closer to me, the muted sound of his boots stamping across the hardwood. "I thought we had an understanding, you and I."

"An understanding?" That actually confuses me.

"First night. Over drinks," Johnny clarifies. "When Calla was telling the story of how we met. Funky Pete's. Throwing clay. And you—" He wags his finger at me. "You didn't say it was a good story. You just . . . sat there. I'm a very perceptive person. I thought, if she stays out of my way, I'll stay out of hers. Even got Nick to keep an eye on you to make sure you didn't fuck this up."

I stop the gulp in my throat. It's painful. It burns. "You told Nick to watch me?"

Johnny smirks, and it is not the smirk of a man who sings Mariah Carey Christmas karaoke, or a man who gleefully admits how much he loves mashed potatoes. He flips like a switch. Or, I guess, like a switchblade. "Why do you think he's been following you around like a sentimental asshole? That's not Nick."

I bite out words. "Are you sure?"

"You've known him for how long? Three days?"

Johnny's enjoying this, toying with me. As I wanted him to. But I didn't think we'd go in this direction. I didn't think we'd be here. *Nick. Sentimental asshole. Following me around.* Maybe my grandmother didn't tell Nick to keep an eye on me, like he said that first night; maybe it was always Johnny. That doesn't really matter, though. We're past that.

"Doesn't matter," I say, underlining the words in my head.

A sharp little laugh from Johnny. "Doesn't it? Because that's Nick to a *T.* Picks out some girl at a bar, tells her she's special, tells her *he's* special." A tendon ticks in his jaw, like he's about to reach out and bite me. Go in for the kill. "Did Nick feed you that line about CSIS?"

Panic wooshes past my ears. Suddenly, the ocean's in there. Humming. Crashing against me. *What* did he just say?

Johnny licks the corner of his mouth with the tip of his tongue. "Yeah, it always works. 'I'll protect you like I protect my country.' All that bullshit. Takes out his badge and women lap it up."

What the . . . What in the . . . ?

I shake my head, not processing, swimming, drowning—but still gripping on to my cover. "Wait, I don't . . . what's CSIS?"

Johnny gives me a slapable smirk. "Oh, so Nick *didn't* use that line on you? That's too bad. Guess he only pulls that one out when he wants to close the deal. Maybe you were easy."

Scorching heat travels through my belly, a sloshing feeling invades my brain, and I . . . I don't . . . I don't want to believe it, but . . .

Oh fuck. Oh fuck, fuck, fuck.

Betrayal feels like this. It feels like being sixteen years old and waiting in a driveway; it feels like standing alone but barely standing. At The Farm, you learn how to crash through a barrier at one hundred miles an hour, vehicle smashing through concrete. You pick the weakest spot. You pick the middle, the heart, the point where the concrete bows, the space that's already cracked. And you drive *right* there, strike there. That's what Nick's done, hasn't he?

He has, hasn't he.

Because there are only two possibilities here. Either Nick isn't affiliated with the Canadian Secret Intelligence Service—and, *oh god*, never has been—or he's Johnny's man on the inside. That's a double cross, no matter how you spin it. And I . . . how could I have been so *fucking* stupid? My mouth dries as I think about all the questions I never asked. All the assumptions I made. Things like . . . Nick's badge. Christ, the *badge*. Why the fuck would he carry that on an undercover mission? How was that even remotely believable? And he . . . he said he took the GPS tracker off Johnny's car. I thought that was to protect me, to avoid suspicion, but what if it was to avoid *tracking*? He literally got himself stabbed for the man! And the wire. Nick didn't want me to wear a wire to the bachelorette party. Of course he didn't. *Of course* he didn't!

Gail's words come back and pierce my skin: *Don't fall for the target.* The target could lie to you. The target could manipulate you. The target could fuck you against a dresser, and say, *You're not unknowable, Sydney*, and you would be *so* far gone, so—

Johnny sniffs. "Nick is more loyal to me than anyone. If I asked him to shoot someone in the middle of the street, he would."

"You do that often?" I manage to grit out, jaw clamping. I feel like if I clench myself together enough, I won't completely fall apart—but *I'm* the concrete barrier. I'm the concrete. And Nick has found my weakest spot.

I told him. I told him about my dad. I told him about everything, and I let him in.

At my words, Johnny quirks his head to the side, moonlight streaming through my window blinds. A shard of it slashes over his five o'clock shadow, the whitish-blond bristles along the edge of his face. Coming one last step closer to me, he pauses, raising a hand above my head and placing it on the bookshelf. It's a stomach-churning movement. A power pose. I stand my ground as he breathes into my face. Cinnamon chewing gum lolls around his mouth. "Now why would you ask a thing like that?"

My response is immediate, cold, even though I'm thinking *Nick, Nick, Sidekick Nick.* Everything he told me. Everything. All the lies. "Why would you *say* a thing like that?"

Johnny's eyes flit over my face, probably deliberating. "You should know," he says, acid in his voice. "This is a mutually as-sured destruction type deal. You take me out of the picture, and I take you down harder. I grind you into the floor."

It's so quiet, you could hear a snowflake drop between us, but just then, bells jingle downstairs—Grandma Ruby traipsing in-side. Nick, chuckling.

God. Nick. The sound of his voice is a sledgehammer.

"Sydney?" my grandma calls up the stairs, her tone merry and bright. "You here? Come help us unpack! We bought more char-cuterie!"

Johnny drops his hand with a gruff, humorless laugh. "That's your cue, Sydney Bean. Let me know if your sister calls, yeah?"

17

I unpack the sausages. I unpack the cheese. I unpack the tiny special grapes and the hard little apples, and all the while my blood is coursing, raging, and I . . . I let myself be vulnerable with a new person. I didn't dole out tiny, calculated pieces of myself; I gave Nick the whole me, the hard parts, the messy, soft under-layer. The first person I've done that with in a long, long time. Almost a decade. He crashed through the barrier with his sweet talk and his stupid fucking honesty game, and I'm picturing him, dark-haired, lusty-eyed, capturing my bottom lip with his teeth, and—

Lies.

Liar.

I don't know Nick. I never knew him. And I don't know what he's planning now.

A cold trickle of fear snakes into my abdomen. If I'm completely uncovered, if I've been burned, what are the chances that Nick will let me get away? Is he just biding his time, waiting for the successful completion of the next attack before he disposes of me? Those moments at the Moose Lodge, maybe he *was* deciding what to do with me: get me on board with him, or get me *completely* off board. Overboard. Duct tape. Into the sea. If Nick is capable of *this*, what else will he try?

I clack my tongue, tasting fury, tasting shame—and unpack all the groceries in a smooth, efficient manner. I barely manage to keep up appearances—but do convince my grandmother that Calla has actually gone to the spa. Grandma Ruby looks almost relieved. "Good," she says, popping one of the unwashed grapes into her mouth. "That girl deserves a break. She works so hard."

Nick's there, too, burning a hole into my side, loading crackers into the pantry. So nonchalantly. Offering me a smile whenever he catches my glance, but I can't force myself to return it. *How dare he. How dare you.* Every time I look at him, I'm back at the inn, his fingertips trailing down my skin, his breath in the crook of my neck, and then my mind snaps to Johnny—to the information he's so graciously shared.

I fell for it. Fell for Nick. I was seduced. *Exactly* like Nick said he was planning.

Charcuterie safely in the fridge, I announce that I'm going to nap before I pass out. My voice doesn't quiver; it's as hard as concrete. I'm good. I'm acting. We're back to this. Still, a line forms on Nick's forehead, and he follows me into the hallway, catching my arm, his voice lowering to a whisper. "Hey, did something else happen?"

I wiggle my arm away, as unsuspiciously but firmly as I can. His touch is light but still wounds my skin; I feel like I'm going to bruise. "No, I'm fine."

"That's not what your face is saying."

My tongue runs along my teeth, a searing pain rushing over the bridge of my nose. "What are my tells, then?"

Slowly, Nick raises a finger and traces the divot in my left cheek. "One of them is right there."

Don't touch me ever again, I think. *Don't you fucking dare.* "Well, thank you for sharing that. Have a good night."

"Wait, Sydney—"

"I'm just *really* tired, okay?" It's all I can do not to break cover again. Break down. Tell him what Johnny said. Tell him that I know, and that he's scum; if I never saw him again, it would be too soon.

Nick takes a step back, like he's been stung. Not like *he's* the wasp. "Yeah, okay. I hope you . . . get a lot of rest, then."

"Thank you," I say again, teeth half-gritted, texting my sister as soon as I lock my bedroom door: **I've told Johnny that you're at the spa. Wentworth by the Sea. Please, please just answer me.**

Of course, I do not sleep. Falling asleep right now feels like a very dangerous idea. Unfortunately, staying awake any longer also seems like a terrible option. I twitch when, hours later, something scratches my door. *It's just Sweetie Pie.* I open up for her, and she tippity-taps past my dresser, visiting me for a nightly checkup. "You want to join me, little noodle?" I whisper, anxious, broken, patting my bedsheets. "Come on, up! *Up!*"

Sweetie Pie obliges, heaving her weight onto the mattress in a magnificent arc. With a thud, she plops herself directly onto my pillow, curling into the perfect doggie donut.

At least I have her. At least there's that.

Seems like I've lost everything and everyone else.

Around two in the morning, I fall asleep in front of my computer, and I dream about a snowball fight. A good old-fashioned snowball fight under the streetlights, Sweetie Pie rising onto her hind legs to catch the soft-packed powder. All of us humans have slipped into our winter hats and mittens, making our way into the biting cold, and I imagine myself with Nick, faux-tackling him into a snowbank. A cute peck on the tip of my cold nose. It's an old-timey montage set to the soundtrack of Nat King Cole. Somewhere in the distance, chestnuts are roasting on an open fire. But then, everything changes: I'm packing snowballs with all the seriousness of a munitions factory worker. When my arm whips forward, I let loose a primal scream. The ball tears through the air with such velocity that I know—when it hits—this will feel a *little* less like a super-friendly game. With an echoing *pop*, the ball smacks Nick in the left shoulder, exploding in a spray of snow shrapnel, and he stumbles backward a few inches, and *Calla, where's Calla, where is my sister?*

Not in her bed.

Still not in the house.

And now it's 8 a.m. on Christmas Eve.

Closing the door to the guest room, I spin around on the upstairs landing, wiping a hand down my face. Yesterday's clothes cling to my body. And I watch as a stream of strangers tramples in and out of our front door, Johnny directing them with enough hand movements to land a plane. This "small family get-together"—this little, laid-back wedding—has transformed into something that would better fit a holiday remake of *Father of the Bride*. First comes the furniture delivery. Dozens and dozens of white, seemingly hand-whittled chairs, stuffed in our living room, almost one on top of the other. All of our furniture's being shunted to the side; movers are carrying our couch up to the attic. There goes Grandma Ruby's reading chair, out to the garage. Sweetie Pie, for her part, is also staring down at the chaos from the landing, jowls quivering in disapproval.

"I know," I tell her, throat tight. "I know, girl."

She glances up at me like, *Should I stop it? Should I woof?*

I don't know what to tell her. I really don't. Grandma Ruby

doesn't, either. Apparently, all the deliveries are news to her as well. Three cakes arrive with tiers of white-frosted flowers. A team assembles to tack additional garlands to our ceiling. Literally tack them. With nails hammering, hooks hooking. A monumental wooden altar is shoved through our garage door, then stuffed between the Christmas trees in the living room. Then there's the tinsel. So much tinsel. I have never seen this much tinsel in my life. It snakes around all the surfaces, around the candles on our dining room table. By the afternoon, we are rivaling Santa's workshop—and nothing feels like ours. Even Grandma Ruby's miniature snow village is given a back seat, shoved atop the corner bookshelf.

I stare at it. At the happy ceramic families. A teeny-tiny station wagon with a Christmas tree strapped to the roof. Miniature people skating on a clear-glass lake, playing hockey with a quarter-inch puck. When Calla and I were younger, we'd spend hours imagining how these fake people lived. These perfect families, who lived in Christmas year-round. Yearlong bliss. Zero cares, zero concerns. Snow-swept cottages and frosted soda shops.

"Have you heard from your sister?" Grandma Ruby asks, sidling up to me in the hour before dinner. She wrings her wrinkled hands, rings glimmering. "I'm starting to get a little worried about her, and our guests should be here soon . . . Sydney, you'd tell me if anything was wrong, wouldn't you?"

"Wrong?" I swallow. "Wrong how?"

More hand-wringing. "I'm just getting this *feeling*. In the pit of my stomach, like I've eaten something way too spicy. Spicy, even for me." Blowing air from her lips, she composes herself and offers me a quick smile. "Never mind. Don't mind me. Maybe I'm just getting too old for this justice of the peace stuff. I keep worrying that I'll stumble over my speech."

My throat's burning, tight. "Whatever you say, I'm sure it'll be perfect."

From the side, she hugs me with a frail-but-strong arm. "I hope so. A lot's riding on tomorrow, isn't it? And tonight! Maybe I should lend you some of my jewelry, Sydney, if you don't have anything. There are some bracelets on my dresser."

Upstairs, I slide two gold bangles over my wristbones and, in the kitchen, disembowel the bell peppers and eviscerate the carrots before moving on to the cheese, grating with particular vigor. Every once in a while, Nick pauses his onion cutting and glances over at my increasingly tall cheese pile. I can't look at him. Can barely stand to be in the same room as him. I hope those onions make him weep.

"That's probably enough, dear," Grandma Ruby says, and I let up, setting the grater down with a *whack*. My phone dings, and I rip it from my pocket, praying it's Calla. It's not. It's my CIA handler, Sandeep, with Vinny's financial records for the last three months—like I requested. Most of the records, Sandeep says, check out. But there's an oddity. A purchase of a mechanic's outfit from an industrial clothing manufacturer. Maybe for when Vinny works on his Mercedes? I thought he brought it to the shop.

I'm also going to pretend, Sandeep adds, **that this conversation never happened. You know you're off this case.**

I will give you six games of Scrabble, I fire back.

Twelve, he responds. **Just don't do anything stupid.**

I thank Sandeep with a quick note, pocketing my phone again, grating more cheese, and trying to appear like I'm focused on dinner preparations. We're having Thanksgiving food. Some of us—*ahem, me*—didn't make it to Thanksgiving this year, and Calla in her infinite thoughtfulness decided it would be nice to have a do-over. Cranberry sauce wobbles in a silver bowl. Rosemary crackers snap in Nick's mouth. Melt-on-your-tongue crescent rolls are yanked, steaming, from the oven. "Wine?" Grandma Ruby asks me, extending a glass.

"Yes." That's a very firm answer. *Yes.*

Drinking on missions is usually a hard no. But I've been kicked off the mission. I've basically lost my sister. The guy I just slept with has double-crossed me. There's a sinking feeling in my stomach that we've missed something about the case, that the armored vehicle heist isn't all that's going down. And my possible future brother-in-law just threatened me next to an Elf on the Shelf.

At this point, wine might help.

I down the first glass in a few gulps, fizzy bubbling popping down my throat. Nick gives me another one of his intelligence professional glances, and hey, if he wants to be a judgmental asshole, fine. Dude doesn't even know how to properly julienne a carrot. That is very possibly not a good enough insult, so I keep it to myself. Smile politely and pretend that everything is A-OK, nothing to see here, perfectly normal holiday.

It is exceedingly normal for George "the Coffee King" Jones and his wife, "the Eagle," to ring our doorbell. Very normal to take their coats and have them kiss me on the cheek and tell me about their drive up from Boston. Super snowy. Heavy traffic. *You must be Sydney.*

"That's me!" I say, way too chipper, leading them inside.

George is like Johnny's much older twin, crossed with the Godfather, crossed with a goose. He's stately and composed, with a honking laugh that comes out immediately when he sees the shitload of tinsel. Which, to be fair, are my thoughts exactly. Anna "the Eagle" Jones is just as Calla described: a carbon copy of Miranda Priestly in *The Devil Wears Prada*, Chanel handbag swinging from her tightly clutched fist. She has radiant white hair and, for some reason, has brought her own turkey baster. Grandma Ruby, I think, is trying very hard not to find this offensive.

She leans into me as they're filtering into the living room, where I think—*oh, fuck*—Johnny is breaking out the Pictionary again. "They're quite an interesting couple, don't you think? Very ..."

"Very very," I say, wondering if there is more wine, and if I've actually just heard the garage door again. Maybe my ears are playing tricks on me, but no—*no*. There are footsteps, too. Calla? *Calla.*

It really is my sister. She's erupted into the house again, heeled boots tapping into the kitchen, and my heart lurches toward her. Almost lurches out of my body. *She's back. She's here.* And she looks ... fine. To anyone else, fine. Hair in tidy curls. Lipstick unsmudged. Immaculate sweater, Christmas plaid. From all the way across the room, though, I can sense the erratic energy pooling under her skin. Call it a sisterly instinct.

"*There* she is!" Johnny's mom yells across the room, joyous, opening her arms.

And Calla sweeps into them dutifully, like absolutely nothing is wrong. Like the last twenty-four hours never even happened. "I'm so sorry I'm late," she apologizes. "I was at the spa."

"Well, it's done wonders! You look refreshed. Like a blushing bride. Doesn't she, George?"

"Johnny's a lucky guy!" Johnny's dad says, thumping Calla on the back; the backslapping must run in the family, and ... *What is happening? What the hell is happening?* Calla isn't looking me in the eye. Absolutely refusing to. Kind of understandable, given everything I've kept from her. But if she's back, that doesn't mean ... that doesn't mean she's still *marrying* him, does it?

"Sorry," I say, pushing past the Joneses, "sorry, I just ..."

I grab Calla and pull her into the biggest hug in human history, squeezing her.

She gives me a slight hug back. Her pulse, though, is pounding off the charts—and the timer is going off in the kitchen. Time for dinner. The rehearsal dinner. Sitting down to eat. When I try to pull her aside for a second, she hisses at me in a voice only I can hear. "Not now. I'm okay. Just . . . wait."

She is not okay.

Wait for what?

All seven of us shuffle into the formal dining room, where Calla sets the table. She places out the best silverware (the glossy forks and serrated servers) alongside Grandma Ruby's ceramic plates with the baby birds, and Nick offers to help carry out the food: a massive and massively well-cooked turkey, a mountain of yeast rolls, and green bean casserole hot from the oven. Wisps of sage scent trail through the space. It smells sensational. I am the farthest thing from hungry.

"Go on, go on, take your seats," Grandma Ruby urges, plopping herself at the head of the table, and I sit in between her and Calla, my gold bracelets clinking.

Sipping champagne near the end of the table, Johnny catches my eye and winks. *Asshole.* I grit my teeth, reaching out for my fresh glass of wine, and swish it around my mouth. Nothing. Nothing is showing on his face. No hint of acknowledgment about what happened last night. What does *he* think is happening here? With Calla? Now that she's back, maybe he believes she *did* go to the spa. A pre-wedding treat. Something normal.

Out of the corner of my eye, I survey my sister. She is either the best actress I've ever met—Oscar worthy, the coolest person possible under pressure—or she has somehow, almost miraculously, managed to convince herself that everything is all right. I'm hoping the former. On the skating rink, she said she was tougher than anyone gave her credit for.

I down my glass. Pour another. Sparkling, sparkling wine.

Just eat the food, I tell myself. *Just eat the food and say nothing.*

But Calla . . . Calla was right. If she's come back, faced all this one way or another, she is tough. She *is*. And I want to give her courage. Give her *something*.

I push back my chair a little.

"What are you doing?" Calla whispers, leaning into me. Panic flits across her eyebrows. "I said no speeches."

No, you didn't.

"And . . . you're sweating," she says. "Why are you sweating?"

You know exactly why I'm sweating. "I'm not sweating."

"Sydney, it's dripping down your face."

Rolling my eyes as if we're playing a game, I dab my forehead with one of the cloth napkins and tug my turtleneck an inch lower. This is the last time I wear Swedish reindeer wool. Stuff does not breathe. "I'm just going to say a few words . . ."

"No! No, *please*. You're—"

She reaches for the sleeve of my sweater, but I'm faster. Rising unevenly, half dragged down at the elbow, I wobble to a stand and clink my wineglass with a butter knife.

"I'd like to make a toast," I say. My smile is warm, friendly.

A hush falls over the dining room until the only sound is "You're a Mean One, Mr. Grinch" thrumming from the speakers.

"Johnny," I say, raising my glass in his direction.

I start giving a speech about how lucky we are to love my sister. Throughout, Calla laughs at the right parts, covers her face at the right moments—and Nick, Nick is hanging on to my every word. I don't want to think about his hands or the hotel room or the way he's looking at me, like he knows me, like we've never been anything but honest with each other.

Bullshit.

Next to me, Calla is tilting her head in a polite way that says both *I love and hate you in equal measure*, and *Sydney, are you drunk?* But I can tell there's something beneath it, a primal fear. Fear of what I'm about to say. How I'm going to finish this little speech.

"When it comes down to it, I would do anything for my sister," I say. "Anything. I'm lucky to love her, like you're lucky to love her. So . . . raise your glasses."

Around the table, seven glasses surge into the chandelier light, and of course, I choose this moment to catch Nick's eye. Double agent Nick. He gives me this gentle nod, as if to say, *Weird speech, Syd, what was that about?* And my throat constricts.

I think I might hate him.

The best man is definitely not the best guy . . . and I don't know how this is going to end for either of us.

"Be good to each other," I add with a final, choked flourish. "Or else, Johnny, I may just have to break every bone in your body, and all that good stuff. Okay? Who wants turkey?"

Everyone. Everyone laughs obligingly, glasses clattering together, and I sink back into my chair. There's movement next to me. Calla and I, we're like a teeter-totter. As I'm going down, she's slowly rising to a stand.

"I'd like to add something," my sister says, the perfect hostess, and my first thought is *uh-oh*. She didn't even want *me* to make a speech. "I was just thinking, most of you know how Johnny and I met, but I'm not sure that all of you know how he proposed."

Eager looks spread around the table, and Nick tries to catch my eye again. Does he sense it as well? That shift in Calla. Something is just the tiniest bit *off*. With Nick, too—now that I'm looking at him fully. At the side of the table, he's discreetly pulled out his phone, reading a message with an almost horrified look on his face.

"Okay," Calla says, smoothing the side of her skirt with one hand, ironing out the tiniest wrinkles. Or maybe removing the clamminess from her palm. "So Johnny and I were out doing some Christmas shopping, even though, honestly, I'd finished ninety percent of my shopping by the Fourth of July."

Some isolated laughter kicks up at this.

"Johnny was acting all nervous," she says, "and I thought it was because he hadn't figured out what to get for me yet for Christmas—but we decided to take a quick walk through the Public Gardens. The snow was just beginning to fall. These really pretty, *perfect* snowflakes. And we stopped in the middle of a perfect bridge. Johnny got on one knee, and he said to me that people in movies always meet the love of their lives on bridges—that even though our families are really different, and we've come from two different directions, it was the honor of his life to meet me in the middle."

Johnny's mom holds her hand over her heart, tearing up, but Calla isn't done.

"Everything about it was perfect. The location. The timing. The speech. The ring." She glances down at her hand like it's disconnected from her body. Like it's someone else's entirely. Still, she smiles, raising her wineglass a little higher, her fingertips so clenched, she's nearly denting the glass. "I'd like to make a toast to Johnny. So perfect—it's unbelievable."

Her final line oozes with warmth. Johnny's parents are thrilled. Look at their son! What a man they've raised. Almost unimaginably perfect. Johnny's happy, too. His glass tilts toward his soon-to-be-blushing bride, and he takes a satisfied, bubbly sip.

But when Calla glances down at me, determination in her eyes, I know. A sister always knows.

Calla hasn't come back to marry Johnny.

She's come back to take the bastard down.

18

Throughout dinner, I bide my time, desperate for this all to be over, desperate to speak to my sister in private. Conversation is a little stilted. Grandma Ruby does the heavy lifting, chatting about the Christmas decorations on Main Street, all the lit-up candy canes that she's positioned on the pavement, and then, out of nowhere, comes the baby talk. Johnny's mom is all about the baby talk. When is Calla thinking of conceiving? Would she consider IVF if she had fertility issues, to ensure that she's continuing the Jones family line? And would she pass the green bean casserole? Grandma Ruby deflects this rather tactlessly—but mercifully—with a story about moose trails on the Canadian border; how she even jumped there conversation-wise is never discussed, but Calla seems grateful for it.

I keep waiting for Calla to get up from the table. Use the powder room. Go fetch another bottle of wine. But she stays firmly rooted in her chair, maintaining the charade. As soon as the yeast roll basket empties, Grandma Ruby asks me if I wouldn't mind refilling it. I give Calla a discreet head bob, hoping she'll follow me into the kitchen. Instead, Nick does.

Something in my stomach ripples.

"I need to talk to you," he says seriously, face wrinkled with worry. Real worry? Fake worry? *Don't believe a thing he says.* "You think we can go outside for a second? Or upstairs?"

I chuck a few rolls into the basket, their doughy heft crashing against the cloth. *Sentimental asshole*, Johnny said. *That's not Nick. Maybe you were easy.* "I don't want to leave dinner for too long. We should—"

"Please, Sydney," he says, dropping his voice to a hushed whisper, hidden under the Christmas music. "I think you've been fed the wrong idea. Actually, I take that back. I *know* you've gotten the wrong idea."

My gaze snaps to him, his face equally tense and desperate. I'm fighting hard to keep up appearances, but the concrete is cracking. Scratch that. The concrete is all over the fucking floor. It's in chunks. It's in dust.

The color leaches from Nick's cheeks. "This is what he does, Sydney, he—" Nick cuts himself off with a biting sigh, neck craning, looking way into the dining room, and suddenly, he's opening the pantry door and gently shoving me inside. One of his hands presses against the small of my back.

"Hey!" What's he planning? What's he going to do next? Rolls abandoned on the countertop, I half trip into the pantry, stumbling over tiny tubs of flour on the floor, heart pounding. "You don't think *this* is suspicious?" I hiss.

Nick shuts the pantry door and yanks on the overhead bulb, yellow light tumbling all around us. He's replaced the CHRISTMAS SWEATER with an actual Christmas sweater, tiny blue-hooved reindeer prancing across his chest; he looks so cheery and so sad. *Don't care.* The pantry walls close in, frosted glass sugar jars and boxes of starch teetering on shelves. "My handler reviewed the latest recording," Nick says, whispering so low, he's barely audible. "That's why I was looking at my phone at dinner. I know what Johnny said to you, and it's *not true*, Sydney. I'm sure you think I've double-crossed you, *triple*-crossed you, but Johnny's just—he's doing what Johnny's does best. He's making people doubt themselves. He's telling you the exact thing you need to hear least."

I cross my arms high over my chest, shoulders bunching. "Well, you don't really know me, so—"

"Don't do that," Nick groans, like I've just punched him in the gut. "*Please* don't do that."

"Do what? We don't know each other. Obviously we don't."

Nick's throat tightens so painfully, I can see it. "I know this looks bad, but if you'd let me explain . . . about a year ago, Johnny had his suspicions. There was a mole in my department who told Johnny about my dad and was starting to pick apart my deep cover. I had to pretend to Johnny that I'd join CSIS *for* him. Follow in my father's footsteps for him, become a double agent for him, be his guy on the inside."

The breath continues to leave my chest. "And you didn't think this was information you should've shared with me?"

"You already were struggling to trust me, and I . . ." His voice breaks. "I didn't want to worry you. I didn't want to give you a reason to doubt, when it's complicated, and it didn't look good. I swear to god, I have never *once* said that to a woman at a bar. Johnny was always joking about how I should use it, but I never did. Please, Sydney. I swear to you. You can still trust me."

"Can I?" I press, voice utterly cold. Because I've already made my decision. I will never trust a single thing he says, ever again.

"Yes," Nick whispers. He breathes out a hard sigh through his nose. "I want you to know everything about me. You're the first new person that I've trusted in about three years, and—"

One of my hands flings up to yank off the light, while the other clasps over Nick's mouth. His lips press fully into my palm, the slight tickles of his breath washing over my skin. A shiver runs straight through my core. I've heard something. Someone has very tactfully tiptoed into the kitchen and is lingering close to the pantry door. Nick and I are entirely motionless, like the sugar jars. We wait. Wait a little longer.

Before Grandma Ruby swings open the door.

To her immense credit, she gives a little jump but does not question the undeniable oddity of this situation. I'm not sure what she thinks we're doing in here—this close together, my hand dropping from Nick's mouth; all she asks is, "Could you pass the extra bag of salt, pumpkin?"

It's right by my head. Silently, I spin, grab, and hand her the seasoning.

"Thank you," she says, shutting the door.

"I should . . ." I tell Nick, never finishing the sentence. His fingertips reach out, brushing mine, and he's still saying words at my back as I flee.

Dinner doesn't last much longer after that. Nick and I filter separately back to the table, leaving that conversation like an untreated wound. Forks clink. We eat a winter salad. Arugula. Somewhere under the table, Sweetie Pie knee-surfs for morsels of passed food; I slip her a scrap of turkey—and then a whole mouthful from the palm of my hand. Johnny carves more of the turkey, picking up the knife and slicing into the bird, chopping thick, jagged pieces—and every once in a while, he sends another flash of a smile in my direction.

You, I think. *You are going down. Down to the ground. Bucko.*

And then, it's done.

Dinner is finally done. Compliments are given to the chef, and to whoever prepared that mountain of macerated cheese (thank you, thank you) before Johnny leaves with his parents. It's bad luck to see the bride much past the rehearsal dinner. Everyone goes their separate ways: Johnny to one of the seaside hotels down the road, alongside Mr. and Mrs. Jones; Nick, to take out the trash for Grandma Ruby in the kitchen; and Calla and me, upstairs. Farther upstairs. Into the attic.

When the door clicks closed, she lets go of an enormous breath, shaking her hands like they're wet and water is flicking off them. "I didn't think I was going to be able to *do* that," she gasps. "I mean, I sort of thought that I could, but this isn't exactly the wedding scenario I dreamed." She captures my gaze, breath cascading in tendrils from her mouth. "Sydney, it is absolutely *freezing* up here."

"Yeah." I nod, letting the honesty go. "But the rest of the house is bugged."

Calla blinks, anger resurfacing. "You bugged our house?"

"No, but it might as well have been me. And I am *so* sorry. Even saying that feels trivial and inconsequential, and I—"

Shaking her head, Calla cuts me off. "No, just . . . stop. I don't want an apology. I just want . . . God, I don't even *know* what I want. For someone to tell me this is all a bad dream. A few days ago, I was thinking to myself, maybe I'm getting cold feet. It's normal to get cold feet. That's what all the blogs say. Of course, I barely had time to read the blogs, because this whole thing has been happening at a million miles an hour!" Calla shakes her head harder. "And I've *hated* that. Absolutely hated that. You're right, I do like to plan, it makes me feel safe—but I just wanted to be this spontaneous person that Johnny wanted me to be, this 'down for anything' person, and . . . Is my vibe check off?"

I don't really know how to answer that. "I don't really know how to answer that," I say.

She massages the base of her throat. "Maybe I'm, like, too used to working with little kids and I don't know how to process adults anymore, but when Johnny and I were driving back, I fell asleep in the passenger seat, and I had the weirdest dream, Sydney. I mean, the *weirdest* dream. It's Christmas morning. We're all sitting around the tree. Suddenly I get this really *sick* feeling. Like something's wrong. When I reach up, my pajama shirt is wet. And sticky. And red. I think, *Oh my god, I'm bleeding, why am I bleeding?* But then I realize it's cranberry sauce. Not even homemade cranberry sauce. The canned kind, with the ridges? And there are just . . . these chunks all over me, and *then* I realize, I'm not in my pajamas at all. I'm in my wedding dress."

She is going to need a lot of therapy. "That sounds awful," I say, utterly sympathetic.

"That's what I thought! I woke up, told Johnny about my dream, and he *laughed*—he thought it was a joke or something—and it just brought all of these other things to the surface. All of these reservations that I'd been shoving down because this was supposed to be *different*, he seemed perfect in so many ways, and I loved the idea of him. Of this chemistry we had, and how he just . . . he just took up the whole room. Suddenly I had this huge social life, and we were going to all these places, and he told me I was 'the one' *super* early. That felt good. That felt like something. He said he'd never leave me, and those were the exact words I needed to hear. But the lie . . . the *lies* . . ." She gulps. "I think he does love me, for real, but I also think I was good for his image. A kindergarten teacher who probably doesn't ask a lot of questions. But I want you to know—I *need* you to know—I *was* asking questions. Right from the very beginning. Johnny just always had an answer for everything. Why were his cousins knocking at the door in the middle of the night? *Marriage trouble.* Why does he own so much duct tape? *He shops at Costco.*"

"He actually does shop at Costco," I admit, nose scrunching. "It's in his file. He's a Gold Star Member."

In tiny, tight circles, Calla rubs a finger between her eyebrows. "I'm numb right now. And furious. I'm trying to process this. I'm failing. I heard what you said at the ice-skating rink—about your job, about Johnny—and suddenly I'm speeding off like some NASCAR driver, and I just wanted time to think about how this all could've gone so, *so* wrong."

I swallow, knowing that we're getting to the extra-hard part. "Where'd you go?"

Calla starts pacing back and forth in the cold. "I just drove around in circles at first. I was mentally skimming over the last few months, remembering all the things Johnny had told me, wondering how much of it was true—like, is it normal to keep handcuffs in your bedroom? I thought it was . . . you know, the other reason. It could've easily been the other reason! I told myself if I broke into his house and didn't find anything *else* like that—"

My breath stills. "You broke into his house?"

"Oh, I have a key. But also, no." She swivels on her heels, changing directions. "I started to get kind of paranoid. If there was even the smallest chance that what you were saying was true— and why the hell would you lie to me about something like that— I didn't want to be followed. So I ditched the Escalade at my friend Tyler's house."

One of my eyebrows quirks. "Your first boyfriend, Tyler?"

"Yeah, he's still in town. That's just the first nonpublic place I thought of. There are woods all around his property. I also sort of invited him to the wedding, which is *ridiculous*, because the wedding's not even going to happen, but he was just standing there—"

"Calla," I say, grabbing her lightly by the shoulders, holding her in place. "Focus."

She nods abruptly. "I took Tyler's car so Johnny couldn't track me, drove all the way to Boston, and went to my apartment. I thought it might trigger some memories, anything that he'd said to me over the course of our relationship, and what felt off. And it did."

"Go on . . ." I press her gently.

"You said I was near one of the crime scenes? In Buffalo? I was visiting Diana. She was selling some of her specialty bear sweaters in this gallery there, and I'd never been to Buffalo . . . and Johnny told me explicitly not to go. Right there in my living room. I didn't understand it. He was *really* adamant about it, but I'd already booked the tickets, and I wanted to see my friend."

Calla gnaws at her lip, her eyes watering. "But he didn't stop me. He knew that if anything went sideways with that heist in Buffalo, it would look *really* bad that I was in the area. I was literally just buying gas at the gas station! That's all. But he must've realized that would look suspicious, and he let me walk right into it. Which means he cared more about the money than me, right? He put his crime over . . . over us. Over whatever we have. And I'm swinging back and forth, because half of me is *so* mad about all the lies, and half of me is totally numb. It's not just that I believed him; it's that I *wanted* to believe him. I wanted all the fairy-tale bullshit and the perfect man who rides in on the white horse out of fucking nowhere."

My head almost rears back. I'm not sure I've ever heard Calla swear. "He did actually say that he wanted to give you a horse at the altar."

"In our *living room*? Where would it fit?" She kneads at her eyes. "Never mind what Sweetie Pie would think. She is *really* afraid of horses." With the sleeve of her sweater, she wipes the bottom of her nose, which has started to run a bit. "I think I just wanted one guy not to disappoint me like Dad did. I know you don't want to see him again . . ."

My stomach tightens. Throat tightens. "It's not that." In fact, I'm picturing it. Him, walking into the foyer in a rumpled blue suit, hair comb-parted. Maybe his hair's longer now. It would be, wouldn't it? And his face would scan the guests, searching for Calla, searching for me. That would be the perfect result. The best ending.

But that's the movie ending. The tidy strings. Real life is messier than that.

"He actually called the house," I breathe out.

Calla catches my gaze, her eyes a little bloodshot, her voice emerging in a rasp. "He did?"

"Yeah." I'm struggling to keep it together. "Yeah, he did. I . . . I, uh, answered the phone, and he didn't recognize my voice, he thought it was Grandma Ruby, and he basically said that he's not coming to the wedding, and I *know* you don't have the father you deserve, and you don't have the sister you deserve—"

In a flash, Calla bursts forward, wrapping her arms around me. It feels like coming home. It feels like forever ago. Her chin settles on my shoulder, and I lean in, breathe in, hold her tight. "No," she says, shaking her head. "Don't say that. You're here, despite everything. Just because I'm not going to get that perfect reunion doesn't mean I've totally lost my faith in *you*. You came back. This—right here—is coming through on who you used to be. Who you've always been."

That just about breaks my heart. Also, heals me a little. Calla's right. I *have* drifted away from myself, but this holiday, it's like I'm stumbling back ashore.

Even just speaking about our dad, out loud . . .

Sometimes you can't heal if you don't recognize the damage.

Sometimes you have to know exactly where it hurts, and why it hurts, before you can start mending yourself.

I speak, throat still raw. "Do you ever just really, *really* miss how it was?"

She nods against my shoulder, hugging me tighter. "All the time," she whispers. "I have this ... memory of Mom and Dad, this specific one that always replays in my head, and it's so clear that I'm not even sure if it's real."

"Tell me," I murmur.

Calla takes a little step back, wiping away a tear with the heel of her hand. "I was really little, because we were still in that condo, way before we moved in with Grandma Ruby, and it must've been Christmas Eve. I think that I thought I heard Santa. Some sort of noise in the living room. So I round the corner, and there's Mom, and there's Dad, and they're just holding each other. That's the whole memory. They're just holding each other by the Christmas tree, these multicolored lights all around them, really bright, and I knew that one day I wanted someone to love me that much."

"That's the thing," I rasp out, instinctively thumbing my tattoo. "You *have* that, Calla. Grandma Ruby and I, we love you to the moon and back ... And I'm sure it's a real memory. That's the biggest thing I remember about them, too. How close they were."

Calla breathes out a sigh, almost like relief. "Good, because ... sometimes I don't know if I'm just remembering stories that Grandma Ruby's told me, or things that I've seen about moms on TV, and with Dad, I have really random images. Like when he signed up for the dunking booth in thirty-degree weather, or him doing my hair with a ... vacuum hose? And the baseball games. I *loved* those baseball games."

My forehead scrunches up. "You did?"

Every summer before school started, Dad, Calla, and I would take in a home game. We'd buy a Cape Hathaway Huskies foam finger and eat the peanuts from shells and wrap ourselves in fleece sweatshirts as the sun set. Dad would kick his feet up on the back of the seat in front of him, his hands behind his head, and he'd say, *This, girls, is the closest thing to happiness.* And it was my happiness, too. My glimmer of it. In the years after he left, Calla and I kept going—but I'd see the after-shadow of him in the stands. Hear his happiness quote, which felt so foreign then. And my grief got me. The CIA became an excuse to stop attending those end-of-summer games, to stop remembering, to stop doing something that cracked me wide open.

"I did," Calla says. "I mean, not the *baseball* part, but everything else."

"Then we'll go," I tell her, meaning it. "We'll start going again. This summer. Or even before that. In the spring. Whenever the season opens, we'll be there. Things will be different from now on."

Calla pauses. She thinks. She says, "I believe you."

It's a simple statement. It's also exactly what I need to hear. And I feel myself mending a little more in all the cracked places. How can she be so loving, so forgiving, when I'm not even ready to forgive myself?

"What do I do, though?" she rasps, leading us back to the present. "About the wedding?"

"What do *you* want to do?" I ask her gently.

"I can't marry him, Syd."

"I know."

"Everyone's coming to the wedding."

I place my hands on her shoulders. "Don't worry about them. Let me worry about them."

"I thought if I came back," Calla says, "I thought if I held Johnny in place, kept all of his family in place for the wedding, that would give you time to . . . work something out. And it would give me time to remember a few more things. There is . . . there's one more thing I remember."

I step back a touch, look at her. "Yeah?"

She chews her lip. "Johnny has a storage unit for his mountain bikes. I found the key last week and asked him about it."

"Okay . . ." I say, pulse rising again.

Calla blinks. "Sydney. He *hates* biking."

F ar down the street, near our neighborhood's gazebo, I dial Gail's number in the snow. My boots crunch as I fast-walk back and forth, rock salt under my heels. She doesn't answer. Someone else does. "You've reached the after-hours offices of Clara's Chicken and Homemade Waffles; how may I direct your call?"

I don't even hesitate. "Put Gail on the phone."

The voice on the other end of the line doesn't waver, either. "Last name? And what department does she work in, please?"

Heart hammering, I massage my forehead with the palm of my hand. "This is Sydney Swift, and it's an emergency. Just transfer me to Gail."

"I'm sorry," the voice says, utterly unaffected, "but we have dozens of departments: marketing, HR, chicken resources—"

I'm fed up with the runaround because *we are running out of time.* "My sister knows about a storage unit."

The response is immediate. "Hold, please!"

A sharp *beep* follows before there's shuffling, and the crisp sound of Gail's voice bleeds over the line. "Sydney."

I dive right in. "Porky's. He's hiding stolen goods at Porky's."

"Have you been drinking?"

"Yes," I say, sparkling wine still coursing through my system.

"Not the point. It's a storage facility off the Massachusetts Turnpike. There's a little pig on the keychain. That's where Johnny's hiding his cut of the stolen goods. I've been racking my brain for days, wondering how the Joneses managed to shift that much high-value contraband without a single trace on the dark web, and that's the thing, Gail—they probably couldn't do it all at once. They'd have to store it somewhere, unload it in batches. And my guess is that's where the rest of the C4 is hidden, too. Because they're not using all of it for some bridge, are they? If we act *tonight*, I'm talking *right now*, we can have all the evidence we need by morning. Before the heist even goes down. Locate the unit, get a warrant, head in with a task force."

"You want me to put together a spontaneous task force," Gail deadpans, "on Christmas Eve."

"On Christmas Eve," I underline. "Who knows how much longer the storage unit will remain operational. If you want to nail them before the next heist, avoid any bloodshed for those armored vehicle drivers and any traffic near that bridge, the window is already closing."

The longest pause in human history ensues.

"Are you still there?" I ask.

"I'm thinking, Sydney." In the background, computer keys clack, and Gail stalls. "Was the Chicken and Homemade Waffles office believable?"

"Thirty percent believable. You would lose most people at 'chicken resources.'"

"We'll reformulate. My assistant, she's new." One final clack on the keys follows. Gail releases a deep sigh. "Theoretically, I could gather a team of four federal officers in the South Boston area. And theoretically, we could obtain a warrant this evening and mobilize in the early hours of the morning, placing a second team outside of your neighborhood—ready to swoop in when the evidence is seized . . . But you'd have to stall until the team arrives. Keep Johnny and the Joneses in place. Maintain the charade."

I nod in the dark. "I can do that."

"You're absolutely positive?"

I nod again. "Just as long as you can get it done before the wedding." I check the clock on my phone, feeling my stomach drop. "Eleven hours and counting."

19

Traditionally, Christmas Eve is my favorite evening of the year. Even as a kid, I'd stay up past midnight, belly stuffed with cheese and my ears trained on the roof, listening for the pitter-patter of reindeer hooves. Now, I'm sitting in the dark on the bride's side of the aisle, one of the uncomfortable ceremony chairs creaking under my butt. My living room has never felt less like my living room. In front of me, the hand-carved altar stands between two Christmas trees, like the gateway to hell.

I take a glug of Santa's eggnog. Grandma Ruby's put it out on the mantel in what reads as a desperate attempt to keep something normal this year, and I've swiped the glass along with a gingersnap. It's very snappy. I'm snapping with it. One thirty-three in the morning, and zero word from Gail. Sure, it takes more than a couple of hours to mobilize a governmental task force on Christmas Eve, but you'd think—

My phone vibrates, and I snatch it from the chair next to me with wrist-breaking speed.

No dice. The text isn't from Gail. It's from Nick: You're not pacing on the other side of the wall, so I guess you're probably sleeping. I hope this doesn't wake you. Another text quickly follows, slicing through me: However I can support you tomorrow, say the word. I'll do it. And I imagine Nick in the darkness of his room, sitting up in bed, angled over the phone, a tortured expression coating his face. The problem—the huge, *huge* problem—is that expression is for Johnny, not for me.

I know that I've lost your trust, comes a third text, and a fourth: But I'm willing to spend as long as it takes to gain it back. Merry Christmas, Sydney.

Merry fucking Christmas, Nick.

I don't reply. I toss the phone to the side with a grunt, close my eyes. A not-so-insignificant part of me wants to stand, race up those stairs, continue this conversation in person—beg him to tell me it isn't true, all over again—but I shouldn't. I wouldn't believe him. I don't. Even if *he* begged. Even if he kissed my neck, or looked at me with those eyelashes, or whispered into my ear that he understood me.

Thinking about him is like a knife in the stomach. Every time I imagine us, together, laughing, in bed, the imprint of his hands on my body, the blade twists.

"Sydney Bean, you're still up?" Grandma Ruby's voice hits me from the corner, a splash of light switching on overhead. She's standing in the doorway in her traditional Christmas pajamas, the ones with the dark green tassels on the sleeves. A mug of something that smells like whiskey is in her hand. "If I'd known, I would've poured you one, too."

"Oh, that's all right," I say, finding my voice, and it really is. I couldn't keep up with her. Grandma Ruby has the alcohol tolerance of a Siberian prison guard.

She plops down beside me with a ragged *oomph*, chair creaking.

"Did you know that I was the justice of the peace for your parents' wedding?"

It comes out of nowhere. I blink. "No, I . . . I don't think you've ever told me that before."

"My first time officiating," Grandma Ruby says, pride dancing in her eyes. "They were a beautiful couple. Just beautiful. And so in love." She pauses thoughtfully. "Sometimes, I do feel angry with your father for leaving, and wonder what I did wrong, if I'd just raised him differently—"

"Grandma, no," I try to jump in, to console her, but she cuts me off with a hand, the ice cube in her mug tinkling.

"Please, I think I need to get this out. What he did was selfish, even though a piece of me does understand that he's in pain. Losing my daughter-in-law, it tore me apart, too. But it was my honor and my duty and my privilege to be there for you girls, to stay strong for you, especially after your dad left. I tried to make you feel so tough that the world couldn't hurt you even if it doled out its best punch. Sometimes I wonder if I taught you to be too resilient, to let that pain just slide on off you, to not really feel it." She appraises me with one eyebrow raised. "Maybe I should've said this years ago, but you're not a Teflon pan, dear. Something's gotta stick."

At this, I actually laugh. "Yeah, I'm realizing that."

"Good," she says, leaning over to kiss my forehead. "Then maybe I've done my job after all. And speaking of, well, speaking of that . . . I've left you something on your nightstand. A Christmas present of sorts. Let me know if you want to go through it together, or if it's something you want to look through alone."

My brow wriggles, confused, but she doesn't say anything else. She stands up, wishing me good night and flicking off the lights. I hear a creak upstairs—maybe Nick, walking—and I think to myself, *At least I have my family. At least I'm not alone anymore.*

In the morning, I'm in the same position: curled up like a dog on the wedding chairs, my back brutally stiff, sciatica shooting down my left leg. The doorbell's just rung. *Shit, shit, shit! How did I fall asleep?* Suppose that's what nearly six sleep-deprived nights in a row will do. *What time is it?* Sunlight streams like daggers into the living room. Frantically blinking, I swipe at my eyes, tap my phone, and—with a shock that feels approximately as swift as a punch to the jaw—realize that my sister is "getting married" in two hours.

The caterers are here.

We might be fucked.

Gail hasn't contacted me. No phone calls. No landline rings. My inbox is conspicuously quiet. In my clothes from last night, I swing open the front door to trays of miniature cheese puffs and bacon-wrapped dates, Sweetie Pie at my heels, her tail wagging; she is more than happy to accept that delivery.

"You can just . . . set everything in the kitchen," I say, pointing, dizzy. "Our dog will show you."

Yanking on my slippers, I head out into the front yard, ankles shuffling through snow, and dial Gail's number. It is a glorious Christmas morning. Couldn't be brighter, merrier, worthier of a sharp, existential scream. "Gail?"

"Sydney," she says.

"What's happened?"

"We're waiting," Gail says calmly.

"Waiting? Waiting on what?"

"A warrant to enter Porky's."

"How much longer?" I press, icy air clawing at my throat. In our neighbor's yard, a gigantic blowup decoration roars to inflatable life; it's a holiday-themed T-Rex, and suddenly feels like an omen.

"As long as it takes for the justice department to finish their Christmas breakfasts, it seems. All you have to do is keep stalling. You said you could do that."

"I did."

"Just last night."

"Right. Good." I swallow, noticing something. "I'm sorry, I have to . . . go. Keep me informed."

Half jogging over in my slippers, I approach the deliveryman, who's hopping down from his silver truck. Printed on the side—in very clear lettering—are the words CAREFUL LIVE ANIMAL, alongside a festive logo. He actually did it. Johnny bought her a horse. Through the thin bars, I see evidence of two furry nostrils, huffing and puffing in the cold air.

"Got a delivery for Mr. Johnny Jones?" the man says. He's wearing a crisp blue jumpsuit with a Christmas tree pin on his chest.

I breathe slowly. "Okay, is it possible to delay this delivery? We can't take ownership of the horse right now."

"Not a horse," the man says, scuffling around the truck and unlatching the gate.

Antlers emerge first. The clip-clop of hooves sound down the ramp, a perfect specimen of a reindeer trotting into view—and *this is fine.* This doesn't complicate things even further. I will stall my sister's wedding with an actual live *reindeer* attached to my hip.

The deliveryman hands me the reins, followed by a clipboard. "Sign here, please."

"I'm sorry," I say, as polite as I can manage, "but I can't sign this. You're a—" I give the reindeer a glance. "You're a tremendous-looking reindeer, but we're about to have a wedding and there's just a lot going on. How much to send him back?"

Rightfully disgruntled, the deliveryman eyes me before

retrieving the clipboard, straight-up forging a signature on the bottom line, and returning to his truck without a word. The reins chafe in my palm as Rudolph bucks. He must sense the tension coursing through every vein in my body. Perceptive animal. "Hello," I tell him.

He nearly pokes my eye out with his left antler.

"Sydney!" Grandma Ruby says, appearing on the front stoop in her robe. Curlers are tightly rolled in her puffy white hair. She calls across the yard and the whoosh sound of the inflatable T-Rex. "Did you order that, pumpkin?"

"Do you think you could go get Nick?" I ask, ducking from the antlers again, managing to maneuver the reindeer into the front yard. In less than an hour, cars will be showing up. Guests arriving to mingle. We're running out of time.

When Nick descends the stairs, he's already showered. Already in his clothes for the day. He stops short on the snowed-over sidewalk, wearing the same dinner jacket from the bachelor party. His black bow tie gleams in the early-morning light, and he is stupidly, exasperatingly handsome. I can almost feel his hands on my hips, the tender kiss on my neck, and the gut punch arrives. What Johnny said. What I've lost and also never had: A man I can put my faith in. A man who'll look me in the eyes and tell me the damn truth. Someone I might be able to come home to, feel completely safe around, feel completely *myself*.

"That is . . . a reindeer," Nick says, obviously unsure whether to laugh or to wince.

"You know how you said you'd do anything to help today?" I say quickly, keeping my voice flat.

Nick nods, moving closer with a serious dip of his chin. "Yeah."

"Well." I hand him the reins. The only thing—and I mean the *only* thing—I can trust him with is a reindeer. "I need you to hold this."

———

Upstairs, Calla is keeping it together almost better than I am. "There you are," she whisper-yells when I plow open the bedroom door. She spins around, and I have to stop myself from full-on gasping. She's standing by the full-length mirror in Grandma Ruby's wedding dress, except the 1960s puffed sleeves have been transformed into a waterfall of white fabric, gracefully skating down her arms. My grandmother's added tulle to the underside of the skirt, so the bottom half is like a cloud. The word *princess* comes to mind in a completely organic way; my little sister is stunning. She's also about to give me a heart attack.

"You put on the dress?" I ask. "I didn't think you'd actually put on the dress."

Calla lifts up the sides, shuffling over to me, voice dropping. "I woke up late, and Grandma Ruby asked why I wasn't getting ready, and I didn't know what to tell her."

"You're not having second thoughts, are you? Because if you're having second thoughts about leaving him—"

"No! No. I just decided it would look less suspicious this way. But they're closing in on them, right? This will all be over soon?"

"Mmm-hmm," I manage. "Soon."

Her face falls. "Syd."

"There's been a delay."

"*Syd.*"

"Just stay up here," I say. "Lock the door. Don't open it for anyone except me, okay? I'll tell Grandma Ruby you're getting ready with your friends, so she should entertain the guests."

"My friends," Calla says, her face falling farther. "Are they here yet?"

"Let me double-check."

"Wait, Sydney! You should probably put on something different, too."

My chin drops as I give myself a once-over: the black jeans and last night's reindeer wool sweater. Maybe *that's* why the reindeer took an instant disliking to me! I smell like a rival. "Yeah. Yeah, I'll do that." I back out the door, shut it, forget to breathe.

I don't have a maid-of-honor dress. Didn't think we'd get this far. The dress is literally the least of my worries, but Calla's right—this morning is about appearances.

Quickly, in Grandma Ruby's closet, I borrow the outfit that looks least like I'm auditioning for a *Golden Girls* reboot (a plain black slip-on with a bumblebee pin) and try to blaze downstairs, but Grandma Ruby catches me in the hall.

"That dress looks . . . familiar," she says, quirking her head. She's already in her justice of the peace outfit: a ruffled pantsuit with sparkle trim. "But never mind! You'd look good in a potato sack. I thought I'd ask if you wanted me to do your hair." She reaches out, tender, and fingers a strand. "I haven't done your hair since you were a little girl."

The movement tugs at my heartstrings so hard that I let her—very quickly—stick a rhinestone hair clip on the side of my head, before she rushes off to do Calla's hair and makeup.

All along our street, cars are assembling. Out the window, I see minivans and Ubers and suspicious black SUVs from Johnny's side. Marco with the scorpion skull tattoo saunters past our mailbox with a large, silver-wrapped present and a bouquet of airport roses, his daughter in tow, while Diana (of the famous Diana and the bears) is waiting for Andre to retie his shoelace on the sidewalk. Andre, with his stack of wedding-slash-Christmas presents as well. Everyone from Johnny's side is bringing *so* many presents. And oh—*dear god*—the reindeer is in the living room.

"Sydney, what is going on?" Nick asks below his breath. He's

appeared at my shoulder, reins gripped in his hands, and can this
man not follow *any* directions?

"It looks like you've let a reindeer into my house," I say, bemused,
feeling like this—this, *finally*—is the part where I wake up.

"I did. Your grandma said if there was a reindeer for the wedding, then a reindeer should be *at* the wedding." Besides Rudolph,
no one else is in the room with us yet; everyone who's arrived is
mingling in the kitchen, listening to the soothing sounds of Nat
King Cole. Still, Nick takes extra precautions and leans in closer,
nearly whispering in my ear. His breath is hot against the side of
my face, and I . . . I can't stand it. "You have that look you get when
things are starting to fall apart, and I know there's no *way* you're
about to let this wedding happen—so why don't you fill me in. I
can help."

"You can't," I say, swallowing fire.

Nick hasn't just lost my trust; he's obliterated it. Can't even
trust him with a reindeer, apparently.

A burst of staccato laughter sounds from the kitchen, and Nick
peers over his shoulder, checking. More guests. More music. Empty
seats, starting to fill. My cousin's kids filter down the aisle, eyes
saucer-wide at the reindeer, and Nick whispers once in my ear,
"Please, *please*, believe me. Whatever's about to happen, I'll do the
right thing."

No, you won't.

"I will," he repeats, like he's peeked inside my head.

The kids gather around, Nick shields them from the reindeer's
antlers, and I slip away again, heart in my throat, double-checking
my phone. Nothing. *Come on, Gail!*

"La-la-la!" Grandma Ruby says in the hallway, warming up for
her wedding speech; she's clutching her justice of the peace notes,
prepared to do the honors, and then Johnny's arriving. Johnny's
here. His parents are here. Andre is here. Vinny.

"Sandy!" he calls out to me, misremembering my name.

Kill me! I want to scream back.

The next ten minutes whip by. Then the next twenty, and twenty more. Five minutes before the ceremony starts, I'm wondering if Calla could realistically jump out the second-story window. Together, maybe we could slide down the drainpipe, disappear past the tennis courts. She can't stay here. What if we get all the way to the part where Grandma Ruby says, "Speak now or forever hold your peace"?

That will never happen.

It won't.

Johnny's ready, dressed in an all-red suit. Yes. Yes, he's done that. Heavy on the burgundy. Heavy on the Christmas. And I'm standing on Calla's side of the altar, clenching my teeth so tightly, I hear a pop in my jaw. The guests are taking their places, including a tall, mustached man who I've never seen in any of the case files; he strolled in at 10 a.m. on the dot and placed a small, white-bowed present by the Christmas tree. Vinny is feeding pieces of crudités to the reindeer. By the wedding cake, Andre is picking up the tiny ceramic humans in the snow village and—for some reason—sniffing them. Calla is two minutes away from descending the stairs.

This isn't just a nightmare. This is *the* nightmare.

It gets worse.

My phone buzzes. As subtle as one can be in front of a crowd of people, I check the message from Gail. It says one pitiful word: *Empty.* A picture is attached to the message: a storage unit off the Massachusetts Turnpike, concrete swept bare, nothing but glistening walls and dead space. No mountain bikes. And definitely no stacks of contraband. No boxes of jewels, no pallets of cash, no C4. A brick drops in my stomach, and I . . . *think.*

I'm thinking. Something's swirling in the back of my brain. If the storage unit is empty . . .

Behind Johnny, Nick struggles to catch my eye. Finally, I let him. I give in. And I mouth, "*Stall.*"

"What?" he mouths back.

"*Stall,*" I breathe again. If Nick wants to play this stupid *I'm innocent* game, let him play it. Let him try to prove it. I'll use him like he's used me. Nick understands what I've said this time, just as Grandma Ruby steps in between us.

Her hands open up to greet the guests, who are quieting down now, eager for a wedding—all firmly in their seats. "It is *so* wonderful to see you all here," she says. "In a moment, we'll—"

"Nick has a speech!" I interject, clapping my hands, gaze swiveling around the room—to the mustached man in the third row. To the three-tiered wedding cake and the Christmas tree at the back of the room. And through the window, out in the driveway, the reindeer van is . . . still there.

"Oh, you do, dear?" Grandma Ruby says as Nick raises one of his eyebrows. "Oh, that's so nice. Step right in the middle, then. We'll swap. Go ahead, don't be shy."

Nick does not stiffen. He plays his part, adjusting his bow tie with a boyish smile. Stepping forward, he gives a grand wave between the two Christmas trees. "Hello, everyone. Hello. I'm Nick. About half of you know that already. Thank you all for coming, especially so last minute, and on Christmas Day, no less!"

Discreetly, I twirl my hand near my hip, urging him to keep going, and start to walk backward—around the left side of the aisle, into the corner of the room.

Toward the white-bowed present.

Peeking out the window, I notice that the reindeer van driver hasn't stuck around.

"Love!" Nick says, clapping his hands like I did. "Uh, I'm not usually a big speech giver, but I . . ." When Nick clears his throat, nerves ricochet down my body. "I really want to give this a chance because, honestly, I love weddings. I love the *food*, and the *emotions*, and seeing everyone brought together by two people who're so committed to each other, they're planning on spending the rest of their lives sharing the same toothpaste. Maybe not the same toothbrush, though. That's going a little too far."

Some light chuckles erupt at the toothbrush comment. I barely hear them.

I'm so focused, it's almost like no one else is in the room.

"But the truth is," he says, "I never understood the couples who get married so quickly. Like Calla and Johnny." Here, a line pops in Johnny's forehead. Nick ignores it. "How can you actually get to know someone in three months? How much can you know a person *ever*?"

I'm still walking backward, panic starting to fizz in my gut.

Panic and pure triumph.

I think . . . I think I might've figured it out. What I've been missing. The van. The blue mechanic's jumpsuit that Vinny purchased. The stranger in the third row.

"Someone I trust," Nick says, "told me a story about love. About this old couple on a cruise ship who were sitting across from each other, just silently eating their cheese. She said *that's* love. Being comfortable. Talking or not having to talk. To know the other person so thoroughly, no words are necessary." Nick's throat bobs, and mine does, too. "I think that was the moment I changed my mind. When she told me that. I was wrong. You can get to know a person in a month, in a few weeks, in a few days, if they let you. If you know it's right. And you'll be fascinated. Falling for someone is like reading a book, and the pages keep turning themselves."

The knot in my throat tightens as tears start to burn in the corners of my eyes.

"Now, this person might drive you a little up the wall sometimes. She might have an excellent right hook, and . . ."

He trails off.

His gaze is fully locked on mine.

At the top of the aisle, I'm standing firm, gripping the white-bowed present with both hands. It has silver foil wrapping. It's light. And my ears are ringing. My breath is coming out in slow, thick streams. If I'm wrong about this . . .

But if I'm *right*.

Johnny snaps his head to look at me, his vision falling on the present. The way I'm holding it. The way I'm staring him down. And I think he knows, in one hideous instant, that I'm about to force his hand. He holds up his palm to stop me, but I'm already picking at the corner of the present.

"It's Christmas morning!" I say, possibly a bit too theatrically. Everyone in their seats turns and stares, including the tall man with the mustache. "And it's a Christmas wedding! We should open a present. Right now."

"Sydney . . ." Johnny warns, taking a few careful steps forward.

But I'm already ripping. Already taking a fistful of paper and rip, rip, *ripping* a long band down the middle. In the hush of the living room, it sounds like the slash of a knife.

Johnny's face pales as I dig into the box.

And emerge with a palmful of diamonds.

"You *fucking* . . ." Johnny says, darkness clouding his face. The corner of his mouth trembles, then stiffens. He's putting the pieces together about me. That I'm not who I said I was. That it's in his best interest to run. And he does run—straight-up bolting around the aisle. The soles of his shoes are even redder than his suit.

Oh, no, you don't—

My body's moving before my mind even processes the next steps. I'm charging, racing after him. Nick weaves around the aisle, so quick, on Johnny's heels. Is he . . . trying to help his boss escape? Keeping him covered from behind? Or—

Nick grabs the top tier of the wedding cake and absolutely flings it at the floor in front of Johnny, like a giant cake Frisbee. It lands with a smash, buttercream frosting slickening the floor by Johnny's shoes, and he slips, slides. Did Nick . . . did Nick just . . . ?

Well, yes, he did. And he's trying to tackle Johnny now, springs off one of the empty seats, but he misses, crashing into the snow village, and no, stop it, the reindeer intercepts me for a good three seconds, long enough for Johnny to grab the spare set of keys to the van and race out the door. I rush to swipe my own keys, still processing what Nick has just done. Still processing that maybe—*maybe*—I do know him after all. This man who told me I was knowable, too.

People can surprise you in all sorts of ways.

And sometimes, those surprises are good.

Shoving the diamonds into my dress pocket (hurray for pockets!), I sprint, snatching my keys on the way outside, where the temperature has warmed to a balmy negative seven degrees. Twenty feet in front of me, Johnny's running, jumping into the front seat of the van, and starting the engine. So it's a race, huh? Keys fumble in my hands as I unlock my door, swinging inside and switching on the ignition. The Prius roars to life. Not the car I would've chosen for a high-speed chase, but—

"I'm coming, too," Nick says, practically throwing himself into the passenger seat. His voice is thick, rough. There's fake snow from the Christmas village on the lapel of his suit, and a determined look on his face, and he . . . tried to *tackle* Johnny. Tried to take him down, hard. Which means . . .

I can either live my entire life trusting no one.

Or I can let someone new in.

I can let *Nick* in.

"Nice speech," I rasp out, a peace offering, a heart offering, no time for anything else. I just throw the car into reverse and speed out of the driveway, avoiding the dozens of parked cars on our road, before slamming the Prius into drive. It purrs indecisively, like *Me? You want me to do what? I think you might be mistaking me for a Porsche?* Then it leaps forward, playing catch-up with Johnny, who is already swinging a left at the end of our street—blasting out of vision.

"Mind filling in some of the gaps?" Nick asks, gripping on to one of the roof handles for stability.

"Those diamonds," I say, gritting my teeth, "are part of an arms deal. Think about it. That guy with the mustache? He's the buyer. He came to trade the diamonds for the weapons. *That's* what the Joneses have been up to. Vinny said that Johnny wanted to evolve the business. I thought he was talking about heists, but this is what the heists are *for*—including the one that's going down near the bridge, if that wasn't a complete misdirection. Money. Pure and simple. Money to buy weapons of mass destruction, to sell to nefarious people. I'll bet you just about anything that the gift shop is one of their new warehouses. The wedding was always a cover, a place to make the first trade, right under the noses of the law. And that *van*—" I point in front of us, at the white reindeer van, rocketing ahead. "That van is chock-full of explosives."

Nick's eyes widen. "Are you kidding me? And we're *chasing* it?"

"I'm sure they're bubble-wrapped."

"Sydney . . ."

"You know they're not going to explode now. They need a spark. Otherwise, they would've exploded with the reindeer." I shake my head, lead foot on the gas. "Vinny bought a blue jump-suit for one of his associates and had him drive the van to the wedding. The buyer was supposed to drop off the diamonds, then drive the van out."

"Where's Johnny headed, then?" Nick asks as I'm mentally reviewing my driving course at The Farm: what to do if I have to make a fast turn over a slick patch of ice; how to safely flip a vehicle.

"My guess? He grabbed the first set of keys he could and now he's panicking. He'll try to stash the van somewhere. Hide as much evidence as he can, along with himself . . . Speaking of evidence, here." One hand on the wheel, I pass Nick the diamonds to store in the glove compartment. If this turns into a footrace, I don't want them weighing me down.

Nick quickly obliges, then whips out his phone, tapping the screen. "He just took a right onto Route 1. Blew through the stop sign."

I keep my breath steady, following Johnny's tracks in the snow, picking up the pace until we're *far* above the speed limit for a residential area. In my rearview mirror, I think I catch the blue flash of Grandma Ruby's Oldsmobile—but no, can't be. "How do you know that?" I press as the Prius makes the Route 1 turn. In front of us, Johnny is clocking in at least 110 miles an hour. Impressive pickup for a reindeer van.

Nick leans forward, squinting at his phone. "I put a tracker on the bottom of his dress shoes last night. Normally I don't mess around with that stuff, because the Joneses always find it, but— Sydney!"

"On it," I mumble, swerving skillfully around a firewood truck that's entering the road. The Prius handles surprisingly well in an emergency.

"I think . . ." Nick begins, widening the map with his fingers. "Yeah, there's an airport nearby."

Barely. More like a short field of snow with one runway and a couple of seaplanes. It's mostly for crab fishermen blowing off some steam on the weekends. But for Johnny, in this situation, it'll do. That was probably the original plan. Unload the contents of the van in a cargo jet, fly it to the dealer's warehouse. Something tumbles in my stomach. "I told you we wouldn't be hugging at the airport," I grit out, foot almost fully down on the gas pedal, speed climbing: *102, 103, 103 and a half.* Okay, *Prius, you can climb a little faster than that!* Up ahead, Johnny is gaining distance, but . . .

"Oooh!" I wince.

"Ooooh!" Nick says.

The van must have hit a patch of ice, because it wibble-wobbles, swerving in a tight zigzag down the dead center of the road. Johnny slows down a hair. Just enough to catch him.

Glass-crusted trees whip by. Snowflakes hit the windshield in sharp, staccato bursts. Right outside the town, we're bumper to bumper. If Johnny slams on his brakes, we're toast.

"He's not going to shoot at us while he's driving, is he?" I muse out loud.

"Johnny isn't great at multitasking," Nick says in a way that is far below the bar of reassurance. "He's much more likely to shoot at us once he stops."

"That makes me feel a lot better," I say, revving the engine and lurching straight forward, slamming the tip of my car against the back of the van.

Hey, this is a rental! I can almost *feel* Johnny say that, and I have the distinct sense that by the time we're done, my car might be returned to the airport in a slightly different condition. The van rocks from side to side, regaining balance, so I do it again— nudging, trying to slow Johnny down.

All of the sudden, he cuts a right, nearly toppling his vehicle, and I follow, both hands clamping the wheel. We're on the back-roads now, lined with wooden A-frames and summer cabins.

Come June, beach towels will flutter on clotheslines, but right now it's just dead silence and wind and us. Should I stay on Johnny's tail until the airport if that's where he's headed? Or should I stop him right now?

"Have you ever been in a car crash?" I ask Nick, breathy.

Nick wipes a hand down his face. "*Speaking* of feeling a lot better."

"Let your body go as limp as you can right before the moment of impact," I say, keeping pace with the back of Johnny's car, scuttling down another side road. Potholes. Big bumps. "Whatever you do, don't tense up. I'm not going to intentionally crash, but—"

I let up on the gas, just enough so we're not bumper to bumper, then carve a very slight right, edging the side of Johnny's car. A little more. Farther. Until we're neck and neck, speeding down the long, tight road. I spin my head to look at Johnny. He spins his head to look at me. Granted, I'm quite a bit lower down, so we can barely see each other, and yet—

Johnny rolls down his window. "I SAID I WOULD GRIND YOU INTO THE FLOOR! AND I WILL GRIND YOU INTO THE *GROUND*!"

"Grind you into the ground," Nick repeats, fists tense despite what I told him. "Original."

"Hold on," I say, steeling myself before jerking the wheel a quarter turn, then back again—pounding Johnny's vehicle from the side. My seat belt clamps hard against my chest, biting in as the jolt reverberates through the whole vehicle.

"WHAT THE FUCK!" Johnny is screaming. "WHAT THE *FUCK*?"

It occurs to me that—for all intents and purposes—if anyone's watching us right now, I look like a maid of honor who witnessed her sister get abandoned at the altar on Christmas Day—and I've taken it rather badly. More seriously than most.

"YOU'RE DAMAGING THE PAINTWORK!" he yells again, right before I strip another set of black lines off the exterior, Prius ricocheting against his van. In my ears are the crunch and squeal of metal, and I think if I can *just* get the angle right, *just* ram him hard enough, he'll be ditch-bound. Immobile for the time being. Enough for the rest of the team to swarm.

Johnny, unfortunately, is smarter than that.

He dramatically stamps on his brakes as we speed past him.

"*Damn* it," Nick swears, craning his neck, watching as Johnny cuts clear across the front yard of what is clearly not a summer home. Twinkle lights are strung between two trees, and he blasts right through them, decorations tangled and whipping against the side of his car. I swallow hard, fighting the anxiety that's quickly scratching up my throat—*he cannot get away, we've come too far to let him get away*—before I make the world's most illegal U-turn, off-road, around a winter greenhouse.

The pit in my stomach gutters. I've remembered something. "He's headed straight towards town. *Shit!* What time is it?"

I glance at the dashboard clock just as Nick says, "Eleven-oh-two."

"No, no, no—the *parade*." I press my foot all the way down on the gas pedal again, snow flying under my tires. We're completely off-roading now, in hot pursuit of Johnny, trees popping up out of nowhere. "There's a big Christmas parade that always starts at eleven, and *yes*, maybe this town does take the holidays a little too seriously, it seems like we have about two hundred different events, but—"

The woods spit us out near the center of town. Just off Main Street. One of Grandma Ruby's lit-up candy canes smashes against my bumper. Shop windows glisten in midwinter light. Beyond that, floats, barges, crowds—and a giant yellow blockade. Johnny stomps on his brakes rather than plowing right through the cement barrier. He's . . . he's cornered! Buildings on both sides. Us behind him. Maybe, *maybe*, this parade is a blessing. Unless he decides to run.

Great, he's decided to run.

After all that, he's had to choose between his goods and himself. He chooses himself. His driver's side door swings open with abandon, and Johnny sprints into the holiday crowd, elbows popping the air; he disappears into an assembly of my high school's marching band. *My* old marching band. They're playing a tuba-heavy rendition of "The Little Drummer Boy."

I've stopped the Prius within an inch of Johnny's car, leaping out as Nick yells, "You take the north side of the street! I'll take the south! And Sydney, just . . . be careful." He fixes me with a gaze that says more than words, and I speed off like a shot in my maid of honor dress, gathering some looks from the older members of the Cape Hathaway Knitting Club, who are perched inside a Christmas-red convertible, crowded around an immense ball of yarn.

Johnny is darting through the chaos, taking the path directly through the parade. For a second, he's caught up in the trumpet section, and I tell myself, *Whatever you do, don't lose sight of his hair!* Right now, his blond curls are catching the sun, and he's just a floating head, frantically yelling something into his cell phone as he runs. He's managed to dial while sprinting—impressive, for someone who "isn't great at multitasking"—but I'm not catching any of the words. He's probably meeting someone on the other side of the parade. Vinny? Andre? Whoever's coming to collect him. Save him. Help him escape.

Not on my watch.

"Ma'am!" someone is yelling at my back. "Miss! No running through the parade!" I barely hear them. On the sidewalk, young children are clapping for the toilet-shaped balloons on the Al's

Plumber float, which I'm rushing past—Johnny about fifteen paces ahead of me and slowing down. For all that muscle, he doesn't seem to have the endurance. Nick and I are closing in as a team, expertly shuffling around people—but the parade is ending. We've almost reached the front of the line, where the crowd thins, where it's a straight shot to the grocery store parking lot. Bet you someone's meeting Johnny there.

Faster, faster—

I push myself—*this is for Calla*—arms swinging, boots pounding the pavement, but it isn't enough. One of the floats lurches to the side and clips my hip as I sprint by. Pain starbursts inside my bone, and yep, that definitely hurts, that—

That's the end.

Johnny has reached the end, where the parade disperses and the barriers open up again. He clears into the parking lot and spins around. A jet-black SUV with tinted windows is waiting for him a few feet away, but Johnny has several words to say to us first. "Don't . . ." he breathes, "move." The gun he's just pulled from his waistband underlines his words. This should tell you everything you need to know about Johnny Jones. Instead of a boutonniere, the man wore a gun to his own wedding.

A spike in my heart hurts even worse than my hip.

Nick stops short, thrusting an arm out to stop me, too. His palm flattens on my stomach, his pulse thudding into my skin.

Behind us, a few people start to scream. They've seen Johnny, seen him draw his weapon. My gut tightens to the size of a fist. If we didn't have evidence against him before, we sure as hell have it now.

"You would've made a *terrible* husband," I spit at him, once again certain that I could've found a more cutting insult. But it'll still keep him engaged. Give us time for the FBI task force to show up. *If they ever do.*

Johnny tilts his head, cocking the gun and pointing the barrel straight at me. Never been in this precise situation before. Zero out of ten, do not recommend it. They tell you on The Farm, though, never plead. Pleading does not wind down the clock. Pleading only gives the aggressor power, makes them pull the trigger faster.

Nick gives an appropriately declarative sentence. "Walk away, Johnny." His voice is practiced and steady, his hand still placed protectively against my stomach, and he's shuffling slowly to block me. I feel a surge of love for him, from the depth of my stomach. "Get in the car, and—"

"No one gets hurt?" Johnny asks, a laugh in his throat. "I think we're a little past that, don't you, Nicky boy?"

"Not really," I mumble, the crowd rapidly dispersing behind me.

"I meant emotionally!" Johnny yells back, having read my lips. "*Emotionally!* You couldn't mind your own damn business, and *you*—" He points the gun at Nick this time, jaw tensing, and something in my chest erupts. "You're chasing me down now, are you? That's what all my loyalty's gotten me? After everything, all these years? You were like family."

"Your idea of family is *seriously* messed up," Nick bats back, and he's right. Of course he's right. Now that he's in the direct line of fire, though, I wish he'd kept his mouth shut. Instinctively, I try to step in front of *him*, which leads him to try and step in front of *me*, and—

"Fine!" Johnny says. "I'll just shoot you both."

There's no time for one last look. One last glance between me and Nick. One last time for me to say, *I love your Christmas sweater. I love how you want to play the ukulele, and how you want to train dogs. I love how I met you in an imperfect situation, but you turned out to be—*

A loud sound follows Johnny's words.

A very, very loud sound.

It is not the shot from a gun. My stomach doesn't even have a moment to drop before the air starts screaming, and Grandma Ruby's electric-blue Oldsmobile T-bones the SUV. It plows right into the back seat, metal shrieking and wrapping around the hood, a deafening crunch, the explosive sound of airbags. *Grandma? Grandma, no!* A cry wells in my throat, and I stumble forward, and . . . Someone else is here, too. Just as the crash happened, just as Johnny spins around, Calla's come out of the alleyway by the Chinese food palace. *How?* How is she here? She must've . . . she must've ridden with Grandma Ruby. Must've jumped out to pursue on foot.

She's in her wedding dress, left sleeve hanging off her shoulder, and she's toting one of Grandma Ruby's gigantic ceramic candy canes. It feels like my pupils widen to the size of dimes. With one propulsive movement, my little sister—the gentlest, kindest person I've ever known—thwacks Johnny right between the shoulder blades.

The women in my family? They might not have the proper training, might not do things as elegantly as federal agents, but *damn*, have they showed up.

Johnny's gun falls to the ground, skittering, and I lunge for it while Nick rushes forward and side-tackles Johnny, successfully this time—dropping him hard against the cold, cold pavement. My grandma stumbles out of the Oldsmobile, dazed, and she just . . . she *did that*. She just crashed that car rather than letting Johnny get away.

And he doesn't get away.

The sky is already filled with the swirl of sirens.

Blue lights, red lights.

Christmas lights.

My head spins as the FBI swarms, black cars rushing to the

scene, and suddenly there's a cloud of federal agents, so much shouting, and Calla? *Calla?* Disarming the gun, I weave through the agents, never losing my sister, and grab her hand. She squeezes it tight, and in the chaos, we rush toward Grandma Ruby—who, to be honest, appears a little worse for wear. Her white hair is cotton ball puffed, sticking out at odd angles, and there's a thin scratch on the plump of her cheek.

"Oh, don't look so worried," she tuts at us, voice loud over Johnny's moans. He's still grumbling under Nick in the background. "That car's built tough, and so am I."

"You just . . ." I almost stutter as Calla says, breathless, "*Grandma*, are you okay? That wasn't part of the plan!"

I blink at them both, federal agents jostling at our backs. Steam is pouring out of the Oldsmobile, almost stinging my eyes. Or maybe I'm crying. I could be crying.

"Calla told me everything, dear," Grandma Ruby clarifies, placing one hand on my shoulder, the other on my sister's. She draws us together, like magnets. "On the way over. About you, about the CIA—and Johnny." She says his name like it tastes terrible. "I had my suspicions about that boy. He told me I shouldn't knit a Christmas sweater for my dog, and I will knit whatever for whoever I damn well please."

Yep, I'm definitely crying now.

And Calla's crying, and the three of us are holding one another, and Grandma Ruby's telling us, "Life's going to throw you knocks, girls. Sometimes it'll throw you hand grenades. But you have each other—you'll *always* have each other. And you're worthy of love. Real, truthful love. Did you hear that? You are *worthy*."

I feel Calla nodding against my shoulder, really leaning in, and I hope she *is* hearing that. I hope she's feeling that. I hope she'll be okay.

"Sydney!"

Nick's voice rises above the din, and I turn toward it, still holding my family. He's by the farthest vehicle, hair mussed, motioning to the back seat of the car. Johnny's inside—and I know that Nick will personally want to take him in. Good. Nick deserves this, really deserves this, after everything that Johnny's put him through.

I give him a sad but triumphant smile.

"Maybe it's not my place," Grandma Ruby chimes in, glancing between me and Nick, "but if you're going to choose a man, one who's willing to take a bullet for you isn't a *bad* option."

20

In the end, there's procedure. There are reports to write, forms to file, all the bureaucracy and the bullshit. Calla takes Grandma Ruby to get checked out at the local hospital (she has a sprained wrist and some rib bruising, but thank god, nothing major), while I'm stuck liaising with FBI officials, passing over the diamonds, and giving my exceedingly long statement. Turns out, Johnny breaks pretty quickly under interrogation, detailing his parents' and his henchmen's involvement in the crimes. At the wedding, they were all taken into custody—and now, they're staying there. Nick texts me that he's going to be a while; his handler has flown in from the Toronto regional office, and CSIS and the FBI are squabbling over who gets credit for the takedown. Doesn't matter either way. Not to me, anyway.

What matters is I have my family back.

At home, well after midnight, after I dot every I and cross every T, I find Grandma Ruby and Calla curled up on the couch together. Someone from the FBI must've helped move out all the wedding chairs—and the altar—because our living room is just as I remember. Warm, cheery, reindeer-less. Plush couch and overstuffed armchairs. There's an open packet of goat cheese resting on the coffee table, and Grandma Ruby has fallen asleep with a spoon clutched in her hand, Calla snoring open-mouthed on her shoulder. Even after this catastrophe of a day, they actually look . . . peaceful. Peaceful in their holiday pajamas and snowman socks.

"Love you," I whisper, heart in my throat, dragging a blanket over them. Keeping them warm. By the Christmas tree, Sweetie Pie licks my toes before I sneak back upstairs, soundless, careful not to wake them. Nick still hasn't returned, and the house is so quiet, just the gentle hum of the furnace, snow-flecked wind hitting the windows. In my old bedroom with the bubblegum-pink sheets, I thwomp back on the mattress with the world's biggest sigh.

My vision catches on a shoebox.

A shoebox, on the corner of my nightstand.

It's been such a wild twenty-four hours, I'd almost forgotten what Grandma Ruby said last night. About a Christmas gift of sorts, waiting for me in my bedroom. For some reason, my pulse picks up—and I reach for it, thin cardboard under my fingers. When I lift the lid, there's a bundle of . . . Christmas cards? Tattered Christmas cards, with a crisp white letter on top.

Swallowing hard, I read the letter first.

Sydney Bean, it begins in Grandma Ruby's handwriting.

I'm not sure if I'm doing the right thing here, and I've debated with myself about it for years, but maybe you and Calla should have these. They're from your father. Every year, he sends a Christmas card to the house. Sometimes they arrive way after the holiday, sometimes around Thanksgiving, and they never say much. My thinking was it would hurt you and Calla to see them, to know he was occasionally in touch but not coming home—not fulfilling his duties as a father. I thought it might be better not to remind you of the pain, to live our lives united and together. But I think I was wrong. I think you need to see that a part of him, no matter how small or how broken, has always held on to you.

Forgive me,
Grandma Ruby

I finish the letter with a knot in my throat, but it's . . . it's the kind that unwinds. Forgive her? Forgive her for what? She gave Calla and me everything.

I finger the first card, taking a deep breath through my nose. The last remnants of glitter cover my hand like silt, and I open it. Dad's name is scrolled at the bottom, his handwriting, which I remember from grocery lists. Little Post-its on tools in the garage.

The next card has a snowy barn on the front—quaint, elegant, with a *Merry Christmas* on the inside. I flip through reindeer prints and village scenes, pictures of silver bells and roasted turkeys, and Grandma Ruby's right—there isn't much. Barely any writing. And maybe, yes, that would've made me sad as a kid. Where are the updates? Where was *he*?

But there, in a card near the bottom of the stack, is one small note. It says, simply, *Please say hello.*

I sniff, tears welling up again, and look down at the card. "Hey, Dad," I say after a long moment, into the silence of my room. Because how can I forgive myself for leaving if I can't, at least a little bit, forgive him?

Placing the card back into the box with care, I shut the lid and slip the whole thing under my bed. I'll show Calla when she's ready. Not now. Not tonight. Tonight is for rest, and sleep, and—

Nick.

All the lights are off when he knocks gently on my bedroom door. I'm still awake, so I answer him, giving a weak but warm "How did it go?"

"As well as it could've," Nick says, obviously exhausted. He's kicked off his shoes, is just in his socks, white shirt, and the tuxedo trousers from this morning. "Can I . . . ?"

"Sure," I whisper, reading his mind, making space for him.

The twin mattress doesn't have that *much* room, especially for his frame, but he climbs into bed with me without another word, hugging me from behind, curling his body around mine. Matching me from head to toe. His arm nestles into my hip crease, and his breath is soft on the back of my neck.

"Is it weird that I missed you?" Nick whispers with a chuckle that comes out more like a wince. What he doesn't say is, *We'll have to get used to that.* His flight out's tomorrow. My flight out's tomorrow. Sure, we can call each other. We can text. But a part of me is terrified that this is all some strange holiday magic. That as soon as he leaves this house, and I leave this house, the spell will be broken.

"Only if it's weird that I missed you, too," I tell him, honest, quiet.

He kisses the space behind my ear, nestling farther into me, and slowly, I turn around to face him, my nose almost to his nose. I like being this close to him. When he reaches up, his thumb swipes a comforting path on my cheek. "You were great today," he says. "Perfect."

"Do me a favor?" I whisper back, wrapping my leg around him. "Never try to die for me again."

He laughs roughly, like he knows better than to argue, and slides his weight even closer to me. Right now, our eye contact might be described as extreme. His pupils lock on to mine, and in this moment, I want nothing—*nothing*—more than him. I think Nick's feeling the same way. His breath starts to come out ragged, his chest rising and falling against mine. And suddenly he's shifting on top of me, my heart beating faster, and my hips rise up to meet him.

"You are really good at that," he groans.

"What, this?" I tease, meeting him again, feeling how hard he's getting. I stoke him through his pants before my fingers turn to his zipper, and—that's enough talking. No more talking. We are all teeth and skin and moans. When Nick drags his tongue up the nape of my neck, I let out an almost inaudible sound—but his fingers still move gently to my lips, reminding me that we need to be quiet, so quiet. Which is honestly *really* difficult. Especially when he slips that same hand under my pajama bottoms, circling a finger in exactly the right spot, and I like . . . just watching him move. Watching his face as we undress, watching how he looks at me, like I'm a present he's just unwrapped on Christmas morning.

His knee nudges open my legs, his muscles in sharp definition, before he drops down and licks a path up my thigh. And that's almost too much. That's almost too teasing.

There's a condom in my nightstand, still miraculously good from my college days, and I help him slip it on, wondering if it'll fit, wondering—

"Is that glow in the dark?" Nick asks, bursting with a laugh.

"Oh, shit. Oh my god." I cover my eyes with my hands, genuinely mortified. "It's a novelty condom. That was . . . I grabbed it as a joke, way back when. But it looks . . ." I peek through my hands. "It doesn't look bad?"

"I'm neon green, Sydney," Nick says, still whisper-laughing.

"Yeah, but in a hot way?"

"*Sydney*," he chuckles, fully grinning now, and if we never see each other again, this is definitely how I want to remember him. About to dissolve in a fit of laughter. Beaming down at me with his dimples and his eyelashes. "I'm going to try to recover from this setback."

"Okay," I say, nodding.

"I think this is salvageable."

"Oh, completely," I say, only half believing it, but Nick's right. Within minutes, he's guiding me over the edge, drawing soft kisses across my collarbone, and it occurs to me with a bittersweet rush: *Wouldn't it be great if we had more nights together, just like this?*

21

NEW YEAR'S EVE

When I arrive at the bench, on the east side of the park, over-looking the river, Gail is already there in a black wind-breaker with a fur-lined hood, her shortish hair blowing around her ears. She could be reading a newspaper in a trench coat and not look any more like a spy. I've never met on an actual park bench before. It almost feels as if we're in the movies, playing our roles. Slowly, I lower myself to the other side of the seat, kicking out my heels and leaning back. Like we're strangers. Like this is a chance meeting.

"So funny to see you here," Gail says, a hint of mirth in her voice. "What a coincidence."

"Thanks for asking me to come," I say, swallowing a little.

Her chin tips up. "Did you know this is where all the greats met? This very park. Fed the ducks over there. I didn't bring any bread, but apparently ducks can't digest bread anyway. If any-thing, we should be tossing them algae. Or fish chunks. But that does seem very messy, doesn't it?"

I sniff out a laugh. She really is kind of humorous, even if she's not trying to be. It's strange that this is only the third time we're meeting in person; she's quickly become one of the people most integral to my life. "You're right. I don't really want to carry fish chunks in my pocket on the Metro."

"Oh, god no. No, you wouldn't. Especially on a warmer day. I think that would be grounds for expulsion from the city. I would personally kick you out." Gail shifts on the park bench, straightening her shoulders. "You look well."

"So do you," I say honestly.

"It's the holidays. I take an hour off work in the evenings. Really restorative . . . Okay, good. Now that the chitchat's all done and dusted, you're probably wondering why I've brought you here."

I sit up a little as the breeze hits the water. "Is my Grandma Ruby marrying a crime lord?"

A real, proper laugh escapes Gail. I've never seen her laugh—just heard her from the other side of a hotel door—but she throws her entire head back, chin to the sky. "You're funny, Sydney. A bit too stubborn sometimes, but funny." She chews on the inside of her cheek, hawkish eyes staring out at the river. "I may have doubted you once or twice since we first met. Now, I don't do apologies. They're soppy. I don't care for them. But if I ever were to give one, it might be to a case officer who showed great resolve in a near impossible familial situation."

The corner of my mouth lifts. "Yeah?"

"Yes. I might also add that, given the circumstances—and now that Johnny Jones is being arraigned—the badge-pulling maneuver might have been a bit harsh. Also, metaphorical badge. Since you have never actually worked for us. I've always found that a bit confusing, haven't you?"

I laugh. "I have never been more confused than I have been in the last couple of weeks. It's made me rethink everything."

Gail nods. "I hear you're no longer employed by the CIA. Was that your decision?"

"It was." Even saying it now, relief floods through me. "I've applied for a few positions at think tanks instead. International diplomacy and conflict-resolution-type stuff. The truth is, I've thought about quitting the CIA for a long time, just didn't know that I could, and I . . . I *really* don't want to keep secrets anymore. About myself, about others. It isn't healthy. I think I only joined the CIA because I wanted to hide."

"Yes, very hidden," Gail says. "Very inconspicuous with the car crash and running through that parade, and the two hundred onlookers, with all the Christmas lights—but yes, I do see what you mean. This job does tend to eat you, whether you want it to or not. How'd they take the news?"

"The CIA? Oh, badly."

"Mmm," Gail says. "Good for you. How is your sister?"

"Healing," I say nonflippantly. It's going to take a long time to recover from everything that happened to her, to learn to trust again. But we're going to tackle everything together. Just like we called Dad together, a few days after Christmas. We talked for over an hour, and it was . . . hard. Hard, but good. The three of us still haven't seen each other again in person, and things will never be the same—but a relationship might *exist*. Right now, that's enough for me.

"Calla's a fighter," I tell Gail. "She's stronger than you think."

"Teachers often are. She is also a sister of yours, so the strength is possibly a given. As is your grandmother's. I was glad to hear that she's recovering well." Gail peers at me, brow furrowing. "Is this what one might call 'a moment'? Are we having a moment?"

I return her gaze, eyebrows pulled together like hers. "I think so, Gail. I think we might be."

Gail clears her throat. "Well, that's that, then. I just have one more piece of intel for you before I go." At this, my stomach actually does a little flip-flop, but Gail dives in quickly. Doesn't beat around the bush. "My sources tell me that your gentleman friend, one Nick Fraser, may or may not have landed in DC on American Flight 2169 out of Boston, and he might have picked up his luggage at Carousel 2, and he has possibly taken the Metro Yellow Line from Ronald Reagan National Airport."

Briefly, I'm legitimately not sure what she's telling me, even though she's laid it all out in explicit detail. Nick. Nick Fraser. He's flown to DC on New Year's Eve. For me?

"I believe, Sydney, that this is what's known as a 'grand gesture.' I imagine there will be flowers involved. But I figured you'd had enough surprises for one holiday, even if the final surprise is a positive one." Gail turns to me, one of her eyebrows raised. "I also thought you might want to meet him as soon as he stepped off the train."

I've worn the wrong shoes for running. My high-heeled boots stamp along the rock-salted sidewalk as I pick up the pace, checking my watch. Gail said that Nick exited baggage claim forty-two minutes ago, which means—yeah, jogging now. I descend the escalator with a rolling gait. "Excuse me, sorry, excuse me," I tell people, bobbing around them.

The Metro floor is still littered with Christmas tree needles. A half-abandoned wreath hangs on the information booth; only the faintest tinge of holiday glitter reflects on the railing. The season's coming to an end. Taped-up flyers advertise the festivities tonight. Fireworks over the Lincoln Memorial. The ball drop. It's almost another year. Time to start over. To be different people.

But I finally feel like I've become the person I *was*.

More open. More trusting. This Christmas, everything changed.

Tapping my fare card on the entryway, I rush through the opened gate and down the stairs to Platform B. A sea of winter coats and shopping bags. Suitcases, last-minute trips. Children in strollers and parents holding hands. My chest starts to ache. *Where's Nick?* At first, I think I've missed him. That I've gotten the wrong Metro car, the wrong platform. Maybe he isn't visiting my apartment first. Maybe he's planning on checking himself into a hotel, or getting a bite to eat, or—my god—not visiting me at all. He could be in DC for business! Something totally unrelated! And here I am, like an absolute fool, neck craning into carriages, waiting for—

Him.

Nick steps onto the platform with his roller bag. He's wearing a longish beige coat, a black beanie, and an expression of utter determination. He hasn't seen me yet. He's too focused on weaving through the crowd, isn't looking my way, and my heart thuds. Keeps thudding as I zigzag around passengers, closing the gap between us, until we are abruptly face-to-face. His facial hair is longer than I've ever seen it. Almost a beard.

He startles, dark eyes wide at the sight of me. "You're—"

"Surprise," I say, suddenly sheepish. We haven't seen each other since the morning after Christmas, when we woke up together, intertwined in bed. We've been texting, though. Just this morning, I sent him a picture of myself wrapped in his CHRISTMAS SWEATER. That was my Christmas present; he'd left it on my dresser, tied with a silver ribbon, and it is quickly becoming my favorite item of clothing.

Nick chuckles. "I thought *I'd* get to be the one to surprise you this time."

"In that case, you should've hidden in my shower."

"Mmm," Nick says, reaching up to tuck a stray hair behind my ear. "I value my life too much for that . . . How'd you know I was coming?"

"Got a hot tip."

"You glad I'm here?" Nick says, fishing, his lips inches from mine.

"Very," I say, travelers rushing around us. "Because the truth is . . . I *think* I might want you for every holiday. New Year's. Christmas. I want you for Arbor Day. Groundhog Day, I'm there. And even the nonholiday holidays. International Talk Like a Pirate Day. We'll buy beers and speak like Long John Silver. Hot Pastrami Sandwich Day—"

With a laugh in the back of his throat, Nick leans forward and kisses me, lips capturing mine. And I want him like this is the first time I've discovered what want truly is—the real meaning behind it, that soul-scraping, gut-gripping, can't-feel-my-face sort of desire. My fingers tangle in the back of his hair, smoothing the skin on his neck, and he moves in closer, until our bodies are flush. Until we're becoming one united, happy person on this random DC subway platform. His thumbs trace the line of my jaw, such a light touch, like snowflakes. "Maybe we should . . ." I say after a long moment, breathless, my head cocking a little toward the escalator.

"Right," Nick says, similarly out of breath. He grins. "We used to be spies. You'd think we'd be better at the 'keeping our actions on the down-low' thing."

"Used to be?" I ask, blinking.

Nick wraps his arm around my shoulders as we stride together, into the next crowd of people, who are already testing out some party poppers. Colorful pieces of paper and glitter speckle my coat. "Turns out," Nick says, stooping to whisper in my ear, "you inspire me."

But there's something else. I can tell there's something else on his face, some element of this visit that I'm missing. On the escalator, I study him, his pupils ever so slightly dilated, his pulse almost imperceptibly thudding in his neck. He chews the bottom of his lip as he gazes at me.

"What?" I say, a smile in the corner of my mouth.

"Nothing," Nick says unconvincingly, shaking his head.

"Oh, come on." I poke his dimple, just as he once poked mine. "You have your own tells."

When the escalator spits us out on the main road, winter is alive and well in the air. The weather has taken a turn for the frosty, and snowflakes are just beginning to fall. They start to dust Nick's beanie, and for some reason, perhaps nervously, he takes off his hat. His dark hair springs out, ruffled, like he's just woken up from a long nap—and I think I might adore him more like this than any other way.

"You have snowflakes on your eyelashes," he almost whispers, the world fading around us.

"You're stalling," I whisper back, because whatever he's come to tell me, he should just say it now.

Nick laughs. He laughs in this private, knowing way, like it could only be a joke between us. "You want to know the truth?" he asks, pausing on the sidewalk. One of his hands reaches out to cup my face, and he looks so incredibly earnest, taking a breath to steady himself. "The truth is, when I left that morning, when I thought we might never see each other again, that I might go back to a place where there was no Sydney, it hit me like . . ."

"Like an Oldsmobile?" I offer, suddenly a bit light-headed.

He nods, wiping a snowflake off my cheek. "Yes. *Exactly* like that. And I realize we haven't known each other for more than a holiday, and we can take this as slow as you want, but I want to be here. I want to be with you. And I just need you to know that . . . that I . . ."

He pins me with the most hopeful glance—and I know. I know it like I know that Sweetie Pie is a good dog, that Christmas trees are green, that this man is the best one I've ever met.

The words rush out of me, rasping. "I love you, too."

"Yeah?" he whispers, his face like summer, and then we're kissing, and he's saying it over and over—on the sidewalk, at my house, later that week, later that month. *I love you, Sydney. I really, really love you.* And I trust him. I'm going to know every inch of him.

And he's going to know me, too.

ACKNOWLEDGMENTS

The idea for *The Takedown* arrived right before the holidays, as I was driving in my car. It came all at once: Sydney, Calla, Johnny, Nick, crowded around the dining room table with secrets between them. I remember laughing out loud; I'd never experienced an idea like that before—one that laid itself out, almost perfectly, like a Christmas dinner.

So, I'm going to thank my parents first, for instilling in me a feverish love of the holidays. My spirit is your spirit. You made our Christmases in Maine (and beyond) extra special, even if we did pick out the worst tree in history. I love all of our traditions, and I love you.

This book is dedicated to the best agent duo an author could have, Claire Wilson and Pete Knapp. Claire, thanks for being there from the very beginning, and for fighting in my corner every step of the way. Your notes—and Pete's—absolutely transformed this story. Pete, I'm so lucky that you jumped on board. I mean it when I say that *The Takedown* would not exist without you two. Huge thanks also to Safae El-Ouahabi, Stuti Telidevara, and everyone at RCW and Park & Fine who made this dream a reality—including the RCW rights team, who have so brilliantly sold *The Takedown* internationally. To each and every editor who saw something in this story, I'm unbelievably grateful.

Speaking of great editors! Kerry Donovan at Berkley and Sanah Ahmed at Orion, I've been blown away by your passion for and insight into Sydney's story. I couldn't ask for a stronger, kinder team, and I'm so, so happy for the privilege of working with you both.

To my husband, Jago, I didn't want to watch all of those spy movies, but I'm kind of glad we did. Our nightly walks were crucial for this narrative. Thank you for your "bad ideas," which always help me come up with good ones. And to my dingo dog, Dany, for lying on my feet while I wrote this book—and for demanding the aforementioned nightly walks.

Lia Liao's cover for Berkley and Carla Orozco's cover for Orion both blew me away; I'm super appreciative that you took on this project.

Michelle Kroes at CAA, I still pinch myself whenever we talk; many thanks to you, Eric Fineman, and Speck and Gordon for championing this project in Hollywood.

Erin Cotter and Kayla Olson, I don't know where this book would've ended up without your support. You both are such beautiful storytellers, and I feel honored to know you. Thanks to Kayla for providing such a fantastic blurb—as well as the wonderfully talented Colleen Oakley and Lizzy Dent.

To the usual suspects, Miss Kim, Ellen Locke, Grandma Pat, and Sandy Johnson—you are my core team, and I'll never forget how you've supported me. To Tom Bonnick, who wasn't my editor for this one, but who's taught me an unbelievable amount about storytelling over the years. Love to my great-grandma Ruby, for much more than the name; you really were a total bad-ass.

Special thanks to the professors at UNC Chapel Hill who suggested that I might make a calmer English professor than I would an intelligence operative. Sorry for that "flowery" paper about

Civil War reconnaissance balloons. You were right: Chaucer was more my thing.

This book is also for all the strong women out there. Dani Speegle, Annie Thorisdottir, Tia-Clair Toomey, and others—you're inspirations. Big shout-out to the women at CrossFit 11:24. It's a privilege to lift next to you every day.

And finally, to Sandra Bullock.

Keep reading for a preview of
Carlie Walker's next romance!

prologue

ROME, ITALY

Night air slaps my face. We're speeding faster on the motor-cycle, swerving around a restaurant with patio tables, and I accidentally clip one, rattling several plates full of antipasti. A glass of Aperol spritz topples. Blood-orange liquid stains the napkins, and—"Sorry! *Scusa!*" I say, both words emerging with a wheeze. No time to stop, though. I'm too focused, too rattled, too aware of Flynn's fingers, which are digging—harder now—into the curve above my hipbones.

"This may be a bad time to tell you!" I shout over my shoulder, unable to stem the terror in my voice. "But I've never driven a motorcycle before!"

"You *think?*" Flynn bleats out, and immediately I picture his face. Pupils dilated, strong eyebrows pulled together, every trace of that smug grin wiped away. "Make a left! Left, Max!"

"I'm trying!" I fire back, easing up on the throttle for just a se-cond, and . . . Where's the turn signal on this thing? *Don't be stupid, Max.* They shouldn't know I'm turning! Makes it more difficult to follow me. Before the traffic light flashes green, I bite the inside of my cheek and just go, blasting across the intersection to a symphony of horns. A man stops short in his Fiat, yelling out the window, *"Morire, signora!"*

I don't speak much Italian, but I know that one! *Die, lady.*

Unfortunately, Fiat man isn't the only one who wishes me dead.

My grip tightens on the motorcycle handlebars. "Are they still following us?"

I feel Flynn turning, pressed against my back. I feel the way his body moves: the sharp flick of his head, the quick glance at the trailing cars. "Three of them now."

Three? A peek at my mirrors reveals—yep, Flynn's right. Two black cars, probably bulletproof, and someone following them on a Vespa. Which almost makes me laugh. Driving a Vespa to an assassination is like bringing a loofah stick to a swordfight.

At least no one is shooting at us.

"Any second," Flynn shouts over the traffic, "they're going to start shooting at us."

"Well . . . *shit*!" I say, because it's the only thing I can get out. I'm usually more articulate than this. More composed than this. To be fair, though, it's only seven o'clock at night—the summer sky has just turned a dusky pink; I haven't even had my evening gelato—and two separate people have already tried to kill me today.

Or rather, two people have tried to kill *Sofia*.

Flynn slips his hands tighter around my waist, gripping me closer, almost cradling me—and I'm not thinking about it. Not thinking about the heat of him, the spicy scent of him, the look on his face last night as he slowly unbuttoned his shirt. At this moment, I know that Flynn is just holding on for the ride. Just praying that I don't end the assignment this way. *This can't be how it ends.* The two of us crashing into a porchetta stand by the Campo de' Fiori or losing control outside of the Piazza del Paradiso, toppling into a group of tourists who'll *click, click, click* their cameras. Then, front-page news. International news. PRIME MINISTER OF SUMMER-LAND VICTIM OF TRAGIC ACCIDENT BEFORE EVEN MORE TRAGIC ASSASSINATION. Or something snappier than that. That's a really shit headline.

"Take the Via Dei Baullari." Flynn's breath is warm in my ear, words almost eaten by the hum of the motorcycle.

"You say that like I know where it is!"

"On your right!"

"*When* on my right?" I bat back, weaving past a Lamborghini and a jewelry store, shiny gold rings winking at us in the windows.

Flynn's chin is almost resting on my shoulder. "Now! Now!"

We make a hard turn, tires gripping the ancient road, and I have a flash of how others are seeing us—a woman in a bright cream pantsuit and heels, a man in a dashing beige jacket, and a busted-up bike that looks newly rescued from a second-rate junkyard. Cars and a Vespa chasing after them. Bullets soon to fly through the air. This isn't how the Italian getaway was supposed to go, was it?

Nope. No, it wasn't.

It would be easy, they said. *A piece of cake*, they said. Just sit there and look polished, and don't open your mouth. Shake hands with the right people. Smile politely, but not like an American; not too wide, not with too many teeth. Do what you're told, and it'll feel like a vacation. *Don't you want a vacation, Max? A simple job in beautiful Italy.*

That was before the disaster of a news conference. Before the fistfight in my bathroom. Before I met the real Flynn and my whole world turned fucking upside-down.

"They're gaining on us," he says, once again into my ear. It's obvious; Flynn is trying hard to steady his voice, trying to be the cool and calm one in this scenario. Despite this, something in his throat gutters. "Our best chance is to make a sharp turn somewhere, pull off where they can't see. Confuse them. Let them pass us . . ."

"Where are the *police*?" I gasp out. "Where's the armed escort? They should be—"

"*There*," Flynn says, but he's talking about a gap between buildings. A little nook by a flower shop, just large enough for a motorcycle. Will they see us in there? Maybe not. Hopefully not. I take the chance, jamming on the brakes, back tire skidding to the left. My pulse hammers in my ears, climbs higher as we slip into the alleyway. I cut the engine. Thick stone walls bear down on us, and the air smells like . . . focaccia. Flowers and focaccia, yeasty and sweet, but I still hold my breath. As if our hunters can hear me. As if one tiny sniffle will give me up.

Luckily, it's a Saturday night in Rome. The streets are stuffed with distractions. Above the sound of tourists laughing, horns beeping, gallery doors squeaking open and closed, there's the distinct noise of two armored cars rattling by the alleyway, fast. Followed by a Vespa, *zzzz-zip*, even faster.

Behind me, Flynn also seems to be holding his breath. His stillness is palpable, not a muscle moving. As soon as the vehicles pass, he loosens a little, whispering, "Close call."

I swallow, gathering myself, feeling blood return to the tips of my fingers. I unclench my fists from the handlebars. "What now?"

I'm asking Flynn, although my body already knows. I'm already swinging my leg off the bike, stamping the ground, traveling forward on foot. We can't stay here. We can't wait for them to reach the main road again, figure out what we've done, and throw their cars in reverse.

"Take off your jacket," Flynn instructs.

"Why?"

"Max, please, just do it."

Still charging forward, I shrug off the cream blazer, satin lining sticky with sweat, and am about to pass it over. About to turn around, hand it to Flynn. At the other end of the alleyway, though, no less than thirty feet ahead, someone appears. Someone moves to block the exit.

My heart lurches to my throat.

This person . . . there's a knife in their hand.

And I *know* them.

1

I have eaten nothing but mac and cheese for three days. No . . . four? What day is it? Wednesday?

Overhead lights flicker in the mini-mart as I chuck three more boxes into my cart. It's not even particularly *good* mac and cheese. Chalky and violently orange, like a fresh highlighter. This is children's food. Prison food. But I guess this is who I am now. Not the person who cooks award-winning meals, who owns her own restaurant, who can get out of bed before two o'clock in the afternoon.

It's inching toward nine p.m., all the summer tourists strolling on the streets outside. If I strain, I can hear the ocean—waves slapping against the harbor, the sharp caw of gulls. Inside, though, there's only the faint clink of glass. The sound of someone haphazardly searching the shelves.

My gaze narrows, flits down the aisle.

A man is staring at me from the hot sauce section, bottle in hand. Do I know him? Don't think so. He's athletic-looking, pushing six foot two, his hair not quite brown but not quite blonde. *Young Ryan Gosling,* my brain inserts, *if Ryan Gosling had been lost at sea.* His beard stubble and rumpled linen shirt say that he, too, could be on his fourth day of mac and cheese.

I wait for him to drop the stare. Keep waiting. *What the hell, dude?* Turning fully toward him, puffing my bangs away from my eyebrows, I grind out a "Yes?"

My bluntness startles him from his stare. "I'm sorry," he says, shaking his head, finally blinking. He inches closer, into the middle ground between us—the dried grains and canned-clams section. "It's just . . . Do you know that you look *exactly* like Sofia Christensen?"

Okay, I've heard that one before. Sofia and I, we have the same posture—rigid in the back, shoulders popping like they could poke holes in something. Beyond that, we have the same face: square jaw and light-blue eyes, with a look that says, *I'm more powerful than you give me credit for.* The only difference is, Sofia Christensen is the youngest female prime minister in history. I'm, as has been established, shopping for bargain-brand macaroni. Right now, I'm also wearing frayed jean shorts and a Maine State Fair T-shirt with a talking acorn on it. Not really Sofia's style.

I nod once at the man, slowly, taking in the pricey pair of sunglasses tucked into his shirt pocket. The guy's a tourist, probably. "I've been told that, yeah," I say, not unkindly, but also not looking to engage any further.

"It's uncanny," he says, obviously awestruck, stepping closer. "With the dimple and the eyes and the—*wow.* You're like twins. Are you related?"

I select a final box of mac and cheese, ready to be on my way. "Nope, it's just one of those random look-alike things, so . . . Good luck with your hot sauce." I scoot around him, eyeing his shopping basket. "That stuff in the yellow bottle is actually really lethal."

"Good tip." He coughs a little, oddly, then says, "Hey, wait up a second. You from around here?"

If that's a line, I'm not having it.

"That's not a line," he clarifies, before hitting me with a brilliant white smile. Hollywood teeth. "I'm just supposed to do one of those boat tours tomorrow from Casco Bay, and it didn't say much on my booking sheet about the exact pick-up spot. I can't reach the guy at the main office—"

"Is it through Portland Pirates Tours?"

"Yeah."

"The owner's like eighty-nine and doesn't do phones. But there'll be signs everywhere. Just go down to Harbor Master Port and look for the windjammer with the blue flag on the front. Can't miss it."

"Great, thanks, that's very helpful . . ."

"Max," I supply, knowing I'll never see him again.

"Max," he repeats. "I'm Jeremy."

I swipe my six boxes of mac and cheese at the self-checkout and pay with a twenty. "Have a good vacation, Jeremy."

But the guy doesn't let it go. "Look," he says, eyes sincere, "I know you probably don't want to hang out with someone you've just met, but on the off chance that you're completely free tomorrow, my friends and I've rented out the whole boat for the day. They've booked caterers and ordered *way* too much food, and if you wanted to join us, we're setting sail at eleven."

"That's very nice of you, but—"

"But you don't like free lobster rolls?" he finishes, raising a brow.

I snort out a hint of a laugh. "You never said there'll be *lobster rolls*. That changes everything."

"Seriously? You'll come, then?"

"No." I shake my head, closing one eye a touch. "Sorry, thanks, but no."

Jeremy looks a little deflated. "Worth a shot. Well, if you change your mind . . ."

I don't. I won't. I'm positive that I'll spend the next day applying for jobs, sending out cover letters with an undertone that reads OH DEAR GOD, PLEASE JUST HIRE ME, before slumping off to part-time work at my uncle's gift shop (specialty: fish figurines). The problem is, when I roll out of bed at an early ten a.m., I decide to throw on my Birkenstocks and take a walk. And that walk leads me to Slate Street, which leads me to York Street, and what do you know—there's the harbor.

It must be the siren call of the free lobster rolls. Must be the fact that it's June, and the weather's perfect, and the salt air is lifting my spirit—just a little—in a way I'd assumed was gone forever. Summer in Maine, before the rush of heavy tourist season, before the wild blueberries even ripen, has always been my favorite. Bike riding, clam baking, sailing . . .

"Max!" In front of me, by the north dock, a Portland Pirates windjammer bobs in the harbor, white sails plump with the breeze. A middle-aged woman is leaning over the starboard railing, shouting my name. "Are you Max?"

Even from yards away, her intensity is tangible. Squinting, I can tell that her clothes are nondescript, nonthreatening—a beige trench coat, blue boating loafers—but her face is sort of sharp. Like the human equivalent of a stick.

Light reflects off the water, blinding me a bit, and ninety-nine percent of my body is telling me *turn around*. Get the hell out of whatever this is about to become. That other one percent of me? That other one percent of me is curious, hungry, and has nothing else worthwhile to do with my day. Besides trench-coat woman, I know every person in this harbor, every boat in sight. Tourists in my hometown don't usually surprise me—and yet, this is the most unordinary thing that's happened in weeks.

Tucking my hands into my jean jacket, pulse pounding a bit harder than I thought it would, I shuffle across the dock and board the windjammer. It rocks unsteadily under my feet, but the woman—she's like a mountain goat. She clambers easily over the decking before introducing herself as today's captain. "So pleased that you could join us."

But . . . who is *us*? Surveying the boat, I see very clearly that Jeremy isn't here yet. Neither are any of his supposed friends. The pit in my stomach says they're not just running late. Especially when the ship's captain whips off a pair of utilitarian, pitch-black sunglasses, hitting me with yet another stare.

"Why don't you make yourself comfortable?" the woman says. Wind in her short chestnut hair, she grabs two champagne flutes from a box by the sail. "Bubbly?"

"I'm not a big drinker."

"Hmm," the woman says, considering this. "More for me, then, I suppose." Which seems like an odd thing for a boat captain to say. What also seems odd—very odd—is that the boat is now moving, without the captain's assistance, slowly pulling out of harbor. "Now that I have your attention, I think it's best if I speak for a short while, and you don't speak, and then we can move on from there. Sound good?"

My chest starts to prickle with heat. "I'm sorry, what's—"

"You're probably familiar with Sofia Christensen, the prime minister of Summerland, that small island nation off the coast of Norway? Someone would very much like to assassinate her. Which is where you come in, as a decoy. To make sure the assassination doesn't happen."

Carlie Walker attended the University of North Carolina at Chapel Hill, where she first majored in Peace, War, and Defense, a feeder program for intelligence services—before realizing that she is way too anxious to be a spy. Having gone on to study at Oxford University and at City, University of London, she worked briefly in publishing before becoming the bestselling author of eight books for children and young adults. She has a registered 250-pound dead lift, volunteers at a cat shelter, and used to spend her Saturdays practicing martial arts. She lives in Marietta, Georgia, with her husband and their American dingo.

Ready to find
your next great read?

Let us help.

Visit prh.com/nextread

Penguin
Random
House